the twisted tree

the twisted tree

SarLew

Bella Bee Publishing, North Carolina

CONTENTS

CONTENTS

DEDICATIONS AND ACKNOWLEDGMENTS

To all the strong women in my life who have inspired my journey.   To Dedee who helped me see the world more vibrantly. To my mom who showed me how to be a strong woman. To my aunts: Faye, Ethel, and Betty who perfected the art of being beautiful, intelligent southern belles. To those that will relate to June's story as their own. To my sister Velina who read all my works with an open heart. To Steve and Karen Vann for encouraging me to write. To Todd Mignola for rooftop chats. To Julius for dealing with my crazy writing style. To Janet and Jeff for pulling me through my own darkness. To Darlene for the spirits. To my sisters from other misters: Tina, Pam, Mick, Diana (Dirty), Deborah, Michelle Leverton, Christy Glenn (where are you both?) Windy, Brandi, Remona, Esther-I-am-a-mother, Elisa, Kim, Cyd, Nance, Tamara B., Tamara T., Angie, Molly, Dahlia (my battle) and Marianne (you all know why). To the Williams Family. To Stuffy! To Butterbean. To Albert and Bobby, thanks for the memories, inspiration and motivation to be the best version of myself possible.

SPECIAL ACKNOWLEDGMENT

To Zee and especially to my strong, intelligent, loving daughter Annabella. I do everything for you!!!

Editor: Julius Vaughn
Front Cover Image: Melpomenem
Illustrations by: Tetiana Garkusha
First printing edition: 2022
Website: www.sarlew.com
Twitter: @authorsarlew
Instagram: author_sarlew
FB: @authorsarlew

Although there are some historical events and/or timelines, this is a work of fiction. Names, characters, businesses, and incidents are the products of the author's imagination. Any resemblance to actual persons, living or dead, or actual events is purely coincidental. The musical artist and businesses that are mentioned are real, but they are in no way, associated with or do they endorse this book. The opinions expressed are those of the characters and should not be confused with that of the author.

Bella Bee Publishing
North Carolina

One

The Scarf

The distant howling of the wind is like a war cry of restless savages preparing for battle. The mountains are layered with fine new snow that drifts away like sand with the passing wind gusts. The swirling white powder dances down to an ice-covered ground creating a hardened surface. The rainbows of colors reflected in the falling translucent crystals are in stark contrast to the steel grey sky. A young June Brown, dressed in Army fatigues, isn't sure how the lack of warmth from her frozen body has melted the snow around her, but it creates a constant source of cold. She lays crouched on the side of a muddy, ice-covered hill waiting to be attacked or to attack; it isn't clear what will happen. That's how things are in Army training.

The constant gusts of wind slide over the hillside to tear at her ivory skin and cause her golden-brown eyes to sting. She is sure the tears will freeze on her face as they slide down her cheeks. She mentally searches her body to find some source of warmth.

Her feet: cold.

Hands: cold.

Head: Also, cold.

However, there is a comforting warmth around her neck. It's an olive-green scarf, which she pulls over her face so that only her eyes are exposed. There is refuge behind this cloak of wool and polyester. His scent still clings to the fibers, like little memories of each moment they have shared. She breathes them in.

Thoughts of him warm her spirit enough to at least make her forget about the cold. She holds the scarf close around her neck and smiles, remembering him saying: "Take this to stay warm, and I'll let you warm up my neck later." The thought of kissing his neck leads her to an uncomfortable level of arousal.

"MOVE! MOVE! MOVE!" barks Sergeant Jackson, startling her out of her daydream. She tries to stand quickly and forge her body forward, only to slip and land face first in the snow. *Damn*, she thinks, now the scarf, her only warmth, is covered in frozen sludge. She finally manages to move, as previously directed, only to be commanded "DOWN!" She falls hard on a rock hidden underneath the snow. Her knee is surely bruised or bleeding but can't be attended to, through four layers of her military uniform.

Her fingers are frozen, which pisses her off. The Army-issued leather gloves with wool inserts do little to combat the cold. She tries to breathe warm air onto her hands, but the relief is minimal. Before the frustration sets in, his scent permeates through the scarf again. She finds contentment in the thought of his smile when he said if she had to go home early, he would break his leg and leave too.

She sits with her squad of soldiers in the snow for hours---waiting...

Finally, awakening from her comatose state, she hears the command, "MOVE!" and surges forward again, trying to keep up as they march through knee-deep snow. This time they march so long that she starts to sweat. Hours pass before they finally stop marching. She takes off her gloves to inspect her hands, which are now purple. Sgt. Jackson is walking around doing goodwill checks and sees her hands. He grabs her by the collar and says, "You are out of here."

"Why?" she clamors. "What did I do?"

"You have hypothermia, Brown. MOVE!"

Hmm, that's why my hands hurt so damn bad, she thinks matter-of-factly. For her, hypothermia is ten times more painful than that falling-asleep feeling she would get when she laid on her arm too long.

She is guided down a snowy bank to a shed where another frozen soldier is waiting. There is no communication between her and Sgt Jackson; he just pats her on the head and walks away. She doesn't know if she will stand there until the mission is over or if someone will come to pick her up, so she kneels with her face buried in the corner- frozen.

Her mind drifts into a fog of memories, and she traces the days way past the guy who gave her the scarf. She thinks back to the night before she left for this training course. She had argued with Alex, her ex. He had agreed to bring her gloves from their storage unit. She had let him borrow her car to make the two-hour drive from Fort Lewis to Portland.

As she sits crouched in the corner of the shed, it all becomes clear. She isn't mad that Alex didn't bring her the gloves or that she let him borrow her car for no reason. She is mad for asking him to bring what had belonged to her, when she should have closed that door with him long before that. She had a perfect pair of nice warm gloves sitting on his counter in the kitchen.

Wrapping her hands up in her new scarf, she realizes that she and Alex have struggled from the very beginning to balance their love, which was always weighted more toward her devotion, despite his apparent doubts.

Two hours pass, and finally, an open-air jeep comes skidding through the snow to retrieve the defeated soldiers. "Specialist, Brown, get in the front and warm those hands," says the Sergeant. June hops into the jeep and leans toward the warm air, and cups her hands to guide the warmth toward her face. She pulls the scarf over her ears and face, and her mind drifts back through the past days. This time she thinks about the day she arrived at training. She and Devan were of the first few people to arrive. He was staying in the building next to hers and saw her the moment she rounded the corner.

He was standing at the top of the stairs, wondering who this golden-haired girl was, bouncing into the building next door. June looked up and smiled at the two guys above her and walked into her assigned building. Devan was sure she was smiling at the guy standing beside him. *That bounce*, he thought as he revealed one of the two dimples that made his smile so engaging.

The bunks were assigned, and that was how June met Anna. She was a tall slim girl who looked like you could break her in half. In the days to come, they would become great friends.

To begin that voyage, they decide to walk around the base taking in the incredible beauty of the surrounding mountain ranges. June shared with Anna her conversation with Alex, and Anna promised to take her mind off of everything negative so they could enjoy their time there.

The next day at breakfast, Anna began to make good on her promise. "June," Anna whispered.

"Yep?"

"How about him?" she pointed to one of the attractive men in their class.

"No, gross," June played along.

Anna looked around the whole cafeteria. "Oh," she chirped excitedly. "How about that guy?"

June looked over and rolled her eyes.

Anna, frustrated, "show me!"

June got a sinking feeling in her stomach. She wanted to choose Alex, but he wasn't an option. Anna realized by June's expression that she had lost focus on the game, so she nudged her and said, "Just for fun; remember? "Pick," she whispered.

"Him definitely."

"Who? Who?" pleaded Anna.

"The one in the green army fatigues."

Anna rolled her eyes this time. All the men in the room had on green army fatigues.

"Juun-nah"

Somberly, June looked around the crowded cafeteria and directed Anna's attention to the brightest smile in the room.

"Ah, you like the brothers," smirked Anna with her mouth twisted to the side.

June had never considered what kind of guy she was attracted to. Alex was brooding and always had an underlying sense of anger about the world, but he told great stories and always commanded the attention of everyone in the room. People genuinely loved that outgoing side of him. It had never occurred to her to focus on his race, although he made those differences very clear to her.

Days passed before June saw Devan again. Anna had done a lot of investigating to find out what time his class went on break. It was the 3rd day at training when they not-so-accidentally bumped into each other. There were genuine laughs when they finally spoke, not those born out of nervousness or anticipation. They seemed to dance around words and phrases like they had practiced all their lives. Their instincts about each other eventually fall short of their realities, but a dance always starts by spinning in vibrant and colorful circles. Anna's interjections into their conversation sealed their fate. Devan would teach June how to plot coordinates for the land-navigation test that was coming up in a few days.

They had to meet in a common area because the male and female soldiers were kept separate during training. June started feeling insecure as they sat in front of a large topographical map. Although she had graduated from basic training and advanced individual training with honors, she had barely graduated high school. She didn't want this fantastic guy to think she was stupid.

Devan's nerves were at their peak also as he discussed cross-sections and resections. He wanted to impress her, but the guy next to them crunching on Doritos made it challenging to concentrate on anything else. This annoying presence somehow soothed their awkward countenances as the time passed. They found a way to communicate their feelings about the Doritos guy without saying a word.

It was dark when they left the orderly room that night. Anna had made an excuse to leave early. Usually, June was terrified to be outside at night. However, that wasn't why she asked Devan if he would walk her over to do her extra duty.

As they walked to the dumpster with a bag of trash that contained two paper towels that Anna had planted there, they couldn't help but walk close enough to bump into each other.

The night sky was dark but clear enough to see the satellites floating by like dancing stars. She loved being alone with him underneath a starry sky, so much so that she didn't even notice the darkness. They were almost at their destination when she reached into Devan's jacket pocket and grabbed his hand. He stopped walking and said, "Do you realize you are holding my hand?" Immediately she pulled her hand away, and her heart sank. She felt like a fool for reading him the wrong way. Only seconds passed before he said, "It isn't a bad thing; I just wanted to make sure it was what I thought." She grabbed his hand again and smiled without confirming or denying his statement. They walked around in broad circles in and out of the paths of buildings, just trying to hold on to the moment. When they had come full circle, back to the female bathroom, he backed her up into the light so he could look at her.

She didn't wear makeup. He wondered if he would even like it if she did. He loved her pale skin and golden-brown eyes. Her nose was slim and sat perfectly above her arched lips; her bottom lip was the most enticing to him. He loved how her short hair bounced around her face and that she bit her lip when she looked at him. He wondered several times if that was unique to him or just something she did.

June felt uncomfortable when he looked at her without speaking. The valance that she carried around seemed to dissolve, and her insecurity crept in. Before she could fall into those insecurities, he lifted her chin and kissed her, gently holding on to her bottom lip with his. *His lips are so warm*, she thought. She was overwhelmed by her physical response to him. He slid his cold hands underneath her coat and held her waist as he continued to kiss her. She couldn't breathe; she didn't want to look at him. She hadn't felt sexual in a long time. *How did he find this part of me so quickly?* She wanted to pull away from him but needed to stay. It hurt deeply to feel her body giving in to him. She didn't trust--period. Suddenly, he pushed her back against the wall and looked away. His mood was displaced from the connection they had just had. *What did I do*, she thought? *Did he read my mind? Was I making some weird face?* He covered his mouth, not looking at her. He wondered if he should have stopped kissing her, because he knew this moment wasn't casual. He didn't know how to start the conversation, and the more words he said, the further it led him from the truth. She only heard *'relationship; a serious relationship.'* She pushed him away and covered her face. Immediately she felt her veil of protection return as her chest tightened. She knew she had no reason to be upset; she hadn't mentioned Alex yet. But she realized she would never have spoken of Alex in the present tense, and she would never have said it was still serious. She composed herself by releasing her bottom lip from the grasp of her teeth. "Do you need a best friend?" she asked blankly.

His laughter was painfully forced. "June, I never planned this."

"Did I? We should get back," she said coldly. *I am so stupid,* she thought. *Why am I so stupid?*

His mind raced through thoughts and words, but he couldn't connect any of them to form a sentence. She grabbed the door to her barracks. "Wait," he said. She looked at the night sky behind him. "I don't like the dark." The door closed between them, and he couldn't go into the female barracks after her.

Anna jumped up when she heard June crawl into the bunk below her. "So?" she asked. She couldn't tell Anna he was taken; she knew how excited she was for her. So, she just said, "perfect!"

June did her best to avoid Devan for a few days. Anna had learned his schedule by heart, so it was difficult to distract her from pushing them closer together. Anna wanted so much for June to find the happiness that she had found with the love of her life. She knew what love looked like and wanted to share that with June. It was the last break of the day when Devan finally caught up with June. "Hey," he said reluctantly. "Can we talk tonight?"

"Sure, what about?" She refused to look at him.

"Us?" he muttered. *Us,* she thinks, as she bites her bottom lip to keep from crying.

Something about the way he said "us" made her want to hear a reasonable explanation that she could hold on to.

She agreed to meet later that night. They walked around the base and found a small outdoor museum of old military vehicles. They sat inside the jeep, and he turned to her with a solemn look on his face. "I don't think we would have such a strong connection if I loved Denise."

That was the first time June had heard her name.

Denise.

It didn't make her feel any better that she had a name. "I don't want...I won't interfere in your relationship." He turned his head toward the wind that had started blowing. "It's getting cold, and there is a storm coming. Do you just want to talk later," suggested Devan?

June squealed at the top of her lungs, "No, I don't want to talk about your girlfriend. I am sorry. I can't do this thing, whatever this thing is."

He didn't respond, and he didn't move, knowing the situation was a lot more complex than he had even admitted. He thought carefully about his next words, because he couldn't imagine not ever seeing her bounce again. He had already grown an insatiable desire for her kisses, and he knew he couldn't let her go for something back home that wasn't working.

The swirling wind in the distant sky engulfed the mountain peaks one by one. The taste of snow was in the air, and the first few flakes fell between them. She looked up at him as he grabbed one of her hands. She loved his dimples when he smiled. She loved that she felt kindness in his eyes. His lips were full, and she still remembered how they felt against hers when they kissed. The attraction was natural and more powerful than she had ever experienced. There was also a gentleness about him that was alluring.

She wasn't familiar with the gentleness of a man. Her father was an abusive man, and she would have never said Alex was physically abusive, but he wasn't supportive or nurturing either. She wondered if she needed that kind of support, because she had stayed with Alex for eight years.

She realized at this moment, standing before this gentle being, that she had never experienced this kind of love before. Although she had come close before her life turned so quickly in the wrong direction. At this moment, she had instantly found a way past her damage to love Devan. However, she would never allow her feelings to influence his decision.

The rapidly approaching snowstorm was a harsh taste of reality. They had to run back to the barracks before deciding about their "us." As soon as June walked into the barracks, Anna pulled her aside. "Girl, Alex keeps calling; he talked to Sgt Jackson and told him he was your husband."

June looked over, and the receiver of the phone was off. Sgt Jackson walked over and said, "Handle your shit, Brown." She lifted the receiver and said hello. She could hear Alex clear his throat.

"Mira," he said. He hadn't called her that in years. She thought about all the letters he had written her when he had been deployed. It seemed like an eternity from this moment. She closed her eyes and listened to his voice as he spoke. *How had he gotten the number there? What did he want?* As if he had read her mind, he said, "I have a friend that got the number, and I wanted to call to apologize for not bringing your gloves. Can we talk about us when you get home?"

"What us, Alex?" Before answering, she heard a woman call him by his nickname, Ali. She swallowed hard and said, "Goodbye, Ali." She hung up the phone and leaned against the receiver. Sgt Jackson touched her shoulder. "Brown?" he said, concerned.

"Shit handled," she said as she pushed by him in tears.

.....⁻ ..⁻⁻⁻ ⁻⁻⁻..

June feels the jeep's tires skid in the snow; they have made it back to the field headquarters. It's another shack with a fireplace and refrigerator. There is some basic medical equipment there, and a young medic approaches her and grabs her hands. "Are you anemic?" he asks. She nods yes, and then shrugs to acknowledge that she doesn't know what that means. The group of two sergeants and the medic decide to force iron-enriched food down her throat until she can't eat anymore. The alternative is to pull her out of the class and send her home only days before graduation. June begs them to go back out to the field with her squad. Her sergeant finally comes in and agrees to take her back. As he puts his hand on her helmet, he says, "Let's go play god." He dangles a key in front of her face. June knew well what the god-key was; she had used MILES gear throughout her military career. The laser-tag exercise used blanks for rounds and unique gear that is activated by the laser on the end of the weapon. Once "killed" by the laser, the soldier needed the god-key to reset the system and silence the alarm.

"Did you get that shit handled?" he says half-jokingly.

"Can I ask you something?" asks June. "About Specialist Devan Bradley and Chief Warrant Officer Brown?" he probes, with one eyebrow raised.

"Who told you about it?" she pauses quickly, remembering that adultery is a serious crime in the military and she is still officially married.

"Brown, it is fine. You are too young to look so sad all the time."

I look sad? She felt she was doing a great job at hiding how she felt.

"Look, it is not my place to offer advice, but Bradley seems a lot nicer than CW2 Brown," he says.

"How did you know he was a Warrant Officer," she asks?

Redirecting, "June," She is shocked that he called her by her first name. "I've been around a long time. Just watch yourself." He hesitates. "Uh, do you know about Denise?"

She felt a little puke in her mouth but didn't respond. "Please make sure you know what you are getting into." *How did he know about Denise?* she worries. He looks over at the young girl, his daughter's age. *How had she gotten herself into such a mess?* "Have fun here," he says abruptly, "Then take it slow once you get back home." He smiles as they pull up to the first outpost. "Wanna be a god?" he asks as he hands her the key.

They walk up to a bunker full of screeching chimes, and she sees Anna holding an M-60 machine gun. Her heart lightens. "You are a badass, Anna," smiles June. "The guys couldn't handle it," she pauses in a pose, "so I took it off their hands." June laughs. The chimes from the miles gear are echoing through the small space in the bunker. Everyone needed to be revived with the god-key except for Anna.

After a few hours of participation, Sgt Jackson takes June back to her outdoor accommodations but not for the nighttime war games. It is freezing, so the medic decides she needs to stay bundled up in her sleeping bag until everyone returns. June feels guilty that Anna has to be out in the cold and that she still has Devan's warm scarf, but she appreciates the time alone to think.

Before she can follow the trail of thoughts in her mind, she feels a burst of cold air as the door to the shack flies open. It is Anna and Devan. They both seem happy to be out doing the war games. Anna climbs up the bunk and says to June, "You have to hear this story."

Devan begins narrating before she can respond: *So, I am sitting out in the cold waiting for what seems like hours in the dark, and I almost feel like they forgot about us. I reach into my pocket to grab some gum, and my flashlight turns on. A barrage of gunfire comes my way. Yep! I single-handedly killed my whole squad.* He can't even finish the story before they all begin to laugh.

June looks at Devan, who is over-dressed in layers of green fatigues. He has taken his helmet off, and she can see that the extreme cold has changed his complexion. His flat nose is red, and his full, soft lips look a little blue from the cold. She remembers kissing those lips just a few days earlier and the shock of his cold hands on her body as he pulled her into him. She scans his face and neck and wants to kiss him now. *She thinks that warm kisses on a cold day are her new favorite thing.* She offers him the scarf he gave her, but he laughs and says, "No, I am still waiting on your promise to warm my neck."

June smiles and says, "I don't think we made that official."

He turns to walk away but stops, "You kept the scarf, didn't you?"

She nods and covers her face with the scarf.

"Oh, by the way," says Devan pushing up his nose with his bent index finger. "John, my battle buddy thinks that anemia is a venereal disease." They both laugh as the group walks out the door.

Alone again, June feels the cold darkness as she thinks about how complicated her life has gotten these past weeks. She wonders if Devan's passion for his story reflects a passion for life. She wonders if they had met in Seattle or Portland if the attraction would have been as strong. *She thinks the battle dress uniform (BDU) does something for a man.* He has stolen her heart smelling like a combination of wool, dirt, and diesel fuel. How could she have resisted him if he was dressed in jeans, a t-shirt, and smelled like Irish Spring soap?

She decides at that moment to do something that feels strange to her. She decides to trust her instincts about Devan and to stop over thinking everything. Before she can sink back into her doubt, Devan comes running through the door again alone. He steps up on the side of the bunk and kisses her. She feels her nose burning and can't hold back her tears. Then oddly, she realizes that she is the one with the warm lips. His cold, wet mouth excites her. She grabs his face and looks into his eyes. "Us?" she questions. He nods his head just as they both hear a loud "Dude!" from John outside.

Things move fast the next few days, wrapping up their last few classes, cleaning their gear, and graduating. June and Devan stop talking about Denise and find a secret spot in the stairwell of one of the unused barracks to talk about themselves. They have only briefly discussed how far apart they live and their desire to continue seeing each other. It is easy to feel those things so far away from both their realities. The closer they come to an end, the more nervous they both feel about the future. The last night they sit on a chair on the landing of the stairwell. The wind keeps howling up the stairs toward where they are sitting. Every time that someone opens the lower door, June cringes.

"What's going on?" asks Devan

"I just feel sick," she says. He understands the gravity of the situation more than she may realize but wants to savor their last moments.

"What if--" she pauses, "What if you change your mind about me?"

"No!" says Devan as he grabs her face and kisses her. "I will not change my mind; I am falling in love with you." She smiles but feels uncomfortable about those words. She redirects the conversation.

"Do you know that I almost didn't make it here to training?"

Devan hides his bottom lip, "What do you mean?"

She explains how she had planned to cancel her training because Alex didn't bring her gloves and the other gear she needed.

"What changed your mind?" he asks.

"My sister randomly called me at 3 am the night before and said her phone had rung, and she thought it was me. I was so upset I was going to cancel, and she talked me into coming."

"I will have to thank her," he says, noticing the time. Devan walks June back to her barracks, swinging her hand wildly in a moment of nervousness and joy. This is their last night. They fly back home tomorrow morning. Devan lies in his bunk staring at the ceiling with a sick feeling in his stomach. He hasn't returned any of Denise's calls in three days.

June's flight leaves at 3 pm. She and Devan meet at the airport and sit together. He changes his flight to have more time with her, and they find a semi-private corner to talk. They talk about him canceling his flight and coming to Portland and vice versa. The time passes quickly, and when he gives her the last possible hug, she buries her head into his shoulder and says, "Don't forget about me." He hands her his phone number and kisses her forehead. "Not possible," he says as he walks away. She watches him disappear down the jet bridge and waits by the gate until his plane pulls away.

June knows she has to go backward before going forward with Devan. She has to figure out how things went so wrong with Alex. She sits gazing out of the airplane window and takes herself back to the beginning.

Two

Alex Brown

Alex grabbed an orange juice from the refrigerator, read the label, and then grabbed water. He added bottled water to his grocery list with his left hand and then used the pen as a chew toy.

Across the room, a rusty screen door opened with a painful screech, and he saw his grandmother gently guide it closed.

"Gram, I will grab some WD40 for that door tomorrow."

"There is some *spray Pam* under the cabinet; it works just fine," she said, waddling into the living room and sinking into her favorite chair.

Alex curiously grabbed the Pam cooking oil and sprayed the hinges; he tested the door and added WD40 to his list. He walked into the bathroom and noticed he was almost out of Noxzema. His Gram had told him to always clean his face with it to look young. He added it to the list.

He had lived with his grandmother for years. It wasn't discussed why. As Alex grew up, the role of mother and grandmother became blurred into the same image of his Gram gently guiding the door closed. Nevertheless, part of him hoped his mother would be proud that he had joined the Army, but his decision somehow justified her distaste for his existence.

He walked into the living room with his list complete and sat beside his grandmother but didn't speak.

She was focused on the TV, which was playing reruns of Sanford and Son. Alex watched his grandmother as the glow of light from the TV illuminated her smile.

"Did you run today?" she asked, not looking at him.

"Yes, ma'am."

"What was your time?"

He dropped his head and didn't answer.

She sat up in her chair and looked at Alex. "You won't get credit for your best, Alex, unless it overshadows theirs."

He didn't speak; he just bit the side of his lip, stood, and then kissed her forehead. As he left the room, the phone rang. His Gram quickly picked it up. She didn't say hello, she just flopped the phone onto the floor and looked at Alex with an understood glance. Alex picked up the phone, knowing it was Vance.

"Sup?"

"Ok, hear me out," pleaded Vance.

"No!" Alex looked at his grandmother for approval.

"Remember Mandy?"

He did.

"We are going to Mike's party, and she wants to bring June."

"Who is June again?"

"You know the girl who kept talking about all that universe bullshit when I met Mandy?"

Alex smiled as they both said, "the philosopher," laughing. He remembered the first time he met *June-The-Philosopher*. Vance and Mandy were close to a climax in the back seat, and June was looking through the sunroof, contemplating how far up in the sky you would have to go to get to where God lived. "No!" Alex reinforced.

"Ok, hear me out?"

"Stop, hold on a minute." He held the phone to his forehead, winked at Gram, and walked out.

Before Alex could speak, Vance pleaded again. "Alex, I know what you will say, and I wouldn't hit you up if David had come through for me."

Alex wasn't a fan of David. He was a heavy drug user and was always plotting to rob an ATM.

"I will meet you at K-mart, but don't call back here if I am a little late. Gram hates you."

Vance laughed.

....⁻ ..⁻⁻⁻ ⁻⁻⁻..

The room was scattered with clothing, shoes, and makeup. June had tried on her fifth dress. She pranced around in her second choice of heels back and forth, looking in the mirror, checking her shape, and smoothing down her dress. *This is it,* she thought: It was a black dress with white and black spandex down the side. She bought it at the mall because she had seen a few college girls trying it on. It was pretty but didn't make her feel overly sexual. Her sister, Darlene, peeked around the corner.

"Sis! Wow! You look amazing," she exclaimed. She took a photo and then walked up to June and grabbed her hand. "So, do you have a date for tonight?" June sighed, "I am not sure. Vance said that a guy named David was meeting us."

Darlene pursed her lips, "June, are you saying you have never met this guy?"

A car horn divided the focus Darlene had directed toward June. They both jumped as June ran past her, escaping.

Vance didn't speak to June when she hopped into the backseat. Mandy took a deep breath and turned to June. "Uh, do you remember when I met Vance at the mall?"

June nodded.

"Remember the other guy, Alex?"

June scrunched her nose.

"June, we asked David, and he doesn't want to come," she blurted.

June looked down at her dress. "Ok, I will just stay here. It's fine."

It wasn't.

"No! It's New Year's Eve. Alex is really excited to see you again." Mandy nudges Vance.

"Uh, sure! Yeah, he liked talking to you about that Jesus shit," said Vance sarcastically.

Mandy pinched his arm.

Vance looked at June in the rearview mirror. "You know Alex is going to be an Army pilot? He leaves in a couple of weeks, so let's just have a fun night".

June looked down at her dress again and nodded.

They met Alex in the K-mart parking lot. June didn't see a car, so she wondered how he had gotten there. He looked different than she remembered. Now he was her date.

Alex was tall, slender, with a milk chocolate complexion and jet-black hair that had been bleached in the front to a golden brown. He was handsome, the skateboarder kind of attractive, dark, and sultry.

June smiled awkwardly and then scooted behind the driver's seat, making room for Alex to sit beside her.

Abruptly, Alex opened the front door and motioned Mandy to the backseat. She looked at Vance for reinforcement, but he motioned her to the back.

"Man! I can't believe you came out. This party is going to be epic."

Alex smiled and glanced back at June. He didn't remember her being so sexy. *That dress:* He blew out a deep breath.

Mandy stared out the window.

June looked down at her dress, then briefly at Alex when he laughed. "Uh, is there drinks at the party, she said awkwardly? Uh, I mean, are there?" she corrected.

Alex turned toward the backseat and looked at the Philosopher without saying a word. *Grams would love her if she weren't white.* He smiled, "What do you drink?"

June sat up straight. "I like Jack and Sundrop," she perked.

She didn't.

Alex didn't respond. He turned around and looked out the window, tapping his lips with his finger.

The four sat quietly in the car as they pulled up a few blocks from the party. No one moved or spoke.

Vance stared out the window, frustrated.

Mandy sat with her arms crossed, pissed off.

June sat with her hand on the doorknob, embarrassed and worried her dress made her look fat.

Alex covered his mouth with his hand, wanting desperately to look back at the Philosopher again.

June opened her door first and stepped out into the cool night. The chill alerted Mandy, and she stepped out of the car too. They both stood rubbing their arms, waiting.

Alex looked at Vance. "Were you really going to trust David to go out with the Philosopher?"

"You said you couldn't come, and I am getting laid tonight." Vance stepped out of the car. "Let's go," he directed as he motioned Alex to get out of the car.

Alex didn't look at the Philosopher; he just pulled his coat close to his chest and ran into the party. Vance kissed Mandy on the cheek, "I will find you in two seconds, I swear." He glanced back to see her reaction as he jogged to catch up with Alex. Mandy was determined to stand outside until Vance returned for her, so June walked into the party alone. She was shocked by all the people crammed into this tiny house. Most of them looked her age, so she searched each room for the "Parent."

There was a bar upstairs, and the guy standing behind it handed her a drink. She took one swallow and then found a trash can to dispose of it. Mandy, who only lasted two full minutes outside in the cold, sat in a chair upstairs. June could tell she was still caught up in her feelings. June kissed her on the cheek and continued her quest to see if there were parents there. As she walked down the stairs, a young attractive guy grabbed her ankle, but his friend swatted his hand away. "She is with Alex," he said sternly.

June, slightly disappointed, continued her search. When she got to the basement, she looked around. *Still no parents; hmmph!*

Her search was halted when she heard a familiar laugh. Alex was standing across the room surrounded by girls, all laughing at the story he was animating. June glanced down at her ankle and wished it was true: *the being with Alex thing.* She swayed back and forth, worrying that Alex might think she was looking for him. Just as he looked up, she found her escape. She opened the basement door and walked out into the cold night.

She always felt hidden beneath the night sky, invisible from the gazes of others. Growing up in the country allowed many late nights staring into the blackness. The twinkling stars always danced around in her eyes, and she loved those rare opportunities when she got to see a satellite moving slowly across the sky. She knew God lived up there somewhere if there was just a spaceship that could travel far enough.

As she peeked through the window at Alex, the chill of the night surrounded her. She hugged herself and leaned against the cold cinder blocks. She closed her eyes and imagined Alex there with her under the stars, but when she opened her eyes and looked back in the window, Alex was gone. She searched the basement for his tall figure but saw nothing but girls crowding in corners *drinking that awful punch,* she assumed. She closed her eyes again and tried harder to imagine him standing next to her.

....⁻ ..⁻⁻ ⁻⁻-..

Alex was distracted several times by the movement outside. He finished his story and then excused himself. He didn't use the basement door to exit. He walked upstairs and then around the house slowly. He was determined to find the source of the bounces of light and shadows. When he turned the corner, he paused. *It's her,* he thought, surprised. Seeing his date leaning against the house with her face pointed upward and her eyes closed, made him smile. He felt instantly attracted to the silhouette of her body, which was beautifully positioned so that the light from the window amplified every curve. His heartbeat accelerated as he watched her—*that dress.*

Alex cleared his throat, and June stood to attention. She couldn't see who was in the darkness, so she reached for the doorknob.

"Pee!"

She almost did.

"Philosopher!"

He had forgotten her name again.

"Oh, hi," she said nervously with her hand still on the doorknob.

"It's almost midnight. You want to sit in the car and get warm?"

June looked through the window at all the girls he was talking to. They were frenziedly looking around the room, then at the clock. It was five minutes until midnight.

Now keenly aware of the cold, Alex grabbed Pee's hand and pulled her toward the car.

June noticed the warmth of Alex's hand and how it consumed hers. She grabbed his arm with her other hand and shuffled close to him, shivering, as they walked back to the car. Alex opened the back seat door, and June got in, scooting across to make room for him. He smiled, closed the door, and got into the front seat. She rubbed her legs and stared out the window, and there it was: a satellite moving across the southern sky. *God was up there.*

Alex cranked the car and turned on the radio. They started the countdown to the New Year by playing "Wild Thing," by Tone Loc. Alex grabbed his thigh and squeezed, then, in one motion, hopped into the back seat and started kissing June. She fell backward toward the door but didn't notice when her head hit the window. His lips were soft, and his eyes were closed. So, she closed hers. *Is this what desire tastes like?* She had been kissed before, but not like this. Strange electricity surged through her body, and she was sure she had pee'd her pants for real this time. Alex slid his hand down her thigh and lifted her leg so he could get closer to her. When he looked up, he noticed how uncomfortable she looked, so he pulled away.

She was left abandoned of his kisses.

Alex reached into the front seat, grabbed his coat, and then turned back to Pee.

"Lift your head," he said gently as he placed his coat behind her. He leaned over her again to kiss her but paused. "What is your name? I am sorry, but I forgot."

"Juniper, but no one calls me that. It's kind of a weird name. I think it came from my grandmother." She realized she was talking too much when she saw him looking vacantly out the window. "They call me June."

He smiled and then kissed a girl named June for the first time. He could feel her body drawing toward him; he knew well what that meant. "Happy New Year," he said as he kissed her, pushing up her dress. June moved down until her back was flat on the back seat. Alex unzipped his pants, then pulled her panties aside and touched her. *Silk.*

"Are you ok with this?" he asked.

She was.

He kissed her neck as he exposed himself and moved closer to her. The tension between them had formed like a fog of passion and desire, which consumed them both. His heartbeat quickened in anticipation, hers in nervousness. Alex closed his eyes as he felt her warmth.

"Ow!" gasped June, lifting her body forward so forcefully that she and Alex hit their heads together. Alex slid to the side of her, holding his head. Then he quickly zipped his pants.

"No, don't stop. I want to," she pleaded, squinting one eye because her head hurt so badly.

"June, have you had sex before?"

She shook her head and twisted her mouth to one side.

Alex covered his mouth with his hand. "I am leaving," he said as the moisture of his heavy breaths pooled in the creases of his hand.

"Now? What did I do?" She pulled down her dress and sat up. "I am sorry. I uh, I didn't even think you liked me."

"June," he said as he tried to record her name in his memory. "You are amazing- surprisingly so, but I am leaving soon, so I don't want to get anything twisted."

"I'm not trying to twist anything," she defended. "I was supposed to have a date with David.

"Stay the hell away from David!" he scolded.

June covered her face and pressed her fingers forcefully into her eyes.

He softened. "June." He wanted to say Juniper. "June, kiss me."

She uncovered her eyes, and he kissed her tears, then her lips. She could taste the salt from her tears in his kiss. As their lips danced around in the warm moisture between them, she noticed a unique smell that their kisses created.

That must be what desire smells like.

He lifted her chin. "If we have sex, it isn't going to be in Vance's smelly ass car."

She suddenly noticed the odor in the car and smiled.

Mandy and Vance were holding hands and laughing when they returned to the car. Alex got out and motioned Mandy to the backseat. "Thank you, Sir," she said, smiling and winking at Vance.

They dropped Alex off at K-mart. He smiled at June and then slapped hands with Vance. "Take her home!" Alex said in a way that Vance understood clearly.

The next stop was at the end of her driveway. Her sister, Darlene, had left the bedroom window open so that she could crawl in. June slowly moved back the covers and crept in with her sister. She put her cold feet on the back of Darlene's legs. *She is so warm.*

"How did it go?" mumbled Darlene.

"Perfect."

....⁻ ..⁻⁻⁻ ⁻⁻⁻..

June and Alex talked almost every day. She would sneak the phone into her room and talk until early morning, sometimes falling asleep on the phone. She marked her calendar: Alex was leaving in three weeks. *That's plenty of time to fall in love.*

Alex invited her to a party his friend was having two weeks before he left for training. June didn't have a car, so Mandy picked her up to go to the party. She decided to wear a dress despite the frigid temperature, just in case the right moment presented itself again. She also borrowed a pair of Darlene's thongs. They were very uncomfortable.

Mandy ran into the house, leaving June standing against the car, adjusting her panties. She squirmed around several times, readjusting, and then decided to take them off. She shuffled into the house, feeling confident but a little drafty. She didn't see Alex, so she walked over to Vance, who pointed upstairs.

June bounced up the stairs and around the corner in the direction of Alex's laughter. She bit her lip and danced into the room with her arms held wide for a hug. Alex was lying on the floor. A girl with brown hair was lying on top of him, and June noticed his hand was between the girl's legs. Alex was moving his hand back and forth, so June assumed they were doing something sexual.

"Hi," June said, lifting her hand once she was noticed.

"Oh, hell, you made it," said Alex, as he jumped up to greet her. He wiped his hand on his pants and pointed to the girl. "This is— Damn, what was your name again?" The girl flipped him off and grabbed her panties off the floor.

"I'm really. I well. Sorry. Nice meeting you," stammered June as the girl walked past her and out the door.

Alex reached out to grab June's hand, but she pulled it away, scrunching her nose and pointing at the bathroom. When he returned, she was gone. He lay back down on the floor and passed out. June ran downstairs, past Vance and Mandy, toward the backyard. The door opened to a cold gust of air that slightly lifted her dress. *Dang, it happened again.* She looked around cautiously and then felt between her legs. It was like someone turned on a faucet. She wanted to ask Darlene why it was happening but was scared she would be mad. She ran through the crowd of people in the kitchen. *They must know. Why are they laughing?* She put her head down and tried not to cry. She bumped into Alex standing by the bathroom.

"Where did you go?" said Alex, as he lifted her chin.

His hands smelled like soap. She looked up at him. "I want to leave, but Mandy won't take me home." She pushed past him and went into the bathroom. She wiped several times until the moisture was gone and then put on the thongs that were in her pocket. She sat on the toilet for a few moments, straightened her skirt, and walked to the sink to wash her hands. *Look in the mirror.* She stared at the water flowing over her hands. *Look in the mirror, Juniper.* She heard Darlene's voice as she lifted her chin and looked in the mirror, and recited the following words: *You are enough. You are perfect. You don't ever have to change who you are to be loved.*

Alex knocked softly as he leaned his head on the bathroom door for support. "Juniper, open the door."

She did.

He guided her up the stairs to a different bedroom. There were candles on the windowsill and Keith Sweat playing in the background. He could tell she was upset, so he offered to get a couple of drinks.

Please don't be Jack and Sundrop.

Alex bolted down the stairs on a mission. As he turned the corner, he saw Mandy and Vance. He tried to maneuver through the crowd, so he didn't have to pass them. His shoulders sank when he heard Vance's elevated voice.

"So, are you finally going to hit that?"

Alex looked at Mandy but didn't respond. He walked slowly to the kitchen, standing at the sink, gripping it tightly. He wanted to have sex that night. He wanted that unforgettable memory to carry him through training. He glanced back at Vance and Mandy as he grabbed two blackberry beers from the cooler. He walked as slowly as possible by Mandy, she looked up at him and smiled. "I brought the blackberry beer. Do you like it?"

He had liked everything she brought.

When he returned, the door was unlocked. He pushed through, hoping June was still there but also wanting her not to be.

She was asleep on the bed.

The wax from one of the candles had cascaded down the wall and pooled on the beige carpet. He walked over to blow out the remaining candles and was comforted by the darkness. He sat quietly on the edge of the bed, wishing it wasn't June in the bed. He closed his eyes and thought about moving *her* hair back as he kissed her neck. He would be sure to move slowly to absorb every moment with her. He longed to feel her heartbeat against his bare chest, but she didn't belong to him. He had lost his chance to know her when he took the front seat with June-the-Philosopher and left her in the backseat with Vance. He drank the last sip of her beer, allowing it to linger on his tongue, and then he covered June with a blanket.

June woke to an empty bed, an empty room, and an irreconcilable feeling of regret. *I shouldn't have let him know it hurt; next time, I won't open my stupid mouth.*

....- ..--- ---..

June looked at the calendar full of X's and crossed off the last one. She tried to call, but Alex's grandmother told her he wasn't there.

He was.

His last promise to June was that he would write to her and give her a phone number so they could stay in touch. He only called once and sent her his address but never responded to her letters.

June had dialed the number Alex had given her many times, but a frustrated voice would always tell her that Alex wasn't there.

On a Saturday, she was at the mall when she saw the sign: US ARMY. She walked through the door and asked the Sergeant, "Can I go to Fort Hood if I enlist?"

He nodded.

June decided to call Alex one last time to tell him she was joining the Army. He had been gone for over a year to Chief Warrant Officer Training and then to flight school at Fort Rucker.

The phone rang several times before she heard a guy answer saying *something, attack helicopter battalion, barracks B.* As politely as she could, she asked to please speak with Chief Warrant Officer Alex Brown. To her surprise, after some clanks and shuffling, she heard his voice.

"This is Brown," he said.

"Wow! I thought there was a sign by the phone saying; If June calls, I am not here," she was joking but could visualize the sign in her head.

"Funny," he said. "What's up?"

"Well, I have written you and uh, called. I was surprised you didn't respond".

"June, talk to Mandy."

She looked at the calendar. She had already sworn in and was leaving for basic training in four days.

"What?" There was a long silence, then a dial-tone.

June immediately called Mandy in tears: a few minutes later, Mandy arrived at June's house with eighteen letters from Alex and a plane ticket in Mandy's name.

Three

The Basics

There were rumors of war as tensions escalated in the Middle East. Since Vietnam, there hadn't been a significant conflict, so when June raised her right hand and swore to "protect and defend," she had no concept of what that meant. At 17, she had followed her heart into war. She had gone to basic training and advanced individual training (AIT) primarily to prove to everyone back home that she could do it. She enlisted to be stationed at Fort Hood, where Alex was, although she could have chosen any other location or occupation based on her Armed Service Vocational Aptitude Battery (ASVAB) scores. The recruiter never encouraged her to rethink her decision. She just pointed to the documents she needed to sign. By her graduation, the Army had already stopped using the military occupation specialty (MOS), which they had just trained her for, so there weren't many available slots left for her job. It had almost been six months since she had spoken to Alex, so she told herself that she didn't care if the Army honored her request to go to Fort hood.

During this time, the Gulf war (Desert Shield/Desert Storm) was ramping up, and there was a hold on troop movement while they prepared to deploy soldiers to the region. June was stuck at AIT for a few weeks after her training was completed, waiting for her future to be determined. She was given the worst jobs to occupy her time. She painted rocks, washed dishes, mowed grass, picked up trash, bleached sidewalks, and did lots of shifts of guard duty. The worst duty was guarding flag poles before the change of command ceremonies. Soldiers would cut the ropes of the flag poles as pranks, so they would place guards there overnight in two-hour shifts.

The air was thick and muggy as she stepped out of her barracks on the way to her last guard shift. The sun gave way to a dark moonless night. June tripped on the curb as the street light flickered in and out of brightness before going completely dark. Her duty was from 1 am to 3 am with Private Miller, another female soldier waiting for assignment. They were dropped off by the parade field to guard the flag poles by the podium. The area was massive: three hundred yards in length and one hundred yards wide. At night, it was a void of impenetrable darkness. June was excited; because she saw shooting stars the last two times she was on duty. Her wish was always the same, to be with Alex.

About an hour into their duty Private Miller said she needed to run back to the barracks for something.

"We have to stay on our guard post until we are relieved," said June.

"Wow, girl." She stretches out the word girl. "You have really drunk the

Kool-Aide, haven't you? I will be back in less than 20 minutes. They will never know unless you go and tell them."

"I won't," chirped June faintly.

Duty aside, June enjoyed the time alone under the stars. It reminded her of New Year's Eve with Alex. She walked around looking for satellites and talking to God. She wasn't *"with"* Alex, but God knew she loved him and would undoubtedly honor her prayers to protect him if he went to war. Her grandmother told her once that she could pray for God to put a hedge of protection around someone, and, as long as she said it in Jesus' name, God would honor her request. So, she closed her eyes. *God, in Jesus' name,* so that she wouldn't forget that part. *I ask for that hedge-thing of angels around Alex to protect him.*

As she walked, with her eyes closed, around the corner, her world faded into darkness, and she fell to the ground like a masterless puppet.

She heard sounds but nothing she could hold on to. She felt tightness around her arms and legs, and they wouldn't function or flee. Her body was numb, but she became keenly aware of the smell of freshly cut grass, dirt, and whiskey. She tasted blood. Before the darkness consumed her, she desperately searched the sky for a satellite or God. But there was only darkness and the taste of whiskey pressed against her quivering lips.

Four

I can't. I just can't

June awoke in an unfamiliar state. She felt the cold grass on her bare legs. Her head was aching, and she could barely focus. She waited in the darkness, believing her replacement guard would soon relieve her: no one came, no one ever came. When she could tell that the sun had risen through her badly swollen eyelids, she tried to stand. The thorns from the Kennedy White roses tore at her skin. She grabbed a handful of the thorns and pulled herself up. She saw the blood streaming down her wrists but felt no pain. She could see the light out of one of her eyes, but the other was swollen shut. Her hands were numb, and she could feel tightness around her arms. *He made perfect tourniquets.*

June found a way to stand and pull up her panties. Her hands were shaking as she searched the ground for her pants. They were covered in blood. She tried frantically to lick her fingers to remove some of the blood and straighten the creases that she had so carefully ironed into them. Then she stood up, as tall as she could, and walked the long four blocks back to the barracks.

Private Miller was asleep in her pajamas. She woke up to see June standing over her, crying. "What the hell? What the actual hell, June?"

June fell to the floor, "You didn't come back."

Private Miller ran down the hall and called the sergeant-of-the-guard, who woke up abruptly. He ran into the room, looking at his watch. He had slept through the guard change. He pointed his finger sternly at June and barked questions at her. June tried to remember what had happened. But she could only remember the smells, the tastes, and the sounds. She tried to stand at attention during his questioning, but her knees failed her.

The sergeant told her to get into her PT gear and come back out to the front of the building.

She followed the order.

She walked systematically to her closet, removed her boots and clothes, and painfully put on a pair of shorts and a t-shirt, but left the tourniquets on her arms because her training told her never to remove them without a doctor present. She returned as directed and was scuttled into the sergeant's personal truck. It was painful to sit, so she leaned to the side. The sergeant noticed the tourniquets but looked at her without expression. "You really got yourself into a mess, Westbrook."

She tried to open her eyes to look at him, but her face had swollen and obstructed her vision. "What did I do?" she muttered, almost in a state of unconsciousness.

"Well, you are in some real shit if you report this."

June sat up the best she could. "What do you mean?"

"The Army will discharge you, probably dishonorably." He had no idea if that was true, but he would be in serious trouble if they found out he had fallen asleep on duty.

"What should I do?" pleaded June.

"Tell them you got drunk and had rough sex but don't remember anything."

"I would never do anything like that," she reasoned. *I am waiting for Alex,* she thought. She grabbed herself between her legs. She was still bleeding. Her face burned as the tears slid down her cheeks. *There is nothing left to be saved.*

The sergeant continued, "Then take your chances, but it's a shame you came all this way and are willing to throw it out the window."

The truck skidded to a stop in front of sick call.

"Get out! Don't forget what I said," he commanded as he drove away.

The Sergeant stepped out of his truck at the parade field; he cautiously looked around and then walked toward the podium. There was a trail of blood from the podium to the rose bushes. He didn't react. He just walked over to the building adjacent to the podium and turned on the water hose. He delicately sprayed the white roses to remove the blood from each petal and then forcibly sprayed the grass. The trail of blood flowed effortlessly through the grass to the drain, and he watched as it disappeared into the sewer. He walked around the area, picking up pieces of June's uniform and a chunk of her hair. He tossed the items in the trash before getting back into his truck.

....- ..--- ---..

The lobby at sick call was full of soldiers in their physical training (PT) uniforms, mostly just trying to get out of doing the morning run. The whispers cut through Westbrook as she walked up to the reception desk and laid down her head. The medic looked up and panicked when she saw Westbrook's bruised face. She ran around the counter and noticed blood streaming down Westbrook's leg and that her arms, neck, and face were blue.

June was immediately given pain medication and an IV, and the tourniquets were carefully removed. She slept peacefully for hours before the pain brought her back to reality. She woke up for the second time in an unfamiliar state. She searched the room frantically for Alex; he wasn't there. A nurse was standing over her, holding her hand. "Honey, can I talk to you?"

June nodded yes.

"What happened to you?"

June recited the *rough-sex* story, but she had no idea how to describe the details of sex. The nurse held back her tears. "I know this wasn't just rough sex. You have a contusion on the back of your head, both your eyes are black, and you have signs of forced trauma around your inner thighs and vaginal area. Honey, I have to report this."

June looked up at the nurse blankly. "We just got a little rough, and I fell and hit my head," she pleaded.

"Well, do you mind if we contact him to see if he's ok?"

"I don't know his name. We met out drinking."

"June, there was no alcohol in your system."

"I need to go to Fort Hood. I am really ok. Please!" June tried to stand but fell into the nurse's arms.

"Ok, June, Ok." The nurse noted her chart and phoned the Military Police (MP). Thirty minutes later, a male sergeant walked into the room. Westbrook tried to cover herself with her arms. She felt scorned, like a child being scolded for doing something wrong. His questions were direct and motivated. She couldn't hear her own words or his. She just repeated the story she had rehearsed. Then strangely, he smiled, slammed closed his notebook, and left.

The nurse confronted the MP in the hallway. "This was clearly a sexual assault."

"What exactly would you like me to do?" the MP snarked.

"Your job, maybe?"

"Look, Miss, if she doesn't want to make a report, maybe it was just rough sex."

The nurse was red in the face when she returned to the room.

"June, please. Please file a report."

June stared at the glass jar of cotton balls on the counter. She could see her reflection in the glass, and it startled her. She attempted to touch her face, but the pain brought his violent grasp to the forefront of her thoughts. Her lip quivered as she looked up at the nurse. "I just want to go to Fort Hood," she said.

"Nothing is stopping you from doing that if you file a report," urged the nurse.

June had already found a division between her recent past and her hope for her future. The words were all carefully placed in their individual boxes. The words she could say, the words she couldn't, and the ones that got her closer to Alex. She focused on that New Year's kiss and the taste of his desire. "I can't," she mumbled. "I just can't."

Five

The Frying Pan

Arriving at Fort Hood was like stepping into a war movie. It was August 1990, and the troops were prepared to go to war in the Middle East. As June was driven to the reception station, she could see soldiers running around with gas masks on, performing drills with their weapons. They were all in line at facilities, turning in their green uniforms for tan-colored desert fatigues. Helicopters were flying overhead, and you could hear the tracks of tanks lining up to be transported to the unfamiliar desert region.

Texas smells like dirt, she thought. The heat from the afternoon rains amplified the smell. June looked up from the backseat of the van at her reflection in the rear-view mirror. Her pale white complexion magnified her blackened eyes. She practiced a smile to prepare for seeing Alex, but it hurt to move her face. The van pulled up to the reception station, and a lovely lady at the desk assigned her a room. She dropped her things and returned to the front desk.

"Is there a way to find out where someone is on base? I have an address," she said to the lady behind the counter.

"Sure, honey, just call this number for the post locator," She winked. "You do know the fellow's name, right?"

"Yes, ma'am."

The lady pushed a phone toward June with a hopeful smile. The post locator found Alex and gave her directions to his barracks.

When she stepped outside, the heat was more unbearable than she had previously realized. She returned to her room and changed out of her jeans into a sundress. As she caught a glimpse of her reflection in the mirror, she paused. *You are enough. You are perfect. You don't ever have to change who you are to be loved.* June looked down at her bruised legs. They looked so dirty. She licked her thumb and tried to rub one of the bruises off her skin. She reluctantly grabbed the jeans and slid them carefully over the bruises.

She was dying of thirst by the time she made the five blocks walk to Alex's barracks. There was a soldier just outside the address she was given.

"Excuse me. Could you please do me a favor?"

The soldier turned to face her. "I'm looking for Warrant Officer Brown, Alex Brown?" The soldier waved her off and started walking away.

"It's ok. I was in a car accident," she said confidently.

He gave her a thumbs-up, and a few minutes later, Alex appeared. "June!"

She covered her face in excitement and shame.

He looked at his watch and then tried to focus on June. He had already gotten orders for Fort Benning and, from there, the Middle East. "Juniper, what the hell happened to you?"

Her eyes burned, but she refused to cry. She just shook her head no.

"Who did this to you, June?" he demanded.

She slowly shook her head no.

"For God's sake, just tell me who did this?"

She shrugged her shoulders.

"June?" He grabbed her face and kissed her forehead, trying to fix something, anything he could.

His grasp was painful but wanted. She wrapped her arms around him and said, "I lied to come here." He had no idea what she meant but stopped pushing. He just softly lifted her chin and smiled at her. "I will come to get you after chow."

She looked at him with her head turned sideways, wondering why he was being so nice to her.

"Chow means dinner, Babe."

"I am in the Army. I know what chow is," she laughed.

....- ..--- ---..

June had rarely worn makeup but borrowed some from another female soldier to hide the dark circles under her eyes. Alex met her after chow and noticed immediately that she was dressed in jeans and a long-sleeved shirt. "Did you bring any shorts?" he inquired gently.

"June, go put on shorts; you will die in this heat."

Unable to say no, she shuffled her feet back to her room and slipped on the sundress. She returned to the lobby with a bounce and a pose as she spun around. He was shocked by her bruises but grabbed her hand. "You look beautiful," he said, meaning it for the first time. He held her hand tightly as they walked across the base, kissing her fingers every few steps. They stopped at an open area full of oak trees. The light breeze in no way combated the dry heat. He could tell she was still not acclimated to the heat, so he grabbed her hand and said, "Come with me." They stopped outside his barracks. A few minutes later, he comes running out with someone's car keys.

"Do you like ice cream?" he said as he dangled the keys close to her face.

"I guess so." She was still confused about why he was being so nice to her. She hadn't talked to him since the night he hung up on her and confessed his love for her best friend.

They sat at a Dairy Queen outside the base, sharing a banana split. She noticed that he really liked the chocolate ice cream, strawberry was his second favorite, and vanilla he could do without. He mixed the caramel sauce, banana and both chocolate and strawberry ice creams but only ate the strawberry topping with the chocolate ice cream.

He glanced up at her between bites. He liked her cute little nose and the mountain peaks that shaped her top lips.

"Would you marry me, Juniper?" He said as he started to fidget in his seat.

She sucked then snorted ice cream out of her nose. "What?"

He rambled on about the war and his family and not having anything to come home to. She was stuck on "would" you marry me. It wasn't "will." *Why wasn't it will*, she thought, as he rambled on?

An awkward amount of time had passed when she realized that he had stopped talking and was staring at her. She played in the left-over swirl of brown, pink, and white cream that had melted in the boat-shaped dish. He was about to withdraw the request when he saw her lift her head and smile. "When?" she asked as she scrunched up her nose.

The next day he picked her up in the same car. She had borrowed a white dress from another soldier in the reception station. It was long enough to cover most of her bruises. They didn't speak on the way to the courthouse.

He was afraid she would change her mind.

She was afraid he would too.

"Did you bring your ID?" he asked as they stood in line?

The guy, that guy... he took it, she remembered. "I have my driver's license." She held it up, hopefully.

"Babe, why didn't you bring your ID? I think we need two forms of ID".

"I have a state ID too, from before I got my driver's license." She frantically looked in her wallet and was relieved it was still valid.

Where is her ID? How did she get on base without an ID? He wanted to push, but they accepted her ID and pointed them toward the courtroom.

The Justice was sitting high on a judge's bench surrounded by dark mahogany wood. He was dressed in a black robe. *Great creases,* she thought. The judge had retired from criminal cases and only performed marriages on Wednesdays. He shuffled through their paperwork.

"So, who do I have before me today?" June looked at Alex, hoping he would speak first.

"This is Juniper Westbrook," he said, "and I am Alex Brown."

The Justice laughed. "Well, Juniper, do you know your name, or is Alex just nervous?"

She stammered. "I do, Sir. That is my name. The name he said is mine."

"Well, Miss June, you are in luck today. Our wedding gift to new brides is a well-seasoned frying pan. If you don't already know how to use one, you will learn quickly."

June felt confused, not by the frying pan remark, but was she already married without saying anything? She looked at her feet. *Does he think Alex hit me, or is that some dumb southern joke? Or is he racist? Oh my god, are we getting married by a racist?*

Alex sensed her anxiety, so he forced a laugh and grabbed her hand.

"I don't mean to rush," said Alex, "but we deploy tomorrow, and I still have a lot of stuff to do." When she heard tomorrow, June tried to drop his hand and attempted to pull away, but he held on to her hand tightly.

"Ok, son. Do you all have rings?"

"No," said Alex.

She wanted a ring. She pulled her hand away from his and grabbed her ring finger. Alex quickly retrieved her hand and squeezed it twice, trying to relay a promise. Her thoughts carried her so far away from the *will you* and *do you*, and she just muttered yes when her hand was squeezed. Alex spun her out of her thoughts when the Justice said, "Kiss your bride." She looked up at Alex as he turned to face her, still gripping tightly to her hand. "Can I kiss my wife?" he asked. She didn't respond but closed her eyes and let his lips touch hers softly.

June dallied outside the door as she saw a white couple walk in to get married. With anticipation, she waited for the frying pan joke, and there it was! She shook her head, *dumb joke.*

The Texas heat was unrelenting. As soon as the courtroom door opened, a wave of sand and dirt filled the room. The external conditions were similar to what she was experiencing physically. She had been thirsty since her plane landed a few days ago. As Alex reached to open her door, she smiled.

"Can we go for ice cream?"

"I'm sorry, June. My commander only gave me an hour to get this done and get back to load our equipment."

Get this done?

She drifted away again on the drive back. As they arrived at his motor pool, she was startled when Alex pulled abruptly off the road and handed her the keys.

"Can you park the car back at my barracks?" Before she could answer, he said, "Just leave the keys with the guy sitting in the hallway on the first floor."

"What's his name?" she asked.

"Babe, it doesn't matter. Gotta go."

She watched him run behind a gated fence filled with perfectly aligned military tanks. The other soldiers were all moving fast, all focused on a specific task, like ants passing each other without regard to the movement of the others around them. A few soldiers saw Alex run across the asphalt toward them. They immediately stopped and started cheering. One of the soldiers grabbed his head and pulled him to the ground. *He looks really happy*, she thought. She, however, felt nothing. She had waited for this her whole life, and absolutely nothing came to her when she tried to figure out how she felt at this moment.

The car was returned, and the keys were given to Specialist Duncan. He was dressed in green fatigues and had a broken leg. This was strangely comforting to her, as she knew he wouldn't steal the car or die in an awful war.

The five blocks walk back to the reception station made her dizzy. When she walked into the lobby, the lady behind the counter said, "Well, Miss-Something. Did you get married today? Is he taking you out tonight?"

June hadn't asked Alex if she would see him again before he was scheduled to leave. She felt the panic rise in her chest. She couldn't breathe. That same darkness that she felt from the blow to her head a few weeks ago rushed over her and made her nauseous. The lady recognized her distress and came around the counter with a cup of cold water just as June fell to the floor.

She woke up in the emergency room. She sat up and grabbed her head. It was throbbing. A nurse came into the room and said, "Hey sweetie, your husband keeps calling to check on you. Are you feeling any better?" She noticed an IV in her arm, and she felt extremely cold for the first time in days. "You were just a little dehydrated. It's hot here, Sweetie; you have to drink lots of water, ok?"

June nodded her head.

"I'm not trying to get in your business, but your husband told me ya'll got married today and that he is leaving tomorrow. Well, what I did was I talked to your husband's commander, and guess what? He is getting ya'll a room tonight before your husband leaves."

June tried to stand up. "I can't have sex," she said without thinking. The nurse walked over and grabbed June's hand.

"I saw your medical record, Honey. The nurse said it wasn't rough sex. Like I said, I am not trying to get in your business, but you can still report what happened to you."

June put her hand up but didn't say anything.

"Ok, then, I hear you. I am gonna talk to Doc Amber and see what I can do."

She returned a few minutes later. "Doc Amber wants to check you out to see how you are doing. Would you be ok if we did a vaginal exam on you, Sweetie?"

The nurse noticed tears rolling down June's cheeks. "It's ok, Honey. I will be right here holding your hand."

"Can you tell me if it looks different down there?" June, asked through her sobs.

The nurse smiled at June. "No, Sweetheart, you look like every other woman I have ever seen."

Doc Amber performed the vaginal exam and indicated that June was healed enough to have intercourse.

June looked at the nurse and said, "It hurts to pee, to bathe, to wipe. I can't." The nurse grabbed her hand again.

"If he loves you, he will wait until he gets back, but doc Amber is giving you some Valium for the pain and a gel that will help with the pain too, if you want to try. But you know there are other things you can do to make him think about you while he is gone." She winked.

What other things? thought June but didn't ask.

They released her to Alex. He was waiting in the lobby with his hat in his hand. He grabbed her as soon as she walked into the lobby and pulled her close to his chest. He repeatedly kissed her head, saying, "I got you now, Babe. I swear I got you." He guided her to the passenger seat of the car. They drove to a hotel off base in complete silence.

She didn't want his last thoughts of her to be sad, so she tried to think of what the other things could be.

Their room was on the second floor. The hotel didn't have an elevator, so Alex offered to carry her upstairs. June was determined to change the mood and bounced up the stairs taunting him to follow her. Their room was 6B. Alex turned the key and guided her in. June walked into the room mentally reciting her imaginary, romantic checklist:

Air-conditioned room- check

Not a dirty car- check

No Mandy- check

Alex, as my husband- check, check

"June, I need to take a shower, then I will run out and get us some food and drinks. What do you want to drink?" She understood that he meant alcohol.

"Anything but whiskey," she said as he walked into the bathroom. "No, Jack and Sundrop?" he joked.

He remembered Jack and Sundrop. She shook her head no in response to his joke.

She had noticed a swimming pool on the way to the room. So, she quietly opened the door and walked over to the pool. The water was a lot warmer than she expected and not nearly as refreshing as the air-conditioned room.

When she returned, the door was cracked open. "Alex, are you in here?" She peeked around the door, shielding herself.

The steam from the shower had filled the room with a winter-like fog. His flight suit had been neatly placed over a green '70s-looking chair, his tan boots in line underneath. He was gone. She slowly opened the door and then slammed it behind her. It was the middle of the afternoon, but she was frightened to be there alone. She sat on the side of the bed and suddenly remembered the Valium. *Fear is pain,* she thought. She retrieved the bottle of pills from a Ziploc bag and took a half, then the other half, then another half, just in case. She thought about using the gel but was afraid he would notice.

Alex returned with two bags. He had been gone for a couple of hours, so June was in a drug-induced sleep when he walked into the room.

He looked at her lying across the bed, still in her white dress. It was pulled tight around her hips, and it excited him to see the shape of her body again. He walked softly across the room and unloaded the bags. He had bought her an orange teddy-bear with a zipper pocket in the front, a mini bottle of whiskey as a joke, blackberry beer, snacks, and lots of water. He tried not to disturb her as he lay down on the bed behind her, but his warmth startled her, and she sat up in bed.

"I'm sorry. How long was I asleep?"

"Take a nap if you want. I can watch some TV." He could tell she was confused by his comment, so he said, "We have time. They shouldn't call me until about 8 pm tonight." June got up and went to the bathroom. Her pee sounded incredibly loud to her, so she released it slowly. She felt the pain of wiping, so she decided to use the gel and then hid the tube in the trash under some toilet paper. When she walked out of the bathroom, she saw the bottle of whiskey.

"What the hell is this, Alex?"

He was startled by her response to his joke. "I thought it would be funny to get you the one thing you didn't want."

She saw in the mirror that her neck had turned bright red. She grabbed the bottle and threw it into the bathroom trash.

"I'm sorry, Babe. Come take a nap with me."

The Valium was still making her sleepy, so she curled up beside him and closed her eyes.

Alex woke up around 7 pm, with June's legs wrapped around him. He gently pulled her hair out of her face and kissed her. She woke up feeling a little blurry from the Valium but returned the kiss. She was pleasantly surprised when she tasted and smelled that same desire. She felt like she was finally with Alex as his hand slid down her hip, pulling up her dress.

He gently touched her pale skin, marked with dark circles of bruises around her shoulders, hips, and thighs. "Don't let me hurt you," he whispered.

She sat up and pulled her dress over her head. She unsnapped her bra but left her panties on. He matched her level of clothing as they continued to kiss. He positioned her underneath him and slowly slid off her panties. "Is this ok, June?"

She stopped his words with more kisses and pulled at his boxer briefs. He moved to her side and licked a few of his fingers, and began to touch her. He watched her carefully for a response. When he licked his fingers again, he noticed his tongue going numb. Alerted by his expression, she grabbed him and pulled him on top of her and then inside her. The pain was shocking, but she didn't make a sound that would discourage him.

She felt each of his movements coursing through her like daggers through her spine. She pulled his head down onto her shoulder and closed her eyes until it was over. As he rose to kiss her, he noticed blood on her stomach, on her inner thighs, all over the bed and all over him. Her lips were trembling.

"Shit, June. Why didn't you tell me to stop?"

"I wanted you to be my first. He doesn't count, right? Since he..." Her lip quivered.

"June, don't ever let me hurt you. Don't ever let anyone hurt you." There was an accusation there that was understood.

"Alex, I know I wasn't your first choice. I wanted you to love me."

He didn't respond.

She stood up and saw her reflection in the mirror. *You are enough. You are perfect. You don't ever have to change who you are to be loved.*

He wrapped his hands around her waist. "You wrote me thirty-five letters in six months. No one has ever loved me that much."

Before she could respond, someone banged on the door, startling them both. Alex kissed the back of June's head and then walked over to open the door.

"Hey Jacob, what's up?" Jacob, Lieutenant Edwards, had been Alex's gunner for six months.

"Dude, Cap is pissed," he said with his hat squeezed tightly. Alex and June looked at the clock at the same time: *9:22!* She grabbed the phone.

"It's dead."

"Just hurry, bro. He gave you 20 minutes to get back to the motor pool. I'll be outside." He looked at the frightened June clinging to her blanket and said, "I'm so sorry, Mrs. Brown."

Alex turned and looked desperately at June.

"Go!" she screamed. She ran to the bathroom and got a warm washcloth to clean off some of the blood that had transferred to him. Then she sat and watched as he got dressed in his flight suit and ran out the door. The echo of the door slamming reverberated through her. She was alone. Then the door opened again, sending her sliding off the bed to the floor. Alex lifts her and puts her back in place on the bed.

"Jacob's wife, Tara, will take you back in the morning." "What time?" Alex screamed toward the car. "At 9 am, June!" Before he closed the door, he said, "Look!" she was in a daze of confusion, and her head was still foggy from the Valium. "Mira!" she looked at him. "I love you," he said. She looked away, then back at him but didn't speak. He ran over and kissed her forehead, then knelt in front of her and lifted her chin. "You don't need to say it, Juniper. I know."

"Don't call me that," she said blankly.

He nodded.

"June, I do love you. You need to know that I love you."

She didn't respond.

Alex was shrouded in confidence as he kissed his wife and then walked to the door. He paused for a response to his confession of love, but the sound of the car horn made him pull the door closed between them.

June sat for an hour before she became aware that the door may be unlocked. She shuffled over, dragging the bed sheets, and latched the chain before jumping into the shower. She stood in a daze, watching the blood cascading down her body and flow into the drain. She used the same washcloth she had used to wipe her blood off Alex's still partially erect penis. "I love you too," she said to her hands.

When she got out of the shower, she grabbed the mini bottle of whiskey and put it in her bag. It was difficult throwing away a gift that Alex had given her, even though she'd never drink it.

The mini-fridge was packed with cold water and blackberry beer. She grabbed water and a beer, then swooped by and grabbed the teddy bear and the bag of snacks. She turned the TV on, only to find apocalyptic deployment news. *Nope!*

She reached over and turned on the radio attached to the clock, now reading: *11:03.*

She drank two beers and three bottles of water before she noticed the orange bear staring at her. "What?" she snarled, but the bear stared blankly at her. Wild Thing by Tone Loc started to play on the radio. She grabbed the bear to hold it close to her heart when she felt something in its front pocket. She unzipped the pocket and saw two tiny Ziploc bags containing two gold wedding bands. She searched for a note but couldn't find one.

"Are these for me?" she asked the bear. He looked at her blankly. She took the smaller ring and tried to put it on her right-hand ring finger. It was too small. She tried to force it before realizing it was supposed to go on the left hand. It fit perfectly. *How did he know her perfect size?* She took out his ring and placed it on her thumb. Mr. Bear approved.

....- ..--- ---..

Alex called before he left Fort Benning for the Middle East.

"Hey, Babe," he said when he heard June's voice. *How can he be so happy about going to war?* she wondered.

"June, I am sorry I had to bail on you. I should have been watching the time."

"I found the rings," she perked.

"Yeah, we can't wear rings in the motor pool. One of the tankers almost lost his finger when replacing a track. Could you hang onto mine? I will be back for it," he paused. "And you."

"You better. Oh, and Ali, take down my address so you can write to me."

"Ali?" he asked.

"You gave me a nickname, so I thought I would give you one too."

"I did?"

"You said, Meeda to me before you left."

"Babe, I said 'Mira,' it is Spanish for 'look.'" He noticed her silence.

"You can call me Ali, Babe. Hey, I have to run. I love you." he said abruptly.

"Wait!" She hesitated. "I love you too, Al-eee."

She could almost feel his smile through the phone. "I will call if I can, but I will definitely write."

She held the phone close to her heart, terrified that those god-words might not protect him.

....- ..--- ---..

Alex sat next to Jacob on the flight over. It was rare that they weren't lost in conversation and laughter, but they both sat silently for hours until Jacob bridged the miles between them.

"So, how are things with June?" Jacob leaned forward and looked at Alex directly.

"Seems great."

"What about that Mandy girl?"

"That's done."

"Is it?" Jacob said sarcastically.

"What's up?" Alex asked in an elevated tone.

"Do you love June?"

"I married her."

"Do you still love Mandy?"

"She wasn't interested after June saw the letters."

"Not really an answer, dude. You might want to get your shit straight before you get back stateside."

"So, Jay, how is Tara?" said Alex, annoyed.

"Kiss my ass, Alex."

Six

The War

June was assigned to a unit that made maps for combat missions. This meant she would remain stateside during the war. She wasn't familiar with a topographical map, but she wondered, as she saw them printing, if any of them showed where Alex was. She was embarrassed that she couldn't answer questions about her new husband. Since he had never written her back, she didn't know very much basic information about the *Army* version of him.

When she got his first letter, she was pleased he had done what she requested and told her all about his position in the Army. She wanted to know the information but secretly just didn't want the other officer's wives to think she didn't know her husband. They already looked down on her for being an enlisted soldier.

June kept Alex's letter in her cargo pocket and read it every few minutes. She had never seen his handwriting. There was something very intimate about reading his handwritten letter. He even drew caricatures of him and her, as male and female smiley faces. His smiley wore a hat, and hers had big lashes and a bow in its hair.

Alex was a 152H, assigned to a unit out of Ft Benning. His helicopter was an AH-64d. Some of the officer's wives said he was the best pilot in the region, and June was proud of him in a distant sort of way. She tried to fill the voids in their relationship with repeated thoughts of the few moments they had had together, but the letters he wrote to

Mandy were a constant source of doubt that fueled all her insecurities. Alex had told Mandy she had always been his first choice but that Vance had really wanted to be with her. She didn't want to be the girl Alex settled for, so she was determined to be the best version of herself when he returned.

....⁻ ..⁻⁻⁻ ⁻⁻⁻..

She had been at her unit for a week when they assigned her guard duty at the map depot.

The Humvee pulled up to the gate that surrounded the depot. The Private gave June a key to the lock, which was held together with a weighted chain wrapped loosely through the gate to keep it closed.

"Your shift is four hours, but lock yourself back in the gate. You will be fine. Just don't turn on the main lights in the depot for security reasons."

"Four hours?" squeaked June.

"Take a nap if you want...but don't let the Iraqis get any of the maps," he smirked.

He waited until June closed the gate and then drove away.

She struggled to open the door of the depot but managed to squeeze through. The door slammed behind her, clanging and vibrating an echo of horror through the building. The darkness tormented June, and having to spend hours in the depot alone made her stomach twist and turn. She had tried to ignore the haunting sensations around random people who walked by her and the horrible nightmares that tormented her almost every night. However, the darkness felt alive and full of the evil that had grabbed her that night. She tried to breathe in and out slowly, but even the sound of her breath was haunting.

You're a soldier, June. She took a deep breath and turned on her flashlight. She slowly started to walk around the perimeter of the building. She jumped several times as her flashlight bounced shadows across the walls of the building. She tried desperately to keep the darkness from consuming her. She tried to focus on the things around her: the smell of the wooden shelves and the lingering smell of the ink from the maps.

There were rows of shelves from the floor to the ceiling, all filled with rolls of maps from countries all around the world. On each row, there was an alphabetic marker. Instead of going straight to Iraq, she stopped by the maps of Egypt, France, and Italy, all places she wished she could go. Somehow, the dreams of traveling diminished her fear of being in the dark. She finished her loop around the world and returned to a desk by the door. She assured herself only a giant could open that door by themselves, and giants run slowly.

Dear Ali, she began to write…

Read this away from the other soldiers. I just want to tell you why I didn't stop you that night. It was because I needed to be with you before you left. Not to mention how hot it was seeing you in your uniform. Thanks for writing to me so quickly. It was nice getting my first letter from you- EVER. I think I will die if I don't hear your voice, so I sent a tape re- corder, tapes, and 9000 batteries so we can send messages to each other. If that is weird, it's ok. At least you can listen to mine. I will buy headphones tomorrow so your bunk buddies don't hear me talking dirty to you.

Ali—Please be safe. I just found you, and I don't want to lose you. Is that ok to say? Also, if you need anything, let me know. Tara and I have been making cookies to send over to your platoon. Please make sure the guys that aren't getting letters get cookies first. It must be hard to be there alone.

I can't believe I have written so many words without saying I love you. I really do.

Your wife,

Mira

She wrote his address on the envelope, neatly folding the letter that she would place in the box of goodies she planned to send him the next day. She sat in silence and realized that Ali made her feel safe. As she started getting sleepy, she decided to walk around the world of maps again. This time she visited a map of Germany. She noticed a town called Bad Kissingen and started laughing. She wondered why anyone would name a whole city after bad kissers?

Before she realized how much time had passed, she heard a vehicle drive up outside. She looked at her watch and was relieved that her time was up. As she locked the clanking chain on the gate and climbed into the vehicle, she saw another female soldier climbing out of the backseat. "Here are all the keys," June said and handed them to her.

"Thanks. Was everything ok in there?" she replied nervously.

"Sure," reassured June. "Do you know that Germany has a town named after bad kissers?"

"What?" The soldier looked confused.

"There is a town in Germany named Bad Kissingen," June laughed.

The soldier rolled her eyes at June and walked away.

The driver looked over his shoulder at June as he laughed.

"Bad means Spa in German," he said.

June was genuinely disappointed. Spa kissing wasn't nearly as funny as bad kissing.

She laid down on her bunk, and immediately her hands started twitching as she fell into a deep sleep. She had a room alone because all of her bunk-mates complained that her screaming kept them awake at night. She hated being noticed that way, so she started a rumor that she had a room alone because her husband was an officer. She could handle their looks about jealousy but not pity.

As she tossed and turned, the darkness crept around her again, and she began to dream. The memories from her relaxed consciousness were vivid and painful. She could hear his voice as he recited her name and social security number over and over. He spoke to her as if he loved her and then punched her in the face. An overwhelming smell and taste of whiskey and blood caused a physical reaction, even in her sleep. At the end of every dream, she was twisted up in her boot laces which came to life to squeeze the breath from her body. June wrapped the sheets tightly around her and slowly started the part of the dream where she dies.

....- ..--- ---..

Tara has promised to take her to the Post Exchange (PX) and to the Post Office that afternoon to mail the cookies and her package to Alex. June had given her a key because the sound of knocking scared the crap out of her. When Tara crept in, the door slammed behind her. June lurched and fell out of bed.

"Oh God," Tara said, covering her mouth. "I am so sorry, girl."

June sat up and held her forehead. "I had an awful dream about him again, and I was bleeding this time."

"June, you are bleeding." Tara ran over to help her up. "We need to take you to the hospital, June. This is happening way too much."

"Ok, but we need to go to the PX and post office first. I don't want Alex to wait an extra day for his stuff."

"June, I am dropping you off at the ER, and I will go mail this crap and come back."

June waited hours in the ER before she saw a familiar face. It was the nurse and doc Amber.

"Hey, Sweetie." What are you getting into now?" asked the nurse smiling.

"I have a lot of pain, and I keep bleeding. My pee hurts, and it all smells funny."

"Well, that is quite the list. Come on back."

When Tara arrived, she sat in the waiting room for an hour before June returned.

"What's going on, girl?" Tara whispered as she guided June to sit beside her.

"Vaginitis, a uterine tear, and an injury where my pee-pee comes out. They also said something about pelvic disease, where you get swollen in there. I have to take antibiotics. They said I have a hair fracture or something in my hip too. I can't run for four weeks; what if I get fat?"

Tara grabbed her head and held it close to her chest. She couldn't hold back her tears. Tara was eight years older than June and had been married to her husband, Jacob, for nine years. She had no words for June or herself.

How could someone do this to this young girl? she thought, as she held her as tight as she could. Finally, she tried to lighten the mood. "You won't get fat, June. That won't start happening for at least ten more years. Do you want ice cream?"

"I can't without Alex."

"Oh!" pipes Tara, "I have a letter for you from Alex." It was stuffed under your door when I went back to grab you some clothes to stay at my house. We will go eat some pie and get smashed."

It had never occurred to June that Tara and Jacob had a house. As they drove off base, she could feel an eerie silence that contrasted significantly from the noise she noticed when she first arrived at Fort Hood. It was nice to drive away from the base for a while. The sound of helicopters had been a constant reminder of Alex being gone.

Tara lived in Harker Heights, which seemed like Paris to June after being stuck on base for weeks. Tara pulled through a drive-thru liqueur store and got them two daiquiris.

"Is that legal?" inquired June.

"The drink or you drinking?"

"The drink. Isn't there an open container law?"

"It's cool. They tape down the straw—closed container," Tara laughed at the shocked look on June's face.

The house was a Spanish style and painted a golden color with a wavy red-tiled roof. There wasn't any grass, only small rocks in the front yard.

June loved the archway that was above the door and most of the windows. She couldn't help but daydream about having a house like that with Alex.

"Take those drinks, girl. I will grab the mail."

June did as she was instructed and walked to the front door. When she stepped into the house, the smell of vanilla surrounded her nose. *I will buy candles next time I am at the PX,* she thought. They sat on the well-worn couch and un-taped their straws. June felt elated as she remembered Alex's unread letter in her back pocket. "Do you mind?" She waved the letter at Tara.

"Girl, please. Go ahead. I need to make a quick phone call anyway."

She slowly opened the letter to ensure she didn't damage the envelope too much. She could feel the familiar grit of sand on the neatly folded pages.

Mira,

I hope you are feeling better. I love you so much. She paused. She feels guilty for not saying I love you sooner, in the letter she had just sent him.

We went on our first mission today. I am sorry I can't tell you where I am exactly or what I do on our missions, but just know that I am always thinking about you. I promise I will share the important stuff when I return. I haven't gotten a letter from you yet, but I know you have a lot going on. She threw down the letter and ran to find Tara. She was talking on the phone, so June waited for a break in her conversation.

"Yes, Babe, I will see you tomorrow. I am hanging out with Chief Brown's wife tonight; she had a rough day. Yeah, you remember the raped girl I told you about."

June put her head against the wall. *Babe? Raped girl?* She turned to walk away and tripped over the dining room chair.

"Let me call you back. I hear June." The phone clicked as June frantically tried to make it back in position on the couch. Tara walked in, slurping down the last sip of her daiquiri.

"Do you like tequila, Little Bit?"

June shrugged her shoulders.

"Tequila it is." Tara returned, swirling around in circles with two glasses of ice. She sighed. "Isn't life funny?"

June looked blankly into the shag carpet. *It kind of sucks*, she thought.

"Here, let's toast to being free." She handed June a glass full of straight tequila.

June turned her head to the side and questioned Tara's comment by twisting her mouth.

"I must already be buzzed. Let's toast to being carefree," Tara reluctantly corrected.

June cringed at the taste of the tequila, but at least it wasn't whiskey. "Have you heard from Jacob?"

"Yes. Why?"

"Has he gotten any letters from you?"

"I write him," she torts.

"No," pleaded June. "Has he said he has gotten your letters?"

"I think so; why?"

"Ali, I mean, Alex said that he hadn't-" She starts crying.

Tara joined her on the couch. "It takes a while for them to sort these things out, with the mail and all. Don't worry. He will probably get ten all in one day."

June grabbed the letter from Alex and continued to read it as Tara walked toward the radio.

"You like R&B?" Tara questioned.

"Yes, please."

...Babe, could you send me sexy photos if you feel comfortable? It would be nice to have something to hold on to. Send one I can show to the boys too. COMPLETLY COVERED!!!! Well, they are calling me. Don't worry. I got plenty of guys watchin' my 6.

*I love you. Ali **** The first time -Surface****

"The first-time surface?" questioned June out loud.

"Oh, I love that song," said Tara.

June instantly remembered the first letter. "Can't Stop- After7?" she thought it was some Army code she didn't understand. He was sending her songs.

"Do you have it," she pleaded. "Or do you have *Can't Stop* by After 7?"

"I got you, girl." She put the first song on.

....- ..--- ---..

Alex loved flying. He had found a sense of purpose when he got his deployment orders. He was a meticulous pilot. His helicopter, Sheila, was the first girl he had ever connected with. Together they were an impenetrable pair. Flying missions in theater was especially exciting to him. He flew hard and low, luring the enemy out of their hiding places. He protected the troops on the ground, and so far, he had counted three possible kills, which he justified by his sense of duty to his country.

He had already flown several missions at night during his first week in theater. Training had prepared him for the flying but not for the sandy conditions. Firing on targets barely seen during sand storms played hard on his conscience. He flew close enough to the ground to hear screams as he turned and banked. He equated those screams with someone hurting June. Somehow every target was that guy that raped her. He was justified in killing *that guy*.

His last possible kill weighed heavily on him. He thought he might have killed a woman holding a child. There was no justification for that, and a shadow of doubt crept into his subconscious. He had always believed that the Universe kept a balance sheet. That very act may have put him in jeopardy. He always flew with Jacob, knowing that Jacob was of strong character. Even though they had only been a team for seven months, Alex trusted him with everything he valued. Alex reasoned that he would be protected as long as Jacob was his gunner.

His third week in theater was when the Operations Commander chose him to fly a special mission. Alex felt this distracted the Commander from his secondary responsibility as gunner.

Night flying in desert conditions was extremely dangerous. The sand and the sky felt inches apart. He needed a hundred percent from his co-pilot, but Cap outranked Alex, so there wasn't much he could say. He performed his checks three times and cleared the mission routes with the same persistency. Jacob, who always stood watch in the operations tent, sensed his anxiety and handed him a cross necklace before he made his way to the tarmac. "I got you, man, even if Cap stole my spot," he laughed as he grabbed Alex and pat his head.

"I can't take that. Didn't your mom give that to you?"

"No, Tara did. God knows she wants me to come home safe." They both laughed.

This mission was more programmed than Alex was used to. He felt a sense of paranoia that he was being given a check ride. He followed his procedures by the book, no sharp banks or fancy maneuvers, just clean flying. He was relieved as they landed from another successful rescue mission.

Alex jumped out of the chopper and immediately ran to Ops to check for mail. The "mail-guy" held up a letter as Alex walked through the door. He smelled it for good measure.

"No scent this time, Chief. You might need to make a special request. Just let me know if I need to inspect your mail for the good stuff."

Alex smiled and snatched the letter out of his hand.

He grabbed a chem-light and found a spot outside their compound. He looked at her handwriting on the envelope, and his heart beat faster. He had read all the thirty-five letters she had sent him at least once, but number thirty-six was from his wife.

He laughed as he realized June scared him more than any mission he had ever been on. He opened the letter slowly and read each word as if it were a breath he needed to survive. He hated himself for the way he had treated her before he joined the military and that he hurt her physically on their wedding night. *I should have never had sex with her*, he thought, a little angry at himself. He read the last words, lingering on *I love you*, then sat and watched satellites slowly moving across the sky. He took the cross necklace out of his pocket, but put it back because he wasn't sure if he believed in God. Looking into the dark sky, he smiled and made a promise to the satellite that he would never hurt June again.

The command, "Chief Brown!" ripped him out of his thoughts of June.

"Debrief."

.... - .. --- --- ..

"I'm shrunk," slurred June as she curled up on the couch.

Tara smiled, covered June with a blanket, and placed a small trash can in front of her.

I'm shrunk too, she thought. Then stumbled back to Jacob's favorite recliner. Tears rolled down her cheeks as she remembered a time when she loved Jacob the way June loved Alex. Eight years of deployments had torn them apart, and the smell of perfume on his uniform unlocked a different side of her. She wanted to divorce him before he left, but he had gotten his orders before the lawyer finished the paperwork. The Soldiers and Sailors Civil Relief Act prevented her from serving him divorce paperwork once he was officially deployed. She didn't have the heart to tell June that the Army would tear apart her relationship with Alex too, so she played the part of a dutiful wife, at least in front of June. When June woke up the following day, Tara was gone. There was a note and twenty dollars for her to take a cab back to the base.

....- ..--- ---..

June received the letter about the "sexy photos" and returned a box including a Playboy, but no photos of her. His response was to return the Playboy, minus three pages that had been stolen and a short note:

Mrs. Juniper Brown,

I was obviously not clear when I requested a sexy photo of YOU. Here is your Playboy. I didn't keep the torn-out pages. They were missing when I returned last night from my mission.

Your anxiously awaiting husband,

Ali

P.S. I am sending you rolls of film. Don't under any circumstance get them developed. Just save them for me, please. Also...

*****My, My, My Johnny Gill**** (in case you need some inspiration)*

....- ..--- ---..

It had been three months and four days when things started to change. June was horribly depressed. Reveille brought the mornings, physical training (PT), chow, and work. Then the days dissolved into mail calls and retreat, which brought her nightmares. Tara wasn't answering her calls, so she spent most of her time in her room alone. Her project was to create a book of all Alex's letters, leaving the back of each page for the letters she wrote him. It would be the start of their great love story.

Since Tara was missing in action, she asked another female soldier; Jacy, to help her take the sexy photos. The song Alex sent to inspire her talked about a red dress, high heels, lipstick, perfume, and the woman's hair down. She listened to the song as they took the photos. Jacy, her pseudo photographer, suggested that she also make a tape of all the songs he was sending her for when he returned.

....- ..--- ---..

When Alex walked into Ops, the mail guy danced around with his letter. "Chief, I have to be honest. I took this one over to my tent and rubbed it on my pillow."

Alex smiled and grabbed the letter. He could smell an unfamiliar but refreshing perfume. The letter was firm, and he could tell instantly that photos were enclosed. He went to the spot where he opened all her letters, but he hesitated to open it this time. The last time he had seen her, she had bruises on her face. He calmed his breathing with three deep breaths, and then he cracked his chem-light and read her letter by the yellow glow. He didn't look at the photos burning his fingertips until the last word was read.

"Damn," he said a little too loudly as he smiled wildly at her photos. He knew she had listened to the song because she was in a red dress that hugged her hips, bent slightly over her bed, with her hair cascading softly over her face. Also included was a photo of her in the white dress he had last seen her in, standing in the park where he had taken her that first day. *Sheila is going to have to take a backseat to this one*, he thought.

Seven

Zain 43

The silence around June had manifested itself as depression, the kind of darkness that can suffocate even the brightest light. For June, the depression consumed her words and ability to organize her thoughts. Five days passed before she realized she hadn't written Alex. As she stared at the blank page, she couldn't find one word to say. She called her sister Dee for help. "Why don't I know what to say?" she muttered on the phone to Dee.

"It's ok, JB. I write him every few days. I just sent a poster and care package. Don't be so hard on yourself."

"It's tough because Tara isn't talking to me. I feel so alone."

"JB, you know you can call me any time you need to talk. We will have sista-time. As for Alex, buy him a few cards. All he needs is the *I love you.*"

June had found that running helped with her depression, so she decided to run to the PX the next day for the cards and some Ziploc bags to store the film Alex had sent her. As she walked into the card area of the PX, she saw Tara.

"Hey, June. I am sorry. I, uh." She looked agitated and kept looking toward the door.

"It's ok. I have been depressed too. This crap is hard."

A flood of information spewed from Tara's mouth. June stood in front of her, sinking back into the darkness. All she heard was that

Tara had sent Alex and Jacob a tape and that she was sorry. June tried desperately to find a number so that she could call Alex, but they were in black-ops, his commander reported.

....⁻ ..⁻⁻⁻ ⁻⁻⁻..

Jacob was glad to finally receive mail from Tara. It had been challenging to watch all the other soldiers getting mail. The distance made him second guess the decisions he had made in his marriage. He knew that he could be a better husband. He felt hopeful that she was writing to work things out between them. She had sent a short note and a videotape. *Make sure you share this with your squad and Alex.* When Alex returned, Jacob got a group of his closest friends and Alex together to watch the video in the debriefing tent. Alex wanted to pull him aside but followed him to the tent- hopeful.

Jacob smiled when he saw Tara. She was wearing a short blue dress. He punched Alex in the shoulder. Alex played over the scenarios in his head. *Her dress was really short. Why would she want other guys to see this?* He reached and grabbed Jacob's shoulder.

"Hey buddy, maybe you should watch this alone. These guys can't handle this much skin." Before Jacob replied, a man grabbed Tara's breast and kissed her neck.

"Out!" barked Alex. "Everyone out!"

A cascade of laughter followed the group as he saw Jacob collapse to his knees. He stopped the tape and then ran to Jacob.

"Man, I'm sorry. I am so sorry. Let's talk to Cap; maybe you can go back?"

"Back to what? "

"Jay, don't go there. I need you in the game, man." Alex squeezed his shoulder tighter.

"Well, Chief, it's pretty clear the game is all I have."

"This shit screws with people, Jay. Just work it out when you are back stateside."

Jacob stood up and composed himself. He squeezed his mouth hard, between his thumb and index finger. As he walked past Alex, he patted him hard on the back. "Roger that," he said reluctantly.

Alex walked over to eject the tape when he saw the note from Tara. *Make sure you share this with Alex.* It had been a week since he had received a letter from June. *Was she on the tape too?* He pressed play and turned off the volume on the TV. It was eight long minutes before the video went to black. He fell to his knees—*no June. Thank God, no June,* he thought with his palms together in a prayer pose.

Alex didn't see Jacob until the following night for the mission brief. He pushed him over to the corner of the tent. "Jacob, you can't ride on this one," whispered Alex.

Jacob knew he had lost his composure, and the consequences pressed hard against his chest.

"I need this, Chief," he urged.

"It's not up to me, Jay. Colonel wants me to take a gunner from Cap's team."

"Damn right, said the young Lieutenant Miller. Hoorah!"

"Man, I am sorry. I should have your six out there."

Alex reached into his pocket, pulled out the cross necklace, and handed it back to Jacob.

"Alex, keep the cross."

"You keep it, Jay." He pulled June's photo out of his pocket and kissed it, winking at Jacob.

"Ok, man, whatever gets you back here in one piece."

The tension was thick, like the dry desert air that stole the moisture out of their mouths. There weren't any words left to say, so Jacob gave Alex a one-arm hug and patted him hard on the back. Alex looked down at the photo of June one last time before he ran out to his helicopter.

Alex tried to stay focused as he flew into the darkness with a stranger as his gunner. They were fifteen minutes out when he felt Sheila jerk hard to the left. Lt. Miller yelled, "We got impact!" The RPG round impacted the tail rotor, which was missing, causing the 64 to be unstable and lose thrust. The aircraft shook violently and began to yaw to the left. Alex tried to fly forward to stabilize, but Sheila was going down. The sand kicked up by the spinning aircraft caused distortions in his night vision, and he was unsure where the land met the sky. He came in faster than he intended and landed off-axis, which caused the aircraft to roll. As the rotor pulled apart, metal and debris fell around the pair. Sheila came to a stop back on her landing gear, like a good girl.

....⁻ ..⁻⁻⁻ ⁻⁻⁻..

Jacob had been in Ops when the call came in that Zain43 had gone off the radar. He immediately thought about June. She was Alex's life force. He grabbed a Sat-phone and ran outside. He rigged it to dial stateside. "Answer!" he screamed into the receiver. The phone rang until the signal went blank. Frantically, he dialed Tara's number. She answered in a drunken fog. "Tara! Listen!"

"Don't yell at me! You have no right– "

"Tara, shut the hell up for once in your life. Chief Brown's helicopter went down tonight. The whole crew is MIA. Go get June; I will call back in two hours. Tara, do you hear me? Two hours!"

"Why do I have to get involved?"

"Are you kidding me right now? Get your ass over to get June, or I swear you will never get a divorce from me."

She tried to call June several times but couldn't reach her, so she went to the liquor store to restock. Jacob called back in two hours only to get her voicemail. He tried June's barracks again, and someone answered.

"I need to speak to Spc. Brown. It's an emergency," his voice was cracking. The soldier blew a bubble and let the receiver hang as she walked back to her room and closed the door.

June, who had just finished a run, stumbled into the barracks. She saw the phone receiver hanging and frantically went to hang it up. *What if Alex is trying to call?* she thought.

As she lifted the receiver, she heard Jacob's voice.

"Is anyone there? Hello!"

June was in shock as she said, "Hello."

"June, I mean Ms. Brown." He paused for an uncomfortable amount of time. Not knowing what to say. "This is Lieutenant Edwards, Alex's gunner." He could barely say the words. We met briefly on your wedding night. I am just calling you to– "

"Where is Alex?" she screamed, interrupting his practiced dialog.

"I don't know. His chopper went down about 2 ½ hours ago, and that is all I know so far."

June leaned forward and puked on the floor. "No!" she screamed. "LT., why aren't you with him?"

Jacob felt the blood drain from his face. "I should be," he said. "I should have his six right now." Jacob was alerted by Captain Humphrey's motioning him over.

June heard yelling in the background and then static. "LT.!" she screamed. No, don't hang up on me!" The door across from the phone opened.

"Brown, keep it down!"

June threw the phone at the soldier, which flew back and hit her. The pain sent her into a spiral of anxiety and emotion. She ran back to her room and grabbed Mr. Bear. She sat rocking back and forth, frantically spinning his ring on her thumb. "He promised he'd come back for the ring and me. He promised," she said to the bear.

Tara got home to three messages, saying, "Tara!" at increasing frustration levels. She unplugged the machine and the phone and went to bed.

....⁻ ..⁻⁻⁻ ⁻⁻⁻..

The dust settled around Sheila, and Alex could hear voices speaking Arabic in the distance, but there was no gunfire. He looked up into the black night and saw the satellite he used to guide him through June's letters, so he knew it must be around 3 am. The glass on the craft was completely shattered, so he reached up to Lt. Miller to check for a pulse. *No!* He rechecked his pulse. Nothing.

"Zain 43 on the ground at zone 22. One possible KIA," Alex said affirmatively. "We need cover ASAP." Two helicopters were already on their way to their last known position. Lt. Jacob Edwards and Cap-Humphrey piloted the rescue copter. CW3. Banks and Cpt. Finger flew cover fire. Sheila was now burning from heavy fire, and Jacob felt sick. Iraqi troops had created a perimeter around the downed helicopter and were firing consistently at any bird in the area. Once he got the ok, Jacob fired savagely back at them, blanketing the area with rounds. Each light that streamed across the night sky stood in revenge for his lost friend and his screwed-up marriage. The vibration of the weapons beat at his chest like restless savages preparing for battle. Finger and Banks continued to fly a defensive circle around the downed craft to provide cover.

Edwards and Humphrey landed beside Sheila, and Alex motioned for them to take Lt. Miller first.

"No can-do, Chief! Strap up," said Captain Humphrey. Alex crawled onto the outside of the aircraft and strapped to the handholds. This was the self-extracting position: nowhere a pilot ever wanted to be. Just as he positioned himself, they began to take fire. At this moment, he realized his arm was broken, but he began to return fire.

"You can't leave him," shouted Alex.

"Don't worry, Chief."

"The two pilots dismounted and drug Lt. Miller to the aircraft and strapped him in."

It was about ten kilometers to the nearest combat hospital. They flew at 80 miles per hour. Alex pulled his scarf over his ears and face, but the wind and sand cut deeply into his skin. He wrapped the scarf tighter and could smell June's perfume through the fibers. *I promised,* he thought. Once given the all-clear, Edwards and Humphrey flew over Sheila to put her down. Jacob looked at Alex before taking the final shot that destroyed the craft. They banked hard to the left and flew toward the hospital.

....⁻ ..⁻⁻⁻ ⁻⁻⁻..

After being treated by the medic, Alex used the Sat-phone to call June. He was pissed that Jacob had contacted her. The phone rang four times before someone answered. He was shocked to hear June's voice.

"Babe," he said smiling.

"Oh my God. Is it really you, Ali?"

He laughed, "Yes, Babe, it's me. I am surprised you answered."

"Are you kidding me? I have been sitting here on the floor all day, threatening anyone that wanted to use the phone. What happened? Are you ok? Lt. Edwards said–" she whimpered.

"Slow down, June. I'm ok." He looked at her photo and then closed his eyes and imagined her in front of him.

"So, what about Sheila?"

Silence.

"Hey, who was your co-pilot?"

Silence.

"Are they sending you home?"

"I want to stay, June."

"Were you injured?"

"I broke my arm."

"Can you fly with a broken arm?"

"No."

"Then why would you stay?"

"It's my team June. Those mother fuckers. "He mumbled something in Arabic that she didn't understand or question.

"Ok, Ali. I am sorry. I am just worried about you."

"I have to go."

"Ok, can you just keep..." before she could finish, she heard static on the line?

....⁻ ..⁻⁻⁻ ⁻⁻⁻..

It was one month before the barrage of troops would return from the region and after she had received her 34th letter and song: "Praying for Time," by George Michael. June looked at the calendar full of Xs and marked off the last day on the calendar. The letter had been dated three weeks before she had received the terrifying call from Lt Edwards. According to the other officer's wives, Alex was on a plane coming home. He had given June vague information about his flight in his letter, so she asked his stateside Commander for the details. She got to the Killeen airport about 30 minutes before his plane was scheduled to arrive. She had brought the book of letters, six cassette tapes full of his songs, and a cooler of cold beer. She finally saw a plane arrive, and the airport announced that Dallas passengers had given up their seats so that the soldiers could return home with their gear. It made her so happy that someone had shown them so much kindness.

She stood back away from the other people waiting for the flight to deplane. She had no idea where their relationship stood or any idea how he was. She hadn't heard from him in three weeks. Each soldier that exited the plane was still covered in sand. She instinctively hugged each of them as they walked past her, and when the last guy left the plane, she stood dazed. *Where is Alex?*

....- ..--- ---..

Lt. Edwards walked slowly toward June with his hat in his hands. "Ms. Brown?" He barely recognized the woman he saw in front of him. His previous image of her was with her face covered in bruises and wrapped in bloody hotel sheets.

June looked up at him and instinctively hugged him. "Where is Alex?" she whispered in his ear.

He briefly hugged her before pushing her back away from him. "Oh, they sent him back early because of his arm. Hasn't he contacted you?"

June spun the gold ring on her thumb as if it would magically make Alex appear in front of her.

She looked around, and the airport had cleared out.

"Sir, do you need a ride?"

Jacob looked around and then at his watch. "Yes, ma'am."

June walked to the car with her head down.

Jacob focused on the hem of her red dress.

"Do you like blackberry beer?" she asked.

"Of course, I do," he lied.

"You are such a liar. Alex told me you only drink Bud Light." She tossed him a Bud Light out of the cooler.

He looked at the can, confused.

"I figured you would need a ride since…" She didn't want to finish the sentence.

"That's very kind of you, Ms. Brown," he said, cracking open the beer.

"Geez, call me June, please."

"I can't do that, ma'am." He puts his hand up and waves, "no disrespect."

"Well, could you do something else for me?"

"Sure."

"Can you find out where Alex is and let me know?"

"Roger!" He clears his throat. "I can do that, ma'am."

June dropped him off at the barracks and drove back to hers alone.

….⁻ ..⁻⁻⁻ ⁻⁻⁻..

June waited for three days to visit Alex after Lt. Edwards had told her where he was. *Even Jesus had needed time in the wilderness to think,* she thought. She put on a white dress with red polka dots and red heels. She had bought a red 1950's purse from the thrift store and finally felt the part of an officer's wife. She walked into the barracks and demanded to see Alex. A private directed her to the sergeant-of-the-guard.

"I need to see Chief Brown," she said sternly.

"Yes, ma'am, but we need to be discrete. He's in a bad way."

June licked her lips, which disappeared before she took a deep breath and exhaled.

He took her down the hall of the enlisted rooms and pointed to his room.

"The soldiers had been leaving food outside his door, but he never ate it."

She looked over her shoulder at the sergeant and opened the door.

"I will wait here for your instructions, ma'am."

Without thinking, she asked, "Why?"

"He's a hero," he said proudly. "He kicked the shit out of those Iraqi bastards."

The room was dark, the smell pungent. She flicked the light switch on and off. It didn't work. She walked over to the window and raised the blinds enough to see her way through the room. There was glass from the light bulb on the floor. She reasoned that is one way to turn off the light. She made notes of his condition and crept out of the room with her list of commands.

"Ok, I need a large trash can, some cleaning supplies, and lots of cold water," she ordered.

"Check," said the sergeant.

June walked slowly to her car and grabbed clothes, wet wipes, a toothbrush and toothpaste, and a backpack. She returned to the room and saw the large trash can and five water bottles outside the door. The sergeant ran down the hall toward her.

"Ma'am, we will clean the room. Don't worry about that."

"Bring the supplies," she sternly insisted.

"Yes, ma'am."

June drug the trash can into the room with the rest of the supplies and started the task of bringing her husband back to life. She gathered the bottles of piss and gently placed those in the bottom of the trash can along with a bag that she refused to open. The entire room smelled like whiskey, which overwhelmed her senses. June leaned over the trash can and puked. Alerted, the Sergeant knocked on the door. "It's fine," she said.

She lit a candle she had brought from the car; vanilla and lavender. Then she knelt beside Alex and started undressing him. He was void of existence as she cleaned his entire body with baby wipes. She washed his face with Noxzema and dressed him in PT gear, easing him onto the floor. After placing his bedding into the trash can, she brushed his teeth and rinsed his mouth with water, which flowed down his face onto the floor. When satisfied with his appearance, she opened the door and found the Sergeant still standing there. "Can I trust you to dispose of this trash with discretion?"

"Of course, ma'am."

"Could you also call Lt. Jacob Edwards and ask him to meet me here at 2000 hrs tonight?" She handed him the number.

"Roger that."

June sat on the floor with Alex's head in her lap until she heard a tap on the door.

"Thanks for coming. I need help getting Alex out of here with some dignity. It's bad enough he chose to camp out in the enlisted barracks."

"Give me a few minutes to coordinate a distraction. I will be right back," said Jacob tapping his finger on his lips.

He calls the Battalion Commander, who owed him a favor. The result was a barracks inspection at 2045. A few minutes later, the halls were filled with the sounds of frantic soldiers running to their rooms.

Jacob walked over to Alex and lifted him. Alex stood but didn't open his eyes. Jacob pulled out the cross from his pocket and put it around Alex's neck. "I guess you do need this, man."

June guided them down the hall and out to her car, holding her head high, still carrying her red purse.

"Should I follow you to your place?" asked Jacob, looking at the hem of her dress.

"Yes, Jacob. That would be great." She touched his arm.

"Ok, June. I'll be on your six. Just lead the way."

Jacob helped Alex to bed and walked into June's kitchen with his hands behind his back. "Is there anything else I can help with?"

June walked over to Jacob and looked up at him. She had never seen this kind of kindness behind his blue eyes. She stared at him silently until it became uncomfortable for both of them. Jacob lifted his hand to touch her shoulder, but she turned away.

"That's all. Thanks. Oh! Here take this." She hands him the cross necklace.

Jacob looks at the cross and kisses it before placing it back in his pocket. He stood outside the door for a few moments looking up at the stars. He saw a star moving across the sky and tracked it for a few minutes before realizing it was a satellite. Jacob took a painful breath, and then, almost instinctively, he turned around and placed his hand on the door. He wanted to open the door and apologize for something, anything that would make her feel better.

June saw Jacob's shadow through the small panes of glass beside the front door. *Why is he still standing outside the door?* She frantically searched the apartment for something he had dropped or his keys.

Nothing!

Slowly, she crawled over to the door and used her shoe to turn off the lights. She waited, holding her breath until she heard his footsteps walking away from the door.

....⁻ ..⁻⁻⁻ ⁻⁻⁻..

Alex slept all day for almost three more days. June wiped his body down every day, but he had started to smell. She decided to wake him so she could change the sheets. She was scared to startle him, so she grabbed a wooden spoon from the kitchen and poked him on the shoulder.

"Ali?"

No response.

"Ali, you don't have to talk, but can you follow me?"

She was surprised that he stood, although blankly, and followed her to the bathroom. She slowly undressed him. She realized how he must have felt seeing her bruised body as she looked at him. He was covered in cuts and bruises that showed through his dark complexion.

She started the shower, guiding him in. He looked through her like she was a window into his past. She touched him gently to wash off the last bits of sand. He wasn't aroused, although she touched the intimate parts of his body. She was meticulous in her task to make him feel alive again. She knew to remain silent and non-reactive: washing, spinning, inspecting until she was satisfied with the result.

Two more days would pass before he came back to her. He awoke on his 9th day home, hungry as hell. He walked into the kitchen of this strange place and saw June sitting at a table drinking coffee.

"Hey, Love," he said as if nothing unusual had occurred. "Do we have vodka?" he asked, searching through the kitchen cabinets.

Startled but non-reactive, she said, "Sure. Do you want coffee with that?"

He smiled. "Yes, please. I'd love some of those eggs and bacon too, if you don't mind. I feel like I haven't eaten in weeks."

He hadn't.

She sat in front of him as he drank his vodka/coffee with eggs and bacon. He put his arm around his plate as if he was protecting it from someone or something. When he looked up at her, he smiled. "Real eggs! Babe, I love the shit out of you."

"My leave is up tomorrow. I have to go back to work," she whispered, disconnected from the man that sat across from her.

"Then I guess we will have to have sex all day today," he said.

Not sure if he was serious, she smiled from the left side of her mouth and bit her thumb.

After the second vodka/coffee, he walked over to her. He pulled her hair back and started kissing her neck. "Are you ready for me, wife?" he propositioned.

"Ready?" she said curiously.

"I don't want to hurt you again."

"Oh! I am experienced now," she said confidently.

He stopped kissing her. "How exactly are you experienced?"

She grabbed his shirt, pulled him into the bedroom, and pointed at the side table.

He pulled open the drawer and saw a wild selection of sex toys. He looked back at June, standing with her arms crossed. "Who are you?"

"Your wife. Now get into bed." She had never used any of the sex toys. Tara had bought them for her on one of their girl's nights. She only unwrapped them, hoping that Ali would be interested in teaching her about the other things the nurse had talked about.

Her teasing words had unleashed his desire as he pushed her hard against the wall. It hurt her ribs, but she didn't say anything to discourage him. He grabbed her face and kissed her forcefully, trying to answer a question about her that he couldn't ask. She knew the answer he was looking for, and she didn't flinch. She just pushed him back onto the bed. She undressed him as he sat on the edge of the bed. He tried to touch her, but she shook her finger no in his face. His smile pleased her. She pulled off his shorts and forced him onto his back. He watched her as she slowly undressed in front of him. He couldn't control his physical reaction to her perfect body. He remembered her curves, but there was something sexier about her now, that she belonged to him.

"Close your eyes, Ali."

He did.

She climbed on top of him and started kissing his face. Avoiding his lips but running her finger slowly through his mouth. She kissed his neck, then whispered, "Do you like this?" He answered by trying to roll her over on her back.

"Keep that up, and I will break your other arm," she played.

He closed his eyes as she gently navigated around his scars. "Don't let me hurt you," she said softly.

His eyes remained closed as she pressed her body against his. Her softness and the sweet smell of her hair excited him, but his mind raced back and forth from pleasure to the day he lost Sheila. He constantly thought if he should have banked left or right, pulled up or down. He saw Jacob in the gunner's seat. Tara had saved his life with her sex tape.

She felt his frustration creeping in but said nothing. She crawled onto him and put him deep inside her. He grabbed her face when he felt her body wrap around him. She pushed forward, then back, trying to connect with him.

"Look at me, Ali," she said as she pushed her hips harder and faster towards his.

"I can't." He pulled his body toward the left.

Her motion slowed to a stop. She knew not to ask why. She didn't want to know why. She just laid her head down on his chest and slowly moved to lie beside him.

After he fell asleep, she walked to the bathroom in pain. Sex still didn't arouse her, and his kiss didn't make her feel passionate toward him, but she loved him so much. As she dripped blood into the toilet, she realized that some things that are taken just couldn't be given back.

....- ..--- ---..

The darkness crept in every night to watch them as they slept. They would kiss without really touching lips and fall asleep with their backs to each other. His nightmares fueled hers. He had woken up choking her so many times that she was afraid to sleep too close to him. They walked in the shadows of each other for months, filling the spaces with two-word sentences.

June was showering for work and, as usual, running late. She rushed into the closet for her uniform. As she turned, still in a rush, Alex was standing blocking the door. She recognized the way he was looking at her. It was how a predator looks at its prey before it pounces to devour it.

"Do you trust me?" he demanded.

"Alex, I am late." She closed her eyes and tried to push past him without reacting. *You can't show weakness to a predator; they are fueled by it.*

"I asked you a question." He put his finger on her nose and pushed.

"Yes, now move."

He grabbed her throat and pushed her against the wall. "And now?"

"Alex, stop!" she insisted.

He lifted her small frame off the ground and then dropped her. "I didn't think so," he said as he walked away.

"Alex, what are you doing?"

"Do you trust me?" he shouted, lifting his hands. "It's a simple fucking question!"

It wasn't.

"Haven't I proved that?" She paused. Her heart was racing. *Don't say it. Don't say it, June!* And then she did. "Did you love Mandy? Were this ring and marriage supposed to be for her? Did she just say no, Alex?"

He grabbed Mr.Bear and walked calmly to the kitchen.

"Give me Mr. Bear. What are you doing with Bear?"

He took a knife from the drawer, and in one powerful slice, he cut off Mr. Bear's head.

June grabbed the pieces of fluff and searched desperately for a needle and thread. "It's ok. I can fix him."

Alex looked at her but didn't see June or his wife. He pushed her against the wall and held the knife firmly at her neck, causing her to bleed.

"Please do it. Please. Just end it," she said as she closed her eyes.

"Don't be late for work," he said, dropping the knife on the floor. June watched Alex's hands as he grabbed his keys and walked toward the door. He was calm. His hands were steady. She didn't move until she heard his jeep starting. It was then she stood slowly, grabbing a towel from the kitchen. She wet the towel and rubbed the moist area with a little dish soap. She removed her uniform jacket and scrubbed away the tiny splatters of blood. The hairdryer was the perfect tool to evaporate the wet spots. *Good as new.* She bandaged her neck with a skin-toned band-aid and practiced the silly story about falling into the bushes outside her apartment.

....- ..--- ---..

Both June and Alex knew that there were unwritten policies about mental health and battle readiness. They both knew that talking to someone wasn't an option. So, they found a new topic to fill the dark spaces between them.

"Why do you think you haven't gotten pregnant?" Alex said randomly over breakfast.

"What?" June said, annoyed.

"I've been home for seven months, and I know nothing is wrong with me."

"Alex, I don't know."

She did.

"Let's try," he insisted, moving her hair back and kissing her neck.

"Are we starting now?" She pulled the collar of her shirt close to her neck to cover the scar he had given her.

"I think we would make beautiful babies," he whispered in her ear.

June closed her eyes and released the grasp she had on her collar. She could visualize their kids running around in circles, pulling at her dress. She could see Alex as their father, but the images disappeared when she tried to imagine herself as their mom.

"What's wrong?" he asked, wiping away her tears with his thumb.

"You'll think I am crazy if I tell you."

"Stop! I don't think you are crazy, June."

She looked blankly at his ear, hoping he wouldn't notice she couldn't look into his eyes. She knew that if she told him that something died inside her the night she was raped, he would think she was crazy. She felt dirty. Unholy. Before she was left to die in the rose bushes, she remembered that *he* had pissed on her like a dog, marking his territory. There was nothing sacred or holy left in her—no place for a miracle.

"Mira!" He turned her face toward his.

June looked at him, hoping for a sign.

"Ice cream?"

....⁻ ..⁻⁻⁻ ⁻⁻⁻..

They had to travel to the Lackland Air Force base in San Antonio for all the fertility testing. It was a three-hour drive each way. June loved taking long drives with Alex. He always made their trips into grand adventures. Things felt right for the first time in a long time. He held her hand into the doctors' appointments and bought her romantic dinners on her fertile days. They had found a way to shine a light on each other, making the darkness less powerful.

On one of their trips down, they found this great place called the River Walk and spent hours strolling along the water, listening to the vibrant music from the local restaurants. It always seemed like a vacation away from the painful struggles in their lives.

Their excitement always peaked at the same time every month, only to suffer a defeating blow when June's pregnancy test would be negative. The disappointment crippled them both. Soon, there was no reason for the long drives to San Antonio, so they fell back into each other's shadows. It might have been over then had she not gotten orders for Korea. Something in the Universe kept pushing them forward while they simultaneously stayed motionless in the same place.

Eight

Screaming Rock

June awoke in a daze. The room was dimly lit, but she had no concept of what time it was. Alex was gone. She wrapped herself in the blanket and walked down the hall to see if he was in the bathroom. It was empty. She came back into the room and frantically looked around for a note—nothing. It was Sunday, so she knew he wasn't flying. They always did aircraft maintenance on Sunday. She sat on the bed with her hands over her face. She had thought they had a great night. She started getting dressed and heard someone in the hallway. She peeked out and saw Alex holding two coffees. He had a backpack over his shoulder. Her heart filled with unspeakable joy.

He walked into the room with a huge smile on his face. "Mira, you're awake? I was sure I would make it back before you woke up. Do you have a headache?"

"A little," she admitted, holding her head.

"Well, here is some coffee, and I grabbed you breakfast from the chow hall."

She smiled approvingly.

"What's in the backpack?" she said with a mouth full of toast.

"Well, Princess Grace," he said, laughing. "I brought your running shoes from home and some workout stuff."

"There is no way I am going for a run, Alex," her mouth still full.

"No, I want to take you somewhere, and you can't wear that black dress."

She finished her food, got dressed, and then followed him outside. Looking down at the coordinated outfit he had brought her from home, she bounced up and down in the shoes. *Good choice!*

"I have to return the dress," she said as she pulled him toward the club. She gently knocked on the back door and asked for Tammy, who was delighted to see her with Alex. She grabbed the dress and winked at her. June looked over and saw Alex with money in his hand. She quickly grabbed his hand and said goodbye, kissing Tammy on the cheek.

"She's my friend, Alex."

"I was just trying to be nice."

"She would have been insulted if you had given her money."

He shrugged his shoulders.

Like many other women, Tammy had been sold into the sex trade. Before they were free to make their own decisions, they had to pay back the money through acts of sex. June and Julian had bought the drinks the night before that would have paid for a night with her. Tammy had enjoyed a whole evening to herself.

Alex guided June through the rural streets until they stood in an opening. They made their way through a grassy meadow before reaching the base of a small mountain. The morning air was still cool and fresh. She pulled his arm into her body as they walked, so that she could feel the warmth of his skin. He rotated his backpack to accommodate her grasp. They were halfway up the mountain when she realized she stunk and hadn't brushed her teeth. She covered her mouth to guard him against her breath. "I should have brushed my teeth." she said, smelling her underarms, "and maybe showered?"

"You smell like sex...my sex, and I brought you something for that rank breath." He laughed, but she was retreating into herself.

"Stop, June. I have smelled your breath before."

For her, this was like their first date. She felt nervous and wanted to impress him.

He reached into the backpack and pulled out a travel-sized toothpaste with a small toothbrush and a water bottle. She loved that he always got the details right in everything he did. She quickly brushed her teeth, and then he grabbed the toothbrush, rinsed it off, and placed it back in a Ziploc bag. She rolled her eyes when she saw the bag.

"What is this mountain called?"

"Dobong Mountain. It's Bukhansan National Park. Some of the guys here call it "Screaming Mountain.""

"Does it scream?"

"There are temples up here, and I guess people come up here to pray, wail and chant."

June looked through the trees toward the top of the mountain. She felt connected to the kind of pain that would make someone want to scream from the top of a mountain, but she couldn't imagine that kind of freedom.

Alex saw that she was fading away from him, so he spun her around and kissed her.

"Fresh," he said.

"I kind of like the taste of me on your lips better," she bantered.

He grabbed her by the front of her sweats and pulled her close, putting his hand in the front of her pants and then sliding his fingers between her legs.

"Why are you still so wet?"

"Chief Brown, I think you are partially responsible for that."

He pushed his fingers deep inside her and watched her body arched toward him again. She bent her head back and exposed her neck, which he kissed. Hearing the sounds from other hikers, he retreated his fingers, sliding the moisture across his lips and kissing her again.

"Better," she said as she spun around and continued to walk up the mountain. He grabbed her hand and turned her back around. "The hike might need to be finished another time," he said, looking down at his pants.

She smiled and took off running down the mountain. She could not compete with his ability to run a 4:20 mile, but she would try. She dodged hikers by pivoting to each side of the trail. He held back and watched her move left to right. At the bottom, she collapsed, feeling sick. He ran to her and reached out his hand to pull her up.

"You'd make a great pilot," he said.

She knew how much that meant, coming from him, but made wings out of her arms and banked left to right as they walked back to La Guardia.

He started the shower as she collapsed on the floor. "You don't have to say anything, but follow me." He reached out his hand.

Did he remember everything?

He waddled her hips back and forth to the bathroom and slowly took off her clothes, then his. As she stepped in, she noticed the water was hotter than he preferred, so she reached to adjust it.

He swatted her hand away playfully. "This is your bath, not mine, Mira" He stepped in behind her, a little uncomfortable by the temperature of the water hitting his back. He gently pulled her head back toward his chest. The water turned her hair into a cascade of silk. He ran his fingers through her hair, then grabbed the shampoo and washed it– meticulously. He used the shampoo sliding down his stomach to scrub her back and between her legs. Then he turned her around and washed her breasts and belly with an apricot body wash. He focused intently on her reactions as he checked behind her ears and cleaned the bottoms of her feet.

She used the soap on her body to lather his, then switched places with him to rinse. They danced for twenty minutes this way until the water turned bitterly cold.

Now wrapped in towels, he began to kiss her, backing her up to the bed. She had a moment of panic as she fell backward on the bed. *What if the pill was what made me wet? What if the sex isn't as good sober?* He must have instinctively known her thoughts as he rolled her onto her stomach and began to kiss her back. He moved slowly and purposefully, kissing and biting softly. He needed to recreate her reaction to him just as much as she needed to feel it. He grabbed her hand and guided it down between her legs. He used his finger to push her finger inside her to get it wet. "Now touch yourself here," he whispered. He put pressure on her finger and began to rotate it in a circle. He could feel her butt press against him, and her breathing became heavy. "If you want to cum faster, use your other hand and put pressure here." He pressed the area on both sides of her clitoris. "If you want to make it last, rotate your finger a little slower, but don't stop completely, or you might lose it." He released her hand and allowed her to control her own pleasure. He continued to kiss her back and neck. "Tell me when you are close." She took a deep breath. "I feel it. Right there." He slowly put himself inside her as he held up her hips. A jolt of electricity raced through her body, and he could feel her throbbing around him before she fell flat on her stomach.

She rolled over and looked into his eyes for the first time, not blankly, not vacantly, but wholly.

He kissed her forehead and asked, "Can I make love to you? Or would you like to watch a porn first?"

"A challenge?" she asked, laughing because she knew she had gotten caught.

"Just one rule: no brothers," he arbitrated.

"Hmm?"

"Well, that would suck for you. That would mean no white girls. That leaves us few options."

"Ok, all women of any race?" he suggested.

"What about all men?"

He tapped his lips and then emphatically said, "No!"

"Dogs? Cats? Horses?" she joked.

"Ok, I got it," he said. "Only groups, so we can focus or fast-forward what is or isn't comfortable."

She reached out to shake his hand, and he pulled her to her feet. He had a remote for the CD player and bit his lip, waiting for her to respond.

The 34 songs. He does love me.

He reached out his hand. "Dance?"

She stood and walked toward him. She felt his arms wrap around her waist and found a resting place just over the scar on his left shoulder. As they stood naked, barely moving, the rest of the world vanished, the room disappeared, and the darkness also vanished.

"Yes," she whispered faintly, to answer his previous question.

He knew she said yes, to more than just the question about making love to her. She said yes to everything between them, to all the darkness around them, and to the porn agreement.

....⁻ ..⁻⁻⁻ ⁻⁻⁻..

Five o'clock came quickly. June had to meet Julian at the motor pool to drive back to Camp Casey. She and Alex had stayed naked as long as possible before June begrudgingly dressed to leave.

"Where is your wedding ring, June?"

She looked down at her bare finger. "You said you wanted a divorce. I didn't hear from you for three months."

"Answer- the- question."

"It's floating at the bottom of my fish tank," she said.

"Are you going to wear it?"

"Do you want a divorce?"

"Wear it, June."

"Not until you put it back on my finger. It's past five, and I have to get to the motor pool to ride back to Camp Casey."

He walked her out of the officer's quarters, where Julian waited for her in the Humvee. She turned to kiss him goodbye, but he had already closed the door.

That's his shit, she thought. *I am not taking on his shit.*

"You look cute. Are you ready to go?"

"Yeah," she said abruptly.

Julian kept looking over at June, who was staring out the window.

"So! Are you going to make me dig the gold out of you?"

"Well, everything was fabulous until he asked me about my wedding ring. He had asked me for a divorce. I hadn't talked to him for three months." She showed him her bare finger.

"Girl, that is normal. You got him all sexed up, and now he wants you back on the chain. You must have done a good job."

"The chain? Like a dog?"

"No, girl! The l-o-v-e chain. He just realized what he has with you and feels a little insecure about it."

"Ok? Now I want some details. How was the X?"

"X?"

He looked at her and dropped his bottom lip dramatically.

"The Ecstasy...Molly?"

Nothing.

"MDMA? Beans?"

Still Nothing.

"Ok, the *methylenedioxy-methamphetamine?" he laughed.*

"That pill?"

He put his finger on his nose. "Ding, ding, ding!"

"Well, I felt weird at first, but then it was like my skin felt so good, his skin felt so good. Does it make you wet?"

"Wet?"

"Well, sex had always hurt because I wasn't wet down there."

"No, I don't believe it does that, boo. That was all you."

She sat looking out the window for a few minutes. "Hey, I think I had an orgasm."

Julian pumped the brakes on the Humvee. "Check it! What did you say?"

"Well, my body started to shake, and then I got this amazing feeling deep in my stomach."

"Dear Lord, baby Jesus, child. Are you telling me this man has never made you cum? Or are you saying you have NEVER had the 'O'?"

"Never before. But twice last night and twice today." She covered her face and then peeked through her hands at him.

Julian was smiling. "Well, Chief Boo Bear does have some game."

"How was your night?" she redirected, feeling uncomfortable about the topic.

"It was good. I have a little piece of somethin' somethin' down here."

"Did he call you daddy?" She burst out laughing.

He smiled. "Don't get me kicked out of the straight, white man's Army."

"Excuse me," she corrected. "Did *'she'* call you daddy?"

"Bish, please. I always make them chant."

Julian pulled up to June's barracks. Another soldier came over to speak to him, and his demeanor completely changed. "Check. Got it. Thanks," he replied to the soldier's questions. June turned her head to the side. It was like seeing someone bleach the vibrant colors out of a shirt. She liked her version of Julian so much better. He looked over at her, staring at him.

"Girl, why are you still in my vehicle?"

"I love you," she said. "The real you."

"I love you too," he said. "Now get!"

June ran upstairs and immediately removed the sign that was by the phone. She replaced it with one that read: *If anyone calls for Brown, please get me or take a message.* She walked into her room and sat on her bed, looking at the fish tank. It had taken three months to heal the hole Alex had put in her heart. *Could one night make everything ok?*

She leaned over to the fish tank. Elmer and Fud seemed to like the shiny gold ring that sat at the bottom of the tank, so she replaced it with a shiny new coin. They approved but didn't say thank you.

Alex knew June hated fresh flowers because they die, so her room was filled with plants and orchids by the end of the week. He had even bought a few fake plants for Elmer and Fud. *They are starting to like him,* she thought.

That Sunday, he took the bus to Camp Casey to see her. He was starved for her taste, for the smell of her hair. He had only been able to find apricot shampoo at the small PX at Camp Red Cloud, so he made that his first stop. He found the shampoo and bought a bottle of wine and chocolates. He had also brought Mr. Bear, who she had left behind in their storage unit. He had purchased a ribbon to hide where it was torn. The damage to Bear was a brutal reminder of a version of himself he wasn't proud of.

He called her barracks and soon saw her coming out the side door.

"Babe!" he alerted with a wave.

"Hello," she said, nervously swinging her body back and forth.

He took her hand and spun her around. She was wearing white capri pants, an orange tank top, and orange polka-dot shoes. He adored her child-like innocence but asked her to change.

"Why?" she protested, slightly offended.

"I want to take you somewhere, but it will ruin those cute pants."

She shuffled up the stairs and put on a pair of cutoff denim shorts but left on the top and shoes. "Still cute," she said as she passed the hallway mirror.

He took her for a walk through the base and out the front gate, where he had a driver take them to a small park near the Dongducheon City Hall.

"I forgot to bring a blanket," he confessed. "Do you mind sitting in the grass?" he pointed to the grass, scrunching his nose.

She didn't mind but was confused that he had forgotten something. He never forgot anything.

"Where is your ring?" she asked, shocked he wasn't wearing it.

"Where is yours, June?" he countered.

She pulled out her necklace, and he saw the gold band he had bought for her. He remembered how he got her ring size by measuring her finger with his pinky. He was still shocked he had guessed her perfect size. She took his hand in hers and kissed the finger with the missing ring. "It's ok," she said. "I mean, I am disappointed, but I... "

He put his finger on her lips and then followed it with a kiss.

He opened the backpack and pulled out Bear.

"Mr. Bear!" she screamed as she ripped it from his hands and kissed it wildly.

"Ok stop. You are making me jealous," he joked.

Alex took Mr.Bear, holding him by his sewn-up neck, and began to speak for him with his lips half-closed. "Hi, June. I bet you are surprised I talk."

She was... and also thrilled.

"Can you put your ring in my pocket so that I can show you a trick?"

She unclasped the necklace, slid off the ring, and put it in Mr. Bear's zipper pocket.

"Now, close your eyes," said Mr. Bear.

She did and covered her face with her hands.

"Ok," said Mr. Bear, "open your eyes."

She felt her eyes stinging and tears starting to form.

"June," said Alex. "Open his pocket."

In the child-like way that he loved so much, he saw her eyes brighten, and she slowly unzipped the pocket.

He laughed at her expression of frustration when she saw the tiny Ziploc bag. Inside were both their rings and the third ring with a sparkling diamond.

"Will you marry me, Juniper Westbrook?" She cringed when she heard her name. *"He"* had said it that night in the dark as he held her down. *"He"* had whispered it in her ears as if they were lovers.

"No," she said. "My name is June Brown."

"No?" he stuttered, looking at the rings.

"Ugh, yes, Alex! But don't ever call me that again."

"By your name?" he asked, confused.

"That's not my name anymore."

She didn't need to say anything else. He pulled her close to his chest and kissed her head repeatedly until she stopped sobbing. "I have wine and chocolate," he whispered as he lifted her chin.

June looked up at Alex, his lip pooched out in place of an official apology. She laughed. "Where is my ring?"

"You mean rings."

He took the rings out of the Ziploc and placed his in her hand, and then he held her rings to his lips. "Amore Eterno." He kissed the rings, then slid them on her finger.

"Is that Spanish too?"

"No, it's Italiano for love eternal."

She put his ring on her thumb. She remembered the weight of it when she had thought she had lost him. She kissed the ring and said, "I promise my eternal love too. She took the ring and slid it down her stomach, then between her legs.

"I will go after that, June."

With her eyes, she dared him.

He pushed her back on the grass and positioned himself over her. He looked into her eyes, followed her arm to her hand, and then slipped the ring from her grasp. He handed it back to her and held out his hand. She placed the perfect gold circle on his finger and then tried to force his hand back down her shorts.

"There is more," he promised.

He stood up and pulled her up to her feet. There was a car waiting for them at the curb. June and Alex jumped in the back, and the driver just took off.

"Does he know where to go? Isn't the base the other way? Alex, where are we going? The base is the other way."

He laughed.

They arrived at a small villa just outside town. There were balloons everywhere and a banner that read: "Congrats!" She looked at Alex and smiled. They walked into the villa, where there was a small courtyard. Julian was standing there alongside another man holding a cake.

"Happy wedding day, girlfriend! I am so glad you said yes, 'cause my ass can't afford to eat this much cake." He leaned into June's ear. "He really loves you." Julian looked up at Alex. "Hello, Chief. Sir."

"You can call me Alex, just not Boo or whatever the hell you said."

"Ok, Boo-bear," he whispered as he walked by.

Alex smiled.

The man, holding the cake, walked over to congratulate June. "Hi, I am Harris."

"Harris something or something Harris?" inquired June.

"Harris Moore."

"So, are you Army?"

"Air Force, Pusan."

June smiled with her nose. Pusan was 4 hours south. This couldn't be Julian's "side-piece" from Uijeongbu. It was then she realized what "a side piece" meant.

She looked over at Alex, who was standing alone. He had done all this for her. He had forgotten about the "rules" and invited her new best gay friend. She walked over, swinging her arms.

"Didn't you want to invite anyone else?"

"Of course, but wouldn't Davis have been your best man or something if we had a wedding?"

She nodded.

"Well, what kind of party would it be if the MPs were arresting people?"

He does love me more than his passion for the rules. She bit her lip.

Julian and Harris stayed for a few hours and then kissed and hugged their ways out the door. "You are staying here tonight. I left the TV on in your room," said Julian on his way out. She slapped his arm and laughed.

Finally, she was alone with her husband for the first time. She walked over and slipped her hand into his. "Can we go to our room?"

"Yes!"

On the room door, she saw a piece of paper over the room number: 6B.

She turned to kiss him.

"If we are going to start over, we should officially start over from our wedding night, right?" said Alex, looking and pointing at the number.

"I shouldn't have taken off my ring," she said.

"I shouldn't have given you a reason to."

They opened the door to the sound of group porn on the TV. June's bottom lip disappeared. Her eyes got wide.

"I want to love you down," he smiled.

"Is that song 35?"

"34... the B side," he laughed.

....ˉ ..ˉˉˉ ˉˉˉ..

Alex felt that being two hours away from June was too far, so he pulled some strings and had her transferred to Camp Red Cloud. It wasn't a common practice to grant such requests, but he had served in Iraq with the Area Commander.

She loved being close to him, now that they had finally found each other. They snuck away for breakfast every morning and tried to spend time together every night. They weren't allowed to live off base officially, but they had a place at their hotel to meet.

One day in the early morning, when she knew that Alex would be flying, she went out for a morning run through the city. It was difficult to breathe in the city because of the smell of fuel from the ondol bricks heating the homes, and the vehicles' exhaust. As she sprinted across the vast five-directional intersection, she felt like she was in the Frogger game. She ran out to the base of Dobong Mountain and decided to climb up to Screaming Rock. She struggled to navigate the terrain in her running shoes, but she was determined to get to this sacred space.

As she neared the Apex of the mountain, she heard the most painful screams. The echoes of their pain clung to the drops of dew that the night had left on the shrubs, that dared to root themselves in the mountain's rock face. She tiptoed closer to the painful cries and watched carefully the art of letting go. She grabbed hold of a briar bush to steady herself, squeezing it tightly, absorbing the physical pain. With her eyes closed, she tried to find that warrior in herself. She searched herself for that powerful woman that could scream from the top of a mountain. She tried to absorb the courage from the voices around her, and then she just opened her eyes and sat silently.

June felt that the pieces of her stability were suspended from the fine silk of a spider's web. Her strength was a fragile mechanism of connections that each had a perfect place that supported her sanity. Her demons were in a box, in the middle of the web. She wanted to ask these women what made them so brave, but it was too beautiful a moment to ruin with words.

Nine

The R.O.K.

June hadn't traveled anywhere to speak of. She was excited when she boarded the US Airways flight to the Republic of Korea. She walked to her seat at the back of the plane, settled in, and closed her eyes.

"Excuse me." A flight attendant tapped her on the shoulder.

"Yes, ma'am?"

The flight attendant seemed offended that June called her ma'am. "You can't sit there. Those seats are blocked."

June looked at her ticket and then up at the seating diagram. They matched. She handed the ticket to the flight attendant. "I am sorry, ma- "she stopped herself. "I am sorry, miss. Can you help me find my correct seat?"

The flight attendant softened when she saw June grab her military backpack.

"Let me check. Wait here."

She heard whispering in the back of the plane, and another flight attendant came out. Her name tag read: Molly.

"Hi, there. Are you a soldier?"

June was dressed in civilian clothes. She wondered how the lady would know she was a soldier. She looked at her ticket, and there wasn't any code. Molly touched her shoulder and pointed at her bag.

June was relieved. "Yes."

"Well, we are all full up in First, but I will do my best to clear you a row so you can sleep. I am sorry about Sherry, the other Stew. She got this trip on reserve, so she isn't in the best mood."

June stayed stuck on the word stew and smiled. She wondered what it meant.

Molly rearranged some other passengers and gave June a row in front of her initially assigned seat. As soon as she moved her things, she noticed that the flight attendants had moved their bags to her original row.

Smart, she thought.

June slept for hours before waking up. When she finally opened her eyes, she was starving and thirsty. She grabbed a water canteen out of her bag and searched desperately for a snack. Molly saw June's distress and touched her lightly on the shoulder. "Do you need anything, dear?"

"Do you have peanuts or anything to eat? I didn't have time to eat before I got to the airport and then I couldn't find my gate. You have to take a train in Dallas to get to different gates."

Molly smiled. "It is a frustrating airport. Let me see what I can do about getting you some food. What do you want to drink?"

June held up her canteen of water. "I am ok for a drink."

Molly walked to the very front of the aircraft and brought back a first-class meal covered in a white dinner cloth for June. She lowered June's tray and placed the meal in front of her. "I brought a bottle of water and red wine too, just in case you don't want to drink out of that green thing you brought." She made a stinky face and stuck out her tongue. June looked at her beat-up canteen and stuffed it back down in her bag. She lifted the white linen from the plate and then covered it quickly. It was a steak. She glanced over at the other passenger she saw eating, and they had a small tray of pasta and a tiny side salad. She scooted out of her seat and walked to the back of the airplane. The curtain was closed, so she whispered. "Molly?"

Molly peeked out from the curtain.

"Hi, I didn't bring any cash. How do I pay for this meal?"

Molly laughed. "It's free, sweetheart."

June looked over at the other passenger's meal and then back at Molly.

"My brother is in the military," she said. "I try to take care of you guys when you are on my flight."

June sat back down and turned her back to the aisle so that the other passengers wouldn't see her food. After each bite, she closed her eyes and sipped her wine like it was the last beverage she'd ever drink. She had no idea why Molly had chosen to be so nice to her, but she felt something she had never experienced before. She felt important.

Later in the flight, June rummaged through her bag to find her medical records. She turned to the pages just after her attack and removed them. She also removed all the physical exams related to her assault and infertility. She wanted a fresh start without being the "raped girl" Tara described. When Molly walked past her, she handed her the papers and asked her to throw them away. Molly took the documents to the galley and glanced at them. She saw the nurse's notes about June's sexual assault, showing them to the other flight attendants. Sherry walked up to June and motioned for her to scoot over. "We accidentally saw what was written on those papers. Are you sure you don't just want to put them in a safe place?"

"The trash is a safe place," said June, crying.

Sherry put her arm around June and pulled her close. "When you are done with your meal, come to the back galley."

June finished her meal and walked to the back galley. She was sure they would report her for trying to destroy her military medical records. She looked at her feet as they directed her to come past the steal grey curtain.

Sherry had pulled out a cart, and June's papers were on top of it. "Tear them up!" she said, with her arms crossed. June looked at her but didn't move.

"Rip them up!" she commanded.

June nervously grabbed the top sheet of paper. She looked over at Molly, who was sobbing and then back down at the piece of paper. She wanted to tear up the paper so badly, but she couldn't, so she handed it to Molly. She read the nurse's words to herself and began to cry more.

"Could you, do it?" asked June.

Molly didn't hesitate to tear the page into tiny pieces. She took a deep breath and handed the tiny pieces back to June. "That felt good," she said as she smiled at June. Sherry picked up the next page and gave it to June, who grabbed the paper and tore it into tiny pieces. Sherry fed her page by page until they were all gone. June took a deep, cleansing breath and covered her face.

Sherry took the scraps of paper and said, "We will file this important paperwork where it belongs." She opened the lav' door and threw the scraps in the toilet. June smiled as Sherry pointed to the flush button. In one gentle press, June flushed everything terrible that had ever happened to her down the toilet.

....⁻ ..⁻⁻⁻ ⁻⁻⁻..

It was a Tuesday when they landed in the Republic of South Korea. June had been assigned to a base called Camp Casey in Dongducheon. New soldiers in the region were called "turtles" because the in-processing and out-processing buildings were only a few feet from each other, but it took a year to get from one building to the next. The duty period for a Korean tour of duty was a one-year assignment.

Everything about Korea excited her. As the bus drove them from the airport in Seoul to Dongducheon, she soaked in this new environment. The smell of garlic lingered in the air. She saw women in elaborate traditional dresses walking out of McDonald's. She couldn't understand how she could feel so safe, so far from home.

Once she was settled in, she started to unpack. She had brought the album she had made of Alex's letters. She sat the first night reading each letter, matched with her response. He had also sent flyers that they had dropped from the aircraft and some Iraqi money. After several hours alone in her room, she counted the letters he had sent. When she got to the end, she realized there were 34. Then she remembered his words: *You wrote me 35 letters in 6 months. No one has ever cared that much about me.*

Her 21st birthday was the next day. Some of the girls in her barracks decided to take her out for her official Soju experience. Soju can be up to 53% alcohol by volume (ABV) and typically causes a stimulant-like effect, as opposed to alcohol which has a depressive effect. Vodka (80 proof) is 40% ABV. They had started with one kettle of soju that quickly became five after playing the Commander's coin game. The rules were simple. The last coin on the counter had to buy drinks: the coin had to be from a Company Commander or higher ranking and given for excellent service. That night she would understand why the three-foot drainage ditches on the side of the road were called "turtle ditches." She had fallen at least four times on the way back to the barracks.

She sat in the shower as the cold water cascaded down her body. It helped with her nausea. She had fallen asleep when she heard someone banging on her door.

"Brown, your husband."

She stumbled to the hallway phone.

"I want a divorce," he said in the place of hello.

"I'm sorry, sweetie, I am *shrunk*. It's my birthday. What about the horse?"

"I'm not coming to Korea, June." She couldn't connect to anything in the tone of his angry voice. They were joint-domicile which meant the Army would send him to be close to her if they could.

"Ok," she slurred. "It's my birthday here--I am 21--not a baby anymore--I can handle it--should I take off my ring? –oh damn, it won't come off! Sorry, I can't divorce you! My ring, it won't come off."

"Seriously, June?" he mockingly laughed.

"Why wouldn't I be serious? I have always wanted a horse." She could feel the water from the shower streaming down her leg.

He hung up the phone, frustrated. He closed his eyes to escape the enemy forces in the room and slid down to the floor with the phone pressed against his head.

"Well, I hope you meant that, Alex. You are just like your father. Running off to the Army for a white girl. Just go ahead and abandon your race for all I care. You've always been a piece of shit!" Alex's mother stormed out of the room.

"She's just mad that you didn't send any money home when she asked you to," said Gram. "Why don't you just find a nice black woman and settle down? This isn't how we raised you, Alex."

Alex just nodded and walked to his childhood bedroom.

June stumbled back to her room before she realized she was naked.

....‾ ..‾‾‾ ‾‾‾..

Three months later, the Army sent Alex to Korea, still married to June. She had come into her own with their separation. He hadn't contacted her for the entire three months, so she felt forced to move forward independently. She had learned basic phrases in Hangul, the Korean language, and fell in love with the food and culture, especially Choco Pies. There was something amazing about being ok without Alex and being so far from the man that raped her. She felt safe to express her sexuality again.

Alex called her once he arrived in Korea, but she had put a note by the phone: *If Alex, Chief Brown or Brown's husband, calls, she is:*

- *in the shower*
- *shopping*
- *in the field*
- *running*
- *out buying Choco Pies*
- *JUST BE CREATIVE.*

A week after Alex arrived, June's First Sergeant called her into his office.

"Brown, I hear your husband is in the country."

She sat silently.

"He called the Company Commander and wanted to know if you were still based here! That's a problem, Brown."

Still silent.

"We are having Corporal Davis drive you down to Camp LaGuardia tomorrow. Handle your shit. Am I clear?"

She took a deep breath in, then out. She wanted to explain everything, but she couldn't do that. She just said, "Yes, First Sergeant."

Corporal Davis met her at the motor pool at 9 am. It was a Saturday. He was a 13F (Fire Support Specialist) but was given the keys to a Humvee in place of the keys he held stateside for the 577. He was a tall African American man with a slim build. She smiled when she saw he had a streak of blonde hidden in his dark black hair, which reminded her of the one Alex used to have.

Davis didn't say anything as she got into the vehicle. They started on their drive to Uijeongbu, home to Camp Red Cloud and Camp LaGuardia. After 10 minutes of silence, he finally spoke.

"Ok, girl. What the hell is going on with you?"

"What?"

"Well, my ass is working on a Saturday to drive you to see your man. What kind of shit is that?"

"I'm really sorry."

"It's fine. The way this traffic looks, we have about two hours for you to fill me in on your saga."

June laughed. Davis had a vibrancy about him that was refreshing.

"So, is Chief Brown your man?" His eyes brightened, and he smiled.

"I am really not sure."

"Well, if you don't want him, hand him over, girl!"

"What?"

"You aren't the only size queen in the vehicle."

Size queen? She felt so stupid that she didn't know what that meant.

"Girl, he has been in the country a week, and I already know his dimensions." He pointed at his crotch.

She got it. She blushed because she had never thought of him that way. This random honesty made her open up.

"It hurts."

"Oh! In the front or the back?"

"Back?"

"Baby! Really?"

Her mouth exploded with the details about her life; the rape, the war, her infertility.

He pulled over.

"You are beautiful and funny and so adorable. Let's figure this shit out, then you hold onto him or tell him to piss off... and if he needs a side-piece while he is here?" She bent forward laughing not knowing what 'side piece' meant.

As they continued the drive, Corporal Davis stopped by a sex shop for lubrication, booked her at a local room-for-rent, and talked her through 'the art of a blowjob.'

"Leave the TV on when you go to sleep," he said as he dropped her off at the gate. She had no idea what he meant, so she waved and said thank you.

She had thought that someone would meet her at the gate, but no one was there. The base was mainly an Attack Helicopter Battalion, but June didn't see any AH64ds. The base only had Cobras, 58's, and a UH -1. She found her way to the Commander's Office and asked where she could find Alex. The Commander invited her into her office.

"Hi, Ms. Brown."

"Hello, Ma'am."

"Brown, first of all! "She paused. "I did not have anything to do with you being summoned here. I am actually offended by it."

"It is ok."

"Actually, no it isn't."

"Why am I here?"

"You are here because they need Chief Brown in the game. They are ramping up for Task-Force-Twenty-One in 1994, and this is a big training exercise."

"Ok?"

"Look, stay together or get a divorce. I don't care. Just don't bring any BS drama to my base. I called Chief Brown. He should be here in 10."

June sat mortified in the lobby until she saw a hut next to the office and decided to wander over. It was a café'.

"Yeoboseyo," she said.

"Hello," said the lady behind the counter. "Are you hungry?"

"How do you say *I am hungry* in Hangul," asked June?

"Baegopa," she smiled.

"What is good?" There was no menu.

"Bibimbap"

"Can I get that to go?"

"Ye," she smiled.

Alex walked into the café as June was taking her to-go box.

"Gamsahamnida," said June with a slight bow.

"Cheonmaneyo," said the lady smiling.

"So, what is this all about?" she said boldly, pushing past Alex.

He just grabbed her arm and guided her out of the café. He was always different around her when he was in uniform: scuttling her around by the arm if she was in civilian clothes and keeping a distance from her if she was in uniform. It may have seemed foreboding to others, but she would always just picture him naked. He didn't say anything as he directed her to the officer's quarters. The tension between them was palpable.

She looked at him as he dragged her along. He stood tall and focused on his task. He looked so good to her. His scars had faded, and he smelled amazing. He was in his flight suit. She had a weakness for how sexy he was in uniform.

They entered the side door of the officer's quarters, and he turned to her. "June, you can't come in here if you have your uniform on. Do you understand?"

"Alex, I know the rules about enlisted and officer's quarters."

"You don't always follow the rules, June."

She was going to reply that he didn't either, but he always did when it came to the military.

His quarters were a lot better than her barracks. He had a private room with a small kitchen and a private bathroom. She immediately thought about Corporal Davis and the room he reserved for her. *Why does Corporal Davis want me to stay off base?*

"June?" Alex forced his way into her thoughts.

Sigh.

"I have CP tonight."

"CP?"

"Courtesy Patrol."

"What is that?"

"We go to the clubs between here and Camp Red Cloud and make sure soldiers aren't getting in trouble."

"Ah, babysitting."

"June, just stay here. You can watch TV."

"No!"

"What?"

"I can be a baby," she paused. "...for you to sit." She pretended to sit on his lap.

He clenched his jaw and moved her hips to a position beside him. He handed her the key to his room, which she placed on the side table by his door.

She found Corporal Davis at the motor pool; he was thrilled to take her on a "thunder-run". A thunder run was another drinking game. There were 12 clubs between Camp La Guardia and Camp Red Cloud. The goal was to drink at each bar, then make it back to Mr.Yi's for

Yakimandu. The trick was that Mr.Yi's closed at midnight, so you had to be quick. She was excited, but she needed something sexy to wear.

Corporal Davis was a.k.a. Julian Davis. He took her to the back door of a nightclub and talked to Tamantha, one of the "working girls." She came out with a tight black dress for June. June walked into the back of the club. The floors were concrete, and each of the girls' areas were only separated by curtains made out of a sheet. Tamatha guided June to her area and held the curtain closed. June could hear someone next door having sex. She tried to ignore the environment she had walked into and appreciated Tamatha's kindness. When she put it on, she felt uncomfortable and fabulous all at the same time. She walked out sheepishly. Julian said, "Girl, that's what Chief needs," as he patted her on the butt. She looked back at Tamantha to thank her. "Call me Tammy," she said.

I'll call you my very first Korean friend. "Gamsahamnida," said June tracing the lines of the dress.

"You are very welcome," said Tammy.

She and Julian went from club-to-club dancing to the best of the '70s, '80s, and '90s music but never heard any of her 34 songs. At the 8th club, she started searching for Alex.

....- ..--- ---..

Alex stomped from club to club, broke up fights, and redirected soldiers back to base. It was 11 pm when he saw June across the street, falling over and laughing. His first instinct was to grab her, but he was on duty. He decided instead to follow her. As he walked into what was her 11th club, he saw her dancing on the stage. There was a shift in the way he thought about her. He had never seen this side of her, swinging her hair and dancing sexually. *This is that bullshit; he* thought accusingly. He waited until she had walked off the stage and then approached her outside the bathroom like he was conducting a police interrogation.

"Having fun?"

"Yep!"

"Are you coming back to my room tonight?" He pulled her shoulders in line with his.

"Nope!"

"June, come back to base!"

"Alex, come to my hotel," she mockingly replied as she handed him the key and the address.

He looked at the card and then at his watch. "I can't be there until 1 am when my patrol ends. I don't want you going there alone."

"Julian is staying there too."

Alex grabbed her chin and forced her to look at him, "June, who is Julian?" Julian walked up behind June and put his chin on her shoulder, "That would be me, Boo-Bear."

"I don't know what rank you are, soldier, but you will address me as Chief or Sir."

"Yes, Sir! Chief!" he said. Then he added, "Boo-Bear," as he danced away.

Alex was furious. He reached to grab Julian's shoulder, and June pushed him back. "He's joking, Alex. You used to be so funny. Please just go and meet me tonight."

Alex turned to walk away.

"Ali!" He turned around, still furious.

"I LOVE THE SHIT OUT OF YOU!" she shouted.

His countenance softened a little. "Behave, Mira!" He stood tall walking toward the door as he brushed by a couple kissing in the corner.

"Excuse you," said Dana holding onto Lt. Meyers for support.

Alex didn't respond but noticed that Meyers was looking in June's direction.

He stood in his line of sight. "Is there a problem, LT?"

Lt. Meyers lifts his hands in surrender and turns back toward Dana.

Alex paused at the door, not wanting to leave June there. He waited until he saw that June had run back to Julian.

"Girl, we have to hurry, or we will never make it back to Mr. Yi's."
As they walked out of the club, Julian looked back. "Girl, did you
see that?"

"What?" asked June.

"Dana and Meyers hip-locked in the corner?"

June shrugged.

"Scandal-licious," he laughed.

Their last drink was a quick shot of lousy tequila, which brought
back horrible memories. June didn't know the status of Tara and
Jacob's relationship, but she could never imagine cheating on Alex. She
thought, *no more tequila ever.* She assumed that was what caused all the
problems with Tara and Jacob.

As they walked back down the crowded street, they saw Alex con-
fronting another soldier. She recognized this version of him well. He
stood taller when he was in uniform, like a superhero. A superhero
wears the uniform to represent a promise to all those they are in charge
of protecting. A promise that they will put themselves in the path of
evil. Alex took that promise seriously.

Julian looped his arm through June's.

"Look, June your boy is all pent up," Julian said matter-of-factly,
pointing at Alex.

June drunkenly giggled. "What does that mean?"

"Girl, if his fine ass were mine, I would take him to that room and
hit that until he called me daddy."

"I hate sex though."

Julian didn't react. He just smiled and tapped her on the nose. "I got
you, boo." He walked into what looked like a video store and came out
with a tiny Ziploc bag, shaking it in her face.

Why is everything put in a Ziploc?

Mr. Yi's was closed, but Julian walked around the building and
tapped on the window, and a few minutes later, the restaurant's front
door opened.

"Hurry," Mr. Yi whispered, looking around nervously. They sat in the dark as Mr. Yi made the best Yaki Mandu she had ever tasted. It was served with an ice-cold Coke, in a bottle.

"Here, Jitterbug," he whispered as he slid the Ziploc bag over to her. The bag had one small pill in it.

"What is that?" she said, slurping her coke through a straw.

"Heaven, girl."

"Is it drugs? We can't take drugs."

"Girl, life is one big ol' drug. Just take the damn thing."

She scrunched her nose and tapped her feet wildly.

"Shh, shh!" said Mr. Yi.

June covered her mouth and nodded an apology in his direction. Then without words, she took the pill and swallowed it.

Julian grabbed her hand and led her out of the restaurant quietly.

They walked, swinging hands, to the hotel.

"I paid for your room, June."

"What? No!"

"Honey, please, it was only 9,000 won."

She did the math in her head. It was about seven dollars.

Julian took her to her room and turned to a news station on the TV. "Just remember, June, don't turn off the TV."

She thought it was a strange request, but she loved this adventure that Julian had taken her on. He blew her a kiss goodbye and left.

The room was small. There was a full-size mattress on the floor in the corner. The blankets were silk and covered in beautiful patterns of exotic birds and huge red roses. The TV was sitting on the table at the foot of the bed. She didn't know enough Hangul to understand the news story, so she just muted the volume. When she spun around, she realized there was no bathroom. She walked back to the front desk and asked, "hwajangsil?" The lady pointed at a door down the hall. When June opened the door, there was only a hole in the floor. *Where do they poop?* she wondered. When she returned to the room, the flashing glow of light from the TV magically reflected off the silk blanket, inviting her to sit. She walked over and sat down. The silk felt so good on her skin. She moved her legs slowly back and forth. Why *is their silk so much softer?* She curled up on the magical, glowing blanket and fell asleep.

....- ..--- ---..

Alex was pissed. He had dealt with drunken soldiers all night, and now this. He pulled the card out of his pocket that June had given him and tossed it on the side table. *She didn't take the key.* He picked up the key and put it back on his key ring. He stood in front of the mirror in his bathroom and noticed there was puke on the shoulder of his uniform. He undressed and jumped into the shower. Despite how mad he was at June for dragging him out to some strange hotel, it never occurred to him not to go.

When he got to her room, the door was unlocked. "What the hell is wrong with her?" he raged under his breath. He saw her curled up on a small bed as he opened the door. The TV was flashing light across her pale skin. He remembered seeing her this way on their wedding night. The shape of her body had always excited him. He undressed, then sat next to her on the bed. "Mira?"

June woke up feeling funny but happy to see Alex. "You came?"

Still angry with her, "Just sleep it off, June. I will watch some TV."

"Don't touch the TV!" she said, remembering Julian's instructions.

Frustrated, he pulled back the blankets and directed her to get under the covers. It only took moments for him to fall asleep. June rolled over too. The night wasn't what she had planned, and the alcohol and the pill soon took her to deep sleep.

When she woke up, it was still dark outside. She could tell by the two-inch window that sat above the weird painting on the wall. It was a happy-looking cat that held up a paw, that looked like a fist.

She looked down at the TV, still flashing light, and saw two women having sex. She looked over at Alex to see if he was watching it. His mouth was slightly open, and he was fast asleep. She thought about changing it but continued to watch as one of the women started touching herself. She tried to mimic her movements, but she couldn't find a spot on her own body that made her feel good. She was, however, incredibly wet, but not like before when she had thought she pee'd herself. *What kind of drug did Julian give me?*

She looked at Alex, who was completely naked. She hadn't remembered him undressing. The light danced around on his brown skin. She had always loved the shape of his body. She moved down the side of the bed slowly and changed the channel to a nature show.

"Alex," she whispered as she kissed his arm. His skin was so soft, and he smelled like apricots. "What, June?" he muddled, annoyed.

She rolled him over to face her, then took his hand and put it between her legs. She slowly moved his fingers around until she saw that he was aroused. Then she pushed him onto his back and climbed on top of him. His warm skin electrified her desire. She opened his mouth and kissed him with her tongue. He grabbed her hips and flipped her over.

"You are so wet."

She nodded and pulled his face to hers. He pushed himself back up and looked at her in the flashes of light and darkness. *Where has she been all these years?*

She lifted her body toward him. She needed to be touched. Her skin had become alive. He grabbed her breast and slowly moved his mouth down her body. He noticed everything about her, how her hips arched upward, as he got closer to her wetness. The way she played with his ears as he kissed her inner thigh. He ached to be inside her, but she gently pushed him in the direction she wanted.

His tongue was warm and well-positioned. She arched her back, and he pulled her hips toward his face. Insatiably he consumed her, occasionally, biting her inner thighs to release the savage craving he had for her.

The warmth and electricity became focused. Her body started to tremble and then released. *What is that, she thought?* She grabbed his ears and gently pulled him up to face her. She kissed him hard. She had never tasted herself on his mouth before, which aroused her. He slowly positioned himself and pushed deep inside her. She was wet and open to him. There was no friction, no resistance. She took all of him and then took him again.

Ten

Independence

There was going to be a huge gala on the 4th of July. They had lined up the attack helicopters for photo ops, and they planned a fireworks display in the sports arena nearby. The day would be full of activities, including a picnic at Camp La Guardia.

Uijeongbu had a sorted history that dates back to the Korean War. The ROK soldiers failed to hold the city against North Korean forces and left a pathway straight to Seoul (the heart) of Korea. Many older cab drivers wouldn't drive to Uijeongbu because of this. It was time that someone celebrated the beauty of this city and its people.

Tammy and Julian had taken June shopping, and she had three outfits for the day. She would wear white shorts and a red top for the picnic and put a blue ribbon in her now long blonde hair. She couldn't find red, white, and blue shoes or even a pair with stars, so she settled on blue.

The second outfit for the officer's gala was a primarily red dress that fit tightly across her hips. It had blue and white inlay down both sides. She found a perfect pair of red heels to complete the aesthetic.

The last outfit was a sexy red bra with stars and stripes and a matching thong. She would have gotten briefs, but there weren't any that matched the outfit.

The Company Commander of Camp La Guardia decided to take Julian as her date because, like most soldiers, she didn't bring her family to Korea. Julian rented a black tuxedo and an electric-blue bowtie for a bit of flare.

June arrived early to the picnic, dressed in her cute outfit. It was always traditional for the officers on base to set up the picnic, cook all the food, and serve the enlisted members the feast. June sat on a blanket blowing up balloons while Alex started preparing the food to put on a large grill made out of 50-gallon oil drums. Alex was wearing grey shorts and a button-up blue shirt, which June had bought him. *No red, white and blue bullshit for me* had been his direction to her.

"What's up, Chief?" questioned Lt. Meyers while watching June on the blanket.

Alex looked over at June. She looked very sexy in her shorts and tank top, lying on her stomach and blowing up balloons.

"What's up, Lt?"

"Well, Chief, this is an officer's event. Isn't your wife enlisted?"

"Well, I'm an officer and MY wife is blowing up balloons," he said blankly.

"It looks bad her being here at all, but I can't do anything about that. However, this is my event. You need to ask her to come back with the rest of the grunts."

"Seriously?" Alex took a deep breath.

"It's a tradition that the officers provide this service to the enlisted," he countered.

Alex threw down the buns he was holding and walked over to June.

"Lt. Myers is offended by your beauty, my love," he said loudly. Could you just come back with Julian and the rest of the soldiers when we are serving the food?"

June looked at Meyers. *What's his thing?* She shrugged her shoulders and released the red balloon that she had blown up but not tied. It *flibbered* and *flabbered* in circles, then fell empty onto the ground.

Alex was smiling at June when he put out a hand to lift her. Then he kissed her so that anyone watching would have felt uncomfortable. She knew it was for the Lt's anguish, so she wrapped her leg around his and slid his hand onto her left butt cheek. "I love you," he whispered, almost laughing.

June found Julian, and they went off base to a bar for a few drinks until the food was prepared.

"Julian, this asshole just kicked me off base, well practically."

"Jitterbug, he's a butter bar."

"Butter bar?"

"Second lieutenant."

She still looked confused.

"He's still got his baby gold bar. He's a brand-new officer and thinks he has to prove something."

She shrugged her shoulders.

"What color is butter, June?" -frustrated.

"Yellow?"

"Yes, but also gold like his rank."

"Oh!" she laughed.

"I can't believe Chief kissed you in public. Mr. *'Call me Sir'* at the nightclub has come a long way."

June smiled. "You helped us both, Julian."

"Look, sweetie, we all need a reboot every once in a while. You both got shit handed to you at a young age. You need each other. I always say, 'the only difference between friends and lovers is the sex', and if that and communication is good, nothing will come between you."

"That's good," she smiled. *Really good.*

"How is Harris?"

"We are done."

"What?"

"He went back stateside, and I don't do that pen pal shit."

"You will with me when I leave."

"No, girl. This is our time. You get those orders back home, and we will hug and kiss goodbye."

"You better keep in touch. I need you."

"You have Chief."

"What? I can't have two gorgeous men in my life?"

"You are the one that likes that group shit, not me." He covered his face and laughed.

She changes the subject. "Ok, well, let's get back and eat some food. I am starving."

"I am sure your man will be too after looking at you in those shorts all day."

Alex was serving hamburgers as they walked through the line with their plates. No one had finished the balloon decorations. She walked up to Alex with a smile from ear to ear. "Hi Chief, I will have a veggie burger."

"We don't have veggie burgers. Would you like a hotdog?"

"That sounds great. Make it really black."

Julian laughed and pushed her forward down the line. "I'll have the same," he said as he winked at Alex.

June sat in a direct line from where Alex was serving, trying her best to entice him without drawing too much attention. As she was slightly resting her middle finger in her mouth, *Butter Bar* blocked her view of Alex.

"Is your name June, or is that short for something?" asked Meyers.

June was thrown off guard by the question. "It's Specialist Brown or Mrs. Alex Brown, Sir."

"It's inappropriate for you to come into the officer's quarters, Specialist...Brown."

June looked around the picnic area and questioned," Oh, is this the officer's quarters, Sir?"

"You know what I mean, Brown."

"Ok, thanks for telling me, she said politely."

"I am talking to the Commander today. You two are ridiculous."

She looked at Julian then back at Butter Bar, "Julian and I are ridiculous?" she questioned sarcastically. Julian leaned on her shoulder and looked up at Butter Bar.

"I like the balloon decorations," Julian said, pointing to the one balloon June had managed to hang. Then he lifted June by her arm and slowly backed away from Butter Bar.

"Take your trash," he barked.

"It's a tradition for the officers to clean up," shouted Alex from the grill. He had been surveying their conversation.

June grabbed their plates. She didn't want to do anything to make things difficult for Alex.

She stayed in Alex's room in the officer's quarters until he finished. Alex smelled like burgers and propane when he got to the room. "How was your charred hotdog?"

"Delicious!"

"Look, I have already cleared it with the Commander for you to come to my room. I told you, just not in your uniform, ok?"

"I know, Ali. He was just so mean."

"He's a butter bar, Mira."

She giggled. "You say that too?"

He walked over to her and kissed her. "I got you. You don't have to fight any battles as long as I am here."

"I can fight," she put up her fist.

He engulfed her fists with his hands and pushed her back against the wall. "Later. We have to do a photo op before the gala."

"Should I put on my dress?"

"No, they want photos in my helicopter."

"With me?"

"Yes, Babe. You get to be my co-pilot today."

"I want to be the pilot."

"The gunner sits it the front," he propositioned as he pulled her butt into his hips.

"Ok, if I get to shoot, I will sit in the front."

Positioned in the 64, they smile as a dozen photos are taken. The day was slipping into twilight as the fireworks began to light up the sky.

Pow! Shuddle! Shreak! Boom! Alex readjusted in his seat. "Are we good?" he questioned the photographer.

"Just a couple more, Chief."

Bang! Zeer! Pop! The darkening sky seemed to amplify the sound of the distant fireworks.

"We good?" Alex barked.

"Ali, are you ok?" whispered June across her shoulder.

"We are done!" he insisted.

"Get out, June!"

She moved quickly. She could sense the uneasiness in his tone. She stepped forward out of the cockpit and couldn't find her footing.

Lt. Meyers ran over and grabbed her ankles. His grasp petrified her movements. She looked helplessly at Alex as Meyers pulled her forward, sliding his grip to her knees, thighs, then buttocks. He swung her around and then slowly guided her down his body.

Alex stood up calmly and then climbed out of the aircraft. June was now on her knees with her hands over her face.

"What's your fucking deal?" He shoved Meyers.

"I was just trying to help *Junie*," Meyers said, holding up his hands.

Alex charged at Meyers.

Julian stepped between the pair and said, "What about those fireworks?"

Alex didn't see or hear Julian. He was focused: doing checks and rechecks, the *trying-to-land-Shiela* kind of focus. The fireworks continued to rage behind him. Zing. Bap-Bap. Pow.

"You're pathetic," said Meyers turning his back to Alex.

Alex ran over to June and tried to help her up. She looked up at him, helpless and consumed by fear. Alex charged forward toward Meyers again.

"He's not worth it, Chief," pleaded Julian as he blocked his path.

Alex pushed forward.

"Chief!"

"Sir!"

"Boo Bear," Julian whispered between his clenched teeth.

Alex looked at Julian and closed his eyes. He buried his head in Julian's shoulder and gasped for breath.

....- ..--- ---..

Julian, Alex, June, and the Commander skipped the gala, but all dressed up to go to the Cabana, the first available bar off base. The Commander was Ms. Angela Glenn. She was a tall, slender woman with slightly grey hair that showed through her blonde highlights. She wore her hair short and close to her neck. She had chosen to wear a formal dress as opposed to the option of wearing her dress blues. Alex wore his blues, with four rows of metals and an expert marksmanship badge. June noticed that he wasn't wearing the Purple Heart he had been awarded in Iraq but didn't mention it.

They sat in the corner of the dark bar, drinking shots and laughing. Angela bought Tammy her drinks after hearing her story, and in return, Tammy brought them food from Mr. Yi's.

Angela's tone was soft and nurturing as she spoke to Alex. "I heard we had a difference of opinion at the airfield."

"Yes, ma'am."

"It's Angela, Alex."

"Trust me. I know how hard it is to be a minority in this man's Army; that is why I didn't bring my partner here. They want to push you until you fail, then they can say you were too weak for the job."

"I can handle all that bullshit." He touched June.

"He found your weakness, didn't he?" she said.

Alex looked at Angela and then looked down.

"Alex, you are a decorated war hero. He's a baby who got out of college and wanted to join the Army to become a man like you."

"Ok," he nodded respectfully. June watched the way he was tugging at the finger he broke in Iraq. She knew he was still volatile.

The alcohol helped to relax Alex. Four shots and two beers later, they had all danced to Hotel California and sang Bohemian Rhapsody.

"I rented our room," whispered June as they all sat back down at the table.

"That's my queue," said Angela.

"Mine too," said Julian. "Let me walk you back, Commander."

June tugged on Alex's arm toward the door.

"Wait," he said. "Do you want the song and letter # 35?"

"I knew it!" she said. "It has always been a competition."

"Well, if we are competing to see who loves each other more, does it matter?"

"Save song and letter 35 for an emergency," she said.

....⁻ ..⁻⁻⁻ ⁻⁻⁻..

June had placed a sticky note with the number 6B on the door, but Alex didn't notice. He staggered into the room and lay face down across the bed. This was their room, their safe place, yet he wasn't there with her. She crawled up beside him and whispered into his ear. "Do you want to talk about Sheila?"

No response.

"I got you," she said. "You don't have to fight any battles as long as I am here."

He turned his face to the side and looked at her. He had tears in his eyes.

"I killed him," he said.

She didn't speak.

She didn't move.

"I should have pulled up. I saw the flash, heard the impact. I should have focused more on the UFD or-, " he stopped.

"Alex, I am here. I am right here." She didn't know what else to say. He fell asleep holding her hand, still in his dress blues. She changed out of her dress into her lingerie because it was the only thing she had brought from his room. She slowly undressed him. She carefully folded his uniform and placed it over the TV. She sat and watched him sleep for a few hours before drifting off into a fragile sleep.

Alex woke up disoriented in his boxer briefs, with June curled up next to him in "American flag" underwear. He smiled. She had found a way to take the darkness out of his life. Her innocence protected him from the demons that possessed his mind, similar to Jacob's protection of him.

He felt that he had ruined her night, so he dressed in his blues and tried to dress her. He could not slide the tight dress past her hips without waking her up. She laughed as she awoke and saw him struggling.

"No one has tried to dress me in my sleep since I was three years old," she said, covering her mouth.

"I'm sorry about the gala. I know you were excited to go." He handed her the toothbrush kit with a bottle of water.

"Did you want to go to the after-party?"

"What time is it?"

"1:20."

"Everything will be closed."

He sat there for a moment, then quickly looked over at June. She looked amazing. The red dress was tasteful but erotic and fit her perfectly. It was tight around her hips, but a split on the side went up to the mid-point of her left thigh.

"Let's play a game he said. You are an exotic princess escorting me to the U.S Embassy."

Oh, I like this. She stands and immediately transforms into an exotic princess.

"Excuse me she says in her best French accent. Are you Mr. Pierre?"

"Yes, I am. Are you my ride to the Embassy?"

"I am your escort," she emphasized. "My name is Anastasia."

He walked around her slowly, running his fingers through her hair. "Can I call you Anna?" he requested.

"You can call me Anastasia," she demanded as she pushed him forward onto the bed. She straddled his waist and held both sides of his face.

"You are pretty handsome for an American. Are you some fancy flyboy?" She flips up his marksmanship badge. She knew he hated that term *flyboy*.

"I am a flyboy," he bantered. He was unmoved by her attempt to derail his mission. "Could we get going?" He lifted her by her waist and moved her to sit beside him on the bed.

"One second," she said, "And then we can go." She turned and bent forward, sliding her panties off. "These are too wet to wear," she taunted. "I hope you don't mind if I go without my panties."

Mr. Pierre stood and slipped off his jacket and laid it neatly on the nightstand.

"I will need you to put your panties back on. I am a married man."

"No, Alex!" squalled June. "That's gross."

"Ok, ok, ok," Alex turned to reset his character.

"Wow, this bra is uncomfortable too," said Anastasia. "Can you help me take it off?"

Mr. Pierre walked over to her and unzipped the back of her dress, then released the clasps on her bra. She slipped it off under her dress.

"That's better, but this dress is so tight around my hips." She places his hands on her hips and backs into his hardness. "Feel how tight it is?"

Mr. Pierre did feel the tightness. He moved her hair back without responding and started kissing her neck, then her shoulder. Her breath was deep and slow as she turned to him to undress him. She opened the front of his pants and slid them down his legs as she knelt in front of him.

"Mr. Pierre," she moaned, "Aren't these uncomfortable too?" She tugged at his underwear.

He slipped them off then lifted her by her shoulders to his mouth. He kissed her wildly as she slid off her dress.

"I want you, June," Alex whispered.

"Anastasia," she said, backing up toward the bed.

"I want you, Anastasia."

"Then take me."

He pushed her down hard onto the bed and then climbed on top of her. He kissed her skin as if he was starving for the moisture, leaving a trail of redness as he made his way down her body. She grabbed his shoulders and tried to pull him back toward her. "Take me now," pleaded Anastasia.

He put his hand near her mouth, and she began to bite his fingers and then slowly lick them. Her body arched forward as he pushed her legs up and open. With his head cradled between her thighs, he began to bite her leg and placed two fingers inside her. She pushed back as he began to lick her. She knew the feeling well. As her heart started to race, the blood rushed down her body to meet him as he sucked and licked her and pulled his fingers forward inside her. She tried to pull him up to her mouth, but he resisted. He wanted this to be about her, at least for now. He could feel her body tense and contract around his fingers. Then her body relaxed, and he slowly crawled back to her side, kissing her softly.

She wasn't finished. She climbed on top of him and looked into his eyes. They stayed focused on each other as she began to move her body back and forth. His desire didn't match her slow, methodical movements, so he rolled her over. He pushed deep inside her, and she pulled back. "Too much?" he asked.

She didn't answer. She just directed his hips harder and deeper. She had begun to crave the pain she felt when he went too far. It answered a question that she had never had the courage to ask herself about pleasure and pain.

His body collapsed, exhausted on her chest. "That was amazing," he sighed.

"You are amazing," she said, kissing his face softly.

Eleven

The Note

Alex was participating in a field exercise for battle readiness when June got orders to report to Fort Lewis. She had only been in Korea for seven months of her one-year tour. She notified her Commander, who talked to the Department of the Army on her behalf. The reassignment was a reorganization of her MOS to transition her field into computer-related technology.

She had to report in four days. She tried desperately to get a message to Alex, but he was in a blacked-out operation outside of Camp Graves. On the last day before her flight, she wrote Alex a letter and tried to stuff it under his door. There wasn't space under the door. She had never taken a key to his room; she wanted him to stay on his toes.

> *Ali,*
>
> *I am not sure what is going on. I got orders to go to Fort Lewis. I will call you when I get there. I love you. Mira*

She was hesitant to write anything too personal because she didn't want anyone else there reading it. She taped the note onto the door and kissed the paper before leaving.

Julian took her to the airport, and she hugged him goodbye and made him promise to call. She gave him another letter to give to Alex when he returned.

She was settled in her room on the 4th floor of her new barracks and repeatedly tried to call Alex, but there was no answer.

When Alex returned from the field, there wasn't a note on his door. He tried to call June before he changed out of his dirty clothes. She didn't answer. He called June's barracks in Korea, and they said she had gone back to the States. He walked to Camp Red Cloud, still in his dirty uniform. She was gone. *Why would she leave?* He replayed their last days, and months, and nothing made sense. He stormed back through the officer's quarters toward his room.

"Trouble in paradise?" said Meyers.

"Kiss my ass." Alex pushed his way past Meyers and walked down the hall toward his room. After a few hours, he decided to try to find Julian. He would know where June was. The Cabana was full of drunken soldiers, singing loudly. He looked around, frustrated. Julian wasn't there. He walked into every bar from LaGuardia to Red Cloud and didn't see Julian, so he started to drink his way back to LaGuardia.

"Wow, Chief, I have never seen you drink this much," said Dana, the ComSec officer. Alex didn't respond.

"Do you want to *stalk*?" she slurred. "Damn, I meant to talk."

No response.

Alex scooted out of his chair and walked out without saying anything. He was almost back at base when he stumbled into a quiet bar. He was relieved by the darkness and slow music playing in the background. He sat in a corner and put his head down. The sound of a glass breaking made him raise his head. He saw Meyers seated at the bar. Meyers motioned him over.

"Look, Chief, come and have a beer."

Alex tried to focus enough to stand up and leave.

"What's going on?" asked Meyers, patting him on the back as he sat beside him.

"She's gone."

"I heard that."

"Did she leave a note?"

"Nothing, it makes no sense."

"You think she met someone?"

Alex hadn't thought that until that moment.

"Look, man, truce. Let's get your mind off things a little."

"No, I'm ok."

"I get it. Just let me buy you a drink. One drink."

"Fuck off!" Alex struggled to stand, then pushed his way by Meyers and found a bathroom. There was a rum and coke at his table when he returned, but Meyers was gone. Alex drank it in three swallows and started his walk back toward base. He realized he had drunk too much as he stumbled through the gate of LaGuardia. He paused and put his head on the fence so that he could focus or puke, it wasn't clear.

"Chief," whispered Dana.

"This asshole is following me. Do you mind if I walk with you?"

Alex felt dizzy and had difficulty breathing, so he didn't respond. She walked with him until the turn to go to her room.

"Have a good night," she said as he staggered forward and fell.

"Chief!"

She tried to pick him up, but his weight was hard to manage. They both fell a few times before reaching his door. She let him slide down the wall as she opened his door. She pushed his body into the doorway and tried to drag him into the room, but he was too heavy. She wiggled his face until his eyes opened.

"Chief, I need your help. I can't lift you."

He struggled to sit up. After several attempts he managed to turn and crawl into the room before passing out again.

....- ..--- ---..

June had called Julian several times before she finally reached him. He had been in Pusan trying to make up with Harris, who had broken up with him, not gone back to the States.

"Julian, did you give Alex the letter? I can't reach him. Are they back from the field yet?"

"I have no idea. I just got back from Pusan."

"He has to be freaking out that I just left. I can't reach him."

"You said that, June. I can't do anything tonight, but I will try to go down there tomorrow."

"Just tell him I love him." I left a note, but he needs to read the letter I gave you."

"I still have it. Tomorrow, June."

"Ok, sorry to call so late."

June paced frantically around the room, holding Mr.Bear and spinning her wedding rings.

....⁻ ..⁻⁻⁻ ⁻⁻⁻..

Dana struggled to help Alex to bed and then sat on the floor. She tried to stand up but kept falling. She finally sat at the end of the bed, mentally preparing herself to walk back to her room. Alex opened his eyes to the blur of a woman sitting at the foot of his bed. He crawled forward to see if it was June.

"Mira!"

"Look at what?" she slurred.

"Mira?"

Dana turned around and looked at Alex. She climbed toward him and kissed him. Alex closed his eyes. He felt his body moving in slow motion, but he couldn't control it. His head was spinning, and he was still having trouble breathing. He fell in and out of consciousness, asking for June each time he woke.

Dana didn't speak, she just kept kissing him. She unzipped his flight suit and noticed he wasn't wearing underwear. She removed hers and climbed on top of him until they both passed out completely.

....⁻ ..⁻⁻⁻ ⁻⁻⁻..

Julian woke up early and decided to deliver a "much-needed" part to the motor pool so that he could deliver June's letter to Alex. He parked outside the officer's quarters and went to the side door closest to Alex's room. He waited for someone to come out, but no one did. He took a deep breath, opened the side door, and then snuck over to Alex's door. It was open, so he stuck his head in.

"Chief?"

No response.

"Alex?" He heard someone moving on the other side of the room, blocked by two lockers for privacy. *Great idea,* he thought. He stood at the end of the bed, and his eyes filled with tears. Alex was naked, and so was this woman beside him. He kicked the end of the bed. "What is going on in here?"

Alex woke up holding his head, not noticing Dana was beside him.

"Hey Julian, why are you here? Where is June?"

Julian stood with his hands on his hips, looking at the woman, then Alex, then her. Alex looked over and saw Dana naked.

"Dana, why are you here? What the hell is going on?"

Dana covered her face with a pillow and then crawled out of bed past Julian. She grabbed her clothes and went into the bathroom.

"Alex?" Julian couldn't breathe. He sat at the foot of the bed with his head in his hands.

"I have to tell June," he said, running out of the room.

"Where the hell is she?" screamed Alex.

When Dana came out of the bathroom, Julian and Alex were gone.

Julian was so upset that he couldn't wait to drive back to Camp Casey to call June. He stopped at the phone center at Red Cloud and dialed her number.

"Hello?" June answered the phone, hoping it was Alex.

"Hey girl," cried Julian.

"What is wrong? Is Alex ok?" she pleaded.

"June, I am sorry. I am so sorry."

"What, Julian? is Alex ok?"

"June, give me a second. Please— June, he had sex with that Dana girl. I walked into his room, and they were naked in his bed."

"What? Did you give him my letter?"

"Really, June? No. I didn't think to give him your pointless letter."

"Julian, could you please give him my phone number?"

"And why would I do that bish? Are you dead inside? He fucked someone."

"Dead inside? Don't you have a side-piece or whatever?"

"June, that isn't what this is, and screw you for making me care about your stupid ass."

"Please give him my number."

"I will, but I will lose yours."

"Julian, stop!"

Silence.

It was 8 pm when Alex called. June answered with a box of tissue in her hand.

"Hello?"

"Mira, I have no idea what is going on. You left without a note."

"Did you sleep with someone?" A soldier walked by June and laughed as he walked past her. "Who did you have sex with, Alex?"

"June, let me talk. I had no idea where you were."

"I told you where I was in the note, Alex."

"No, you didn't."

"Alex, I told you I was at Fort Lewis and would call you when I got settled."

"June, I didn't get a note, and I have no memory of anything with that girl. I don't know what the hell is going on?" screams Alex.

"You had sex with another woman Alex. Seems pretty clear to me." She hung up and slid to the floor in tears.

Twelve

Was it all a Lie?

June suffered a massive episode of depression and started seeing another therapist. The lady wasn't a doctor, she had a Master's degree in counseling and focused on talk therapy. June also started taking an antidepressant that her Veteran Affairs doctor prescribed. She felt stable even though she and Alex hadn't spoken in almost eight months.

Washington was a fantastic place to live. She had found a few favorite hiking spots outside Olympia and settled into a new apartment. She didn't take off her wedding rings. She switched them to her right hand. She felt it was a great compromise, considering the unknown state of her marriage.

Alex had gone to a much darker place. He couldn't sleep without vivid nightmares about Sheila going down. He had started drinking every weekend, and his new gunner was worried about his battle readiness. He couldn't find the balance he had with June, so he tried his best to survive until he got back stateside.

"Brown, phone," said a soldier knocking on her door. She hoped it was Julian as she walked to the phone.

"Mira."

She pulled the phone away from her ear to create distance between them.

"I got my orders for Fort Lewis. You must not hate me too much because you didn't withdraw our joint domicile."

She hadn't realized that was an option.

"Can we talk? Mira, talk to me."

"Please call me June."

"June, just promise we can talk when I get there."

"Hmm! Do promises mean anything to you?"

He breathed in and out slowly. "I will be there in four days, June."

"I'm getting out of the Army in a week. I already signed the paperwork to join the Oregon National Guard, but you'll love it here, Alex."

"June, just promise me we can talk. I will drive to Oregon if I need to."

She hung up the phone. She couldn't have responded if she had wanted to. Her lips were quivering, and she couldn't breathe.

....- ..--- ---..

Although she was furious at Alex, it never occurred to her not to pick him up at the airport. She wore shorts to show off her new tan and a red tank top. She stood behind a barrier at his gate and watched the passengers deplane. Dozens of passengers deplaned before she saw his tall frame walking up the jet bridge. *Damn, he's in uniform.*

Two flight attendants followed him out smiling. "Thank you for your service," one of the women said as she put a piece of paper in Alex's hand. He looked at the paper. "I am happily married...but thank you," he said, returning the paper to her.

Is he happily married? She looked down at her wedding rings. She thought about moving them back to her left hand, but that felt too easy. She moved out from behind the wall and stood silent.

Alex ran to June and swung her around. "You look amazing, Babe." She closed her eyes and tried to find that place where the Universe hadn't created this massive void between them.

The flight attendant looked away, then at Alex holding June's hand. "She's not that cute," she said.

The pilot from the crew walked up behind her. "Maggie, you used to be that cute too."

She rolled her eyes, knowing that wasn't a compliment.

"Let's get your bags," said June pointing toward baggage claim. He took her hand and saw she was still wearing her rings. It never occurred to him that they were on the wrong hand.

He looked over at her several times, and he didn't recognize this version of her. She wasn't soft and innocent or sexy and vibrant. She was balanced and confident. He wasn't sure he knew how to act around this version of June, which made him extremely self-aware.

"I got us a room so that we can talk. You don't report until tomorrow, right?"

"That's right." He almost said, ma'am.

The drive was completely silent.

June had a plan and was focused on sticking to it.

Alex was terrified he would say the wrong thing.

June's bags were already packed in the trunk of her new car. When they pulled up to the hotel, she grabbed a carry-on bag to take into the hotel. He checked the room number to see if she had covered it with 6B. She hadn't. However, when he walked into the room, it was softly lit, and there was an R&B station playing on the radio. He didn't wait for her to drop her bag or say anything.

"June, I love you." He took her hand, walked her to the bed, and kissed her.

She didn't speak. She just let him kiss her. She let him undress her. She let him have sex with her. Then without notice, she got up and got dressed, then sat at the edge of the bed. "I have one question. Please be honest."

This girl you slept with. I get that it was a drunken, whatever. "Did you have sex with her again after that?"

He clenched his teeth. He knew he couldn't lie to her. He had only kept something going with Dana to fill the chasm he felt not talking to June had created. He justified it because he had nothing to balance the darkness, so he found what he thought was a temporary replacement for the stability he had with June. Korea was like the timeout of war, he assumed. Things were kept on hold until a soldier returned stateside. He had thought that coming home to June would be enough to make things better between them.

He looked at her but didn't say anything, and she knew the answer. "So, you ruined us. I have to say I am a little shocked. I had thought that Korea healed us, and I guess it just healed me." Her demeanor changed, and she stood up. "We got on-base housing. I have some of my stuff stored there. Can you keep it until I get settled?"

He nodded.

"Get dressed; I will drop you off."

June dropped Alex off at their on-base housing and handed him the keys.

"June."

She drove away with the door partially open.

Alex walked into the house with his head down. The smell of vanilla and lavender filled the space. He wasn't sure why that scent was so familiar to him. As he walked into the kitchen, he saw a neat row of cobalt blue towels on the stove's handle. One still had a sales tag hanging on it. The kitchen that came in basic Army beige was decorated with a flare of color that represented everything he knew about June. There were photos of them on the refrigerator in blue cobalt frames on the kitchen counter. He was drawn to a magnet on the refrigerator door: *I want a man that fights for me, not with me.* He opened one of the cabinets and saw two boxes of Choco Pies. He had no idea she loved them so much. He opened the refrigerator and saw that it was full of groceries. All of his favorite things had carefully been picked out, and the veggie drawer was full of blackberry beer. He grabbed one and a fried chicken leg and searched for the living room. There were burning candles lit by the TV.

She expected us to come home soon.

He sat on the couch and stared at the TV. The flicker of light drew his attention to some DVDs on the counter. He knew, without understanding Korean, that it was group porn.

He walked upstairs to the bathroom and saw that June had taken the right side of the sink and given the left to him. There was a massive jar of Noxzema on his side. His eyes started to burn.

He took the beer to the bedroom. There were more photos of them on the nightstand with a small key. He looked around the room and noticed a wardrobe in the corner, he tried the key. The wardrobe was full of costumes. On either side of the door were the names *Pierre and Anastasia.*

He started feeling dizzy. He knew he couldn't stay there. He changed his clothes and walked over to the officer's club. As he walked through the door, he heard two very familiar voices. He followed the vibrations, and they led him to June and Jacob playing pool. June was lying across the table laughing. He watched her walk to the bar, glance in his direction, and then go to the bathroom. He had just kissed and touched her body. It felt so out of place to see her laughing with Jacob in that space.

"Do I need to ask what is going on here?" demanded Alex in a whisper to Jacob.

Jacob placed his hand on Alex's shoulder and squeezed. "Don't go there, Alex."

Alex removed Jacob's hand, accepting any challenge that was being presented.

"She's drunk. She was going to drive to Oregon, and I called Jan at the on-base hotel and got her a room."

The bartender drops off two blackberry beers at the table.

"You like that shit?" asked Jacob, sipping his Bud Light.

"No, I hate it," said Alex.

Jacob closed his eyes, his lips disappeared, and Alex realized that June was standing behind him.

June looked up at Alex with tears in her eyes. "Was it all a lie? Did you intend to have sex with Dana the whole time we were in Korea?"

June's voice was elevated in a way that made Jacob uneasy. He scanned the room and noticed the Brigade Commander in the corner; Jacob nodded to Alex to go outside, and he followed him.

"Alex, I've been there. I get it. Just give her some time. I know she loves you. Did you see the house?"

"Did you see the house?" Alex barked.

"Damn, Alex, get out of your head."

"I can't be at that house, man. All this shit is unreal."

"Let me call Jan. I will be right back." Jacob ran back into the club, looking for June.

She had left the money for the drinks he had bought her on the table with a tip.

She was gone.

Thirteen

...About That Scarf

June is happy to finally get home from training and out of her head about her past. She frees herself from the scarf she has tucked tightly around her neck, as she walks into her apartment. The room is filled with the smells of vanilla and lavender, and her best friend Pippa has stocked her refrigerator with blackberry beer and fresh eggs for breakfast.

She grabs the beers and lines them up on her kitchen counter. She stands with her arms crossed, staring at the bottles. The moisture from the cold beer reacts to the room's warm climate, and the bottles start to form small drops of water on the outside. She touches the moisture with her finger and realizes that it wasn't always a lie. Still, she takes her arm and corrals all the bottles into the trash. Satisfied with her achievement, she orders a pizza and turns on the TV. The apartment feels peaceful and safe. Three hours and four slices of pizza later, she decides to call Devan. The phone rings several times before a woman answers.

"Hello?"

June's heart starts racing, and her mouth speaks before her mind can think.

"Devan, there? I have his scarf."

"This is his wife! Did he tell you he has a wife?"

Wife? June instinctively hangs up the phone. She can't draw enough air into her lungs. She looks on her bed, grabs Mr. Bear, and buries her face.

Suddenly, that familiar darkness surrounds her again, and she reels in an emotional squall. Mr. Bear does his best to calm her, but she squeezes him so tight he can barely breathe. He is grateful when she finally rubs her snot on his head and tosses him across the room.

The phone ringing startles her, and she falls off the side of the bed. She stumbles madly and runs across the room to answer it.

It is Alex. "Babe, are you ok? You sound upset."

"What do you want? What!"

"Can I call you tomorrow?"

"No!"

"Yes."

"Shit!"

Alex laughs a little. He misses her quirkiness.

She holds the phone close to her face without speaking.

He doesn't hang up; he just listens to her crying and wonders if the tears are for him.

She is alerted by the sound of a call waiting on the line. "I have to go," she whispers.

They have said goodbye so many times in the past, but this time he feels it. "Mira," he says as she switches to the other call.

It is Devan. June can hear screaming in the background.

"I'm driving down."

"To Portland?"

"Yes, I will be there later tonight."

Before she can respond, she hears a dial tone. She tries frantically to call him back but keeps getting an answering machine. The storm builds again, drowning her in emotions.

She tries to sleep, but her mind races through scenarios about Devan, Alex, and her rape. She realizes that she forgot to lock her front door, so she gets out of bed and shuffles to the door. As she reaches for the doorknob, she hears a loud banging. "Portland Police! Open up!"

Police? She opens the door slightly with the chain pulled tight. "Can I help you, officer?"

"Ma'am, we are looking for Devan Hartford. Is he here?"

June is so confused she isn't sure what to say.

"Ma'am, would you mind if we came inside and had a look around?"

"Of course not. "June unlatches the door and then thinks she should have, asked for some sort of ID.

The phone rings again, startling June. The police officers look suspiciously at her as she runs to answer the phone. It is Alex.

"I need my Jeep back. I forgot I have to renew the registration this week. I also need to get our stuff out of the house. My Commander is pissed to find out you aren't here. I'm in the officer's quarters by the PX."

"I need to call you back whispers June. The police are here."

"June, what the hell is going on? Do you need me to come down there?"

"I will call you back," she whispers again.

The police officers check all the rooms and even look under the bed. One of the officers examines the snot on Mr. Bears' head and then throws him back in the corner.

"Ma'am, when was the last time you saw Mr. Hartford?"

June looks at her watch. "At the airport today in Salt Lake City, Utah. I think it was before three. Yes, my flight left at three."

"You haven't seen him tonight?"

"No." She is getting nervous about the questions, so she stops providing details.

"We have a missing person's report, and his wife states she suspects foul play. She gave us your address as his last known location."

Foul play? She smiles inappropriately.

"Again, Miss, when is the last time you saw Mr. Hartford?"

June pinched the bridge of her nose. The phone rings again, and she grabs it before the officer can stop her.

She's relieved to hear Devan's voice.

He sighs. "So, how do I get to where you are?"

She doesn't respond; she just hands the police officer the phone.

"Portland, Police."

"What? Where is June?"

"Sir, who is this?"

"Devan," he says with hesitance.

"Where are you, Sir?"

Devan doesn't know his exact location. "I think highway 205 exit 10."

"Are you en route to this location?"

"Well, I need directions, which is why I am calling."

The police officer gives Devan directions to their location and hangs up the phone without allowing June to speak to him. She raises her arms in protest to the police officer and then walks around him toward the bathroom.

"Ma'am, we will need you to stay where we can see you."

June leaves the bathroom door open but goes to pee.

When Devan arrives, he walks into the apartment without knocking. June shakes her head in dismay and sits down on the kitchen floor. She looks at the trash can and then at the police officers, barreling questions at Devan. She slowly pulls the trash can over to her and digs out a blackberry beer.

pshhitt!

They all three look sharply at June.

Devan follows the police officers to the door and closes it, waving and apologizing to the officers. He looks over at June, who is still sitting on the floor. "Can I have one of those?" he asks as he slides down the kitchen cabinet to the floor.

June digs out another beer and hands it to Devan. They laugh a little when they hear the *pshhitt*. June taps Devan's beer and casually asks, "How was your drive down?"

Devan describes his adventure leaving and making the three-hour drive down to Portland. June yawns, points at the couch and goes to bed.

Staring at the ceiling, she feels a tightness in her chest. She sneaks into the living room and turns down the volume on the answering machine. It would be too weird to talk to Alex if he calls back, but she doesn't want to miss a message from him either.

When she wakes up the following day, there are 19 messages.

"June, this is Pippa; some woman called at 4 am saying you stole her husband or something. I told the bitch... "June deletes the message as she looks across the room at Devan, who is fully dressed and sitting on the floor.

"June, this is April from work. A woman called last night- "delete.

"Mira," her heart sinks. "A lady named Denise called me last night; I am not sure what is going on but be careful. Who is Devan? Babe, I hope you are ok; just call me." She deletes the rest of the messages without listening to them.

"I will go," says Devan.

June is gripping her hair tightly in her hands.

"How the hell did she get my work phone number or the number for Alex?"

She immediately thinks of training. Surely, they wouldn't have given out her personal information. She is terrified that the man who raped her could just call and find out everything about her. She calls the training center, and they had faxed all her information to Denise. She immediately calls her mom.

"Momma, did you get a phone call last night."

"June, I can't handle this kind of stress. When you got messed up with Alex, I knew that this was going to come back on me."

"Mom, it's not coming back on you. Let me have your number changed."

"I have had this same number for thirty years, and now I have to change it? No, I won't kowtow in the corner because you are cheating with some woman's husband. You should be damn ashamed of yourself. I raised you better than this."

"Mom, it's a long story. I just want to make sure you are ok."

"Well, I am not ok. That girl called four times, screaming at me. It was 3 am, June."

"I am so sorry, Mom. What can I do?"

"Stop screwing up your life. First, you go and get yourself raped, and now all this. You are putting yourself in these positions. Is this guy black too?"

"Mom, that doesn't matter."

"Well, maybe the good Lord is trying to tell you something. You should probably listen this time."

"Mom, I have to go to work. I am sorry. I love you."

"Well, for the love of Christ, don't lose your job."

June holds the phone, waiting for an I love you.

"Well, go on now, June."

"Ok, Mom. I love you."

The phone is silent then she hears a dial tone.

June sees Devan grabbing his things to leave.

"Sit down! Stay here until I get home. You should probably call your mom. Your crazy wife called mine."

"June."

"Don't! I can't right now."

June pulls up at the café and sees the word 'whore' painted in red paint on the windows and copies of Devan's marriage certificate taped to the door. She walks into the front door, and her boss April motions her back.

"June, I hope your training thing went well."

"Yes, ma'am, it did."

"Well, I guess maybe it went too well. Do I need to explain the kind of phone call I received last night?"

"No ma'am. I will clean the windows. I have no idea how this got so out of control."

"June, I love you, honey, but I have to let you go. Josh doesn't want this kind of drama around here."

June takes a deep breath. "I am so sorry."

June finds a hardware supply store to buy paint remover for the windows. It takes her three hours to remove all the paint. Her hands are bright red and she has paint on her face and hair. She wants to go home and wash off the paint remover, but she can't deal with that much confrontation. She grabs the marriage certificate off the window and folds it neatly before putting it into her pocket.

She decides to go for a walk in the Japanese Gardens. She walks down the winding paths staring up at the vibrant leaves. Fall has wrapped its arms around the trees for one last time, showing its beauty in vibrant oranges, reds, and yellows. There is a smell of chestnut on the moist and mossy ground. She walks across a small arched bridge that stands over a still pond. The trees and shrubbery overhang the pond, so it appears as if everything is floating peacefully around her. As she walks across a small knoll, the tall evergreen trees frame all of this vibrancy, which calls her into a beautiful painting of color.

She closes her eyes and tries to breathe in the beauty, the color, anything to free her from the darkness creeping around her. Her journey leads her to a small waterfall. She sits and listens to the water hitting the flat surface of the pond. *I need a fountain,* she thinks. She is restless, so she keeps walking until she sees a beautiful tree. The tree's base is solid and robust, but it becomes confused a foot off the ground; the limbs twist in random directions–indecisive. Its dark lines are determined, and its leaves show a bright red lipstick color. She wants to have the confidence of this tree. She wants to feel beautiful enough to bend and twist in any direction she chooses. She wants the courage of those women on the mountain to scream and cry. Anastasia is the closest she has ever come to the confidence of this tree. She kneels in front of the tree but refuses to touch it.

She knows that the foundation of what her mother said is true. She has made all the decisions in her life based on a man. She is so confused about what she wants or who she is.

The tree calls to her that it wants to talk to her, to hear her problems, so she lies on the leaf-covered ground at the base of the tree and looks up through the dark branches and red leaves at the pale blue sky.

"What did Alex do to our lives? Why do I still want him so badly? Is Devan any different? He's married." She takes the marriage certificate out of her pocket and looks at his signature. "He wasn't forced to marry Denise," she says aloud to the tree.

The tree sits patiently, listening to her every word. It never interrupts her with advice or thoughts of its own. It just sways above her until she is finished.

She stands and looks at her new friend one last time. "Can I have this?" she says, picking up a fallen leaf. The tree doesn't answer or object.

When she returns to the apartment, Devan isn't there. It is nice to be in her space alone. She plops on the bed where Mr. Bear is sitting. *You are the only man I need*, she thinks, kissing the bear.

She is asleep when Devan returns. He has brought her gifts and more blackberry beer. She wakes up and motions for him to come and sit on the bed. He starts to explain things about himself and Denise, but June stops him.

"These are the facts: I am married to Alex. You are married to Denise. I lost my job because of all this. Why would we continue to be together?"

"Do you want me to answer?"

She nods.

"June, I have never felt the way I did when I saw you walking into the building that day. You have this amazing light that energizes me in ways that I can't even understand. I couldn't. I can't let you go. I will file for divorce today if that is what you want."

June closes her eyes and runs her fingers through her hair, pulling slightly. *Divorce?* Even the thought of it makes her anxious. She has never thought about divorcing Alex, even during the eight months they didn't speak. She doesn't want to be responsible for a divorce, much less two.

"Devan I can't make decisions for you and I don't need you to get divorced to prove something to me."

He lowers his head and then says, "I have gifts!" He has bought her a blue scarf, the ingredients for dinner, candles, wine, and a box of chocolates.

"Can I make us dinner?"

She sees the dimple that makes his smile so adorable. He is wounded more on the inside than he has been by the scratches from his wife. He doesn't need to tell her that he is sorry for everything. She can see it in the fading light behind his eyes.

"Let's do it together," she smiles.

They make spaghetti with garlic bread and a salad. June doesn't have a table, so they make a picnic on the floor. They talk about training mostly since that is the only positive experience they share. They laugh about the flashlight and how cold it was. She feels comfortable, almost at home.

The next day is Saturday, and Devan, asks if he can ride up with her to Fort Lewis since his parents live there. She wants to say no. She wants to see Alex alone, so she is relieved when he asks if she minded if he stayed with his parents.

June is quiet for most of the drive while Devan talks about hiking, Seattle, and his love for computers. June drops Devan off at a cute house with a bright red door. She loves the Asian-style garden in the front of the house. She is drawn to the secret walkway around the right side of the house. She notices the sound of a water fountain. She remembered how peaceful the one was at the Japanese Garden. This scene is in stark contrast to the anxious feeling she feels inside.

June still has privileges to go onto the base, so she drives directly to the officer's quarters. She sees her car in front of the officer's quarters, so she parks beside it. She pulls her wedding bands out of her pocket and puts them on. She notices a huge scratch on the side of her car. Alex is always so careful. She is confused and a little angry. She doesn't hesitate to go to his room since she now considers herself a civilian.

Alex opens the door before she knocks.

"What is going on? Why were the police at your house?"

She had forgotten to call him back and explain but doesn't have the energy to do so now.

"Alex, I brought your Jeep back. Here are your keys."

"Sit down, June, just for a minute."

She smiles when she sees a stack of Choco Pie boxes on the dresser.

"Wow, are these for me?"

They aren't.

"Yeah, they are for you," he mumbles as he comes over to the bed and sits beside her.

"How did we get here?" he says.

"Do I need to draw you a picture, Alex?"

"June, stop! Please. I don't remember anything about that night except Julian waking me up."

"Alex, you are so intelligent. You understand the minor details about everything you do. Has it ever occurred to you that Dana drugged you?"

Alex lay back on the bed. He looks over, and June has put her hands behind her head and is staring at the ceiling. Tears are rolling down her cheeks into her hair. He wipes her tears with his thumb and then kisses his finger. Then he climbs on top of her and leans down to her ear. "Amore Eterno?"

She looks up at him crying. She has promised forever too. She takes his face in her hands and pulls him to her lips. Their kisses are deep and painful. He has missed the passion between them, the way June always knows what he wants. She pulls aggressively at his pants until he removes them. He opens her jeans and puts his hand between her legs. "You are always so wet," he whispers. She hurries to take off her pants and takes his hands to put them on her breasts. She desperately feels around his hand for his wedding ring and then pushes him off. "Where is your ring?" She stands up before he can answer and walks over to his dresser, frantically searching for the ring. "Where is it, Ali?" He still doesn't answer. She opens the top drawer and notices a picture frame turned upside down. "Is this her?" June studies the photo carefully. "Damn, Ali, this girl was with Meyers."

"What?"

"She was all over him at the Cabana the night we did the thunder-run."

"It doesn't matter, June."

"Are you serious right now?" She throws the photo at him shattering it on the wall.

"June, I don't even know how to say this."

"Then don't, Ali, don't say it!" she screams, holding back a torrent of tears.

Alex walks over and puts June's head on his chest. "I am so sorry, June." He pauses and holds her as tight as he can.

"Dana is pregnant."

As if imprinted on a sharp knife, those words cut a perfect circle into her stomach and rip out everything it means to her to be a woman. June falls to her knees, screaming and crying. Alex drops down to the floor with her. He holds her shivering body until she stops crying. "I am so sorry, June. I am not even sure how all this happened."

"You had sex with another woman!" she says as she pushes him away. She stands up slowly and grabs her keys. Her legs can barely hold her up. She pulls at her rings until she gets them off her finger and then places them on his dresser.

Alex doesn't follow her. He just starts picking up the pieces of glass. June stops in the stairwell, then turns around and runs back up the stairs. She flings his door open and grabs the boxes of Choco Pies, fumbling them onto the floor and kicking the last few boxes out of the door.

The cool fresh air blowing across her face is like a breath she can't take. When she finally breathes in, she collapses onto the ground. It takes several minutes for her to gain enough strength to stand.

When she finally stands, she dusts the gravel off her pants and picks up the boxes of Choco Pies, stacking them neatly on top of each other. She opens one of the boxes before she gets to her car and starts eating a pie. "You can have Alex!" she screams toward the officer's quarters, with a mouth full of her treat. "But you can't have my fucking Choco Pies!"

June drives quietly to Devan's parents trying not to think about Alex having a baby with someone else. As she gets out of the car, she collapses from the weight of yet another trauma.

Devan runs over to June. "Jesus, did he hurt you?" He tries to pick up June, but her body is heavy with defeat. She hears the question but has no idea how to answer it. *Of course, Alex hurt me.* She just doesn't have the words to say how much. She manages to get to all fours and then slowly stands.

Devan's mother runs to June and waives Devan away.

"Gwaenchanh-a," she says as if she understands that kind of pain.

June looks up and sees the most beautiful woman she has ever seen. Her kindness shows through her skin and her voice brings June peace. All of the questions and the doubt she has about Devan dissolve at that moment. *Nothing evil or hateful could come from such a beautiful being.*

As tall as she can, June stands up and looks at Devan. "Can you drive?"

He did.

She directs him to a small community of houses in a remote area of Fort Lewis. "I need to grab my stuff. Can you wait in the car?"

He is frustrated and confused but nods his head.

There isn't much left in the house. The tapes she had made of their songs, the books of their letters, and a couple of boxes of clothes, photos, and the porn tapes. She puts the boxes outside and then returns for the books.

They had never slept there, never made dinner in the kitchen. The cobalt blue towels she had bought for the kitchen still hung from the stove, unsoiled. She knew Alex had been there when she saw the black-berry beer bottles and Choco Pie wrappers in the trash. The fire of emotion builds behind her eyes again when she thinks about him bringing Dana there to eat her Choco Pies. She puts the key on the counter and runs out, locking the door behind her. Devan comes over to help her load the boxes into the car.

"Oh my god, no! no!"

"What, June? What is wrong?"

"I left our books."

He knows he isn't part of that "our."

"Check the windows! Please just check the windows," she pleads.

Devan walks around the house, and none of the windows are unlocked. He feels helpless and somehow responsible.

"June, do you want me to break the window?"

She does, but knows it won't change anything.

"Just take me home," she says. "I need to go home."

Neither speaks for the first hour of the drive back to Portland. June stares out at the dark landscape. The grey sky has changed even the evergreen trees to a variant of grey. She hears a faint rumble of thunder, as the rain starts sliding its way down the window. She traces each drop from the top to the bottom of the window, where it pools and then floods backward.

"June, do want to talk?"

"Please just drive." She curls up into the smallest version of herself and falls asleep.

Devan leaves June in the car for a few minutes, then comes out to get her. She walks in dazed; her apartment doesn't feel safe anymore. He takes her to the bathroom, where he has run her a bubble bath. On the edge of the tub is a blackberry beer. She sits on the toilet listening to the bubbles fizz and pop and then lifts her arms like a child to be undressed. Devan doesn't think about what this means. He just helps her get undressed and into the bath.

She looks into his kind eyes and sees that his light has returned. "I'll take tequila," she says, handing him the beer. He searches every cabinet in the kitchen, and he can't find anything suitable to mix with tequila, so he grabs a coke from the refrigerator and adds ice. When he returns, she is bent forward with her face in the water, sobbing and choking on the water. He instinctively jumps in the tub behind her, fully dressed, and pulls her up. He moves the soapy wet hair out of her face. It takes an hour before she leans back on his chest and wipes her nose on his sleeve.

"That's sexy," he says.

"What, being fully clothed in a bathtub with a naked woman?"

"No, the snot on my sleeve. It's been a fantasy of mine for a long time." She swirls around. "That's great. I have plenty of snot."

He tries not to look at her breast covered in bubbles or notice how her wet hair is painted around her face. He is glad that he is fully clothed.

She stands up and takes a drink of her tequila and coke. "It's not bad," she says. He watches as she dries off, washes her face, and brushes her teeth, not knowing if he should move. He doesn't understand how her mood has changed so quickly. It seems like she has turned a page and found a new chapter. When she leaves the bathroom, she closes the door, and he stands up. He doesn't have a spare set of clothes in the bathroom, so he wraps himself in one of her cobalt blue towels and tries to wring the water out of his clothes. He walks out of the bathroom cautiously. "I just need to grab some clothes. Sorry." She grabs his hand as he passes her. "Thank you."

The next day she asks Devan to stay with his parents for a while so she can think. He leaves her a message every day, but she doesn't have the words that it takes to return his calls. It's two months before she decides to call Alex. She has found a few words for him.

"I hate you," she says before he can even say hello.

"I know, June."

"You don't. You don't know. You broke my heart."

"Did you get my letter?"

"No, I haven't checked my mail in weeks."

"Please check it and call me after."

June hangs up the phone and runs to her mailbox. It is packed with junk and newspapers. She sorts her mail over the trash until she sees the letter. She opens the envelope and it's just a CD and not an actual letter. On the CD is the number 35. She holds the CD tightly remembering that song 35 was for "an emergency." She slowly puts the CD into the player in her car and hears, "On Bended Knee," by *Boyz II Men*.

She listens to the song three times, crying more each time. Then without thinking, she just starts driving north until she is at the gate of Fort Lewis. She no longer has base privileges, so she checks in at the entrance, and they phone Alex to get approval. She sees the thumbs up and suddenly becomes nervous.

He is waiting outside the barracks when she pulls up. "Can I take you somewhere?"

"No, can we just go up to your room?"

"June, can you just hop in the Jeep?"

"I really can't. Just talk to me here."

"June, you were right about Dana. She said it was Meyers' idea but that she cared for me or some bullshit. I don't know how to sort this entire thing out, but you are my wife, June. That means something to me."

She rolls her eyes, but he is saying exactly what she has wanted to hear for so long.

"Come upstairs. It's cold out here."

She follows Alex up the stairs to his room. She checks the drawers for photos and then looks under the bed and in his closet; there are no photos, no traces of Dana.

"June, I don't know how to wake up without you. I keep having nightmares. I try every night to save Sheila, to save you, and I crash every time. I wake up soaked in sweat looking for you, and you aren't there to tell me it's just a dream. I haven't slept in over a week. They grounded me until I can get my shit together."

"I want to throw up every time I think of you having a child with her. I don't think I can ever get past that."

He reaches into his pocket, pulls out her rings, and places them on the dresser. "Can you try?"

"I hate you," she says in a shaken voice.

"I hate me too."

She traces an imaginary line down his arm to his wrist, remembering where he had broken it. She grabs his hand, it feels right.

"Alex, I feel like I waited my whole life for you to love me. I really thought that you were all I ever needed. I think we are perfect for each other in a lot of ways. Something was taken from me the night I was raped, and knowing Dana has your child is a constant reminder of what I lost."

He knows that any words he says will only take more away from her, so he just leans against her. June senses that he is exhausted, so she guides him to the bed. "Sleep. I will be right here when you wake up." He curls up in her lap with his arms tightly around her waist. She wipes his tears away, then hers. In minutes she can feel the full weight of his body and see his hands twitching. He is wearing his wedding ring, so she reaches over to the dresser and puts on hers. She holds her hand beside his and tries to feel happy, even if it isn't real. She watches his eyes go into REM and wonders if he is dreaming.

Her finger traces the hairline around his face and pauses at the scar over his right eye. She remembers how deep the cut was there when he had returned from Iraq. They had left small pieces of metal under his skin, and they would come to the surface over the years. He used to save the small pieces because they were part of Sheila. June leans against the wall and closes her eyes. She tries to sync her breaths with his. She slowly drifts off to sleep.

June wakes up to see Alex looking at her, smiling.

"You stayed."

She laughs. "I promised I would. How did you sleep?"

"Like a bear. I don't think I had any dreams."

She covers her mouth. "Toothbrush?"

He gives her the Ziploc he had packed just in case she came up. It has been in his closet for a week as a reminder that she hadn't responded to his letter.

"How did you sleep, June?"

"Ok. Can I say something to you, and you just listen?"

"Sure."

"I want you back so badly. I love you so much, and I don't know how I will survive without you if I leave."

He takes her hands and notices she is wearing her rings. He rotates the rings back and forth as she continues.

"If I stay, it hurts everyone: you, Dana, the baby."

He looks up at her. "Mira, I don't want to let you go."

"Listen, please. Your daughter."

Without thinking, he interrupts, "Son."

Why is that worse? She stops talking.

"June, my son will always be my son. You can still be my wife."

She takes a deep breath and tries to hold back her tears. "That is great for you but not for your son or Dana. I hate her, trust me. But your son is part of you, and I could never hate him. So, I need you to file for a divorce. I lost my job so I can't afford to do it."

"Dana, I won't." He covers his mouth with both hands and closes his eyes.

"Here is my address." She puts a piece of paper on the dresser and then places her rings on top.

Fourteen

Different Guy

June and Devan both get divorced, and June has reenlisted in the Army because she has no other real skills to support herself. She is stationed back at Fort Hood, but she can't bear the memories of being on base, so she suggests that Devan marry her so they can live off base. She also wants to separate Devan from her life in the Army, which belongs to Alex and her. She still occasionally talks to Alex, believing they have become really good friends. The truth is that they need each other to balance the darkness. There is finality in letting go that neither can bear.

Devan has gotten out of the military entirely but can't find a job right away in Killeen, so he opens a coffee shop at the mall. June loves that he smells like coffee when he comes home.

"June, can I use this tiny bottle of whiskey you have carried around for years?" asks Devan as he plunders through the kitchen cabinets.

"No!"

"I don't have wine for the pasta sauce."

"Then go buy wine."

Devan continues his search until he finds some grape Kool-Aide. *This should work.*

June walks into the kitchen as he sprinkles Kool-Aide into the pasta sauce. She sticks her finger in the sauce. "Yum."

He swings her around and kisses the sauce off her lips. "I agree, that is delicious." He lifts her onto the counter lifting up her shirt.

"Dev, I am starving."

"Me too." He kisses her harder.

"I need to eat."

"Me too." He tugs at her pants.

"Turn off the stove," she says, running to the bedroom.

Devan is very gentle with everything he touches, especially June.

He slowly backs June up to the bed, unlaces her combat boots, and then takes off her socks. She takes off her outer jacket, then her t-shirt, and then stands to remove her pants. He smiles when he sees her rainbow-colored underwear, a drastic contrast to her green and brown uniform.

"Devan, I need a shower."

"Nope, I like you dirty." He takes off his pants, then his shirt, and climbs on top of her. He kisses the side of her face, then her neck. He slowly lifts her breast into his mouth, biting her gently. She moves backward and tries to pull his head back to her face, but he continues his way down her body to her hips.

"I don't like that," she whispers.

She did, just not with him.

"Tell me what you like." He says as he spreads her legs apart.

She wants him to stop but knows he wants to please her. "Put your tongue here," She points to the spot. He isn't doing it hard enough, and she is more focused on instructing him than enjoying it. "Give me your hand."

He did.

She licks between his fingers the ways she wants him to lick her. He follows her directions, and she starts to feel that amazing feeling again. She lifts her hips to meet his lips––his tongue.

"Oh, god don't move," she moans.

He freezes in place, waiting.

"No, don't stop moving your tongue. Just don't move from that spot."

"Oh, my god. Don't stop," she pleads. "Oh my god." Her body falls flat, and her heart beats loudly. He lifts his head, then his arms in victory.

June smiles. "You are so stupid. Get up here."

June loves having sex with Devan, but it doesn't feed her darkness. He is a perfectly ordinary guy with very few issues. He comes from great parents and has a huge supportive family who loves her. She is the only one damaged. She is terrified to share her darkness with him, so she wears it like a cloak, suffocating her spirit.

....⁻ ..⁻⁻⁻ ⁻⁻⁻..

June is assigned to an attack helicopter battalion. She knows Alex is based in North Carolina, but she always watches as she sees pilots stepping out of an AH 64. She has become a network specialist as part of Task-Force-Twenty-One. She is at the airfield to distribute the new Standard Operating Procedures that she co-wrote on how to use the latest computer systems. She waits in the field Ops building for the pilots to come in so she can brief them on the new system.

"June?"

"Oh my god, is that you?" She reaches to hug Jacob before she realizes she is in uniform.

"Captain Jacob Edwards at your service," he says, pointing to his new rank.

She holds out her collar too.

"Ah, I see you made rank too. Sergeant Brown."

She looks down at her feet. "It's Hartford."

"What? Where is Chief?"

"Fort Bragg. We..." Her lip starts to quiver.

"No, June! What happened? He loved you so much." He briefly wonders if Mandy is involved.

She reaches for a piece of paper and writes down Alex's number. "You'll need to talk to him. I am not really sure."

"I will, June, but tell me about Hartford."

"He's sweet."

He waits for more and then realizes there may not be anymore. "Give me a hug. I am really sorry. I hope you are happy."

June hugs him a little too tightly. "I hope you are happy too, Jacob."

Jacob calls Alex right away. It has been over four years since he saw him at Fort Lewis, and he hasn't spoken to him since.

"Chief Brown," Alex answers. *Why did she give me his work number?*

"Chief!"

"LT.?"

"That's Captain Edwards to you bitch."

"That's awesome, Jacob. How the hell are you?"

"I am great. I am here at Fort Hood. Hey, I just saw June."

"Really?" He takes a deep breath.

"Yep. She says yaw split up but wouldn't say why. June loves you. I can't imagine there is much you could have done that she wouldn't have forgiven you for."

"Hey, I have a son. He's going on two," answering the question.

Jacob got it. "That's great, man. Wow, you must be thrilled."

Alex takes a deep breath. He doesn't know how to explain what happened, and he doesn't want to talk about it with Jacob. He has always given Jacob a hard time about cheating on Tara, and it makes him sick to think he has done the same thing.

For Jacob, there is no judgment. He understands too well how deployments, distance, and the Army's stress can weigh on a relationship.

"Jay, I don't know. It all seems so far away from where I am now."

"Listen, Alex. I am not the person to tell you how to handle this, but June doesn't seem like she has gotten past it. Maybe you should just cut ties with her so that she can move on?"

Alex has no intention of ever letting go of June. He still loves her. He still needs her. She is his pendulum. He feels that his punishment is that she is with someone else. The discomfort fuels his need to hold on to her in any way he can.

"She calls me when she has nightmares. How can I not answer?"

"If you didn't answer, maybe she'd wake up her new husband. Just let her move on!"

"Jacob, that would be like cutting off my arm. My good one."

"Then cut off your damn arm. You don't get to have everything your way. The new wife... and I am assuming, the kid June couldn't give you. The whole happily ever after. On the other hand, she is straddling this chasm between what she can't have with you and what she won't have with him. Unless you let her go."

Alex takes a deep breath. "So, how long have you been at Fort Hood?"

"Goodbye, Alex. I truly wish you the best."

"Jacob, let me explain."

Jacob already hung up the phone. He can't believe that Alex could have cheated on June. He had counted on them to make it. He wants to call her, to hug her, but it isn't his place to do those things either.

....⁻ ..⁻⁻⁻ ⁻⁻⁻..

June wipes her tears before walking into the house. She goes straight to the bathroom and buries her face in the cobalt blue towel.

"June, some of my friends from work want to play cards tonight."

"Go ahead, that is fine."

"June, with us."

"Ok, I need to shower first." Since her attack, everything seems to give her a bladder or vaginal infection. She is on a strict policy to bathe constantly, pee after sex, and make sure the man she is with is as germ-free as possible. It is a constant reminder of how filthy she feels she has become.

She gets out of the shower and puts on a sundress.

"Wow, that is sexy for friends," says Devan.

"Well, we could stay here," she teases.

"No, we are going to meet my friends and have fun. You look like you had a bad day."

"I saw Jacob."

"Who is that again?"

"Alex's gunner in Iraq."

"I thought he died."

"No, he didn't." June doesn't want to explain. "Different guy."

She can't believe that they drove up in Jacob's old neighborhood. *Is this some kind of sign?* Devan's friend lives three houses down from where Jacob and Tara lived. She still remembered the night she sat in Tara's living room, reading Alex's letter and figuring out that he was sending her songs. It feels like yesterday and a million years ago.

They play spades and hearts; two games June has mastered in the military. She and Devan are a great team. She can talk across the board in a way that no one suspects. He doesn't like when she cheats but loves seeing her happy.

Michael and Elizabeth have been married for twenty-three years. They have four children, all grown, and travel all over the world. Michael is a retired engineer who works part-time at the mall, and Elizabeth has always been a stay-at-home mom. *They are like shadows of the other person*, June thinks, remembering how that felt with Alex. They are there but not taking up any space in the other person's life.

"So, June, are you guys thinking about kids yet?" asks Elizabeth.

Devan wraps his feet around June's as he watches her reaction.

"No ma'am, I can't have kids."

"Well honey, only God gets to decide that. You can always try. You guys are such a cute couple. You should try."

God did decide.

"Liz, mind your business," says Michael grabbing her wrist.

"Well, there is nothing wrong with trying, Michael," she clamors.

"Liz, I need your help in the kitchen," urges Michael.

He scurries her off to the kitchen, and Devan moves to sit beside June. "Are you ok? I am sorry. I should have said something to them."

"Let's try," she says. "God may have changed his mind about me."

"Really? No. Really?" questions Devan.

Liz walks back into the room. "Honey, I am so sorry. Mike just told me that you were raped and that your husband left you for a woman that was carrying his child. That is just awful."

June looks at Devan coldly and walks out to the car.

"Devan, I am sorry," says Liz. I didn't know it was a secret. She probably needs to talk to someone about all that. Poor thing."

"I guess we are going. I will see you Monday, Michael."

Michael pats him on the back and follows him to the door. "Liz means well," he says. "It's just that her mouth hasn't consulted with her brain in decades."

Devan smiles and hesitantly walks toward the car.

June is livid. She is pacing back and forth and has found a cigarette somewhere and is smoking it.

"You smoke now?" asks Devan, a little disgusted.

"Are you kidding me? You tell random people I was raped, and you want to question me about smoking?"

"He's a friend."

"Oh, so that gives you the right to expose all my hurtful secrets?" She blew the smoke of her last drag into his face.

"I needed to talk to someone," bargains Devan.

"Oh, you need to talk to someone about MY rape and MY inability to have a baby and MY husband cheating on me."

"You mean your ex-husband."

"That is your takeaway from what I just said? Take me home."

"June."

"Take. Me. Home."

June falls asleep on the couch while Devan works on the bank receipts for the coffee shop. He has grown accustomed to her mood swings and refusal to talk. However, he is confused about the on and off switch that seems connected to her desire for physical contact. Even her bounce has lost its buoyancy.

....¯ ..¯¯¯ ¯¯¯..

Oddly, June immediately makes appointments for the fertility clinic. During her new rounds of testing, she takes Clomid for two months and HSG shots to inspire ovulation. Her ovaries shutting down are only part of the problem. She has tremendous scarring in her uterus, and the doctors feel she couldn't sustain a pregnancy. Every time her period comes, she feels like she has lost another child. She cries for hours in the bathroom and won't eat for days. The doctors finally did all the testing possible.

"Hi, Sergeant Hartford. I don't know if you remember me, I am Dr. Amber. We met several years ago when...," she pauses. "I am having difficulty finding the tests I had performed in your medical record."

June takes a deep breath. She remembers ripping up those pages on the plane to Korea. She shrugs her shoulders. "I remember you." June smiles.

"I am sorry to say that we haven't gotten a positive result. It appears that your reproductive organs have shut down. There aren't many options if we can't encourage your body to ovulate."

"Couldn't you just take the eggs?"

"We can't take them if your body doesn't respond to making them."

June sits quietly, looking at the model of the human reproductive system. She has grown numb to hearing bad news.

She calls Devan and leaves a message saying, "No."

Devan is devastated that he has agreed to put her through this again. She seemed so encouraged that it had made him hopeful too. He loves June and wants a family with her. He thinks about getting her flowers, then remembers she hates them because they die. So, he buys her a tiny orange kitten.

June arrives home early and goes straight to the shower without saying hello to Devan. He gets comfortable on the couch with the kitten beside him and anxiously waits for her to come back into the room. After several minutes he walks into the bedroom and sees her sleeping on the bed. She still has her bath towel wrapped around her. He wants to wake her with the kitten but knows she must be devastated. It is 7 pm when she finally walks into the living room, still in her towel.

"Hey, Dev. I am sorry. I was exhausted." She looks over at Devan, smiling wildly and pointing at the puff of fur. "Is that? Is that a baby? You got me a baby?"

Devan nods proudly.

June runs and sits in Devan's lap and grabs the puff. She looks into its eyes, then at its butt. "It's a girl." She kisses Devan passionately and then looks at the puff. "We kiss a lot," she says. Devan can't agree with that statement, but he is thrilled that June is smiling again.

"What are you going to name her?" Devan inquires.

Her first thought is Sheila, then Anastasia. "Let's name her Cheese."

"Cheese?" he questions as he rubs his nose with his index finger.

"Yes! And we will go back tomorrow and find her a brother, Ham."

June looks at Devan as she kisses Cheese. He is smiling like the first day she had ever seen him. His eyes are bright and focused on her interactions with the puff. It is strangely erotic to her that he bought her a kitten. She crawls over to him and wraps her legs around his waist. She kisses him hard, with every ounce of passion inside her. He slows her down by touching her face and then pulls her head gently back with his hands laced through her long blonde hair.

"I want you so badly," she whispers in his ear as she kisses him.

"And you will have me, just not that way." He thinks that to give in to her passion means unlocking her darkness. He doesn't realize that her darkness is woven so deeply inside her that to deprive it suffocates her too.

She unzips his pants to expose him, and then she climbs on top of him, forcing his arms backward with her weight. Her smell and the feeling of her damp hair on his face break the barrier he has placed between them. He wraps his arms around her waist and moves her to the floor.

The puff tries to join them, but June tantalizes her with her fingers as Devan continues to kiss her.

They undress together, laughing as they fall over each other. He feels her body arch toward him as he kisses her neck and shoulder. He finds an openness about her during sex that he doesn't know in any other aspect of their life together. It is intoxicating to be with her. She draws him deep within herself and exposes to him everything vulnerable about her.

She wraps her legs around his waist and pulls him close to her, then lightly releases her pressure to allow him to arch his back away from her.

"Look at me," she whispers.

He does.

She looks deeply into his eyes, searching for something that she can connect to. She desperately wants to connect him to the pleasure she is feeling, to the joy he brought her by bringing home the puff.

She feels his rhythm moving at a different pace than hers, so when he closes his eyes, she closes hers. She waits for that feeling she has become so attuned to. Her heart beats faster, and the energy moves down her body but stalls at her hips. She moves and squirms until he releases her, and then she flips onto her stomach. She presses her hips toward him with each thrust, trying to recapture the feeling.

Nothing.

She reaches down between her legs and touches herself, putting the required pressure on that perfect spot.

She can't get there.

"Faster!"

His pace doesn't change.

"Harder, Devan!"

His movements stay focused as he gently kisses her back.

She buries her head in her pillow and bites down as hard as possible, holding her breath. She can feel the electricity moving down her body again. She wants to release the breath, but she's afraid she will lose the feeling.

She's almost there. She wants to give Devan everything inside her. She feels the sensation in her thighs, so she pushes back toward him. He puts his hands on her hips, and the feeling starts to flee again. Her eyes sting. She closes them tightly and goes to that place she knows well, that dark place that feels safe to her. That place that she has only ever been to with Alex.

"That was amazing." Devan pants as he collapses on top of her.

Fifteen

Two Beans

The rain pounds fiercely on the tarmac as the sky turns a yellow hue. The last of the helicopters are landing before the heart of the storm reaches the area. The sun-baked concrete releases a cloud of steam forced down by the helicopter propellers. It rises savagely into the air in swirls of dancing moisture.

June lingers in the Operations area looking for Jacob. Alex has stopped returning her calls, and she wants to see if he'd ever called him.

Jacob sees her standing in the window, looking hopelessly at the storm approaching and then back down at the line of helicopters. When she looks in his direction, he motions her over. She runs across the field and stops suddenly to salute him.

"Sir."

"At ease." He allows the other pilots to pass then he speaks again. "Hey girl, how are things going?"

"Ok."

"What are you doing out here today? More paperwork to hand out?"

"No, I wanted to talk to you."

"You did?" he says, surprised.

"Yes. Did you ever talk to Alex? He stopped returning my calls." She had planned the conversation to go more smoothly, but her pounding heart led the charge.

"June, I did talk to him. Don't you think it would be best if you both moved on? You said Hartford is sweet, and I know you are the best. Give it a chance to work."

"Yeah, but what did Alex say?"

"June, he's happy." He hadn't verified if Alex was happy when he talked to him, but he wanted to help June move forward in her life.

"I can't do it without him. It's like he is the glue holding all my broken pieces together, and if he's gone, I will fall apart."

"June, you won't fall apart. Isn't Hartford your glue too?"

"He is sweet, but it's hard to be with someone so perfect. It amplifies everything that is wrong with me."

"June, there isn't anything wrong with you. You have suffered a great deal of trauma, and I promise you that Hartford isn't perfect."

"Have you talked to Tara?" She covers her face. "I am sorry, that just slipped out. I didn't mean to bring her up."

"June, it's ok. She's fine. She married the guy."

"Wow! What happened to all of us?"

"We focused more on ourselves than we did the people we love. That is why I don't want you to throw things away with Hartford. What is his first name?"

"Devan."

"Well, give him my best. I have to catch up with these guys. We are heading downtown. Hey, you should come and bring Declan. The place is called The Canteen."

"Devan."

"Oh, right; maybe I should just call him Hartford," he laughs.

"I will ask Hartford," she smiles.

....⁻ ..⁻⁻⁻ ⁻⁻⁻..

June stops by the PX to buy a new dress. She buys Devan something nice too. He usually wears jeans and Birkenstocks, but she wants him to make a good impression on Jacob. She rushes into the house and calls Devan at the coffee shop.

"Two Beans Coffee Shop, this is Devan". They had named the Coffee shop *Two Beans* because you got two chocolate-covered coffee beans with every coffee.

"Let's go out."

Devan is surprised by her enthusiasm to do something fun. "I am here until ten. Could you take a cab, and I will meet you there?"

"Ok, I will leave you something to wear on the bed."

It frustrates him that she doesn't think he knows how to dress to go out, but he has learned to ride the wave of good moods with June without question.

June gets dressed slowly as she drinks a glass of red wine. Her dress is cut low in the front, exposing just enough of her breast to still be classy. It is tight around her waist and short enough to show her well-developed thighs.

She straightens her hair and wears makeup, which is conservative except for her red lipstick. She thinks about wearing heels but decides to wear a pair of white go-go boots she had found on sale at the PX.

The Canteen isn't what she expects. It is a nightclub with male and female pole dancers and a massive wrap-around bar. It is dark except for the strobe lights and the blue glow of lights underneath the bar's glass. Her dress beamed brightly underneath the black lights.

"Three o'clock!" nudges Jacob's gunner, Peter.

"Damn." Jacob looks over and sees a sexy woman dressed in white.

"Dibs," says Peter trying to stand up.

As she walks to the bar, the flashes of light on June's face reveal a familiar smile.

"Hold up Peter, she's married."

"And?"

"That's Chief Brown's ex-wife."

"I thought he was married to an enlisted puke?"

"That's her, Sgt Hartford now. You have seen her at the airfield. She handed out the new SOP."

"Well, I guess I will have to spend more time in Ops," says Peter smiling hugely.

"Your ass needs more time at the range, the way you are shooting."

Jacob stands up and walks over to June, who is standing alone in the club's entryway.

"That dress is dangerous. Where is Damon?" Jacob shouts over the music.

June looks down at her dress and tugs a little at her skirt to make it longer. "Devan's working. He will be here later."

Jacob grabs the back of June's neck and pulls her gently toward the bar.

"Well, sit with us, so I don't have to kill any of these mother-fuckers for trying to hit on you."

June smiles. Alex had always talked like that about her.

"What are you drinking?" asks Jacob.

June looks over, and the four guys at the bar are drinking beer. She has only liked blackberry beer and is hesitant to seem too girly if she asks for wine. "Tequila?"

"Oh hell," says Peter, looking suspiciously at Jacob.

Jacob orders a round of shots for the group. June looks at the salt shaker and lime, confused. She removes the lime and takes the shot. The guys erupt in laughter, and then they all follow her lead. Three shots later, June excuses herself to go to the bathroom.

She looks at herself in the mirror. She feels sexy. She hopes that Devan will like her new dress and the cabernet-colored lipstick she has bought. She walks into the first stall, and a lady is sitting on the toilet, fully clothed.

"Oh, sorry," says June.

"E?" the lady questions holding up a tiny Ziploc bag.

"You know all the plastic from those little bags is killing the ocean life," June snarks. It is then she realizes that the lady is selling Ecstasy. Oh, how she loved that night with Alex.

"Yes, two." She says, looking over her shoulder.

"Two beans it is," says the girl handing them to June.

She takes the bags and uses the next stall to pee. Standing by the sink, she places the baggies on the sink, washes her hands, and then swallows one of the pills. She crushes the other pill up in the bag, using her teeth.

She waits in the bathroom for the Ecstasy to start working. She intends to ask for a refund if it isn't the same drug she had taken in Korea.

Jacob looks at his watch. June has been gone for 30 minutes, so he walks toward the bathroom to check on her. He sees a woman coming out of the bathroom and asks her to check on June.

"Hey! Girl in the white dress! Your man is looking for you."

June looks up and sees Jacob peeking into the bathroom. "Different guy," she muddles. She walks out of the bathroom a little disoriented. The flashing lights seem to have been amplified and are a little unnerving. "Can we go outside for a minute?"

Jacob assumes she is going to be sick from all the tequila, so he walks outside with her. The pilots at the bar cheer as he walks by with his hand around her waist. He flips them off.

June feels his arm sink into her skin. His hand is so warm and covers most of her lower back. He takes her toward his Jeep and leans her against the front bumper. She can feel the strength in his grip as he guides her backward. She looks up at him. He has grown out a short beard and mustache that is neatly trimmed. He has crystal blue eyes, which she had forgotten about. There is a tiny raise in his nose that makes her think it has been broken. *I bet he fought for Tara*, she thinks, as she touches his nose.

"Who did this, and did you kick his ass?" she inquires.

He felt his nose. Alex had accidentally elbowed him while they were playing football in Iraq. "I actually got my ass kicked," he laughs without answering who had done it. "Are you ok, June?"

She stands and wraps her arms around his neck. He tries not to look at her. He can feel her tiny body pressed against his. He gently takes her arms away from his neck. We should go back and wait for Devan. She grabs his face and pulls his lips to meet hers. She has never kissed anyone with a beard. It feels incredible on her face, and his resistance to her kiss soon falls into a passion.

She tastes like tequila, but something else makes her kiss intoxicating. She wraps one of her legs around his, throwing him off balance. He pulls back. "June, you are amazing. Trust me, I would love to take you home with me, but I love your hot-little-ass too much to contribute to any more drama in your life."

June is startled that she kissed Jacob. It feels more like a betrayal to Alex than to Devan. "Jacob, I am so sorry. I feel so stupid."

He put his finger on her lips. "I am thrilled I had the pleasure of kissing you, June. Don't allow this to be something bigger than it is."

"Ok," she smiles. She wants to say that she enjoyed the kiss too, but she broods past him and goes back into the club.

Devan is sitting at the bar talking to Peter when June walks in. He bought her a rum and coke. As he slides it toward her, he hesitates. He has put Ecstasy in her drink. She has repeatedly shared her experience with Alex on Beans, and he wants that same experience with her. He feels reassured that the guy in the bathroom said it wasn't very strong.

"Hey Babe, these are my, she corrects–– the pilots in my unit."   Peter stands up and introduces himself, and Jacob grabs Devan's shoulder and says, "Glad to finally meet Mr. June," he has forgotten his name again.

Devan puts out his hand. "Devan will be fine, thank you."

Jacob sits down beside Devan and away from June. He realizes that she feels the effects of more than just tequila, and he doesn't want her to get into trouble with Devan.

"June says you own a coffee shop at the mall. That is awesome. I've always wanted my own business."

"It's harder than it may seem."

"Would you mind if I stopped by to check it out?"

Devan is excited to be able to share his success. So often, he is just seen as June's dependent and not as an equal part of the Army culture. He had served eight years in the Reserves before meeting June.

"So, what do you fly?"

June is annoyed by this question. "He was Alex's gunner, Devan! He flies a 64."

Jacob interjects, "It's even difficult for me to remember the nomenclatures of every helicopter, June." He knows it is important to her because it is something else that *belonged* to Alex. Jacob gets up to use the bathroom and brushes by June as he touches his lips. He can still taste her.

"June, you don't have to *snark* at me every time something goes wrong in your world." Devan rarely stands up for himself, but he wants to have a fun night with his wife for once.

June slides her hand between his legs, then stands up and rotates his stool around so she can stand closer to him. "I love you. Let's dance, but order a drink first. The bartender is exceptionally slow."

"I need to go to the bathroom, really quick. Can you just get me a rum and coke?"

"You mean tequila and coke, don't you?"

Devan kisses her on the cheek. "That's funny."

June waits for the drink, staring anxiously at the bathroom, then at the pilots. The bartender is having a conversation at the other end of the bar. She starts chewing on her fingernail and almost speaks up when he turns and waves at her that he is making her drink. The bartender brings over the drink and places it on a coaster. He winks at June in a way that makes her feel exposed. She waits for him to turn around and then takes the drink and walks toward the bathroom. On her way across the dimly lit pathway, she opens the Ziploc and empties the contents into the drink. She stirs it with her finger and then licks her finger to see if it tastes differently. She is startled to look up and see Jacob standing in front of her.

"You are trouble," he says, squeezing her shoulder.

Am I? humph!

Devan follows Jacob out of the bathroom and sees him touching June. "What's his deal?"

June shrugs her shoulders and hands him the drink.

Devan gulps the drink in two swallows. "Let's dance." He takes June's hand, spins her around, and follows her to the dance floor. They dance closely even though the song isn't appropriate for their slow movements. June looks up at Devan and absorbs every touch. The warmth of his hands on her lower back sends surges of electricity through her hips and thighs. Devan starts to feel his heart racing but attributes it to the sexy woman in front of him.

She has dressed him in all black and herself in all white, which is the opposite of their true nature. Jacob and the other pilots close out their tabs and pay for Devan's drink. Jacob pauses as he leaves to see if June looks in his direction, but she has her head on Devan's shoulder with her eyes closed.

Devan leans heavily on June. "I'm not feeling very well," he says. "Would it be ok if we left? It looks like your friends are already gone."

June looks around feverishly for Jacob. He is gone.

Why didn't he say goodbye? Shit, is he pissed that I kissed him?

She put Devan's arm over her shoulder, and they walk over to the bar to pay for the drink.

"Your husband paid for it," says the bartender sarcastically.

June rolls her eyes and walks Devan to the car.

"I can't drive," he says. My heart is racing, and I feel sick. That drink was intense."

June walks back into the bar and asks the bartender to call a cab.

"Maybe next time you are going to drug him, you should wait until you get home," he says.

June wants to flip him off but needs him to call the cab.

....- ..--- ---..

June wakes Devan up when they get back to the apartment. She drags him into the apartment and drops him on the floor. She cannot wake him up and feels too fuzzy to be able to get him into bed.

She instinctively gets to the shower but doesn't have the wherewithal to take off her clothes. She turns on the shower and gets in. The weight of her water-soaked clothes feels fantastic on her skin. She can follow the path of each drop as it slides down her body. She closes her eyes and focuses on her boots which are filling with water. When the water temperature turns cold, she turns off the water and sits on the tub's edge. She undresses, leaving her wet clothes in a puddle on the floor. She doesn't bother drying off, she just crawls into the bed and notices that Devan is there.

....- ..--- ---..

Devan wakes up as the light comes streaming through their bedroom window. He isn't sure what time it is and is disoriented by the wet sheets. June is curled into a naked ball beside him. He feels stupid that he had taken the Ecstasy from the guy in the bathroom. He just wanted to do something adventurous with June. He tries to roll over and go back to sleep when he is suddenly keenly aware of his erection. He crawls over to June, kisses her back, and unravels her body from the tight coil she has created with the sheets.

Ham and Cheese stand up, turn in a circle, and then lay back down at the end of the bed. June still feels fuzzy as she wakes up. Devan is kissing her slowly, softly. This time she craves it. Each kiss is like a lightning storm rushing down her spine, then through her hips. *Take your time,* she thinks. He moves her body to his pleasure, rolling her over on her stomach and then lifting her hips toward him. He finds a path of moisture that leads his fingers inside her. She pushes her body toward his, she wants him inside her, but he gently touches her until her body responds to his touch. He wraps his other arm around her waist to hold her up as the surges of pleasure become focused and directed to her inner thighs. He feels her body shake, get tense, then relax. She exhales and collapses forward onto his arm. He rolls to her side and kisses her as if there is something about her taste that will expire. It is enough for him to please her.

"More," she says, tucking her body in line with his. She reaches between her legs and positions him to have sex with her. He pushes his hips forward, then moves her hair and kisses her neck. He has never felt this much pleasure, not even with her. She is vulnerable and open, and he falls in love with her again. June falls asleep with Devan still inside her, finally trusting him to love her.

They both wake up at the same time with cotton-mouths. Devan jumps up and gets them a bottle of water. Telepathically they both think of the night before and the fantastic sex.

"I have to be honest," they both say in sync.

"You first," says June laughing.

"Please don't be mad. This guy in the bathroom."

June stops him.

"Did you drug my drink?"

Devan clinches his teeth and shakes his head yes.

June falls forward laughing. "I drugged you too."

"What?" asks Devan.

"I put E in your drink."

"Hell, that is why I felt so horrible. I took E in the bathroom."

"Wow, two Beans. We could have died," smirks June.

"Well, good thing you believe in reincarnation," says Devan.

"Are you starving?" she asks.

"Rooty Tooty Fresh and Fruity?" asks Devan.

"Absolutely."

....⁻ ..⁻⁻⁻ ⁻⁻⁻..

Devan and June feel like a couple for the first time since they have been married. She loves that he has finally stepped outside his perfect box to drug her. His indiscretion has made her feel more secure that she doesn't have to be perfect. They go on hikes in the hills outside Fort Hood, and he teaches her how to swim. She has thought of Alex very little the past few months. A peace settles around them and their two babies, Ham and Cheese. June is finally happy, and the darkness that has always lurked around her seems to have faded slightly.

....⁻ ..⁻⁻⁻ ⁻⁻⁻..

Devan shows up at Two Beans early to set up the displays. Jacob is waiting outside. Devan is taken back by Jacob being there, even though he had invited him the night they went to the club.

"Hey man, you need any help?" Jacob reaches to grab one of the boxes out of Devan's trunk before he can reply.

"Hey, Jacob. We aren't open for another hour, but I could put on some coffee."

"Sounds great."

Devan nervously grabs the coffee for the brewer and spills half of it on the floor.

Jacob laughs, "I will have mine in a cup if you don't mind." His joke falls flat onto the floor next to the spilled coffee.

Devan cleans the mess and starts brewing the coffee. "I have A LOT of things to do before we open," says Devan.

"I get it. I just wanted to see the place and talk to you about June."

Devan a little defensive, "What about June?" He hands Jacob a coffee.

"Do you have any cream and sugar?" asks Jacob casually.

"What about June?"

"Well, I know her mostly through Alex. We served together in Iraq. I am not sure how much June told you about all that."

"She told me everything," he chomps.

Jacob takes a sip of his black coffee and scrunches his face before realizing it. Devan grabs the cream and sugar and slams them down on the counter beside him.

"Thanks! Could I get a spoon or something too?"

Devan turns around in an about-face movement and takes a deep breath. He grabs a wooden stir stick and hands it to Jacob. "Anything else?"

"No, this is perfect. As I was saying, I know June mostly through Alex. I am assuming you know about her rape and his crash in Iraq."

Devan closes his eyes. "Yes."

"Well, Alex was pretty fed up when he got back from Iraq, and I can imagine she was too after what happened to her. That is why their relationship worked."

"What?" Devan asks, annoyed.

"Darkness feeds darkness, but it consumes the light."

Devan walks into the back of the café and starts unloading boxes. He has no idea what Jacob is talking about, nor does he care. June is fine. Things are great. So, he could shove his 'darkness feeds darkness' up his ass.

"Hey Devan, I am not trying to get deep with you. You just have to know that scars run deep. If you want to hold onto what you and June--"

"Stop!" Devan interrupts, putting up his hand. "You have no right to come into my store and tell me how to be with my wife."

"Devan, I care for June and what happened with Alex crushed another part of her spirit. I am just trying to protect her and you."

"Protect her from who? Alex?"

Jacob doesn't answer. He knows how strong the connection is between June and Alex but would never divulge that to Devan. "Thanks to you, she may have a chance to be happy. Don't mess that up by being naïve that things are fine. June needs to talk to someone about her rape and losing Alex."

"Who? You?"

"No, preferably a professional."

"So, you come in here and think you can tell me my wife is crazy and needs a shrink? Get the hell out of here."

"Devan, that isn't what I said. She needs support."

"Jacob, I have plenty to do here. Thanks for coming by."

"The coffee is great." Jacob stands up and puts five dollars on the counter before leaving.

Sixteen

Ham and Cheese

Cheese doesn't really like Ham. He is a younger kitten and doesn't respect the boundaries she had established on the one day she was at the house alone. She remembered loving Devan and June instantly and had found a perfect spot at the end of their bed. The next day, out of nowhere, they brought another kitten into the house. Cheese feels betrayed and hisses at the kitten to let him know he isn't welcome there. Ham, is too ignorant to understand that she is in charge and constantly wages attacks against Cheese. He plays with toys that were hers before he arrived.

They put the same collar on him as they had on her, with the same goldfish with their names and numbers separated with dashes, which didn't make sense. She realizes she is the superior kitten because she has more letters on her fish than Ham. Ham also feels he is the special kitten because his letters are bigger than Cheese's. They have battled on and off for a year, claiming and relenting territory, only to repeat the same efforts the next day. They always fight as to which of them will greet June when she comes home from work. Cheese typically wins the battle, but June lovingly distributes her affections evenly.

It is a Monday and Cheese has gotten her fill of Ham's antics. She chases him out the door left open while Devan brings in the groceries. Finally, she will run him off, and she can return home to her happy family of three. He is a little faster than she is, but she targets his tail and catches up quickly.

The car can't stop in time to avoid the two kittens that randomly run out into the road. Devan looks up when he hears the screech of brakes. He runs over when he hears the neighbor scream, "oh, no!" He tries to pick them up, but their bodies are crushed. He falls to his knees with tears in his eyes. "How did they get out? Why did they run in the road?" he mumbles.

His heart races, realizing June will be home in three hours. He wonders if he should call her at work.

No, bad idea.

He recovers their bodies, wraps them in scarves, and places them in two boxes. He feverishly takes a bucket of soap and water and cleans all the blood from the street, dodging cars and flipping off anyone who blows their horn. He collects all their toys, even those hidden under the couch. He boxes everything up with the baby blankets that June had bought them: one pink, one blue. Then he waits. He waits for their world to change. He has finally found a place with June that is safe and healthy, and he knows that the moment she realizes she lost her babies that he will lose her again.

He hears the car door shut, and he frantically looks around the room for any more toys. He doesn't know if he should tell her as soon as she opens the door. *Maybe she won't notice right away,* he thinks. The key slowly turns, and he can see the doorknob move. He nervously stands up, putting his hands in his pockets, then behind his back. June opens the door and sees Devan standing oddly with his hands behind his back.

"Hi?" she says.

"The kittens are dead," he blurts out.

"What?" She drops her bags and frantically looks around for Ham and Cheese. "Stop, Devan. Where are my babies?"

"The car! It! They--"

"Devan, where are my puffs?"

"A car hit them." He points toward the road then he covers his eyes.

"How did they get out?"

He knows exactly how he had let them out but can't say it. Devan just stands with his hands behind his back, looking at his shoes, like a child.

"Did they learn to open the door?" shouts June.

"I was bringing in the groceries," he whispers.

She looks at him without saying a word. Her face is flooded with heat, and her eyes are stinging. "And I thought about having a child with you," she screams as she runs into the bedroom.

Devan sinks inside himself. He wants to follow her, but he knows she is right. He should have been more careful. He sits by the closed bedroom door, listening to her sob, scream, and fall silent. He peaks into the room after an hour of silence. She is curled up in that same ball that he had unraveled a few weeks before. Her hands are over her face. He takes the puff's blanket from the foot of the bed and covers her with it. He then sits next to her, waiting for her to wake up.

Hours pass and Devan has fallen asleep. When he wakes up, June isn't on the bed. He comes into the living room, and she isn't there. When he realizes she's gone, he looks in the freezer. The puffs are still there.

Seventeen

6B

June drives through the front gate of Fort Hood and through all the streets that are familiar to her. The base is quiet at this time of evening. She drives past the airfield, where she had dropped Alex off the night before he went to war. She can still picture his smile as he looks back at her. She drives out to Dana's Peak Park and sits looking at Stillhouse Hollow Lake. She and Alex had gone swimming there once until something slimy touched his foot. She laughs softly, thinking about his reaction. She had thought: *My attack helicopter pilot, scared of a plastic bag in the lake.* She hates the name of the park now. *Why would they give such a beautiful park such a horrible name?*

She is frustrated and just wants to feel close to Alex, so she drives to their hotel. She walks into the small lobby and sees a young guy behind the counter. An older man is in the office behind him. June walks toward the guy hesitantly.

"Hi," she looks at his name tag. "Hi, Jeff. I was wondering if I could rent a room?"

"Sure, for how many nights?" Jeff starts to type on the computer in front of him.

"Well, I wanted to rent a room for one night," says June.

"Ok," says Jeff. "We have several available. Do you want one near the pool?"

June whispers, "Can I get room 6B?"

The manager immediately stands up and shakes his head no to Jeff, sternly looking at June.

"We don't rent specific rooms upon request," Jeff says sharply, nodding at the manager.

June hates male aggression. She turns around and walks out to her car. Jeff follows her outside. "It was a suicide," he says, lighting a cigarette.

"Here? What room?"

"2A, I think. A guy wanted to die in the last place he had sex with his girlfriend. I guess that is a thing."

"Is it?"

"Well, who would want a specific room if they are alone?" he questions, flicking his cigarette across the parking lot.

"I get it. Well, thanks anyway."

June drives around to room 6B and sees that there are no lights on. It is dark enough outside that there would have been lights on if someone had rented the room.

Her ringing phone startles her. Devan has been calling every thirty minutes, so she almost tossed the phone when she saw that the call was from *Mr. Pierre*. Dana has called her several times using Alex's phone, so she is hesitant just to say hello.

"Hola," she answers.

"Hola, Mira," Alex laughs.

"Alex?" Tears immediately stream down her face. She hasn't spoken to him in almost a year. She closes her eyes and absorbs the space between them.

"Yes, it's me. Look, I am sorry I haven't been in touch. Dana monitors my phone calls, and I don't need that bullshit with her."

"How is little Alex?" she asks.

"He's great. He's starting to talk now. June, that isn't why I called."

"Ok. Why did you call?"

"I miss the hell out of you. I honestly don't know how we got here, Mira."

June holds back her sobs, trying to listen.

"You are part of who I am, just as much as my son is. I am not trying to screw things up with you and ol'boy, but I still love you."

I love you too, she thinks silently. She traces his name on her phone.

"June, I arranged to come to Fort Hood to do a training exercise for three days next week. Can I see you? We could go for ice cream."

"I'm not sure," says June biting her lip.

He knows she may not see him. He can feel the distance in her voice. "June, I tried to hold on to us. I'm sorry about Korea. I really can't say what the right decision is to make. I love my son and wouldn't change having him in my life, but I love you and would change everything if it meant still being with you."

She looks up at room 6B. She remembers the night he first said I love you and that she didn't say it back to him. Her heart starts to beat noticeably in her chest. She feels a panicked urgency. "I love you too, Alex."

Alex smiles loudly.

"Well, I will call you as soon as I land in Dallas."

"Ok, but I am still not promising I can see you."

He knows that her saying I love you is a promise enough. He doesn't feel guilty about loving June. Dana has taken her from him. He is willing to stay with Dana for the sake of his son but justifies that he doesn't have to love her the way he loves June.

....⁻ ..⁻⁻⁻ ⁻⁻⁻..

June pulls into the parking lot of her apartment. She has stopped at the grocery store to get wine and a box-chicken. It is Devan's favorite, just a little spicy. She bounces into the house and sees him sitting on the couch, talking on the phone. She tip-toes passed him and notices his face is red and his nose is running. She grabs a paper towel from the kitchen and hands it to him, kissing him on the forehead.

"Ok, I have to go," he says before hanging up the phone.

"I got wine and chicken," says June.

Devan is frustrated and confused. She has been gone for four hours without a word. He has tried to call her several times and filled her voice mail with messages. "June, where have you been?"

"I needed to go to the grocery store."

He had just gotten groceries but didn't want to question her obscure mood. She brings him a plate full of chicken and a glass of wine with one ice cube, the way he likes it.

"Do you want to talk about Ham and Cheese?" he questions cautiously.

"No, let's just find a nice place to bury them. Where are they now?"

"I put them in the freezer."

She twists her mouth sideways. "Ok, maybe we bury them tonight and then...uh throw out all the stuff in the freezer."

"Grab them, and let's go."

Devan looks down at his wine and chicken. But without question, he sets them aside, runs into the kitchen, and grabs the puffs out of the freezer.

They drive to Clear Creek Golf Course and bury Ham and Cheese by the lake. June thinks it will be a nice spot to be buried, and it will never be overgrown with weeds.

The car ride back is quiet, so June turns on the radio. Devan turns it off. "Are you ok?" he asks.

"I am. I wasn't, but I am now."

"What happened? You just left."

"I needed a minute, Alex."

"It's Devan."

"Devan," she says abruptly. "I needed a minute."

He looks out the window as it starts to rain. He traces the drops down to the puddle formed at the base of the window.

"June, do you need to talk to someone about your rape and Alex?"

"Alex?" she felt a sense of guilt flood over her.

"Yes, and the rape."

"I already talked to you about everything," she proclaims.

"Yeah, but maybe a professional can help you deal with some of the dark stuff."

June feels her face getting red and a tightness around her neck. *Why is he ruining everything by bringing up my rape and Alex?* "So, now you think I am crazy?"

"No, June, that isn't what I said. I just think you need to talk to someone about the trauma."

"It's MY TRAUMA, so don't I get to decide that?"

"Of course, you do, June."

"Why haven't you ever given me a nickname?" she redirects.

"I don't know, June. I never thought of one."

"Exactly!"

Devan is confused, but he doesn't respond. He looks back at the window at the rain sliding down to a puddle.

....⁻ ..⁻⁻⁻ ⁻⁻⁻..

Alex arrives at the airport early because he hasn't been given a seat assignment. When the agent hands him the ticket, she shrugs and says, "Sorry, we are oversold. This is the only seat I have left."

Alex smiles, "No worries. Thank you, ma'am."

Once he boards, he crams his tall frame into the tiny middle seat and closes his eyes. The lady sitting beside him is too large for her seat and keeps trying to lift the armrest. "I need that," he says politely. "I need to support the arm I broke in Iraq." As soon as he says the words, he wishes he could retract them. She is obviously angry about the war and almost everything else in life. Alex keeps trying to close his eyes between her rantings, but her voice penetrates his subconscious.

Without requesting it, a flight attendant brings him a rum and coke and says, "Thank you for your service," very loudly. The people across the aisle clap softly and give him thumbs up. He drinks the rum and coke with his eyes closed and thinks he can finally think about June, but the woman beside him won't let it go. Finally, a flight attendant comes up to him and asks him to gather his belongings and follow her. They walk to first-class, and a man gets up and says, "Thank you for your service, son."

Alex thanks the man but then hesitates. He leans into the man's ear. "There isn't much room to sit back there."

He laughs. "I am a pilot; I'll just ride up front."

"I'm a pilot too, well helicopters," says Alex proudly.

"You are braver than me. Did you see any action?"

"Nope," Alex looks back at the flight attendant for balance.

"Well, Jim, we will put the cart out as soon as I get our hero settled. Just wait in the galley."

"Yes, ma'am!" he says, winking at Alex.

Alex settles into 6B and stretches out his legs. *What are the chances?* He closes his eyes and retraces his life with June. He misses her softness and the child-like way she looks at life. She can see rainbows and butter-flies in even the darkest circumstances.

He has no intentions of leaving Dana. He knows if he did, that he would never have the relationship with his son that he wanted. He has no desire to hurt June's relationship either, despite how horrible it felt for him to think of her with someone else. He has convinced himself that he can hold onto everyone and everything.

When he opens his eyes he notices that his drink is gone, and the tray table has been put up. *Those flight attendants are amazing*, he thinks. *They read minds and move around without making a sound.*

He told Dana the conference is in Dallas because she still keeps track of where June lives. She asked to come with him, but it was "so last minute" they couldn't get her and the baby a ticket for a reasonable price.

He rents a car and drives three hours to Killeen. On the way, he decides to rent a room at the hotel they stayed at the night before he left for Iraq. He drops his stuff in the room and then drives onto the base to see Jacob.

Jacob has just landed, and June runs out to meet him. She is dressed in a flight suit. She crawls up into Jacob's helicopter in the gunner position. Jacob is in the pilot's seat. A photographer starts taking photos of her and Jacob in the helicopter for the 4th of July picnic flyer. Alex pulls up as Jacob is helping June out of the gunner's seat. The anger he felt when Meyers grabbed June is still consuming him when he sees Jacob swing her around. She laughs as she takes Jacob's arm and walks off the airfield.

"Mira!"

Her heart sinks when she looks up and sees Alex waiving from the edge of the field. She feels nauseous. She wasn't expecting him to violate her space. It is supposed to be her decision whether or not to see him.

Jacob's lips vanish between his beard and mustache. He hasn't spoken to Alex since the phone call a couple of years back. He squeezes June's shoulder and says, "Return my flight suit," as he walks away.

Alex doesn't try to stop him. He wants to see June.

He walks toward her smiling, "I always told you that you'd make a great pilot. That should be my last name on that flight suit, though."

"You mean Devan's name."

"Well, Brown suits you better."

Seriously?

June covers her face. "You know why I kept your name. It has nothing to do with you."

It mostly didn't.

"Mira, it's ok. I didn't mind that you kept my name. I gave it to you, didn't I?" He puts his arm around her head and pulls her close to him, kissing the top of her head. Her hair smells just like it always had, clean but not flowery. He breathes her in completely, and holds his breath as long as possible. She sinks into him and wraps her arms around his waist before realizing what she has done.

"Are you done here?" he asks.

"Yes, I just have to take off this flight suit."

"Great idea," he says, looking at Edwards' name over her breast.

She unzips the flight suit and steps out of it. She is wearing shorts and a tank top underneath, but he is aroused by seeing her undress.

"Ice cream?" He questions, trying to distract himself.

"Alex. I didn't say I would see you. You just showed up here and took that away from me too."

He is sad that she hasn't called him Ali.

"I came to see Jacob. I didn't know you were in the same battalion."

"Then go see Jacob. Here is his address." She writes his address on a piece of paper.

Why does she know Jacob's address?

"Ok, but I will call you later!"

"No, Alex."

"June, I came here to see you."

"You just said you came here to see Jacob."

"I came to the airfield to see Jacob. I came to Fort Hood to see you."

She doesn't respond.

"Come see me, if you can. I am in 2A at our hotel."

June covers her mouth in shock. "No! Gross! Someone died in that room."

"What? Never mind, I will change rooms to 6B; I just thought that would be weird."

"They won't let you do that," says June matter-of-factly.

"To hell, they won't. I will be in 6B."

June shrugs her shoulders. *Jeff isn't going to do that.*

....- ..--- ---..

June drives the long way home. She waits too long at the stoplight in front of their hotel, and the driver behind her blows their horn.

She jumps, looks at the hotel, and then puts on her turn signal to go toward home.

Devan is working late. He has left her a voicemail saying he will be home around 11 pm. She takes a shower, then drives to the café. There is a sign on the door: *Closed for inventory*. She goes to the back and uses her key to open the door. Devan isn't there. She tries to call him, but he isn't answering his phone. She drives toward her apartment, past *their* hotel. The light is on in room 6B. She takes a profound breath, then drives home. Devan isn't there either. She calls him again and leaves a message.

The house is quiet without Ham and Cheese. Devan has offered to get her another kitten, but she refuses to replace her babies. She sits in darkness until her phone ringing startles her. She looks at the clock. It is 10:32. It's Devan.

"Hey Junie," he tries the name out for her approval.

"No!" She rolls her eyes, remembering Meyers had called her that.

"June, I am trying to surprise you with something, but I got stuck here in Dallas. I won't be back until tomorrow, but I should be back in time for the picnic."

"Why are you in Dallas? You said you were working."

"It's a surprise."

"Ok, but why Dallas?"

"June, trust me. It's worth it."

"Ok, well, I love you," she says, frustrated.

"I love you too, J-muffin. Have a good night."

No!

June hangs up the phone and immediately thinks about Alex. She could just go by and talk to him. He has come from North Carolina to see her. She thinks about calling him but decides to drive over. She stops for Bud Light since she knows he hated her blackberry beer. She knocks on the door of 6B, sure that it wouldn't be Alex, but he opens the door.

"Wow, Jeff!" barks June, pushing her way into the room.

"Who the hell is Jeff?"

"Nothing! Asshole!"

"Now I'm an asshole?" he laughs.

"No. Jeff is the asshole."

He has missed the quirkiness, which she carries around like a parade flag.

"I brought beer and snacks. You didn't get any last time we stayed in this room."

"I got plenty last time we were here," he says, glancing at the bed.

She blushes as she looks at the bed. All she remembers was the blood. *Maybe, Jeff told people there was a murder in 6B, too*, she thinks, giggling a little.

Alex opens two of the beers, handing one to June. "How long can you stay?"

June looks down at the beer and thinks about leaving. She looks at Alex, sitting on the bed, and thinks about staying. She puts down her beer and walks with purpose toward the door.

"June, please just sit for a second."

Her hand is on the doorknob, turning it. He walks over and stands behind her, putting his hand on hers. "Go if you need to, Mira."

Electricity surges through her heart as if she has been shocked by an AED.

She does need to go, she turns the knob and opens the door, but she can't close it between them. She stands in the precipice between Devan and Alex, crying. Alex pulls her back inside and closes the door. He moves the hair out of her face and then dries her tears with his shirt. "Can we sit? I just want to talk."

She stands on her tiptoes and kisses him. She can't stay if they talk. If there is a line, she needs to run across it, not stand and stare at it for hours. He feels her urgency and kisses her back without saying a word. She quickly undresses, so her guilt won't extinguish the fire. He follows her lead and undresses. She traces his familiar scars, kissing each one as they fall onto the bed. She craves his smell, the taste of his lips, and the force of his hips pushing against hers. She wants him hard and fast, but he moves slowly. He kisses her as if it is his very last kiss. She doesn't know how to respond to this version of him.

He craves her too. He is intoxicated by the look she has in her eyes when she looks up at him. She has never judged him, no matter what he has done. He searches for her judgment now and can't find it. *How can she love me so unconditionally,* he thinks as he kisses her face?

He feels the guilt for both of them. Not about cheating on Dana, but about what it will do to June. He can't have sex with her. It feels like a violation of her trust. So, he lies beside her and scoots her into her favorite spot between his chest and arm. "Mira's pocket," he says. It's reserved for you."

"You promise?" she asks, crying.

"You don't see the sign?"

"No, what does it say?"

"Step the fuck off."

They both laugh. June wraps herself in the sheet trying to hide.

"Can I ask you why you don't want me?"

He exposes himself playfully. He is visibly aroused. "I want the hell out of you. It's just that I have screwed your life up enough."

"It's important to say goodbye to us that way," she says, bargaining.

"I promise you, Mira, if we go there, we will never say goodbye."

"Then take me there, Ali," she says, climbing on top of him.

Eighteen

Turbulence

Devan has waited at the Dallas Fort Worth airport for three hours, constantly checking the monitors for updated flight information. He searches through the lists of canceled and delayed flights which have followed the torrent of rain that has passed through the area. Flight 241 from Seattle is delayed until 11:30 pm. He looks at his watch, and it is already 10:30, so he picks up his phone to call June. He drank a few beers at the bar while he was waiting. He struggles to focus on the numbers on his phone and realizes that the two-for-one special may not have been the best idea. He talks to June, but can't focus on the words. He isn't sure if he fell asleep talking to her, but he wakes up and his phone is on the floor.

The airport is quiet, which seems unusual. He finds a corner and sets his watch for 11:15. As he drifts off to sleep, he gets excited about his surprise for June. He feels he has resolved all her issues with just a few phone calls. Flight 241 will make her happy again.

Devan's watch fails to wake him up at 11:15. At midnight, he feels someone kicking his foot.

"Devan?"

"Yes," says Devan sleepily.

"This weather is something. I thought we were goners a couple of times. The turbulence was horrible."

"Well, I am glad you made it. I got us a hotel for the night. We can just make it for the picnic tomorrow if we leave at 9ish," says Devan.

"Did you tell her?"

"Nope," says Devan. "She's going to freak."

....- ..--- ---..

June has to be on base early to get ready for the picnic. She is blowing up balloons and putting out decorations most of the morning, which leaves her little time for guilt. She decorates the same way she would have in Korea had Butter Bar not stopped her. She loves being creative. She makes a flag on the fence out of Dixie cups and coordinates the red-white-and-blue balloons around the pavilion. She is wearing an all-white tank top and shorts, with a pair of red-white-and-blue Keds. The same officer's wives that had befriended her when she was married to Alex now refused to help her decorate for the event.

Around noon, she looks around for Devan, but he hasn't arrived yet. He isn't answering his phone either. She is concerned, but the silence leaves room for her thoughts of Alex. She can still smell him on her skin, making her crave more of him.

Her thoughts are interrupted by the buzzing of her phone in her pocket. "Where are you?" she barks.

"Traffic," says Devan.

"Well, get here before it's over."

"I'm about twenty minutes away."

June hangs up without saying goodbye. She is frustrated that Devan doesn't understand how important the picnic is to her. As she is stomping over to the outdoor bathroom, she sees Alex talking to Jacob. She waves at Jacob, who nods but doesn't wave back. She hopes that Alex won't tell him about their night together. She needs her connection to Jacob to stay pure. He had done the right thing by pushing her away when she kissed him. She feels he will be disappointed in her if he knows her truth. When she walks out of the bathroom, Alex and Jacob are standing by the water fountain. She looks around nervously.

"Damn, girl. You are killing me with those shorts," whispers Alex.

"Shut up and go away," she grunts, looking at Jacob to see his facial expression.

"Come see me tonight," whispers Alex.

"No!"

"Then come with me now."

"I can't."

He leans close to her ear, "Amore Eterno."

She remembers him saying that when they got back together at their impromptu wedding in Korea. She takes a deep breath, then pushes him away.

He grabs her hand and squeezes it as she walks away.

She is lost in the moment as his taste lingers in her mouth. Then she is startled again by her phone: "Devan?"

"June, where are you?"

"The bathroom near the fence with the flag on it," she says proudly.

"Close your eyes," says Devan.

"Why?"

"Close your eyes!"

She does and covers her face so that she won't cheat.

"Hey, June Bug," says Julian.

Damn, why didn't I think of June Bug, thinks Devan?

"Oh my god!" she says with her eyes still closed, crying.

Julian walks over and hugs her. "This one tracked my ass down," pointing at Devan, who is smiling and shrugging his shoulders.

"Devan, why? Oh my god."

"You need someone you trust to talk to," says Devan.

She puts her arms around Devan's waist and buries her face in his shoulder, crying. *I suck,* she thinks.

"Let me get in on some of that," says Julian, holding out his arms. "I have missed your simple-ass."

She gives Julian the finger and mouths, *"f-you."*

Alex decides to leave when he sees June kissing Devan. He also doesn't want the confrontation from Julian, so he goes back to their room and waits.

Julian rarely misses any details. When Devan leaves for a plate of food, he pulls June aside.

"So, what the hell are you thinking rubbing up on Alex like that? Are you still messing around with him?" demands Julian.

June covers her mouth. "I do need to talk to you."

"Girl, not about that. I'm not the one. Damn, you smell like him too. Did you even bother to shower or brush your teeth?"

"Julian, I'm twisted. I can't breathe without him. As stupid as it sounds, I can't be with Devan without him."

"Stupid is right. Devan stalked me for your ass. If I had known you were doing this same bullshit, I would have never come here."

"I love Devan. I need him too. I just don't know how to be that normal girl."

"Then fake it, bitch, like the rest of us!"

"Can I tell you how amazing it was last night?" pleads June, with her hands together.

"No! No one cares about your cheating ass."

She takes Julian's hand. "Thanks for coming back to me. I missed your simple-ass too."

Julian laughs. "I love you and want the best for you, and in my eyes, that isn't Alex."

"Ok, but it was so amazing."

"You are going to make me slap you, aren't you?"

June smiles. "Should I tell Devan?"

"Hell-to-the-no! Never tell that man you just broke his damn heart. Confessions are selfish. You absorb your bitter-ass guilt and live with it."

Should I feel guilty? she wonders. *No! I feel whole and peaceful.* Being close to Alex removes the clutch of darkness around her throat. Alex absorbs her fear and she can't balance that kind of freedom with any form of guilt.

The picnic ends at 2 pm, so June starts cleaning up when Jacob walks over to help.

"You know, it's customary for the officers to clean up," says Jacob, grabbing her trash bag.

"Yes, I have heard that applies to decorations too."

"June, you did a fabulous job with the decorations. Maybe that's a career for you after the military?"

"Oh, so I couldn't do anything like becoming a helicopter pilot? Is that what you are saying?"

"Damn, June. I am saying you did an amazing job. I am sure you will be a hell of a pilot too if that is what you want to do."

"I don't, but I could."

Jacob smiles.

"What did you talk to Alex about?" she asks––Probing.

"He said he came here to apologize, but I didn't hear that in anything he said."

"Jacob, you are his best friend. Guys just don't know how to talk to each other."

"June, he came here to see you."

June feels uncomfortable; she looks around to see where Devan is. "Why would you say that?"

"Well, he said 'damn' when he saw you in those shorts, and he told me he is at the Suites. Isn't that where I picked him up the night we were deployed?"

June shrugs her shoulders.

"Look, I am not trying to get all up in your shit, but if you want to be with Alex, be with him. "

"I love Devan," she says sincerely.

"Not in the way he loves you, June. There will come a point in your life when your claim that, 'I am all fucked up' will no longer be a valid excuse for bad behavior."

"So, what do I do?"

"I am not the person that can answer that for you, but figuring out why you can't let go of Alex, is a start."

"You hate me, don't you?"

"I love the absolute shit out of you, June, or I would mind my own business."

She hugs Jacob and takes a deep breath.

"I love the absolute shit out of you too, Jacob."

She stops by the Suites to say goodbye to Alex, but her goodbye is only a kiss goodnight. No words. No finality. And it isn't the kind of kiss you use to say goodbye.

He falls asleep, touching his lips and thinking about June. It is the first night in a long time that he doesn't wake up crashing Sheila into the sand. *How can I let her go?*

Nineteen

The Price to Stay

June wakes up just as they are driving across the Texas state line. Devan hears her gasp for air, then lurch forward. "Are you ok?" asks Devan.

"Where are we?"

"Still in redneck country. We should probably not stop until we get to Colorado."

June has finished her second tour in the Army and can't imagine reenlisting again. There is too much about the military that reminds her of the highest and lowest points in her life. She and Devan are moving to Washington State to be close to his family and friends. Their relationship is stronger than ever. June is balanced and stable because of her continued connection to Alex. She doesn't need to lean too heavily on Devan, and he doesn't feel he needs to support her more than he can bear.

Devan thinks her shift in stability is because of Julian, and he is proud to have been a part of bringing them back together.

They drive until they reach the Natural Fort in Carr County, near the Wyoming State line. June thinks it will be a great place to have sex, but she starts itching after rubbing up against the sandstone. She fidgets around enough, complaining about her butt burning, that Devan agrees to stop in Cheyenne, Wyoming.

They rent a room and go to a local café for dinner. They wait thirty-five minutes for the waitress to come to the table. She says they are closing early. June looks at the 24-hour sign on the door and back at the waitress, but Devan gets the message and motions her toward the door. He pulls June to the car, and she complains that, "they can't do that."

"You can have yourself some dinner if you are willing to hang from that tree over thar'," says Devan sarcastically.

"Devan, stop. They might actually do it," June only half-jokingly proclaims.

The rest of the drive to Devan's sister Christy's house is full of incredible landscape and excellent conversation. June is falling in love with Devan in the way she thought Jacob described Devan loving her. She has decided not to see Alex anymore, but talking to him couldn't hurt.

Devan plans to stay at Christy's for a couple of weeks while they both find jobs. The coffee shop isn't an option in Lakeland, where they planned to live. When they arrive, Christy is annoyed.

"Hey, Sis, what is wrong?" asks Devan, recognizing she isn't happy.

"Well, David has agreed that you both could stay here, but now he's acting like a baby about it all."

"Chris, we can go to a hotel; it's fine," says Devan.

June looks at him with a scrunched face. They only have a little bit of money left in the bank.

"No, he has to deal with his shit. I am not carrying it around with me. I told him that you were staying–period."

June smiles, relieved.

Devan shook his head. "We should just go. It will be fine."

June interjects, "Thanks for letting us stay. We will get out of your way as soon as possible." She pushes past Devan and walks into the house with her bag.

"I like her," says Christy, smiling.

....- ..--- ---..

It is three weeks and two days when David walks into the bathroom to pee while June is in the shower.

"I am in here," says June into the air.

"I have to pee," shouts David, as if she was in another room.

June smells the waft of whiskey that floats through the room behind him. She sinks into the tub and curls into a ball. She doesn't speak or breathe. She waits for the flush, prays for the flush, and then sees his hand slide slowly across the shower curtain as he leaves. June waits seven minutes, crouched in the shower before she finds the courage to peek out. Her hands are shaking as she locks the bathroom door. After getting dressed, she frantically runs to their designated room and starts packing her clothes. Devan interrupts her frenzy with good news; he has found a job working for the State's revitalization program.

"Great, we have to leave here now!" says June, still shaking.

"June, what the hell? Are you ok?" asks Devan, who is visibly concerned.

"No! David just walked in on me in the shower."

"June, are you sure?"

"Really? Are you asking me that?" she screams.

"June, calm down. I am sure it was an accident," debates Devan.

"I am sure my rape was an accident too, asshole."

"Really, June? Are you going to put me in that category of all the men you hate?"

"All the men? Are rapists and perverts all the men?" she screams.

"June, I have known David since high school. He is a nice guy. You are being a little crazy."

She stands silent and looks at the floor. *I may be overreacting, but why isn't Devan fighting for me like Alex fought for her when Meyers touched her?* She slides down the wall and looks up at Devan, sitting on the edge of the bed.

"We have to move out," she says.

"We will try when I get my first check in a few weeks," says Devan.

"Tonight," insists June.

"I can't do this right now, June. Can you just pull yourself together for a few weeks?"

"I am leaving tonight. I couldn't stop my rape, but I should never have to feel unsafe again. I feel like that here."

Christy is listening by the door. She pushes open the door and points her finger at June. "You are a whore. David told me that you stepped out of the shower when he went in to use the bathroom by accident."

"Hold on a minute! Christy, calm down! June would never do that," asserts Devan.

"Devan, you are so damn blind! She has been calling that Alex guy almost every night she has been here. She sneaks into the garage and calls him." She grabs June's phone and reads off Mr. Pierre's number, then hands the phone to Devan.

Devan looks at her phone, then back at June. "Are you still talking to Alex?"

She shrugs her shoulders.

"Every night!" he says as he scrolls through the recent calls on her phone.

"She slept with him too," says Christy.

June turns to stand up, taking her phone from Devan. She holds it close to her heart but doesn't say anything.

Devan lifts her chin, almost asking her about Alex, but instead, he turns to Christy.

"Can you give us a minute, Chris?"

"Devan, I am not sure I want your whore to stay here anymore."

"Chris, stop! She's not a whore, and we all know David drinks too much."

June pulls away from Devan. *Couldn't he have said that to her when I brought this up?* she thinks.

Christy slams the door shut, and Devan walks over to June, curled in a ball on the bed. He tries to unravel her, but she retracts back into her protected position. "June, can we all just talk about this? It's a huge misunderstanding. I am sure David didn't try to molest you, and that you haven't had sex with Alex."

"I did. We. Did."

"When?" asks Devan rolling over with his back toward June.

"I'm going to stay with Pippa tonight."

"Well, take this with you," he hands her his wedding ring.

She takes the ring and places it on her thumb. It doesn't belong there, so she puts it on top of the dresser. She grazes Devan's shoulder as she walks past him. "I love you. Maybe just not the way you are capable of loving me. I hope you are never in a position to understand what that means."

He buries his face in the pillow and says, "You are a whore!"

She believes him.

....- ..--- ---..

June stays with Pippa for a week. She has found a job at a Veteran's organization and gotten an apartment. There are plenty of beautiful apartment complexes in the Portland area, but she has particular requirements. She wanted a second-floor apartment with a parking space directly in front of it, so she doesn't have to walk through any dark passageways. She also got an extra lock put on the front door, even though it will cost her a $300 deposit when she leaves. She got an alarm system installed for $70 a month, just in case anyone tried to climb up the side of the building to get into her second-story windows. She never talks to her neighbors and tries to avoid seeing them in the parking lot just to be safe. She thinks about getting a cat, but she isn't sure how long she will stay there.

Devan has changed his cell phone number after her repeated calls. She writes him a letter that is returned, so she calls and leaves him messages at work. She tries to explain to him why she slept with Alex, but it doesn't matter to Devan. Betrayal is permanent in his mind. He has his work number changed, and the receptionist is notified not to take any messages from her.

June changes her number too. Alex has been calling for several weeks, and she can't find the words to say to him. She has finally found the guilt that had lain so dormant in her spirit. She understands that 'pack-it-down' guilt that Julian had talked about. He was right; confessions are selfish. She should have just left Devan instead of telling him the truth.

Devan calling her a whore answers the questions she has never wanted to ask herself. Did she do something to justify being raped? She remembers losing all the connections to her feelings until she met Julian. He gave her a drug that allowed her to feel conscious for the first time. It freed her from the battle her mind waged between feeling sexy and deserving to be raped.

Because he helped her find herself, she has forced him to stay in her life despite his rule about pen pals. They talk every night at 9 pm so that she can fall asleep feeling safe.

"Hey, Julian. You know it's ok if you can't always call me."

"Girl, I call you, so I don't feel scared,"

June smiles.

"So, who are you dating this week?" asks June.

"Well, there is a sex club here. So, I've had a few hook-ups."

"Thanks for the insightful details, but those are your side-pieces, right?"

"June, I hate to educate your simple-ass, but it doesn't work that way. I will settle down when I meet my Alex."

"You hate Alex."

"I don't. I hated how Alex treated you. I think he was perfect for you, besides the fucked-up-getting-another-girl-pregnant-bullshit."

"What?" she probes.

"Baby girl, Devan loved your light, as long as it was shinin' bright. Alex loved your darkness too."

"He wanted me back that day at the picnic and six months ago when I left Devan." I haven't talked to him since then. I feel like I should just let him be happy with Dana and his son."

"There you go, thinking for other people again. June, he's a grown ass man. If he is what you want, take him. Dana has no hold on him."

"I love you, Julian. I hope you find your Alex soon."

"I love you too, June Bug."

....- ..--- ---..

June gets a call at work from Devan. She wonders if Julian gave him her number but doesn't ask. He wants to see her. Without hesitation, she gives him her address, and they plan a day to meet. He doesn't volunteer his new phone number, so June makes sure she is home all day just in case.

The knock on the door startles her. She takes a few deep breaths and peeks out of the peephole. Devan is standing with his hands in his pockets, looking around nervously. He knocks again. June slowly opens the door but doesn't say anything.

"Thanks for agreeing to see me," he says.

"We have assigned parking. Where did you park?"

"Oh, I think I parked in a numbered space."

"Give me your keys. I will move your car."

June walks out of the apartment to a crisp fall night. As she hops into Devan's car, she doesn't sense the impending darkness on the horizon. She turns on the dome light, so she can see to adjust the seat. The car smells like cologne, but nothing he had worn with her. She looks in his console and sees that it is Joop. She parks the car in a visitor space and looks deeper into the console. She finds a cassette player and notices there is a tape inside. She looks around and then rewinds the tape a little. *I am at a bar in Seattle, and I finally feel ready to move on. I met this girl at work, and I am thinking about asking her out.*

June plays the tape until it goes silent. She carefully places it back in the console, trying to make it look undisturbed. She has no idea what to feel as she walks back into the apartment.

"Do you want to watch TV while I take a quick shower?" asks June so faintly he barely heard her.

"Sure, I will find us a good movie to watch."

June is taken back by the casual tone in his voice. This is the same man that thought she was a whore just a few short months ago. He hated her so severely that he changed all of his phone numbers and put her on the no-call list.

She locks the bathroom door and then steps out of the shower to unlock it. She steps back out of the shower with soap in her hair to lock the door again. She knows it is 9 pm when she hears the phone ring. She grabs it quickly and whispers, "I can't talk. Devan showed up here."

"Girl, call me as soon as he leaves. Unless he doesn't leave, call me when he's knocked out from all that lovin' you put on him."

"Julian, that isn't funny. Well, maybe it is!" she smiles.

June gets dressed in the bathroom and casually walks into the living room. Devan has found a movie and has it on pause, waiting. He has made some cheese and crackers and opened a bottle of wine. *It feels like a date.* June sits down and watches the movie in silence, taking small bites of the cheese and crackers; like a mouse.

"Remember when we were at that restaurant in Wyoming? They could have killed both of us," he laughs.

June plays along. "I know; I wanted to use the bathroom so badly but was afraid you would disappear before I got back."

Devan and June relive all their stories from a third-person perspective. They both sit silently when they get to the end of their story.

The silence grows to be a dark wall between them. Finally, June stands up awkwardly and says she needs to go to bed. She offers him to sleep on the couch or in her bed with her. Devan stays in the living room, watching TV.

An hour or so later, June hears the front door open. She sneaks into the living room to see if he has left. She listens at the door. He is talking on the phone.

"I won't be back tonight," he says. "I know you don't understand, but this is something I need to do."

Kill her? she wonders.

"Please, I will call you tomorrow."

June rushes to get back into bed before the door opens. She waits, but Devan doesn't come into the bedroom. She feels an urge to go to him, to plead with him to take her back, but she can't. She waits until he comes to bed with her and then falls asleep. When she wakes up in the morning, he is gone. He left the front door unlocked.

Twenty

Our Tree?

June joined a gym and goes for a run on the treadmill at the first light of every day. She is still hesitant to run outside or leave home while it is dark, but she likes the gym. It is a chance to listen to music and escape to the place that the Molly had taken her without the side effects. She has cut her hair short and dyed it dark brown.

Devan has filed for divorce, and she has to drive up to Washington to sign the papers in two days. There isn't anything to divide, they have already gone through all of their personal items, and he doesn't want any photos or letters. She kept them because she remembers how hurt she was to lose the letters from Alex. *Words that are attached to feelings should always be preserved.* So, she stows them in a box, putting them in the back of her closet.

June has made Devan a mix-tape on a CD with all the songs that remind her of their time together. She thinks it is a great way to say the words he will never allow her to say to his face. She arrives at the law office early and waits for Devan to show up. When he arrives, there is a woman in the car with him. June wonders if it is the woman he spoke about on the tape. She is really cute, with short bouncy hair that makes her look very smart. June steps out of the car and waves in Devan's direction.

"Hey June," he says emotionless.

June just nods. She is afraid if she speaks that, she will burst into tears. He perceives it as indifference.

They walk into the law office and sit in front of an inappropriately dressed lawyer. June is confused as to why he isn't wearing a suit. He is dressed in a wrinkled t-shirt and jean shorts.

"Are you the lawyer?" asks June, looking side-ways at Devan.

"Yes, ma'am."

Devan smiles a little when June says, "Humph!"

"Ok, I understand that you have divided all your assets and that there are no children involved," says the lawyer.

June puts her hand on her stomach.

Devan says, "That is correct."

June's mind wanders a little as she plays out the scenario of having children with Devan.

"Ok, just sign here. Ladies first." He pushes the paperwork to June.

She looks it over and gets a sick feeling in her stomach. She looks at Devan with panic on her face. The lawyer has requested the court restore June's maiden name: Juniper Westbrook.

"I can't use that name," she says, panicking.

"Ok, so are you going to keep your current name?" asks the lawyer.

June looks at Devan for approval, but he says nothing. Devan looks out the window so he doesn't have to acknowledge her. An awkward amount of time passes before she says, "No, uh. Can I just take back the name Brown?"

The lawyer makes the correction and then hands the new document to June. She signs it and then passes it to Devan.

"You are a piece of work," he says as he signs the papers.

"What?" peeps June.

"You're taking HIS name back?"

"You are divorcing me. You know I can't use my name, and you didn't offer for me to keep yours."

The lawyer looks at Devan." Do I need to change the paper-work back to Hartford?"

Devan looks at June and then down at his feet. "No, she can have him."

June stands up. "I don't need your permission, Devan. I was changing my name out of respect because things didn't work out with us."

Devan doesn't reply. He just gets up and heads for the door.

"Do you need a copy of the paperwork?" asks the lawyer.

"No, "he says slamming the door. He takes two steps then turns back and mouths *I am sorry* to the lawyer as he peeks back through the door.

The lawyer looks at June, sitting with her face in her hands, crying. "No matter how smoothly you think things will go, a divorce is like ripping off one of your limbs," he says.

June nods. She feels a loss of mobility in her arms and legs. The lawyer hands her a copy of the signed paperwork. "You will need this to change your name on your license and social security card."

She doesn't respond. She just takes the paperwork and walks back out to her car. It takes an hour for her to crank the car. She is lost somewhere between losing Alex and Devan and trying to find herself, which culminates in her inability to move.

Devan drives home in silence, despite the repeated questions from his new girlfriend. He hates June for leaving, but this betrayal will never be forgiven. He replayed how stupid the name *June Brown* is repeatedly in his head.

June notices that her phone is vibrating. She looks down and sees *Mom* through her tear-filled eyes.

"Hey, Mommy," she answers.

"Juniper Leeann, whatever your last name is these days. Why haven't you called me?"

"Mom, Devan, and I got divorced today."

"Well, that's nice. We planted three rows of peas and two of corn because the deer always come up and eat the corn. I want to get a dog, but you know how your dad is."

He isn't her dad, but she couldn't say that to her mom. It is the man she had chosen as their dad when hers left.

"Mom, did you hear me?"

"Hear you what, Juniper? You hadn't said nothin'."

"Mom, Devan, and I got a divorce today."

"Well, what do you want me to say about that? I know you don't want to hear from me on it."

"Mom, I am really sad."

"Now, aren't we all Juniper? You just need to get yourself together and stop worrying about all those boys."

"Mom, can you call me June?"

"I will call you by your God-given name."

"Did God name me Juniper, or did you?"

"I swear. You are lucky we serve a gracious God. He should have stricken you down ten times in this here phone call alone. June, see, there I did it. Why haven't you called?"

"Mom, I promise to call more. I have just been really sad."

"You don't think it makes me sad when you don't call?"

"I will. I love you."

"Ok, June, call me tomorrow."

Only a few people know her name is Juniper: her family, the two men who are now her ex-husbands, and *him*. She hated it and has never allowed anyone outside her family to use it to address her. It is a clanging cymbal that lingers in her ears after hearing her rapist repeat it over and over again as if they were lovers.

....- ..--- ---..

June decides to stay at a hotel in Washington. She is too emotional to drive and feels incredibly exhausted. She had packed a bag, just in case Devan changed his mind about the divorce and wanted to spend time with her.

She undresses to change but can't find the energy to complete the task, so she crawls into bed naked. Within minutes, her body is twitching into a deep sleep. She has another nightmare about being twisted up, but it was a twisted tree this time. As she runs closer to the tree, she sees that it is twisted by vines embedded into its trunk. She tries her best to free the tree from the vines, but they keep growing back. Finally, she finds a knife and cuts the vines at the tree's base. They untwist and fall to the ground, but the tree turns black and dies. She awakes soaked in sweat and her heart racing.

She lies still, staring at the ceiling, strangely aroused by her nightmare. She runs her fingers through her hair and then touches her face. Alex likes her nose. She remembers him using his thumb to open her mouth before kissing her.

Then she thinks about how Devan looked at her the first time they kissed. They were connected instantly and passionately. She touches her breasts, pushing them up and pulling hard at her nipples. She follows the shape of her body down her sides to her hips.

She sees Alex looking up at her from between her legs. He would always spread her legs open and push them forward. She reaches between her legs and finds some moisture for her finger. She begins to rotate her finger slowly around. It sends vibrations through her spine.

She laughs when she thinks of giving Devan instructions the first time, he tasted her.

She has found the perfect spot, so she uses her other hand to apply pressure around the area, forcing the blood flow to the center, as Alex had taught her. She is almost there when she thinks about Jacob and how he grabs the back of her neck with one hand. She thinks about their drug-ridden kiss and how he gently pushed her away...

June sits straight up in bed. "Why am I thinking about Jacob?" she says under her breath. Then she dialed his number without hesitation.

"Lieutenant Colonel Edwards," he answers.

"What? You got promoted AGAIN?"

"June?"

"Yes, sir. I feel like I should salute you over the phone."

"Please do," he laughs. "Where are you, June?" He walks over and closes his office door.

"Right now, in a hotel in Washington, but I live in Portland. I just got divorced," she stutters awkwardly.

"June, no. I am so sorry. Where do you find these guys? The military?"

She laughs.

"I have a weakness for a man in uniform."

Jacob looks down at his.

"I don't think I will ever get married again," she says randomly.

"Maybe you should say, I don't think I will ever get divorced again. You have to give a guy a little hope."

"Does a guy want hope?" she inquires.

"I am not sure I could handle you, June. You are insatiable."

She looks up the word insatiable on her phone. It didn't sound positive. She didn't know what to say after that.

"I am stationed at Fort Lewis," he breaks the silence.

"Really?"

"Yes, ma'am. Do you still run?"

"I'd die if I didn't."

"Well, text me your address, and I will pick you up at 6 am for a run. We are having an event at Point Defiance Park in Tacoma."

"I didn't bring running shoes up here."

"What size do you wear? I will stop by the PX on my way home."

She smiles. "8 ½."

"Jesus, how do you walk around with such clown feet?" he jokes.

She looks at her bare feet. They are cute. "So, should I ask what size shoes you wear?" she touts.

"You are quick. Let's see how you do on our run tomorrow."

"Can you bring me a toothbrush too? I forgot mine."

"Wow, and you said you'd never get married again. You are great at the can-you-stop-by-the-store thing."

June is excited about her running adventure with Jacob. She wonders if he can run a 4:20 mile like Alex.

As soon as she hangs up the phone, it rings again. No one had her new number that would be calling so late. She looks down at it. It read: unknown. June slowly lifts the phone to her ear but doesn't speak.

"Ma'am, this is the operator. We are required to inform you that you are receiving a call from Fort Leavenworth Penitentiary."

June sees the room go dark as she hangs up the phone in a panic. It immediately rings again from an unknown caller. She throws the phone across the room and runs to the bathroom, where she curls up in the tub. She isn't sure she has locked the security bar on the door, and she knows the curtains are open. She low crawls over to the curtains to pull them shut, then crawls back to the bathroom. She sleeps in the tub until she hears a knock at the door, which sends her over the side of the tub onto the tile floor. She had been so scared that she hadn't put on her clothes. She runs to the door and sees Jacob looking around and then at his watch.

"I am naked. I am going to crack the door. Wait 30 seconds, then come in."

He takes a deep breath and grabs his mouth, and squeezes. He waits precisely one minute before opening the door with his eyes closed. "Are you ready?" he says.

"I had a kind-of weird night."

"Really? What's up?" He grabs the back of her neck with one hand and pulls her close to his chest, which sends electricity through her body.

"I got a call from Leavenworth."

"Who do you know there?"

"No one, unless it's Alex."

"June, Alex has done some questionable shit, but nothing that would put him in prison."

"Well, I haven't talked to him in almost a year."

"Really," he says hopefully.

"Have you?" She doesn't look at him for a response.

"Yes, about three months ago. I was in California, where he is on a special assignment. I can text him if that would make you feel better."

"No, I am sure it is a fluke."

"I still have some friends in the Central Intelligence Division. Should I look into it?" He is asking but has already planned on following up with them.

"No, it's ok. Let's go run!" She doesn't want him to know that she is terrified.

....- ..--- ---..

The day is gorgeous for a run. A slight cool morning breeze helps them breathe easier and get into a pace. For him, she runs slowly, but the view is impeccable. They run the outer loop, which is 5.1 miles. They cool down near the rose garden. Jacob has brought a picnic lunch with a lot of water and some wine.

"I know a good spot," he says.

Jacob has made a mental note about June's quirky preferences without being conscious of it. He knew never to put anything in a Ziploc bag and that she hates whiskey for some reason. He knew her full name was Juniper Leeann Brown but realized she always insisted on people calling her June.

He puts down the blanket for the picnic and unpacks all the food. June notices that the Tupperware is coordinated. All the fruit is in a green container. All the vegetables are in blue containers. The cheese and crackers are separated, and he used aluminum foil to wrap up the crackers.

No Ziplocs!

Jacob grabs her hand after they eat and pulls her up to meet him. There is an awkward moment when their chests touch, so he spins her around and starts walking through the park. June swings his hand back and forth as he spins her around. Abruptly, June stops and covers her face. He turns her to face him and moves her hands to her side.

"What's wrong, Jay-bee?"

A nickname.

She points at a mangled tree in the park. "I have dreams about this tree," June says.

Jacob walks over to the tree. He traces the lines of the twisted pieces as far up as he can reach. "It's a great tree," he says. "They must be great dreams or a premonition about our date."

"Is this a date?" she asks.

Jacob feels an unusual sense of self-awareness. "Let's just call it a run for now," he says, grabbing the back of her neck.

"Could we at least make this our tree?" she petitions.

He doesn't respond. He just stands there for a moment and soaks in her innocence.

....- ..--- ---..

Jacob and Alex had a constant competition regarding everything possible. They both ran a 4:20 mile, except for a few seconds that would bounce between each race. They both bought the exact same Jeep and compared upgrades each time they saw each other. They even compared possible kills in Iraq but would never admit that publicly. Despite the brutal competition between them, they never crossed paths when it came to women. He knows that June is off-limits, despite his attraction to her.

After returning her safely back to her hotel. He vows to keep her at a distance. He struggles to make space in his conscientiousness for a scenario in which he dated June. He finds it difficult to speak with her or interact personally without having romantic feelings toward her. So, he doesn't call.

....- ..--- ---..

June focuses on running. She has become so separated from her emotions that it never occurs to her to be upset when Jacob stops responding. It is an early morning run down Yakima Street when she slows down to read the sign at the Yakima Pub: Penny Bud Light on Draft. "Bleck, it's not worth it," she laughs. She walks back to her apartment, suddenly hurt that Jacob hasn't returned her calls.

Three days pass before she decides to drive up to Fort Lewis. She reasons that since she has lost her benefits to go on post, if she shows up, he can let her in or ignore the request. It's his choice.

She pulls off the highway, about a mile from the gate to Fort Lewis. *Why does it have to be his choice? I want a choice.* She dials his number.

"Edwards," he answers.

"I like you, Jacob. If you don't feel the same, that's fine–– but say that! This black-ops crap isn't fair!"

He laughs at *"black-ops."*

"Will you go on a date with me tonight?" she asks firmly.

He takes a deep breath. He doesn't want to say no. "I have a Corp run in the morning, so I can't drive to Portland tonight."

"I'm here. Do you have another excuse, or should I hang up now?"

Jacob clears the room and asks his secretary to close the door.

"Yes," he sighs, "Alex," he says with a commanding voice.

"The Alex that cheated and has another woman's baby, Alex?"

"He's still my *Battle* June."

"So, we both get to be alone because of Alex? Why don't I get a choice? Why don't you?"

She checks her phone to see if he has hung up.

"I will call the gate. They will clear you to come in. I'm at the airfield."

....- ..--- ---..

June sees Jacob standing outside the Ops office with his hat in his hands. She walks slowly toward him, wanting to run. They don't speak. He grabs the back of her neck and pulls her into his office. He holds her close to his chest, breathing her in. He can't remember ever wanting anything as much as he wants her. He suddenly understands Alex's possession of her and the hopelessness that Devan felt trying to hold onto her. To him, she represents the essence of the wildness that all women struggle to embrace. He knows she is more than he deserves, so his intentions stay firm as he walks slowly into this, despite also wanting to run.

....⁻ ..⁻⁻⁻ ⁻⁻⁻..

Jacob comes down for every race held in the Portland area so that he can run with June. He even runs the Girl Power Half Marathon with her. He could have placed in all the races but always chooses to run with June.

It is a Saturday, on her 26th birthday, that he let his guard down with her. He waits as she takes a shower, then he takes his. When he finishes, he opens the door to her, still standing with a towel wrapped around her.

"June, don't do it," he warns.

She smiles as she drops her towel and then spins around. She has a heart tattoo on her left shoulder with the words, amore eterno underneath. He touches her passionately for the first time as he traces the outline of the heart. "What does this mean?" he asks.

"It is Italian for eternal love."

He knows what it means and why she has it. "Have you been to Italy?"

She smirks, "No way. I just got my passport. I hope to go someday, though."

Maybe I can take you, he thinks. When he was married to Tara, he had been assigned to Longare Army Base in Vincenza, Italy, and fallen in love with the country. They had bought a condo on the coast in Rimini, but he hasn't been there since his divorce. He could visualize June standing on the balcony in her towel.

June noticing his distracted mind throws her towel at his head, which brings him back to reality.

There is a sensuality about her that fills the room. Jacob knows that she has a vulnerability that requires a unique sensitivity. He struggles with crossing the boundary of being attracted to Alex's wife and his own craving to be with her. He would never cross a line between a friendship and a woman, but he justifies that she is no longer Alex's wife, and she had never belonged to Devan. His hesitation now is that he will lose himself in her and that she has already lost herself in Alex.

June turns around and moves closer to Jacob. "You make me nervous," she says.

"Why?"

"You seem perfect, and I am so far from that. It's why I screwed up Devan's life so badly."

Jacob smiles and then pulls her close to him. "Jay-bee, you don't have to take on the weight of the world. We are all adults. It takes two people to decide to make a relationship work and two people to give up on it."

"Do you want to go to dinner?" he asks her as she stands naked in front of him. He felt he should give her an option or give himself one, to get out of their impending circumstance.

"No, but I am starving. Let's order a pizza and stay naked."

He backs her up against the wall and lifts her chin. He holds his face close to hers, breathing in her exhales and tasting the moisture of her breath. She finds it strangely erotic to stand so close to him and not kiss. She wants to pull him toward her, but he has created a barrier of energy and heat between them. He is waiting for something, some sign. His eyes are closed when she looks up at him. She runs her finger from the bridge to the tip of his nose. He opens his eyes. "You make me nervous too," he whispers.

"Why?"

"Because you have no idea how perfect you actually are."

They laugh into a kiss that ignites the passion between them. He backs her up to the bed and gently lays her down. He crawls toward her, kissing a trail of incandescence reflecting from the light cascading into the room onto her pale skin. She doesn't touch him. She absorbs his energy and passion. When he reaches her lips, he kisses her slowly, holding onto her bottom lip with each exhale. She looks into his eyes and feels mystified. She doesn't just want him inside her; she wants him to consume her. She wants to have his stability, his confidence, and his courage. She combats the insecurity that bleeds into her thoughts by asking him to talk to her.

"I love your lips and how your body arches toward me when I kiss your neck. That look you give me is intoxicating. I have wanted you since the night you first kissed me. I wanted you every time I saw you on the airfield, but it was never sex that I wanted. Do you understand that?"

She understands.

He wants to tell her he is in love with her, but he still feels her holding back. He assumes it is for Alex. "June, do you want to have sex with me?"

"Yes!"

Jacob takes off his towel, and the space between them dissolves. As he feels the warmth of being inside her, he says, "This will be quick." Her anticipation for the moment makes an orgasm quick for her too. They lay pasted together by sweat and passion until the pizza guy rings the doorbell.

Twenty-One

Losing Everything

June is excited about her new friendship with Jacob. At his suggestion, she starts seeing a psychologist once a week. Her name is Abelle, and she works for the Veteran's organization that June has been working for.

This is June's 8th session, and she feels frustrated. She wants to know what is wrong with her so that she can move on with her life. "So, I told you about the dream of the tree. I had it again last night."

"Refresh my memory."

June wonders if she ever listened to her or is just focused on the clock behind her hidden in a landscape photo.

"I keep having these same reoccurring dreams about this tree. I think these vines are twisted, or the bark is overlapping but looks distressed. When I walk close to the tree, I can hear it crying. I try to untangle the vines, but they keep moving and twisting tighter around the tree. When I am trying to cut the vines, I get entangled with the tree, and it starts squeezing me so tightly that I can't breathe. I saw the same tree on the run with Jacob."

"Which husband is Jacob?"

June looks at the wall behind Abelle. "Do you know what my dream means?" asks June.

"Well, I don't do psychoanalysis, so I don't believe in interpreting dreams. Maybe you have just seen that tree before somewhere?"

June wonders why Abelle became a therapist. *Aren't they supposed to tell you what is wrong and then fix it?* "So, what is wrong with me?"

"June, a diagnosis isn't important. What is bothering you today?"

To June, a diagnosis is essential. She needs to know how her life got so messed up and why she can't escape the darkness that looms around her.

"Well, talking to you for one thing. I have been here eight times, and all we do is talk about how screwed up my life is, but we don't fix it."

"What do you think would fix it, June?"

"Well, I don't know. That is why I am here."

"Do you want to talk about your sexual assault?"

"Nope, and it was rape."

"Well, that may help you understand some of your feelings in these other relationships."

"So, you are saying my rape was a relationship?"

"No, but it could have altered your beliefs about relationships."

"I think that is stupid. My rape didn't make Alex cheat on me."

"What did you do after he cheated?"

"I moved on with Devan."

"From what you have told me, it doesn't sound like you moved on June."

"I'd like to move on, but we have such a strong connection."

"Hasn't he remarried?"

"Do you always have to focus on the negative parts of my life?" June crosses her arms around the pillow that was on the chair.

"June, I can tell you are getting frustrated. Would you like to talk about that?"

"No. Look. I don't think this is working. I still feel like shit. Sorry–– crap. As long as I feel this way, I will never have anything."

"June, that is progress. What would make you happy?"

Alex is the first thing that comes to her mind, but she says, "Ice cream."

"That's awesome. So, when you leave here, go get ice cream."

June gets up and looks at the clock. It has been exactly fifty minutes, so she knows it is time to go.

She doesn't want to tell Jacob that the therapy isn't working, so she devises a plan to figure things out for herself. She finds out where Alex is assigned in California and buys a ticket to see him. She arrives early and waits for him to show up at his office outside Edward's Airforce Base.

He arrives in his Jeep. She notices a few improvements to his Jeep that Jacob doesn't have. She makes notes so that she can recommend those features to Jacob. After he parks, she slowly gets out of her car, sneaks around the vehicles in the parking lot, and approaches Alex.

"Ali?"

"What are you doing here, June?" he says, looking around nervously.

"I wanted to see you."

"Is that why you changed your phone number?"

"I've been going to therapy."

"What the hell for?"

"Well, Jacob–– "

He didn't allow her to finish. "What the hell are you doing? Are you hooking up with Jay as some kind of revenge bullshit?"

"Jacob and I are just friends," she defends.

He rolls his eyes, "June. I have to get to work."

"Can I talk to you after?"

"Where are you staying?"

She hands him a business card from the hotel.

"I can come by around 5 pm, but I can't stay long. Dana is here with me."

"Ok," she whispers faintly.

They both stand silently, looking at their feet, for an awkward amount of time. Alex looks up and points to the door of his office. "I need––"He can't finish the statement. "I'll see you later."

The hotel is nice, but she goes to a local store for flowers and candles. She bought a CD player, in case she wanted to play the 35 songs. When she is finished decorating, she stands back and surveys her efforts. *It looks like home.*

It is 6:20 when Alex nervously knocks on the door of her room. He has been a wreck since he felt she had abandoned him. His nightmares have returned, and being home full-time doesn't allow him the time he needs to manage his stress load.

June answers the door in a long t-shirt and cut-off sweats. To him, she has never looked so sexy. He pulls her close to him as soon as the door closes. He doesn't speak. He just breathes her in. June buries her head into *Mira's pocket* and closes her eyes. He smells the same as he always has. That connection to him is rooted in her core.

"Can I talk to you?" she whispers.

"Sure." He motions her to the chairs in the room.

She takes his hands and kisses them. He feels very conscientious about where he is and how Dana would feel about it if she knew. He looks around anxiously, and June feels disconnected from him. She lifts his chin and kisses him in a way that only she can. She can feel him flooding back in her direction as she crawls into his lap.

Alex rests his face against June's and relives all those moments he had with her. She feels like home, but she has left him alone for almost two years. That is unforgivable. He picks her up and tosses her to the bed.

"Did you come here to fuck me?"

She is shocked by his unexplained aggression and unsure how to answer his question. She becomes increasingly nervous as he forcefully touches her. It is disconnected from anything she knows about him, but she has never said no to Alex. She clinches her teeth and allows him to devour her. He grabs her throat and pushes her forward on the bed. "Is this what you want?"

She doesn't answer. She tries her best not to cry because she can feel his pain. She saw the same look in Devan's eyes the day they divorced, and she took back Alex's name.

Alex undresses her, even though he sees her fear. His desperation consumes him. She closes her eyes, then feels the pressure on her body release. She looks up, and he is putting on a condom. *I am a whore*, she thinks. "What are you doing?"

He looks at her, confused. "Being safe."

Now he's being safe? "Against what, exactly?"

He doesn't know how to answer that. He just wants a barrier between them.

June panics. She feels the distance between them again. "What if I want to have your baby?"

His façade of anger dissolves. He has always wanted children with June.

"June, what does that look like? Did you find out you can have kids?"

June knows the answer to both of those questions but motions him over. To her, the condom is a betrayal. It is him choosing Dana over her. He has never done that before.

Alex is wedged between the stability he has found with Dana and the arousal and the volatility of June. They have grown up together in the worst circumstances. They have always watched out for each other unconditionally, but she also stopped talking to him and changed her phone number. He and Dana had a rough start, but she is stable and strong. She loves him and their family, and he feels the pressure of losing that if he goes to that place with June.

He remembers telling her: *if we go there, we will never say goodbye.* But now he wants to say goodbye. He wants to get up and walk out the door. But instead, he takes off the condom and tries to make a baby with June.

As they lay naked together, June finds the courage to ask Alex to come back to her. Because he has tried so hard to win her back, he pauses before speaking. "June, if you had, asked me two years ago, I would have dropped everything for you, but you left me so many times when I needed you, and Dana has never left. I can't be with you. I can't do that to Dana or our family."

June takes a deep breath. She feels the blood rush to her face. "Now you stand on morality and loyalty? Why was it so difficult for you to protect our love and family? Do you honestly think that Dana's reaction to you getting someone pregnant would be different from mine?"

"June, I don't know. I know that my connection with you is a thousand times stronger than what Dana and I have, and you still left me."

"I think you left me, Alex. When you cheated and gave another woman our baby."

"I am sorry, June. I wish I could change it all, but this is all we will ever be now."

"What? Meeting at a hotel to have sex?"

"I was thinking, friends."

"Friends that have to sneak around or friends that you can tell your wife about?"

"June, you had a chance to save our marriage. You said you couldn't handle it."

"What I couldn't handle, if we are being honest, is that you cheated, neglected to wear a condom, and got another woman pregnant."

"June, it's more complicated than that."

"I will throw up if you don't just go."

"Mira, you are and will always be my *Amore Eterno*. We don't always get to choose our circumstances. I promise you that I will never give anyone my heart the way I gave it to you. That is all I can give you now."

She pushes Alex toward the door. "I hope you know the kind of pain I feel someday."

"June, I just can't handle your crazy anymore. I am sorry for everything I did to contribute to this, but I want to move on." As she slams the door in his face, he places his head on the sticky note she had put over the room number, which read: 6B.

....⁻ ..⁻⁻⁻ ⁻⁻⁻..

June tries to call Devan as soon as Alex has left the room. Christy has given her his number when she caught David with a 19-yr-old girl from his gym class.

"Devan, I know you won't ever answer my call, but I want to say I am so sorry. I am screwed up in a way that I never understood until this moment. I won't call you again, but I hope the girl in the car makes you incredibly happy."

Two minutes and forty-three seconds later, June's phone rang. It is Devan.

"June, thanks for calling. I wish you would move on and leave me alone. I say that but also that I wish you the best, even if it is with Alex. Please respect my privacy and don't call Christy again. She sent you a package with the rest of your things. I hope that is enough for you to leave us all alone."

June gasps for breath. Her first instinct is to call Jacob, but she doesn't want him to know how screwed up she is, so she texts him.

"Things are going great with therapy. I hope we can "run" again soon."

He responds immediately. "Anytime, my love."

June drives to the grocery store and buys three bottles of wine. She starts drinking one on the way back to the hotel. She stumbles into her room and lies on the bed, where she and Alex had just had sex. After half a bottle of wine, she determined that it felt like Alex fucked her, probably because Devan was right when he said she was a whore.

She can smell his cologne on the sheets and wraps her body in them until it cuts off her circulation. She sinks deeply inside herself as she wraps the sheet around her neck and pulls it tightly.

....- ..--- ---..

Jacob has read June's text at least a dozen times before convincing himself to drive to Portland to surprise her. He arrives at her apartment at about 8 pm, and she doesn't answer the door. He decides to call her.

June is almost done with the third bottle of wine when her phone rings. "It's me," she slurs.

"June, where are you?"

"In my room."

"I am outside your apartment. You didn't answer."

"Because I am in California."

There is a long pause. June looks at the phone to see if it is still connected.

"So, how is Alex?"

"He's married and can't handle my crazy."

"June, are you ok?"

"Yes, Devan sent me a package. Is it there?"

"I have no idea June."

"Ok, so go to apartment 101 and talk to the nice lady there. She has my keys. Check my mailbox number 82, and call me back."

Jacob did just that.

"Ok, June. I have a small envelope from a Christy but nothing from Devan."

"Open it."

He did.

"What is it?"

"June, I will leave it on your counter."

"What is it?"

Jacob sighs and throws back his head, "It's his wedding ring."

"Ok, I am done. I am so done. I am sorry, Jay."

June hangs up the phone and looks in her makeup bag. The Valiums that Doc Amber had given her to have sex with Alex are still intact in a tiny Ziploc. She swallows two, then three more, and curls up in her protective position.

Jacob immediately calls Alex when June hangs up the phone. He doesn't offer a greeting. "Do you know where June is?"

"Why are you fucking around with June?" says Alex.

"Alex, I am worried about her. She doesn't sound good. She said she was in Cali. Do you know where she is or not?"

"Yes."

"Can you go and check on her?"

"I really can't."

"I swear to God, Alex. Get your ass over there and check on her. I can't get there until tomorrow. Please help me out."

"I can't. Dana is already pissed I was late rolling up in this bitch."

"You better hope she is ok, or I will take it out of your ass."

Alex just hangs up the phone.

Jacob paces around in June's apartment before deciding to call Alex back. "Hey, man, I am sorry. Just tell me where she is," says Jacob sincerely.

Alex gave him the address. He hangs up and calls the Kern County Sheriff's Department.

"Kern County Sheriff's Department. How can I help you?"

Jacob hangs up the phone. He isn't sure they will check on June if he just asks them to. She has Alex's last name. He redials Alex's number.

"What?" Alex answers.

"Look, man, we go way back. I have never asked you for any-thing. Can you call Kern County Sheriff's Department and have them do a welfare check on June? I am concerned about her."

"You have lost your damn mind. You ruined your marriage, and now you are trying to ruin mine, with June."

"Yours? With June? I thought you were divorced because you cheated and got another woman pregnant?"

Alex doesn't reply.

"You are a piece of work. What did you say to her tonight? I could barely understand her, and she said you couldn't deal with her crazy."

"I never said that."

"Go check on her, Alex."

"Jay, you have crossed a line. Stay away from June!"

"Oh, your virtue precedes you." Jacob hangs up the phone and calls the Sheriff's Department again.

"Kern County Sheriff's Department. How can I help you?"

"Hello, my name is Alex Brown, and my wife just called and said she was going to kill herself. I am in Oregon. Can you send someone over to check on her?" says Jacob.

"Sir, let me get you to dispatch."

"Dispatch."

"Hello, my name is Alex Brown, and my wife just called and said she was going to kill herself. I am in Oregon. Can you send someone over to check on her?" repeats Jacob.

"I can send someone out. What is her address?"

Jacob gives them the address. "Can you call me and let me know if she is ok?"

"Are you her next of kin?"

"Yes, I am her husband," he replies.

The Sheriff knocks on June's door, but there is no answer. He gets the manager, who opens the door and finds June passed out on the floor. He shakes her but gets no response. Her lips are blue, and she is in a comatose state. He is concerned that she is suffering from respiratory depression and calls for an EMT.

June is taken to the hospital for an overdose. The ER physician immediately gives her a dose of Flumazenil. The Sheriff gives a note to the nurse in charge to call "Alex" at Jacob's number. The nurse walks into the room and sees a young girl curled in a ball on the hospital bed. She has dark circles around her eyes. She can't help but think of her daughter, who is also twenty-six. She goes to the nurses' station and calls "Alex."

Jacob answers the phone when he sees the number with a Cali area code.

"Hello. Do you have June?"

"Hi. This is Merida at Kern Medical. I am calling for Alex?"

"This is Alex," says Jacob nervously.

"Hi, Alex. I wanted to update you on your wife, but I need you to verify some information about her first."

Jacob text Alex as he is talking to Merida. *June is in the hospital. I called, but they are asking for personal information. Can you send me her social, D.O.B., and full name?*

"Alex read the text and responds immediately with the information."

"Yes, ma'am," says Jacob. "What do you need to know?"

She asks for June's full name and date of birth. He gave her the information that Alex had given him.

Alex text back, "What hospital?"

Jacob doesn't want to respond, but he text: "Kern Medical." To him, it is more important to take care of June than to fight with Alex over her. Alex leaves to go to the hospital, even though Dana is angry about his unexplained departure.

The nurse explains to Jacob that June has overdosed on Valium and alcohol and was initially in respiratory distress, but the counteracting medication has put her in stable condition. She also questions him whether June has any mental or emotional conditions that would cause her to harm herself.

He adamantly says, "No!" He knows June doesn't need any more struggles on her plate. When the nurse hangs up, Jacob calls and books a flight to Bakersfield airport for the next morning.

Alex arrives at the hospital and asks the receptionist to see Juniper Brown. After checking his ID, the receptionist gives him a pass that he uses to get to June in the Emergency Room. The same nurse that had talked to Jacob approaches him.

"Hi, Mr. Brown. I thought we wouldn't see you until tomorrow?"

Alex is confused but doesn't ask any questions except to see June. When he walks into the room, he sees her curled in a ball and feels responsible. He stands by her bed and looks down at her. Her hair has fallen into her face. He brushes it back and then kisses her on the forehead. *What did you do?* He thinks. *What did I do to you?*

He walks up to the nurse. "Can you tell me what happened to June?"

"Didn't I just speak to you on the phone?" she inquires.

"No."

She looks at his badge, and it reads, "ID-verified." So, she continued. "As I said on the phone, she overdosed on a combination of Valium and alcohol. The treating physician gave her a drug to counteract the Valium, and now she is in stable condition." She touches Alex on the shoulder. "I am so sorry to tell you that she lost the baby."

"Baby?"

The nurse hesitates to continue. "Yes, you are aware that she was twelve weeks pregnant?"

"Sure, yeah. Thanks for telling me." Alex is furious, and he feels gutted. He finally understands how June must have felt when he told her that Dana was pregnant. He walks back into June's room and watches her sleep. He wonders if Jacob is the father. *It must be Jacob.* He isn't sure if that makes things better or worse. His mind traces back the moments with her: the disappointment when they couldn't get pregnant and the fantastic relationship they had in Korea. After looking at her for hours, he pulls the blanket back to look at her stomach. It is flat. He wonders if she knew she was pregnant. *She couldn't have known.* He feels the acid rise from his stomach. He knows this will destroy her.

Why should I care that she lost Jacob's baby? He pushes up his nose with his finger, trying not to cry.

He can hate her for getting pregnant, hate her for not waiting for him, and hate her for being with Jacob. He can hate her for all those things, and he needs to hate her to walk out of her room.

....- ..--- ---..

June wakes up disoriented. She looks around and sees nothing familiar. She tries to stand up, but she feels dizzy.

"Slow down, sweetheart," says the nurse, checking on her.

"Where am I? What's going on?"

"They brought you in last night. You had a lot of alcohol and benzodiazepine in your system."

"What is that?"

She looks at June's chart and sees that she has lost her baby. "It is Valium, but let me grab your doctor."

A young woman came into the room, looking down at June's chart. "Hi, Ms. Brown. I am Dr. Hyeseth. We need to send you over to an OBGYN for a D&C and then to the 6th floor for a Psych evaluation. After that, I see no problem releasing you."

"What's a D&C?"

The doctor looked up from the chart at the nurse. "Didn't the nurse go over your chart with you?"

"No! I just woke up two seconds ago."

The doctor came and sat on the side of June's bed. "I am sorry to say this to you June, but you lost the baby."

"Baby?"

"You were twelve weeks pregnant when they brought you in last night."

June grabs her stomach and starts crying so forcefully that she vomits. The nurse rubs her back and moves her hair away from her face. "You are so young, sweetie. You can have another baby. They said your husband was here last night. Did you want me to call him?"

June is confused but nods yes.

The only number they have on file is for Jacob. He has landed in Bakersfield and is driving to the hospital when they call him.

"Mr. Brown?"

It kills Jacob to have to respond to Alex's name. "Yes. Is June ok?"

"She is a little emotional. Did the nurse talk to you last night about what is going on with her?"

"Yes, over the phone."

"I am a little confused. Weren't you here last night?"

Jacob knew she was talking about Alex. He must have come to the hospital.

"Oh, yes. She talked to me. So, why is June so upset?"

The nurse is taken back that he isn't also upset about losing his baby. "Well, pregnancy creates a firestorm of different emotions, but losing a baby is very traumatic."

Jacob pulls over on the side of the highway. "Excuse me, how far along was she?"

"The doctor says about twelve weeks."

Although he remains composed, he feels the loss at his core. "Ok, I will be there in about thirty minutes to see her."

The nurse returns to June's room. "Your husband, Alex, says he will be here in thirty minutes. I will have him wait in your room."

June feels weird about seeing Alex, but she doesn't want to be alone. She has the D&C and psychological evaluation. She has had eight weeks of experience answering the questions about her mental health, thanks to Abelle.

When she returns to her room, Alex isn't there. She tries to call him, but he doesn't answer. She has five messages from Jacob. She listens to them and can tell he is upset. She almost dials his number but hangs up. She doesn't want him to see this side of her. How will she tell him she killed his baby?

Jacob has arrived at the hospital but knows he can't go in to see June as Alex without some sort of ID. He has tried to call Alex, but he isn't answering. He decides to say he is a friend of the family. The receptionist doesn't have him on the list that Alex has left for authorized visitors.

"I am sorry. You aren't on the list."

"Could you go and ask her if I can come up to see her?"

"Sir, I am sorry. We have to go by the list." The receptionist motions him to move aside and allow the person behind him to come forward.

Jacob finds a chair and sits with his head in his hands for hours. He finally decides to try to call June again and she answers.

"Oh, my god. Are you ok?"

"Of course, what are you up to?" she perks.

"Jay bee, I am at the hospital, but they won't let me see you. Alex didn't put my name on some list."

June feels overwhelmed by her emotions again. Alex has been there, and now she has to confront Jacob about the baby. "I will; ask the nurse if she can come to get you."

She rings the nurse, who agrees to escort Jacob to her room.

Jacob runs over to the bed and hugs her, kissing her repeatedly on the forehead. The nurse goes back to the nurses' station. "Psst!" she says to get the other nurses' attention. She points at June's room. "The husband came last night, and now this guy?" The other nurses laugh.

Jacob doesn't want to let go of June, but she needs space to breathe. She starts crying every time she tries to speak. "June, I know about the baby, and it's ok."

"It's not," she holds her stomach as her lip quivers uncontrollably.

He crawls into her bed, behind her, and wraps himself around her. She leans into him and closes her eyes. He wants to tell her that he loves her even more now, but he just holds her in silence.

Alex doesn't return to the hospital, and Jacob refuses to leave. He takes care of all the arrangements to fly back to Portland with June in first class. *She deserves to feel special.*

....⁻ ..⁻⁻⁻ ⁻⁻⁻..

It isn't until he finally leaves to go back to Fort Lewis, that she can breathe in all that happened. She doesn't do much of anything for two days. She doesn't answer her phone. After rejecting repeated calls, she turns it off completely. She walks down to the local convenience store and buys a book of babies' names.

The nursing staff felt so horrible for June that they had the remains of her baby cremated. They gave her the remains in a small box. She writes on the box. *"Your daddy and I would have loved you. Ballentine Elizabeth Edwards. We would have called you Bee for short."*

She sneaks into the Rose Garden and buries Bee by the Kennedy White Roses. She has always felt like the roses helped her stand up the morning after her rape. She thinks that they will protect Ballentine if she is buried near them. She picks one of the roses and sends it with a letter to Jacob.

Jay,

Don't ask me how I know, but I think we would have had a little girl. I buried her in the Rose Garden. Here is one of the roses. I named her Ballentine Elizabeth Edwards. You can refer to her as Bee-bug. If you want, I will take you to where she is buried. I am sure she will love it if her daddy visits her.

I love you.

Jay Bee

As Jacob reads her letter, he releases an audible sigh. He had never really wanted children until he held June in the hospital. He traces the words; I love you, with his finger and takes another deep breath.

He has the rose framed and has them make a small plaque that reads: Ballentine Elizabeth Edwards, my favorite BEE.

He continues to reach out to June, but she isn't responding. He calls her almost every day until her phone indicates her mailbox is full. He knows she needs space, but he is terrified of losing her.

Twenty-Two

Who Raped Juniper Westbrook? (Part 1)

Jacob changes his focus from contacting June to helping her in any way he can. He thinks that if he can find out who raped her, it will give her peace of mind. He has his friend in the JAG Corp looking into the situation.

There are some significant issues with their efforts. She never filed a police report, so the rape kit that the nurse had taken at the clinic has long been discarded. It will be hard to prove anything legally with no physical evidence, but he still wants to confront the person who has ruined June's life. It isn't a hopeless cause. He knows a basic description from what June remembers, and is sure it is a soldier since her training base is closed to civilians. The guy had also kept June's ID card, so Jacob thinks he is probably a predator. He plans to look into other rape cases on the base. He starts his research at the sick call June went to, where he finds the nurse that had examined June.

The nurse can't reveal any of June's personal information, but Jacob convinces her to search her memory for anything unusual that could have happened that day.

"There is nothing unusual other than the rape itself. She came in, and I treated her, took a rape kit, and called the MP's," says the nurse.

"Do you remember the MP's name?"

"I don't, but I wrote it in her medical record."

Jacob knows that the medical record wouldn't help since June removed the pages that referred to her rape. She had fully disclosed what she considered a crime on one of their runs.

Jacob drives over to the pavilion where the incident occurred. They have just completed a change of command ceremony, so the decorations blow softly in the wind. The flag is still raised, and the chairs are aligned in perfect rows. He wonders who had cleaned up all the blood from June's attack. Had they still had their scheduled Change of Command the next day, knowing what had happened to her? He stands looking out at the parade field and wonders what the thought process of a rapist would be. It made him physically sick. He walks into an area of rose bushes and pukes. He stands with his arms crossed, looking across the field. He remembers June saying she had been dragged over to the rose bushes. He walks over to the Kennedy White Roses and grabs a handful of them, tearing the petals off their stems. The blood from the thorns drips down his hand onto the ground. He covers his face and starts crying. He is hurt and angry and wants nothing more than to hold June in his arms again.

Then he wonders why she would bury Bee under white roses when something so horrible happened to her there. He is determined to move his daughter's remains to a more suitable place.

When a few soldiers come over to collect the rows of chairs, Jacob composes himself. He looks across the field, staring through a blur from the sting of tears in his eyes. He starts to run down a checklist of questions: *How did this guy know she was here alone? Had he followed her? Did he know her?* Then it hit him. He ran across the field toward three rows of barracks directly across the pavilion. The barracks are officers' quarters. *Could someone have been watching June that night?* He looks across the field. It would have been possible to see her during the day but not at night. Unless they had night vision goggles, but those are only good for about 30 yards. He feels the barracks are somehow connected. *Maybe he was walking home to the barracks and saw her there alone?*

He walks back to his rental car and drives to his hotel. He calls his friend from JAG, and she agrees to look into who was living in the barracks at the time of June's rape. There would have been over one-hundred soldiers living there at the time. He has no idea if a list of names will help him out. Since it will take a few weeks to get the names, he decides to fly back to Fort Lewis the next morning.

Twenty-Three

Dance out Your Crazy

It takes June four months to tell Pippa about the miscarriage. She and June have been friends through both of June's marriages. Pippa has never tried to give June advice, but she sees her slipping into a very dark place. She recommends that June go to her therapist who specializes in alternative therapies. June arrives at her first therapy session with Hanna Garber, who has a Masters in Mental Health Counseling. *She isn't a shrink like Abelle,* thinks June. June waits in the lobby, trying to listen through the door. She hears nothing, which is a great relief to her.

There is tea, coffee, and a collection of books and magazines in the lobby. June makes some tea; it is lemon and makes her mouth pucker. She adds some honey. *Still gross.*

She has made a list of notes of what she wants to talk about. She knows that therapists say you have an hour appointment but only really talk to you for fifty minutes. She could visibly see the ten minutes slipping away from her with every session with Abelle. She has become obsessed with squeezing as much information as possible into her allotted time. She has even bought a stopwatch so that she won't run out of time in the middle of a major breakthrough.

A woman comes out of the office and grabs a book off the shelf. She doesn't look at June, who tries to wave at her. She fidgets in her seat until she sees an older woman peeking out of a door.

"June?" asks Hanna

"Yes, that is me."

"Would you like to bring in a cup of tea?"

June looks down at the awful-tasting tea. "No, I am finished." June follows her down a short hallway to a room full of windows. She can see the trees and green shrubs swaying in the wind. It is really peaceful. June notices some stuffed dolls and other items that she is sure Hanna uses for counseling children. The walls have a mix of art, some that June liked and others she found disturbing. She looks behind the very comfortable couch, and the wall is blank. *Where is the hidden clock?*

"June, do you see that bell beside you on the table?"

June nods.

"If we start talking about something you aren't comfortable with and want to stop, you can tell me or ring that bell. Ok?"

June practices ringing the bell. It only makes a tiny little *ting*.

"Ok, I usually leave an hour between clients, so don't worry about the time. I just brought you in earlier today because I want to do a free introductory session to see if we are a good fit for each other."

"Free?"

"Yes, June. If I am not the right therapist for you, I don't want to waste your time or money."

June already loves her.

"So, let's talk about what brought you here today. I know that is a broad question, so maybe we could start with how you feel today."

"I don't know where to start, but I am trying to figure out whether or not to call Jacob back. He has left me twenty-three messages. My voicemail filled up, so he may have called more."

"Can you tell me who Jacob is to you?"

"I don't know."

"Ok, so how did you meet Jacob?"

"He is my husband's best friend. They were in Iraq together."

"You put on your intake form that you are divorced. Is that accurate?"

"Yes, Alex is my ex. Well...Devan is my ex too."

"OK, let's focus on Jacob since you brought him up. Why is it that you feel you are having trouble contacting him?"

"It's so complicated. I think I tried to kill myself, and when I woke up in the hospital, they said I had lost Jacob's baby."

"I am sorry you lost your baby, June. Any kind of loss is difficult, but the loss of a child is especially hard. Were you two trying to have a baby?"

"No. It was an accident...well, I was told I couldn't have kids. The point is, I just don't want to screw up his life like I did Devan's and Alex's."

"What makes you think you screwed up their lives?"

"They told me I did."

Hanna smiles. "That is their truth, June. It doesn't have to be yours. So, what do you think would happen if you called Jacob?"

"He would want to see me."

"Do you not want to see him?'

June looks down at her hands, then at the bell. She doesn't respond.

"June, our goal is to find your truth and have you live that authentically. You are free to tell me whatever that is. I will never judge you."

"Part of me still wants to be with Alex, and Jacob is his best friend."

"So, do I understand that you feel like being with Jacob would be a betrayal to Alex?"

ting. ting.

"June, I am very proud of you. These are some difficult topics, and you confronted them very bravely. Would you like to continue next week?"

June nods yes.

....- ..--- ---..

Pippa is waiting in front of Hanna's office. "So, how did it go? She is great, isn't she?"

"I liked her. I think I will come back next week," says June.

"Sounds fab, June. Now go home, and I will pick you up at 10 pm. We are going out."

June decides to write Jacob a note and mail it to him instead of talking to him on the phone. It reads: *I am learning my truth, but I am not sure what it is yet. I know I love you! I hope that is enough for now. Jay-bee.*

She puts the note in an envelope and takes it down to the apartment's mailboxes. Her neighbor, Amira, is getting her mail. She is a strange girl: quirky. She doesn't say much, but June loves her sense of style. She is wearing a cutoff pair of denim shorts and black nylons underneath. She has on a pair of combat-looking boots and a black tank top over a white one. June has always liked to dress simply, but this looks fun.

"Amira, where did you get your outfit?"

"From my drawer in my apartment." She looks confused.

June laughs. "No, sweetie, where did you buy it?"

Amira looks down at her clothes and then back up at June. "I only shop at the vintage store on Hawthorne. I know no demons are working there."

"Ok, great talk. I will check it out." June bites her lip and scrunches up her nose.

....- ..--- ---..

June goes to the vintage store in the Hawthorne District and finds the perfect outfit. She finds a pair of camouflage shorts and a tank top that reads: *Make love, not war.* She steals the idea of the nylons and finds a similar pair of boots to the ones she saw Amira wearing. She decides to take a photo of herself dressed up and sends it to Jacob. He replies, "You are killing me. You look amazing." He is happy to hear from her but isn't going to push.

"I sent you a note," she replies.

"Thank you, my love."

She kisses his words and then walks down to meet Pippa.

Pippa hands June a pill as soon as she gets into the car. "Wanna do some E?"

June smiles. She thinks about the unforgettable memories she has taking Molly. "Hell No! That shit gets me in trouble." She puts the pill in the cupholder between them.

"Isn't that the idea, to go out and get crazy?" asks Pippa

"I have enough crazy to deal with."

The club looks plain from the outside, but June can hear the thump of bass every time someone goes through the door. There is a huge 24 painted in a graffiti style on the outside of the building. Club 24 is the hottest dance spot in town, and there is an hour's wait to get in. Pippa knows one of the bouncers. He pulls them out of the line and scoots them through a side door. She kisses him very provocatively as a thank you.

"What's that about?" asks June.

"My truth is complicated," she says, laughing.

Isn't that the truth for all of us?

June and Pippa danced to every song, with a shot of tequila in between. June staggers to the bathroom for the fourth time. She plops down on the toilet seat before realizing it is covered in urine. She is disgusted, but she finishes peeing before hobbling to the sink to wash off the urine. She hasn't realized that the bathrooms at this club are unisex, so when a man walks in with her butt exposed, she jumps to her feet. Her nylons cause her to pivot forward, falling face-first into the man.

"Well, Juniper. That's a hell of a greeting."

June pushes backward and looks at the man. *How does he know my name?* She hurries out of the bathroom, but he follows her and pins her against the wall. He puts his hand up her skirt and tries to kiss her.

Pippa is watching June and thinks she is just drunk. The guy rips her nylons and puts his fingers inside her. She freezes, unable to make a sound. She closes her eyes as he kisses her clinched lips. "You are so wet," he says. "I knew you wanted it."

It's pee, she thinks, as she tries to pull away from him.

Pippa walks over feeling weird about the encounter, so she asks June if she is ok. June looks helplessly at her. Pippa knees the man in the balls from behind then grabs June and runs for the door. "Who the hell is that guy?"

"I don't know, but he called me Juniper."

"Who is Juniper?"

"Me."

"Really? How do I not know that?"

"Exactly!"

Pippa volunteers to stay with June, but she convinces her to leave. She doesn't want to be alone, but she doesn't want to talk to Pippa either. She wants Alex.

She dials his number, knowing he won't answer. She has tried to call him several times since she was in California, and he has never responded. She knows he must be pissed at her for being pregnant and asking him to have a child with her. He must know it was Jacob's baby.

The phone rang once.

Then again.

Alex answers. He is in such a deep sleep state that he hasn't looked to see who is calling.

"Ali?"

Alex jumps out of bed looking to see if Dana has woken up. She is sound to sleep. He sneaks out of the room, slowly turning the door-knob, so it doesn't make a sound. He goes outside to his Jeep before saying anything.

"June, why are you calling me? What the hell time is it?"

"3 am"

"Ali, this guy started kissing me and–"

"What?"

"He called me Juniper. How did he know my real name?"

"June, how the hell am I supposed to know." He is trying to stay distant from her and her issues, from the tug of her crying voice. The thought of Jacob touching his wife sent him into a torrent of uncontrollable anger. Just as Dana had taken June's child, he feels that Jacob has taken his. He finally understands the kind of pain June felt when Dana got pregnant. He justifies it as a more significant betrayal because Jacob was his gunner, his best friend, his *Battle*.

June fills the silence with tears.

"June, I am sorry something happened to scare you tonight. Please be careful, but you can't just call me in the future. Please send me a text: 428, and I will let you know if I can talk."

His son was born on 04/28. She smiles. "I am sorry. I panicked.

"June, did you report this to anyone?"

"No, we just ran out."

He wonders if this was an excuse to call him, but he doesn't care. He needed to hear her voice. "June, what club was it? I will call and ask some questions tomorrow."

"Club 24."

"I take it because you called me that you aren't talking to Jacob anymore?"

She doesn't answer.

He doesn't repeat the question.

"Lock your doors, and try to get to sleep, Mira."

Her breath staggers as she cries uncontrollably. "O...K..."

....- ..--- ---..

Jacob has never seen June dance. He lay in his bed, staring at the ceiling, imagining her dancing around in her camouflage shorts. He has looked at the photo she sent him at least twenty times. A part of him wants to possess her and keep her away from the rest of the world; however, he knows that will kill her beautiful spirit. He remembers seeing Alex lead her around the base, and he promises himself that he will always walk beside her. He looks at the clock. It is 4 am. He wants so badly to call her, but he knows she won't answer. At 4:22, he gives in to his desire and dials her number. She picks up on the first ring. She thinks it might be Alex calling her back.

Jacob isn't sure what to say. "June?"

There is a second of disappointment, but warmth runs through her body. "Hey, Jay. I am glad you called!"

He is glad too. "Are you back home safe?"

She doesn't feel safe. "Yeah, I got home about 3 am."

"Oh, I am sorry. Did I wake you?"

"No, I was just staring at the ceiling. I am really drunk."

"I can tell. Your words are blending together a little. It's cute."

June wonders if Alex could tell she had been drinking too. She tries to enunciate her words better. Jacob laughs out loud when he hears her dragging out her words.

"What?" she questions

"I adore you."

Adore? She thinks. *Why hasn't he said he loves me? Maybe he didn't. Maybe I am too damaged for him.*

"Is adore how you feel about your helicopter?" she snarks.

He gets the point. "Would it be weird if I drove down?"

"Here? Tonight?"

"Yes, ma'am."

She pops up in bed. "Aren't you in the car yet?"

He starts getting dressed, throwing things in his bag, as he runs out the door.

"Get some sleep. I still have your key. I meant to give it back to you, I promise. Can I just come in, or do you want me to call?"

"Bring me my toothbrush when you wake me up."

Jacob makes a really strong coffee but needs to stop twice for more. He hasn't slept in two days, and the dark drive to Portland is hypnotizing him to sleep.

Fred Meyer's is open when he drives into town. The store name doesn't escape his attention but June is more important than his distaste for the name. He buys June some flowers and Listerine breath strips.

He feels awkward just walking into her apartment, so he eases the door open quietly and calls for June, who is in an unconscious state of sleep.

Her apartment is a warzone of clothes that she had tried on, makeup on the bathroom counter, and a half-eaten pizza. He took a slice and ate it. He hasn't eaten all day either. As he finishes the last bite, he cups his mouth and breathes out. He closes one eye and looks down at the pizza. *Who puts onions on pizza?* He takes one of the breath strips and places it on his tongue. He hopes it works as well as he thinks it does. He finds a vase for the flowers. *Why do people keep them under the kitchen sink?*

He doesn't want to startle June, so he tries to make a noise to wake her.

Nothing.

He decides to just slip into her bed beside her, but then he notices she is naked, which immediately arouses him. He takes a pillow from the bed and opts to lie down on the floor beside her.

....- ..--- ---..

June wakes up and looks at the clock. It is 7 am, and she has to pee. She looks around and then at the clock again. *Maybe he decided not to come.* She jumps out of bed and falls onto Jacob. "Shit! What are you doing on the floor?" she exclaims.

"You are naked."

She looks down at her naked body. She doesn't remember taking off her clothes but did remember sitting in pee at the club.

"You've obviously seen me naked. Where is my toothbrush?" She covers her mouth. He hands her the strips. She puts one in her mouth and dissolves it. "Do they work?"

"I hope so. I had some of your onion pizza."

"Gross, there are onions on it?"

They both laugh.

"Kiss me, and tell me if it works. I have to take a shower. I sat in pee."

He stands up and brushes the hair out of her face. He lifts her chin and cautiously kisses her, testing the effectiveness of the breath strips.

She feels as if she is dissolving into his lips, her heart races, and she feels that cleansing feeling like she had just gone for a run.

Whew! They work. "Can I join you in the shower? I have been a bum all day."

"You can come in after I have been in there two minutes. Look at the clock, not a second before."

She sees the flowers and doesn't mind that they are fresh cut. *They are beautiful*, she thinks.

He salutes her. "Yes, ma'am." He tries his best not to think about a naked June in the shower. He searches his mind for the worst possible image. *Tara and Alex,* that did it. It is the longest two minutes he has ever experienced.

June jumps into the shower and washes from head to toe. She inserts a vaginal contraceptive and looks at the clock. It takes thirty minutes to activate. Two minutes and thirty-four seconds pass before he opens the door to the bathroom. A waft of steam comes floating out of the bathroom into the hallway. He peeks around the shower curtain and sees her covered in soap. Her hair is like a cascading fountain flowing down to the small of her back. He thinks, *Tara and Alex, Tara and Alex*, as he steps in behind her. She turns around, a little disappointed that he isn't aroused. *Maybe he doesn't think I am sexy anymore?*

"Is the water too hot?" she asks, knowing that Alex never liked it hot.

"You could make it hotter if you want."

She bites her lip and inches up the temperature to how she likes it. She switches places with him and hands him her loofah. She covers her eyes. "You have two minutes."

He laughs and completes the job in forty-five seconds. Then he pulls her into the warm water with him, kissing her through the flood of water. There is no way that the thoughts of Tara and Alex can save him now. His desire for her consumes him. She is pleased that he is visibly attracted to her. "I missed you," she says as she touches him.

I missed her too, so why can't I say it? He wonders.

The water turns bitterly cold, so they jump out and dry each other off. She looks at the clock. She still needs ten minutes to activate the birth control. They are both wrapped in purple towels. She has refused ever to buy blue ones again. *They have to be bad luck.*

As if he had known about the ten minutes, he plays "Fall Into Me," by Emerson Drive from his Zune. He reaches out his hand for her to dance. June has never listened to country music, but the lyrics pull her close to him. *Song 1,* she thinks. Her heart races in a way that makes her extremely nervous. He moves her body slowly in circles, pulling her hips toward his. As the song fades into silence, he lifts her chin and looks into her golden-brown eyes. "I love you, Jay bee."

She shakes her head no as she starts crying. "I can't ruin you too. I might actually be a crazy person."

"Well, then I will just have to dance out all your crazy."

She looks at the clock. Forty-five minutes. "Could you sex it out of me?"

He takes her hand and guides her to the bed. "Music?" he asks.

"Yeah, let's do more of that country stuff. It suits you."

He puts on a playlist and slips into the sheets next to her. "What do you like?" he asks as he kisses her neck.

"I like that."

He finds a path down her body, asking "and this?" with each new area. She absorbs every touch. She wishes she hadn't used birth control. There is an intrinsic need she has to be with him. He is sustenance. He doesn't lead her around like Alex, and she doesn't lead him like Devan. He stays with her, somewhere in the middle.

June feels connected with Jacob during sex. He is amazing at oral sex. She comes four times before he crawls toward her.

"Damn. I am done. What do you want from me now?" she pants.

"I want it all, June."

Her eyes sting with impending tears. She wants to give it all to him. "I will give you all I have, but you will have to take it tonight."

He flips her over and pulls her hips toward his.

....- ..--- ---..

The phone rings at 10 am. It is Alex. June looks over at Jacob, who is curled up with her pillow, and declines the call. A few seconds later, her phone vibrates, indicating a voice message. She struggles with whether or not to listen. She can still smell Jacob on her skin and taste him in her mouth. She throws the phone against the wall and shakes Jacob awake.

"I love Alex. I do. I still do."

"Do you still love Tara?"

Jacob hasn't thought about Tara in a long time. He waits until he feels he has an honest answer and says, "I do love her as a memory. I wish the best for her. I wasn't perfect in all that."

"I called Alex last night, before you called me. A guy touched me last night at the club and called me Juniper. I didn't know him. I was freaked out. Alex said he would call the club today to find out who it was."

"Who touched you, June?"

"I didn't know him, but Alex said he would call the club today."

"Call him back, June. Do you want me to leave?"

"No, can you talk to him for me?"

"June, I know you still feel connected to Alex. I know you called him because he feels safe to you. I also know I have to earn that. Call him."

June stands in that precipice again, between two men she loves. Alex is all she has ever known. "I need to call him, but you are my focus. You are my reality. Can you sit here and listen as I talk to him?"

Jacob has no desire to hear her talking to Alex, but he also knows this is how that trust is built.

"June, you should talk to him alone. He will be pissed if he ever knows I am listening."

"But I don't trust him. I trust you. Should I not call him back?"

"Call him. Take notes, and then we can talk about it."

Jacob gets dressed and walks out to the courtyard so that June can call Alex.

"428?"

"Check!"

"June?" Alex answers.

"Yeah. Did you call the club?"

"I did. The bouncer said there were no reported incidents last night. Maybe he saw your ID when you came into the club?"

"We came in the side door."

"June, did he look familiar to you?"

"No. I don't know. I was really drunk."

"June, why don't you call the police and report it?"

"Yeah, ok. Ok. I will do that."

She has no intention of reporting it.

....⁻ ..⁻⁻⁻ ⁻⁻⁻..

Jacob loves the courtyard area of the apartments. It is full of flowers, and he finds it a peaceful juxtaposition to the old brick façade of the building. He sees a woman sitting at a bistro table, and he walks up to her.

"Who are you? Do you live here? I have never seen you before." She seems overly anxious.

"Well." Jacob smiles, "I am Jacob. I don't live here, but my–" He hesitates to say, girlfriend. "I know, June."

"Oh," she says, relieved. "I am Amira."

"Hi Amira, how long have you lived here?"

"Gotta go before the demon mailman comes."

"Excuse me?"

"Just walk outside to get back into the building, so you don't have to walk through the mailroom."

"Roger that!"

June suddenly has an overwhelming urge to be close to Jacob. She throws down the phone without saying goodbye and runs out the door.

Alex says hello a few times before hanging up, frustrated.

June passes Amira on the stairwell.

"Hey, I saw your friend in the courtyard. He is a little weird; he called me Roger."

"Jacob? Really? That is weird."

"The mailman should be here any second. You might want to go outside and use the gate to get into the courtyard."

She almost said *"roger that"* and realized that must have been what Jacob said. She knows there is no point in trying to explain, so she just squeezes Amira's arm and says, "Thanks for watching out."

....- ..--- ---..

June grabs Jacob's waist from behind and squeezes him as tightly as possible.

He turns around and hugs her. "I met a girl named Amira down here. She said something about demons and the mailman?"

"Wasn't her outfit super cute?"

Jacob is curious why June isn't tracking with his conversation, but he plays along. "I am not sure, I didn't pay attention to what she was wearing, but she was extremely nervous."

"She's cool."

"So, how did it go with Alex?"

He didn't find out much. She covers her face.

"Jacob, I called Alex last night because I wanted him to save me."

Jacob takes a deep breath. "How do you feel Alex can save you, June?"

"He knows what the darkness looks like. He knows what it feels like. Did he ever tell you he tried to kill me in his sleep?"

"No, he didn't."

"Jay, I wanted him to kill me. I wanted to die every time he strangled me. I wanted to die, so the darkness died too."

He pulls June tighter to his chest and kisses her head repeatedly.

"June, you aren't part of the darkness. It is something that happened to you. It doesn't become who you are."

It does, and Alex understands that.

June loosens her grasp and barely holds Jacob's hand as they walk back to her apartment.

Jacob can feel her slipping away. It's like someone is covering her light with a blanket. He feels panicked. "June, I know that Devan and Alex had stipulations on how and why they love you. I promise you that my love doesn't have those conditions. Go away from me or stay with me. It won't change my love for you." He puts on another song, "To Make You Feel my Love," by Garth Brooks, and pulls her close to him.

"Ok, if you are going to start playing songs for me, you need to make a list of them so I don't forget."

"June, are you asking me for a love tape?"

"Just put some damn songs on a CD, Jay."

Twenty-Four

Who Raped Juniper Westbrook? (Part 2)

Jacob calls Alex on his way home. Alex feels confident that June is no longer seeing him, so he answers the phone. "What's up, Jay?"

"Hey man, I just wanted to talk to you about a couple of things."

"Go ahead. Oh, Wait! As long as it's not about June," he petitions.

"Alex, it is about June. I have been looking into who raped her. I have a couple of leads, but I need some information from you."

"Jacob, why the hell do you care who raped June?"

"You don't care? You wouldn't want to kick the motherfucker's ass?"

Alex has thought about that many times. He still remembers how June looked when she first came to Fort Hood.

"What do you need to know?"

"I got a list of names from JAG, of the people that lived in the barracks across from where she was raped. Could you just look at the list and see if any names stand out to you?"

"Sure. Do you still have my email address?"

"Yeah, man. I got it."

Jacob has a ravenous determination to figure out who has hurt June. He is well aware of the struggles she had faced before he fell in love with her, and believes he can somehow fix things for her.

Alex thinks it is better to leave the past alone. He avoids any thoughts of Iraq or what had happened to June. He has no intentions of looking at the list of names.

····⁻ ··⁻⁻⁻ ⁻⁻⁻··

June arrives early for her therapy session. She wants to try the lemon tea again. She hated it before, but there was also something about it that made her feel sophisticated. Hanna is standing at the bookshelf, restocking books. She is a beautiful woman. She always wears long flowing dresses and has a pair of red glasses perched neatly in her grey hair. She doesn't wear jewelry, so June isn't sure if she is married. She guesses that Hanna is about forty years old.

"Hi June, you are a little early. Do you mind if I finish my task before we start?"

June is relieved that she will have time for tea. She walks over and makes a cup. "Would you like a tea Hanna?"

"I would love one. I just put out a mandarin orange."

Orange tea? How weird, thought June, but it smells incredible.

"Do you want honey?"

"No. It is naturally sweet."

June wishes she had tried the orange tea, as her cheeks pucker with each sip of the lemon tea. Hanna takes the tea from June and walks back toward the counseling room. "Could you give me a couple of minutes to meditate, and then I will come to get you?"

"Sure." June isn't sure what meditating means, but it sounds nice. Her phone vibrates in her pocket. She looks, and it is a text from Alex. She thinks about saving it until after counseling, but she can't resist.

"Let's have a baby together!" She tries to focus on the words to make sure she has read them correctly.

Is he serious?

Alex knows exactly how June will react to his text. There is a part of him that wants to have a baby with June, but more than that, he doesn't want her to have a baby with Jacob. It makes him nauseous to think that June was ever pregnant with someone else's child, especially Jacob's. He wants a tie to her that can never be severed, and he doesn't care what it does to his relationship with Dana.

"Can I come to see you?" texts Alex.

June doesn't respond. She can't. There aren't words for the conflict she is feeling inside. Hanna peeks around the corner. "Are you ready to chat?" she asks.

June nods her head and starts talking as they walk down the hallway. "I wanted to talk to you about Jacob, but I just got a text from Alex." She hands Hanna her phone. Hanna tries her best not to react, but she doesn't like the text she reads. June sits on the couch and faces Hanna, seated in a Papasan chair with her feet curled up.

"Ok, June. Let's unravel some of what is going on with you."

"I'd love that," sighs June.

"Do you want to start with Jacob or this text you got from Alex?"

"Alex."

"June, do you want to have a baby with Alex?"

"I really do."

"Can I ask you why?"

June looks at her finger, where her wedding ring used to be. She takes in a deep breath and exhales audibly. "I miss him. She took him from me, and I miss him."

"So, do you want Alex to come back to you? Has he said that he would leave Dana?"

June shrugs her shoulders. "I guess, maybe?"

"What about Jacob? You said you were excited to talk about him before you got this text from Alex."

"He came down a few days ago and it felt really good being with him until Alex called me back, with the information about the guy who touched me at the club."

"Someone touched you? Sexually?" Hanna puts her feet on the ground and leans toward June.

"Yes, and he knew my full name, which freaked me out. They said there were no incidents at the club. Maybe it's because we ran out."

"Are you filing charges against him?"

"No, I was really drunk."

"June, that doesn't matter. No one has the right to touch you without your permission–– ever!"

June thinks about the last time she had been with Alex. She should have said no to Alex when he was so aggressive with her. "I don't know how to say no."

"June, say it now."

"Say what?"

"Say no, as loudly as you can."

June looks around and feels very uncomfortable. She looks at the bell and leans in that direction.

"Say no, June," Hanna says with intention.

June covers her face and shakes her head no. Hanna moves to the couch beside June. She grabs her hand and holds it tightly.

"Find your voice June. Say the word NO."

June grabs the bell––

Ting!

....- ..--- ---..

June sits in the car, staring at her phone. She starts to text Alex "428" but then puts down the phone. She picks up her phone again and calls Jacob.

"Hey, sunshine!" he answers.

"Hey. I need to talk to you. Can I come up there?"

Jacob gets a sick feeling. "What about?"

"I don't want to talk on the phone. Can I come up?"

"June, you don't need to ask me that. Drop in on me anytime. I don't have anything to hide." His lips disappear when he says that. He has a lot he is hiding from her. He has no idea how she will react if she finds out he is trying to find her rapist. He hasn't stopped to think he should have asked her first.

June hangs up the phone and texts Alex, "428."

He responds, "What's up?"

"Can I think about the baby thing and you coming up?"

"Mira, I already booked a flight for next weekend. It didn't occur to me you would say no."

"I am not saying no. Next weekend is fine. We can talk then."

"Ok. I will text you when I get to the airport."

June deletes his text message. It feels weird to her, but Alex is the *other* guy.

....⁻ ..⁻⁻⁻ ⁻⁻⁻..

A slow, methodical rain slides down the windshield, hypnotizing her into a trance-like state. Before she knows it, she has made it to Jacob's condo in Olympia. She loves Olympia. It is the state capital but a very small town on the water. She can imagine running on the trails around town if she lived there. Maybe they could go for a run before she talks to him? She calls to ask.

"Can we go for a run?" she says before he says hello.

"Of course, babe. Let me throw something on."

She instantly feels the moisture between her legs as she thinks about Jacob possibly being naked. "What are you wearing now?"

"Sex or a run, June?"

"Both."

Tara and Alex, Tara and Alex. "Just get your ass up here, and we can go for a run first."

....⁻ ..⁻⁻⁻ ⁻⁻⁻..

They ran down the path parallel to Marine Drive, then around to Percival Landing Park. They both collapse on the wet grass.

The rain has stopped but left a cool breeze that quickly reduces the temperature of their soaked bodies.

Jacob loves seeing her damp hair clinging to her face, and her bright red nose. He moves her hair and kisses her snotty face, then her lips. *Warm kisses on a cold day,* she thinks. *It is still my favorite thing.*

"Are you hungry?" he asks.

She puts her hand between his legs and nods yes.

"Onion pizza?" he laughs.

"Perfect."

They kiss their way into his condo. He pushes her up against the wall and lifts her hips. She wraps her legs around him. "Take me to the shower," she says.

His bathroom is spotless, and there is a window squeegee that he uses to clean off the water drops. He is meticulous, like Alex. She suddenly understands why they are such a good team. "Do you like anal sex?" she says, to break her thoughts of Alex.

Tara and Alex, Tara and Alex...

"I have always wanted to try it," she says. "I heard it is amazing."

Tara and Alex, Tara and Alex...

He kisses her forehead. "I would try anything with you, June."

"We need a first," she says.

"Ballentine Elizabeth Edwards is a first," he says before thinking about where his words will take her. He is surprised when June looks up at him. "You made me a real mommy."

He pulls her close and tightly to his chest. "God, I love you, June."

"What's your middle name," she asks randomly.

"Matthew."

"Your parents did that Christian thing. He doesn't answer.

"What do you believe in, June?"

"I went to church. I just don't understand a God that allows people to be raped. I asked Him to help me, to send someone to help me. No one came. No one ever came."

June buries her head in Jacobs's chest. "I think I want to meditate; is that a religion?"

"I think they meditate in Buddhism." He looks at her tearing eyes, and kisses her nose. "I made your love tape. Wanna hear it?"

"Yes, but you stink. Can we shower first?"

He smells under his arm. "Yeah, sheesh."

Jacob jumps out of the shower, grabbing the last towel when he hears the doorbell ring for the pizza. He asks them to leave it outside the door because his thoughts of *Tara and Alex* aren't working. June is standing behind him dripping on his floor when he turns around. *Why didn't she dry off?* he thinks as he watches a puddle collect around her feet. She looks down at his hard penis showing through the towel. "What? The pizza guy couldn't help you out with that?"

Jacob smiles. "He offered. I am just previously engaged."

He watches the puddle getting bigger around June's feet. "Why didn't you dry off?"

"There are no towels in the bathroom."

"Shit! Sorry!" He runs to the laundry closet and throws her a towel.

She laughs.

"What?" he questions sarcastically.

"It's nice to know you aren't perfect."

"Oh, but I am, June." He pushes her still-soaked body back toward the bed, using a remote to start the CD he had made her. She loves being romanced by him. She has never felt so wanted.

He laps up the water that has made a puddle on her stomach, takes a towel, and slowly dries her off, starting with her feet. When he reaches her waist, he sits her up and dries each arm, her hair, and between her legs. She takes the towel and dries his body too, noticing every scar and kissing it.

He has a similar body shape to Alex: tall, slim, but very muscular, like a basketball player. There are apparent differences between the two. Jacob has pale skin, traced with sunburned freckles. His reddish-blonde hair is showing some grey around his ears. He also has full lips, but they are a lot firmer than Alex's.

She climbs into his lap and kisses him wildly as she moves her hips up and down. Running has always made her feel more provocative, and running with him is like foreplay. He never leaves her side, even though she knows he could run much faster. She holds onto his ears and plays games with his tongue. Her warmth and wetness make it extremely difficult to maintain any kind of stamina, but there is no way he will think about Tara or Alex when he is inside June. He tries football, but it is distracting to how amazing this experience is. He is almost there, so he lifts her off him and places her gently on her back. He thinks about what she said in the shower about anal sex but is versed enough to know that it doesn't just happen. So, he kisses his way down her body and finds that spot that only he has ever found without June guiding him. He licks his fingers and puts them inside her as his warm flat tongue takes her to that place. She squirms and rolls onto her stomach pushing her hips toward him. Her heart races, as she feels his movements inside her. He uses his fingers to place pressure on her ass as she comes. "Are you kidding me?" she screams. "That was awesome. Let's do it."

"June, it won't feel amazing. We have to warm up to that. Fingers first."

"How do you know?"

"I've done it."

"What?"

"With a toy, June."

She frowns at him like a child. "With Tara?"

"No, actually--" He stops.

"Did you really cheat on Tara?"

He shakes his head yes. "It's not something I am proud of."

"So, this," she points at them both. "This is hard for you?"

He knows what he should say, but it isn't hard for him to be with June. He knows what an amazing woman she is and how Alex has screwed things up with her. He justifies that had Alex just moved on. He wouldn't have tried to protect June and never would have invited her and Devan to come out dancing. He fell in love with her when she kissed him outside the bar. He can still remember the taste of tequila on her lips and the savage look in her eyes.

June sits up. "Can you grab the pizza so we can talk?"

Jacob brings the pizza, some red wine, and a bottle of water. They sit naked on the bed, eating pizza and drinking wine from the bottle. "Jacob, I want there to be complete honesty between us." He almost chokes on his pizza.

"Alex is coming up next weekend to see me."

Jacob's expression falls flat. He can feel the anger heating his skin. "Why June?"

"He says he wanted to talk to me." She pauses. "And that he wants to have a baby with me."

Jacob stands up and turns his back to June. He doesn't want her to read into his reaction, so he turns back around and sits back down, holding his jaw to cover his mouth. Then he does something that soldiers instinctively learn to do. He disconnects from his emotions and focuses on the basic facts of the situation. He plays out the fundamentals that he remembered reading in the Art of War. Sun Tzu said, "Move not unless you see an advantage; use not your troops unless there is something to be gained; fight not unless the position is critical."

"June, I don't want you to see Alex, and I absolutely don't want you to have a baby with him. What does that look like, June?"

Hanna had asked her the same question. *Could I be with Alex if he didn't leave Dana?*

"I love you, Jacob. I just need to be able to say no to Alex and mean it."

You can't win this battle. Don't pick up your weapon. Wait for the enemy's weapon to dull. Alex's efforts are divided between his wife, son, and love for June.

Jacob looks at the stack of papers in the corner of his desk. He wonders if Alex will tell June he has been looking into her rape. Of course, he will. It is the Art of War.

"Ok, I am sure he will tell you this, so I want to be the one."
"What?"

"I have been trying to find out who raped you. I just made some calls to a JAG friend to look into it and asked Alex a few questions."

June stands silently in the corner, covering her face. Jacob turns her to face him and pulls her close to his chest. "I will stop, June. I was just trying to help you."

"You can't help me by lying to me. It is impossible for me to trust anyone, and now I have to put you on that list."

Her words cut through him. He has never seen his actions as a violation of her trust. He sees it now.

"Jay-bee, I am so sorry." He can feel the darkness creeping around her. He sees it consuming her. She stares blankly into the corner with tears streaming down her face. *I am such an ass*, he thinks. "June, I swear on my last breath that I won't ask another question about your rape. You can take all the documents I found and burn them."

"Let me see them."

Jacob feels helpless. He hands her the file of documents.

She flips through the pages of names. They all blurred into each other through her tears. She turns to the last page of names and throws the papers across the room.

"What? June."

She runs to the corner and grabs the last page, pointing at a name
"Is that who raped you?"

She rocks back and forth, covering her face. "Call Alex. Just call Alex."

Jacob takes his phone into the kitchen and calls Alex.

"Look at those papers I sent you."

"Hello!"

"Look at the last page. June just saw them. Who is Adam Meyers?"

Alex goes to his computer and looks through the names, seeing Meyers' name.

"Holy shit," he says. "He drugged me in Korea."

Jacob is frustrated that, once again, Alex is focusing on himself. "And he raped June!"

"Where is she?"

"She is here."

"Why the hell is she there, Jay?"

He doesn't respond, he just takes the phone to June. Jacob sits at the end of the bed, listening to her cry and Alex scream. Jacob wants to hold her and wipe away her tears, but she is curled up in a ball with Alex.

Twenty-Five

Step Back From the Edge

June takes the Max to pick up Alex. It drops off two blocks from her apartment, so she can't justify driving. She wears the white shorts and tank top she had worn at the picnic at Fort Hood because Alex had loved them so much.

She realizes from looking at the flight arrivals that his plane has already landed. She stands in a hypnotized gaze, watching the passengers lining up at where his baggage will come out. She sees his tall frame in the distance and bounces over to meet him.

"Why are you wearing that?" he says, looking at her shorts.

"You loved this the last time I wore it."

Alex grabs June's arm and pulls her into a corner. "June, you are drawing attention to yourself. What do you think men think when you dress like that?"

"I dressed like this for you."

"I don't want you to look like a whore, June."

That word again.

She looks down at her shorts and tries to pull them to cover more of her legs. He walks in front of her to the Max and doesn't speak until she motions to him that it is their stop.

She changes into a pair of sweatpants as soon as she gets into her apartment. Alex paces around the apartment, looking at his phone. "I have to call Dana. I will be right back."

June sits, then stands, and then sits again.

The door flings open, then slams shut. "Why are you fucking around with Jay?"

"Are we going to have an honest conversation about fucking around?"

"Dana isn't your best friend, June."

"No, she isn't Alex, but you were."

He walks into the kitchen and looks into the refrigerator. "Are you hungry?"

"Sure," she shrugs.

"Let me make you dinner."

"Can you cook?"

He would never confess that Dana expected it. "Mira, I am a grown ass man. Of course, I can cook. Do you like lasagna?"

It feels strange to her that he doesn't know that lasagna is her favorite food. Since they have only lived together for a short time, she has never seen this domestic side of him. She has never experienced him in the role of husband. They have always been married lovers, traveling all over the world, fading in and out of each other's lives.

They walk to the grocery store downtown, swinging hands and laughing. There is a particular way they hold hands, with their fingers oddly intertwined. It is something else they only shared with each other. Alex starts animating stories of his time in Korea after she left. It makes June uneasy because she isn't sure if those moments had been shared with Dana.

As they return to the apartment, June sees Amira. She is dressed in a hot pink tutu, with black laced nylons and a bright yellow shirt. She is wearing the same combat boots June loves so much. The usually stand-offish Amira, runs up to Alex and hugs him tightly. Alex is hesitant to embrace her back until he sees June nod and smile.

"Don't leave your son," she whispers eerily. "He's gonna need you."

Alex gets an uneasy feeling in his stomach. He unclasps himself from Amira and points for June to go up the stairs. June looks at Amira sternly. Amira sticks out her bottom lip and waves goodbye to Alex.

"What did Amira say?"

"Nothing!" He pushes her forward up the stairs.

June unpacks the groceries and pours them both a glass of wine. *Why did Amira have to ruin things with her craziness?*

Alex walks over to June and puts his head on her shoulder, snuggling into her neck. She feels the weight of whatever Amira has said to him as she cradles his head but doesn't speak. Alex wraps her scent around him like a scarf protecting him from the bitter winds and sands of the desert. She is the reason he has survived all these years. He can't get close enough to her to satisfy his urge to hide from the world.

"I am sorry I said those things to you at the airport." He is too ashamed to repeat the words now. "I am mad at myself that I couldn't protect you from Meyers and that I didn't punch the shit out of him when I had the chance. I was such a fool that night you disappeared. I should have never let my guard down around him. He stole something from you that can't be given back. Mira, I lost some things too. I lost that connection we had when we were in Korea. I lost the love I used to see in your eyes when you looked at me. Most of all, I lost your trust. When I saw you in the hospital, I knew that ultimately, I was the reason you ended up there. It killed me to know you had been with Jacob, and that God would give you his baby when he hadn't given you mine." He stops talking, and June can feel his silent tears on her shoulder.

Breathe, just breathe. June clears her throat as she pulls away to look at Alex. "Do you remember when we took the vehicle from the motor pool in Korea to go for a drive? We parked on that dirt road and started making out. The gear shift kept getting in the way, so we got out and leaned on the bumper of the Humvee. You turned me around and pulled off my shorts. I still remember how amazing it felt to have you inside me. I was almost at a climax when you pushed me down on the ground face first."

He laughs.

"Yeah, I stood there alone in the middle of the woods as three tanks came barreling down that damn tank trail, cheering me on. I can only imagine how that story was passed around."

June laughs so hard she snorts. "And––" she can't finish the story because she is laughing so hard. "And!" Alex interjects. "I stood there, like an asshole standing at attention, with my dick in my hand."

June falls to the floor. She can't breathe. "You... You know. You can't make this shit up," she says, wiping the tears from her eyes."

"I miss Korea," he says, taking a deep breath.

She understands.

"Hey, did you ever go to that Screaming Rock place?" she asks.

"No, once you left, I didn't do any hiking."

She wonders why but doesn't ask.

"I went up there one morning. It broke my heart seeing all those women screaming and crying, but I wish I had the courage to do that."

"Do you have a car? I know a place."

"In Oregon, or are we catching a flight?"

"Just get your car, Mira."

Alex drives to Sublimity, Oregon. He stops at a convenience store to grab a few things and tosses them in the trunk before going to Silver Falls.

June connects to this version of Alex. There isn't the usual circumstantial crevasse separating them from each other. She watches Alex hop out of the car and run around to open her door. He pulls her up from the car and kisses her as if he needs her to breathe.

They hike out to North Falls, with him holding her hand and swinging the bag of stuff he bought. The mountains hide the last gleams of light from the sun, so he breaks a chem-light to light their path. The wet gravel crunches and pops with each of their footsteps. Alex leads June behind the raging waterfall, stopping at a wet cavernous space. The glow from the yellow chem-light dances between the mossy patches and smooth wet rock face. There is a smell of chestnut that June loves, which is lingering in the air. He positions her in the center of the falls, facing the raging water, and grabs her waist from behind. They both close their eyes and listen to the water falling in desperation toward the rocks. The mist covers them in a fine layer of moisture. June starts to shiver, so Alex pulls her close to his chest.

"Are you ready, June?"

"For what?" she tries to turn to face him, but he holds her waist tightly.

"Are you ready to scream?"

She holds her breath until her lungs burn.

"I got you, Mira! Let it go."

Her body shivers. "I can't."

He holds her even tighter.

"Don't let Meyers take your voice too."

She gasps for breath, trying to lean forward. "I got you, Mira!" He pulls the hair out of her face and repeatedly kisses the back of her head.

"I can't."

He releases his grasp and turns her around to face him. She is whimpering and gasping for breath. He lifts her chin and smiles at her. "I have never believed in anyone the way I believe in you. You are a badass, Mira. I have never told Dana about Sheila or the woman and child I thought I killed. We survived that together. It is part of who we are, not a part of what I have with her."

She covers her face.

He turns her back around and holds on to her waist, whispering. "In three...two...one...."

She doesn't make a sound but hears him scream at the top of his lungs. She senses the same kind of pain coming from him that she felt from the women on Screaming Rock. June, you have to release this pressure you hold onto, if not for yourself or me, for Ballentine.

How does he know her name?

She spins in a familiar squall. He can feel her heartbeat quicken as she gasps in and out for breath. "Why? I fucking hate you. Why?" she screams, trying to pull away.

He holds her tightly.

"What did I do?" she rages. She pulls forward towards the falls. Alex loses his footing and releases her. She looks back at him–– hopeless. The same way she had looked at him when Meyers grabbed her on the airfield in Korea.

"June! Step back from the edge!"

She leans toward the falls, reaching out her hand to try to touch the raging water.

"Mira, do you hear me? Don't fucking move!"

June feels peaceful for the first time since she felt that blow to the back of her head, the night Meyers took everything from her. She takes another step towards the falls.

Alex calculates and recalculates her movements and the distance he is from her. He is focused on her feet, knowing that the water will take her from him if she steps forward. There is no time to second guess his decision to bring her there. He takes a deep breath and holds out his hand. "Mira, wait. I am going to reach into this bag. Please don't move."

June is lost in the maelstrom of emotions pulling her toward the edge.

The rustling of the bag echoes through the cavern. June doesn't look at Alex. She is focused on the falls. She is trying to find the kind of courage she saw and heard on Screaming Rock.

Alex's hands are shaking. He knows there is only one opportunity to pull June back. He trains his focus on her as the music from the CD player reverberates through the space, bouncing off the walls and dancing around June. "Cry for You", by Jodeci, is song 36. It's the most important song he has ever played for her.

He watches her, terrified to move. He is watching, waiting for God to reveal the pathway back to her. He is praying for the path to save his wife, to save Sheila, and to save himself. He looks in June's direction and sees her clinch her fist. He moves strategically toward her until he can grab her waist.

He pulls back as hard as possible, and they both fall back onto the ground. June struggles to stand, to escape his grasp. She thrashes and kicks Alex, who just holds onto her the best he can.

"LET ME GO! ALEX, JUST LET ME GO!"

Alex sweeps her feet out from under her as she tries to stand. She falls backward onto him, and he grabs her waist and rolls her over so that she is underneath him. June curls up into her protective position. Her breaths are short and labored. Alex scoops her up, like he would his son, and kisses the side of her face. "I got you, Mira." He carries her back to the car, leaving the bag containing a stuffed bear, wine, chocolate, and their wedding rings.

Twenty-Six

You Can't Chose Both

Alex drives them back from Sublimity and tucks June into bed. He watches her sleep for hours, ignoring the texts and phone calls he keeps getting from Dana. Alex dozes off several times before falling asleep in the Papasan chair. He wakes up around 7 am, as the morning sun cascades dancing rainbows of light through the old lead glass windows. He struggles to get out of the chair and falls forward to the ground. He looks over at the bed, and June hasn't moved. He grabs her keys from the kitchen counter and decides to go to the coffee shop for some coffee and pastries. As he walks down SW Taylor St., toward the coffee shop, he listens to the messages from Dana. Her anger permeates through the phone and into Alex's conscience.

It is an easy decision for him to choose June over Dana, but it is much harder to choose June or his son. Amira's words cling to him as a haunting reminder of what he could lose. The guilt for coming to Portland settles around him. June is once again open and vulnerable with him, and he knows that leaving her now would be another betrayal of the unconditional trust she has always given him. It weighs heavily on him that he can't have June and his son. Dana has made it clear that he can't have both.

June wakes up and looks around the room. Alex is gone. There is part of her that feels relieved. Alex is connected to all the pain that eats away her ability to survive. When they are together, she carries the weight of his darkness and hers. She has learned to manage her own by packing it down and parsing out her feelings into manageable doses. She has no barriers with Alex. She has given him full access to her since their time in Korea. He is so attuned to the vibrations of her spirit that he sees any wall she tries to put up and walks right through it. It's like the scale of justice that used to be perfectly balanced between them has been weighted to his side by his son. She knew that nothing she could give him would balance them again: Nothing but her death.

She stumbles toward the bathroom as she lifts her shirt. She has a line of bruises around her waist, where Alex held on to her. It feels like a tattoo that represents his love for her. She grabs the bottle of tequila and takes a shot. The taste brings Jacob to the forefront of her mind. She had drunk tequila with Tara at the end of her relationship with Jacob. She also had shots with Jacob and considered the night she kissed him the beginning of their relationship. She presses the tequila bottle to her lips and drinks gulp after gulp.

She wants to text Jacob but knows he must hate her. She looks in the mirror and then opens the medicine cabinet. Xanax. Abelle had given her Xanax for anxiety. She definitely feels anxious. She takes a handful.

She sits in the shower as the water runs across her naked body. The Xanax and tequila slow her world to a manageable state. It is forty-three minutes before Alex pushes open the bathroom door. June is face down in the shower, breathing slowly. He tries to pick her up, and she falls back into the tub. *Why the fuck did I leave her alone?* He pulls her to the floor and dries her off. He tries to dress her, but she is gasping for breath, falling again. He dials 911 and waits for the paramedics to arrive. The paramedic asks, "What did she take?"

"I don't know." He opens the medicine cabinet and corrals all the bottles into a bag that was lining the trash can. "Here!" he says to the medic.

The paramedic loads June's lifeless body onto the ambulance. "Hey man, take her to the VA hospital. She is a soldier. Also, make sure they put Jacob Edwards on the visitors' list."

"Who are you to her, Sir?"

"I am Alex Brown, her husband." Alex waits until they pull away to text Jacob.

His text: *June's on her way to the VA hospital in PDX. I am so sorry I have to leave. Dana texted that my son is sick.*

He wasn't.

Jacob is on a run when he gets the text. He runs back to his Jeep and starts the drive to Portland. He calls Alex on the way.

"Sup?"

"Alex, what is going on?"

"Man, I honestly can't put words to it."

"What happened? Why is she in the hospital?"

"I think she took Xanax and drank ½ a bottle of tequila."

"Why would she do that, Alex?" There was a deliberate accusation there.

"Jacob, I just need to know if you can be there for her, period?"

Jacob knows the question is much bigger than whether or not he can be there for her at the hospital. His eyes start to sting. "I got her, man!"

"Check. I have to head back as soon as possible. It's my son, Jay."

He thinks about Ballentine. He understands completely.

....- ..--- ---..

Jacob arrives at 11 am. As he walks to the reception desk at the hospital, he hesitates but is relieved when the receptionist says that he is on *the list.* He walks into the room, and June is sitting up in the bed smiling, eating a cupcake. She motions him over with a mouth full of pink icing. She says, "Wan a cup cay?" She points to the other cupcake on the side table. He is starving. It hadn't occurred to him to stop to get something to eat. He is still wearing his running clothes, smelling like a year's worth of teenage gym socks.

He eats the cupcake in two bites, licking his fingers. He brought her a toothbrush and toothpaste because he knew she would ask for them. He also got some alcohol wipes and deodorant for his funk, and fresh-cut Gerber Daisies because the only other options at the hospital gift shop were roses.

"Alex left," he says softly.

"Thank God," she says, now with a mouth full of toothpaste.

"Really?"

"Yes. It's too painful to be around him." She starts to cry.

"Are you ok?"

"Please, just tell me I haven't ruined things between us."

He grabs her head and pulls it close to his chest. "I got you, Jay-bee."

The nurse comes into the room. "You must be Mr. Brown."

"Maybe you should change your name," he whispers.

"It's ok," says June. "We are together."

"Well, I see you were seeing Abelle here at the VA, but you missed several appointments before stopping to come in at all."

"Yeah, I am seeing Hanna now."

"Is she a psychologist here at the VA?"

"No. She is a civilian Mental Health Counselor."

The nurse twists her mouth. "Ok, well, we will have Abelle come down for your Psych Eval so that we can release you."

June feels uncomfortable about Jacob hearing her talk to Abelle. He senses her apprehension and assumes his being there violates her privacy.

"Jay-bee, do you mind if I go down and return some phone calls? My Garrison Commander has called me three times but not left a message."

"Yes, go. Please. Sure. Go."

Jacob walks out of the room to make the phone call.

Abelle comes into the room and asks June a few questions about her desire to live or die, signs a piece of paper, and gives it to the nurse. June rolls her eyes as she looks at the clock and realizes it only took her seven minutes to determine she isn't suicidal when she actually had been.

Jacob walks back into the room, looking down at his feet.

"What's wrong?" asks June, smiling.

"June, I know this is horrific timing, but I am being deployed. I am pretty sure it is to Afghanistan. They made me lead Operations Commander, so I won't be flying much if that is a consolation."

It isn't.

June turns away from Jacob. He crawls into her bed behind her and holds her until she falls asleep.

Twenty-Seven

Enduring Freedom

It isn't going to win him a popularity contest, but Jacob decides to stay with June until they ramp up the deployment in a week. He wants to solidify their relationship because he doesn't know how long he will be deployed. They are getting dressed to go out dancing at a local country bar called Fiddle-Stix. June walks into her living room wearing jeans, tennis shoes, and a long-sleeved black shirt. Jacob smiles and looks down at his cowboy boots. "You don't have any shit kickers?" he asks.

"Shit kickers?" She turns her head sideways.

"Boots?"

"Oh, I have black ones," she brings out her combat-looking boots.

"Cowgirl boots, June?"

"No, why would I have cowgirl boots? I have been married to two different black men for the past decade."

"African-Americans do wear cowboy boots, June."

"Mine didn't."

He knows for a fact that Alex did but grabs her hand. "Let's go shopping," he says. He takes her to a store that only sells western gear. She is amazed at how many different pairs of boots they have. They are beautiful.

"So, what do you like?" she asks.

"Who cares what I like, June? Pick the pair you want."

June picks up a pair she likes. She peeks at the price on the heel. They cost $300. She barely makes ends meet, working part-time at the VA. There was no way she could afford that much for shoes.

Jacob is attuned to June's vibes. He walks over to her and hands her his credit card. "These are on me," he says, picking up the boots she likes.

"Jacob, I can't do that," she says.

He lifts his hands to surrender. "You have the freedom to do whatever you want, Jay-bee. I am just trying to be nice. I want you to have them if you love them, and I know you do. Your eyes twinkle, and you bounce when you are happy."

June remembers what Hanna had told her in one of her sessions: *Allow people to be nice to you and don't accept it when they aren't.*

"Ok, you can buy me boots, but don't assume it means anything."

Jacob smiles. He loves the child-like tone in her voice. "What if I bought your entire outfit?"

June takes a deep breath and exhales. "Ok, but you have to tell me which one you like."

"I can do that. I like everything, even what you are wearing now."

"That isn't fair. Pick out three things," she demands, pointing at the women's clothes.

He picks out one pair of really sexy shorts, then a skirt and a pair of jeans.

She looks at his selections and tosses the shorts to the side.

"Come on, June, just try them on," he pleads, dropping down to his knees.

"I don't want to look like a whore," she whispers.

Jacob's countenance changes. "June, why would you think that makes you look like a whore? You can look sexy and not be or look like a whore, Jay bee."

"Alex and Devan both said–– "

Jacob holds up his hand for her to stop. Those two names in one sentence are more than he can handle. He takes June's head into his chest and takes a deep breath. "June, you should be able to walk down the street naked if you want. No man has the right to tell you how to dress or use that as an excuse to hurt you. Please don't allow me or anyone else to dictate what you wear. I would think you were sexy if you were covered in a tarp."

"They do sell those here," she laughs. She tries on the shorts but only allows him to see them inside her dressing room. Nothing can save him from his physical response to her. "We are buying those, babe. You can just wear them around the house if you want."

"Take them with you. I wouldn't wear them for anyone else." She also gets a pair of jeans, the boots with the cobalt blue inlay, and the skirt he had picked out for her. She decides to wear the skirt, boots, and a black long-sleeve shirt that fits tightly around her waist.

He watches her dress and feels elated to be with her. It feels to him that all the barriers between them have been removed.

They walk into the club hand in hand. He offers her tequila, but she doesn't want to drink anything. She wants to remember each of the moments she has left with Jacob before he leaves. They dance to every slow song, and June even tries line dancing but fails horribly.

"I need to go pee," she says.

"Well, don't buy any drugs in there and try to take advantage of me," he jokes.

She leans into his ear, "I don't need drugs to be with you, Jay."

He feels lightning race through his chest. He turns and kisses her softly on the cheek.

When she comes out of the bathroom, he takes her and leads her out of the club to his Jeep. He stands, filling the space between the door and the passenger's seat. He puts both hands on her face and kisses her hard. "I want you so badly." She takes his hand and slides it under her skirt. "You are killing me," he says. "You feel amazing."

She reaches into the front of his pants and pulls him toward her. "I want you too," she whispers as he kisses her neck. "Get in! Let's drive over there by the woods."

She briefly thinks about the tank trail and smiles.

He can barely sit in the Jeep to drive it. She laughs as he groans in pain. "Oh, it's funny to you that I am in pain?"

She nods and scrunches up her nose. As soon as he parks, she jumps out and runs to the front of the Jeep. She sits on the bumper and takes off her panties, throwing them at him. He catches them just as they are hitting his face. "You smell so f-ing good," he says through clenched teeth. He pushes his body against hers as she wraps her legs around him. He pushes her back against the Jeep and unzips his pants. She looks at him and smiles. "Is this what you imagined that night I kissed you outside the Canteen?"

It was.

She pulls his hips toward her, and they both take a deep breath as they connected. She feels a rush of blood flush her face as she tries to absorb him. They move in perfect sync with each other, breathing in and out to the rhythm of their heartbeats. She leans back onto the Jeep as he pulls her hips forward to meet his. The warmth of the engine amplifies her desire for him. He pulls her back up to kiss her. Her eyes are closed.

"Look at me, June."

She does.

Return Address

Jacob leaves the following Tuesday. June kisses him goodbye on the tarmac as he boards his plane to Afghanistan. She has made sure he packed her sexy shorts, plenty of paper to write her and some sexy photos she had taken and put in an envelope that read: In case of emergency. He, of course, opens the envelope as soon as the aircraft door closes.

Tara and Alex...

He wonders if Alex has also been deployed. He can't imagine going to war without him. There is something about going to battle with someone that can't be explained to anyone that hasn't experienced it.

Your *Battle* is closer than family. They are your arm or leg and a direct connection to you. They make it possible for you to take that next step toward the enemy. Part of him wonders if he would have given up June if Alex had asked him directly.

....- ..--- ---..

He falls asleep on the first part of the flight but is awakened by a Private asking him to come to the back room of the plane for a briefing. The last time he went to war, he flew over on a C-130. This plane is like Airforce One. They have fully reclined seats and briefing rooms that would put the Pentagon's to shame.

Jacob is given a list of his soldiers' names, positions, and next-of-kin. He is briefed on the mission and his responsibilities. He has a sense of pride in leading a team. Since 9/11 the face of war has changed, and so have the responsibilities of being a soldier. He is older now and feels more prepared for what he faces, but he worries about the fragility of June. He won't be able to protect her from her darkness while he is away.

He takes the stack of papers, lays them on his chest, and falls back to sleep. An hour later, he jumps up and flips wildly through the pages, looking for the name Alex Brown. He isn't there, so he casually looks through the rest of the names, and there he is: Captain Adam Meyers. *How is he still in the Army?* Jacob throws the list against the wall and starts a letter to June.

....- ..--- ---..

June has taken all of Jacob's plants from his condo. He left her the key and asked her to check on things and open all his mail. He wants to be sure she knows he can be trusted. She had started to apply for jobs in the area but loves Portland so much that she declines it when offered a position in Olympia. The plants hate Portland and die immediately. She keeps the pots so she can replace them with new vibrant plants before he returns.

It is eighteen days before she gets a letter from Jacob. He has finally gotten settled and can give her an address. He included some sand in his letter and asked her to save it. He says he loves her one thousand times more than each grain of sand. She finds a crystal blue vase and starts collecting the sand grains.

Days drag into months, and June spends most of her time learning about meditation and running as much as possible. Pippa offers to take her out on her birthday, but she feels uncomfortable going out of her apartment.

Jacob has found a way to call June on her birthday. It has been six months since she has heard his voice. The line is fuzzy, but she can understand him.

"Jay bee!"

"Hey, my love."

"Happy Birthday to you. You live in a zoo. You look like a monkey, and you smell like one too."

"Jay, that would be you!"

"So, what are you doing for your 29th birthday?"

"I am getting old."

"You are just getting to the perfect age, June."

"For what?"

"To settle down and have a family."

"I have a family with you, Jay"

"And our Bee bug," he reminds.

She falls silent.

"I don't have long, my love. I just want you to know you are in my every thought. Every step I take here is one that comes back to you."

"I'm dying," she professes.

"I know. Please just be strong for me. I will be home as soon as I can. I sent you a special gift. I hope you will accept it."

"Of course, I will you dummy."

"I love you more than all the stars in the sky."

"And I love you more than all the grains of sand in that desert you are in."

"You always have to win, don't you?"

She laughs and the line goes silent.

Two days later, June receives a call from the Ford Dealership. They pick her up and take her to the showroom. "What color Mustang would you like, ma'am?"

"I can't afford a Mustang," she says sheepishly.

"Ma'am, I am sorry. I should have told you it's paid for. Jacob Edwards has already signed all the paperwork. We have been waiting six months to call you. It's been a big deal for us all to be a part of this for you."

June puts her face in her hands. *This is why he was worried I wouldn't accept it.* She walks around the showroom with childlike excitement in her eyes. Then she sees it: a cobalt blue Mustang. It is perfect. She motions the guy over. "Is this one too much?"

"Ma'am, there is no limit, and he left a note that you can pick any car or truck here if you want, it doesn't have to be a Mustang."

June shakes her head, "It has to be a Mustang," she says.

"Janice, you won the bet!" he screams across the room!"

Everyone cheers.

"Happy Birthday," says the sales rep. "And thank your husband again for his service and business."

She almost says that he isn't her husband, but she likes the thought of it. She wonders if Jacob has told them she is his wife. He has never talked about marriage or children besides referring to Ballentine as his daughter. A small part of her had hoped that the gift had been a ring and an engagement, but he would have never done that without being there. He cares too much about the details.

She drives home, realizing she has nowhere to park. She sold her car when Jacob left and has been driving his Jeep around. She finds street parking for the Jeep and takes her new baby to the garage. She sits for an hour in the car, listening to the radio. She can't figure out how to set the stations, so she looks in the glove compartment for the manual. There is an envelope taped to the manual in Jacob's writing. *"Look in the trunk! Love, Jacob."*

She pops the trunk and sees a huge box wrapped in blue paper. There is a card with a Gerber daisy on the front. She told him it was her favorite flower when he brought them to her at the hospital.

She kisses her baby goodnight and carries the box back to her apartment. She tosses the box on the bed, then lies down beside it. There is something final about opening it. She doesn't know when she will hear from Jacob again, so she wants to make this moment last. She decides to wait until she receives a letter from him to open the box.

....⁻ ..⁻⁻⁻ ⁻⁻⁻..

On Wednesday, she gets a call from Devan, asking if he can come by and see her. The randomness of the phone call makes her curious, so she agrees to see him. He arrives and asks her if she could parallel park his car. She knows he can park his car, but she takes the keys and follows him out. She sees Amira standing on the sidewalk in front of her apartment. She appears to be lost. June taps her on the shoulder.

"Are you ok, Amira?"

Amira turns toward them and screams, "Shit! Fuck!" and runs around the corner.

June looks at Devan, who is laughing. "What is up with her?"

June shrugs her shoulders but wants to check on Amira. Devan redirects her attention. "I am delighted you agreed to see me."

"I have to be honest… I am shocked you want to see me."

He follows her upstairs to her apartment.

June feels nervous about having Devan there but doesn't ask him to leave.

He reaches to take her hand, but she pulls it away and stands up. "Do you want a tequila or something?"

"Only if you are serving it with coke." She is no longer in that space with him, that she feels nostalgic reminders are appropriate.

June readjusts herself and moves a little further away from Devan. She smiles awkwardly as she bites her bottom lip. "Uh, Sorry, I am all out of coke."

She isn't.

He takes the tequila and sips it slowly. "June, are you ok with me being here?"

"Sure thing. What's up?" She looks at the door and hopes it will magically open.

"I have been thinking about us a lot lately."

Us? she thinks.

"June, I need to know if there is still a chance for us to work things out."

"Devan, I haven't heard from you in years. You told me to leave your family alone, and I have done that."

"Do you remember when we were in training? We had an amazing connection with each other. I just can't imagine that it was an accident."

"I love Jacob," she blurts.

"The pilot?"

"Yes, we became great friends, and now we are dating, well, he is deployed, but I consider us dating."

"So, you cheat on me with Alex and then cheat on Alex with his best friend?"

She notices his facial expression has completely changed. She backs away from him and sits in the chair closest to the door. "Devan, I am sorry. Alex ended things with me, and I don't think I should have to explain who I am dating to you. You divorced me."

He stands up and walks toward her. "I still love you, June."

She looks into his eyes and sees a glimpse of darkness. "Can you excuse me? I need to go to the bathroom really quickly." She walks out her apartment door and runs down the stairs to Amira's room.

Amira peeks out of the chained door. "Hurry, come in."

June walks into her apartment. The hallway is dark, and she sees rows of bookshelves containing hundreds of vintage-looking books. Amira motions her down the hallway to her living area. Crosses, evil eyes, and Fatima's hand hang on her walls.

"Are you ok?" asks June.

Amira is always hesitant about confiding in strangers. She just sits quietly in front of June.

"That guy I came in with used to be my husband," June confesses.

Amira cringes her face.

"I don't think he's unattractive," says June.

Silence.

"I feel uncomfortable with him in my apartment since I am dating Jacob. You met Jacob, right?"

Amira nods and smiles.

"It's just strange that Devan would show up after telling me he hated me and ask me to get back with him."

Silence.

"I just really want him to go away."

"If I only had the box. Gavin lost the box," rants Amira as she rocks back and forth.

"The box: what box are you talking about?"

Amira doesn't answer the question. She just jumps up and rummages through her dresser. She pulls out a Ziploc bag with a pill in it. She hands it to June.

"What's this?" June asks, looking at the pill.

"It makes them go away," says Amira.

Do you want me to give this to Devan?

Amira grabs the bag from June and puts it back into her dresser drawer. She pushes June toward the door.

"Amira, I am sorry. Did you want me to take the pill?"

Silence. Pushing.

"Ok, I am leaving. Sheesh."

June walks back upstairs and goes straight into the bathroom. She sits on the closed toilet seat with her head in her hands. She taps her feet wildly and then stands up and looks in the mirror. "No," she whispers, scrunching her nose. She spins around a few times and then walks back into the living room. Before Devan can speak, she runs back downstairs to Amira's apartment.

Amira opens the door with the pill in her hand and a glass of water and then slams the door in June's face. June looks at the pill. She has no idea what it is, but if it will help her talk to Devan? She swallows it and then waits by Amira's door to see what happens.

....⁻ ..⁻⁻ ⁻⁻⁻..

"Hey June," says Gavin knocking on Amira's door.

June looks up at him but doesn't speak. Her world is spinning in small circles, then larger ones.

"What's wrong with her?" Gavin asks as Amira opens the door.

"I gave her one of your demon pills."

"Amira, you can't give those to anyone! I told you! Help me get her up to her apartment."

"I am not going up there. You take her."

Gavin lifts June and helps her back to her apartment. Devan stands up when he comes in.

"What is wrong with her?"

Gavin, a little nervous, "I think she drank too much." He looks on the counter and sees the bottle of tequila. "She drank too much tequila. Are you ok with staying with her; she needs someone to stay with her for at least 3-6 hours."

Devan thinks the time frame is very specific but doesn't ask any questions. He paces around June's room, waiting for her to wake up. He sees the gift in the corner and reads the letter on her dresser. He is furious.

June leans over the side of the bed and pukes but isn't aroused enough to wake up completely. Devan tries to talk to her, but she isn't responsive. He cleans up the puke, then undresses her and covers her with a clean blanket. He doesn't want to stay for five more hours. He writes a note for the girl downstairs and walks out of the apartment. He pauses in the hallway and comes back into June's apartment. He sorts back through the letters on her dresser, circling the return address with his finger.

Amira hears a knock on the door and runs to open it, thinking it is Gavin. She freezes as she sees Devan standing in her doorway. She doesn't hear what he is saying. She pushes the door closed between them and runs into her safe room.

It's morning before June wakes up. She looks around frantically, and Devan is gone. She stands up before she realizes she is naked. She covers her mouth: *Did I?*

She has no memory of even coming back up to her apartment. She puts her finger inside herself and tries to smell it to see if she has had sex. She can't smell anything. She searches the room desperately until she finds her phone.

"Hey, this is Devan. Leave a message."

"Devan, I uh, just call me, please. It is important."

June gets dressed and runs down to Amira's apartment. She knocks loudly. Amira drags her feet to the door and looks out the peephole. She's relieved it is June.

"Amira, what was that pill you gave me?"

"I don't know. Gavin gets them for me."

June runs down to Gavin's apartment. "Gavin, I need to know what that pill was that Amira gave me," she says instead of hello.

Gavin looks up and down the hall and then, with a jerk, pulls June into his apartment.

His hallway is dark like Amira's, but he has posters of these horrible creatures on his walls. It feels a little creepy. "Amira knows better than to give those pills to other people. Your friend freaked her out."

"What was it?"

He twists his hands together, then squeezes his mouth before he says, "Flunitrazepam."

"I have never heard of that," she says.

"Yeah, you have."

She looks confused.

"It's a Roofee."

"The date rape drug? Why would she give me the date rape drug?" June covers her face.

"They help her with her bad visions, in an off-label sort of way."

"Oh my god, I don't remember anything. I woke up completely naked."

Gavin covers his face with one hand and pushes June out of his apartment with the other. "So, you take random pills people give you without asking any questions?"

She does.

Twenty-Nine

Colonel Edwards

June paces around the birthday present and then rips into it desperately. There are a series of boxes that get smaller and smaller until she reaches a tiny box that fits in the palm of her shaking hands. She opens the box, and it is the biggest diamond she has ever seen; it is shaped like a heart. She looks over at the bed, still wet from what she is sure was sex with Devan. She rips off the sheets and throws them in the corner, then lays on the bed beside the ring. Jacob only liked sleeping closest to the door, so that is the side she placed the ring. There is a note inside.

This is my promise that you are my forever. Diamonds are made of carbon that can withstand a great deal of pressure and turn out beautifully, just like you. They say carbon is synonymous with life. Since we are all 18% carbon, it means God designed us to take the pressure life gives us and become beautiful too. You are my love and my life. I will be home to you soon. Jay

p.s I hope you picked the cobalt blue mustang I special ordered for you.

June can't breathe. She knows that once he finds out that she put herself in the position that she did with Devan that he will never forgive her.

...⁻ ..⁻⁻⁻ ⁻⁻⁻..

Jacob has insisted on doing a few rescue missions, but he stays pretty busy as the Operations Commander. He makes rank after only two months in-country and is now a full bird colonel. He sent the wings that were pinned on him in the ceremony to June.

He shares a tent with two other officers but misses being in the big tent with all the pilots. He visits on occasion to feel like he is still in sync with them. He has kept track of Meyers, who is stationed in a subordinate unit twenty kilometers away.

"Any status on the transfer request for Captain Meyers?" asks Jacob.

"Sir, we have enough pilots here, we'd have a logistics nightmare acquiring a new helicopter to get him here."

"I am sure you can make it happen. Check with the crews and see if anyone wants to transfer over there?"

"Check, Sir!"

Jacob notices his hands are shaking, so he puts both hands in his pockets and walks out of the Operations tent. As the sun sets low in the western sky, it will be getting bitterly cold soon, so he grabs a scarf from his bag. June's shorts fall out of the bag. He had insisted she wear them before he packed them. He keeps them in a Ziploc bag so they will still smell like her, but he will never tell her about the Ziploc.

....⁻ ..⁻⁻⁻ ⁻⁻⁻..

June has taken Jacob's Jeep back to his condo because she can't stand seeing it there without him. She parks in the visitor's space to unload her groceries.

Amira is in the lobby but doesn't help her open the door.

"Is the demon with you?" she asks coldly.

"The demon?" asks June laughing.

"Yeah, that's why I gave you that pill."

"Devan?"

She nods and hands her the note from Devan. June reads the note: *You were amazing last night; sorry I had to leave.* "Crap," she says under her breath.

"Amira, you think Devan is a demon?"

"He is. Be careful."

"Ok, Amira, have a great day," June says sympathetically. *Wow, she is a weird one,* thinks June.

June checks her mail before going upstairs. There are three letters from Jacob. The sand from two of the letters has compromised the seam of the envelope, and the sand spills out on the floor. She tries scooping it up, but the carpet fibers hold onto the precious dust. She runs upstairs and brings down duct tape to pick up every speck that she can. She lies with her face on the carpet, looking for any sand she has missed.

Amira walks by the mail room and giggles. *She is a weird one,* she thinks, looking at June crouched on the floor.

June dusts the last bit of sand in the blue jar and begins to read the letters. She remembers the gritty feeling of the paper from all the letters Alex had written her. She wants to save Jacob's letters too, but in a more memorable way. She decides she will have them scanned and make them into a book. She will include all the photos they have taken together and silly quotes of all the funny things he says.

She isn't sure if she should tell Jacob about Devan. She remembers what Julian had said about confessions being selfish. She had followed his guideline, but it all ended disastrously with Devan anyway. Even if Jacob did forgive her, she isn't sure she can ever forgive herself. As she sorts through all his letters and envelopes, she realizes one is missing. She frantically searches for it but can't find it.

....- ..--- ---..

Jacob is growing tired of the war and the relentless battle for a stronghold in the country, that will only be taken back the following week. He can only measure his success by the lives he saves and the days that bring him closer to returning to June. He looks at his watch as he runs into the Operations tent with a determined look on his face.

"Captain Meyers reporting, as requested, Sir."

Jacob waits an uncomfortable amount of time before saluting him. "At ease, Captain."

"Sir, I am honored to be a part of your team, but I am just curious how you heard about me?" He reaches out to shake Jacob's hand.

Jacob doesn't extend his hand. I make it a point to be familiar with all the soldiers under my command. You can bunk with us for the night, and then we will get you settled in the pilots' quarters first light, says Jacob."

Meyers salutes him and turns to leave.

"Hey, Cap! Wait up! Could you drop your bags and go on a quick scout mission with Chief Smith? He can show you what we are up to, and when you return, I will debrief you."

Meyers looks at his watch. It is 1 am. "Yes, Sir!"

Jacob feels that he has been holding his breath the whole time he was talking to Meyers. He uses some of the meditation techniques that June had made him practice after she had attended a weekend retreat at someplace called Breitenbush.

He had stood in the place where June was raped by something that was pure evil. There is no doubt that the same evil has just been standing in front of him, trying to shake his hand. As soon as he hears that Meyers and Smith have taken off, he excuses himself and casually walks over to the officer's tent. He positions a private outside to ensure that no one comes in or out.

His breathing is calm and steady as he meticulously searches Meyers' bag for anything that would tie him to June. He is sure he will find June's ID, but it isn't there. He kicks the bag repeatedly until the private inquires if he is ok.

He restores all the items to the bag, places them in the same position on the cot, straightens his uniform, runs his fingers through his hair, and returns to Ops.

Meyers and Smith land and start walking back toward Ops.

"So, what is up with the Bird?" asks Meyers.

"If you are referring to Colonel Edwards, I would suggest you drop the informalities," says Chief Smith.

"So, he's a hard-ass?"

Smith stops walking and faces Meyers. "Captain Meyers, you will find you won't get very far with that attitude around here. Colonel Edwards is very well respected, and for a good reason. If you can't get in line with that, you may want to transfer back to the little boys' camp."

When they walk into Ops, Jacob motions them over to a table covered with a topographic map of the region. He discusses the areas of patrol, the hot spots for insurgence, and the areas they hope to capture and maintain in their next mission. He explains the efforts the ground troops are making and how they are supporting them with aerial coverage. Then he dismisses them to shower, chow, and sleep until 0800.

....- ..--- ---..

Jacob has to hear June's voice. It has been two months since he has spoken to her, and tonight a letter or tape recording isn't enough. He wants to hear her breathing, make her laugh, and hear that she loves him. He doesn't have to be Colonel Edwards to her. He is just Jacob.

"June?"

"Oh my god, is it really you?"

Jacob smiles. "Yes, Jay-bee, who else would be calling you from a restricted line?"

"Well, I am famous, you know?"

"Really? Famous for what?"

"You know!"

"That could make you famous, June. God knows I am a fan."

Desperately she says, "I love you, baby. I didn't get to say that again before I lost you last time."

"June, I know you love me."

Her heart sinks. She hates herself.

"Jacob..."

"Babe, I don't have much time. I just needed to hear your sweet voice and imagine you bouncing around your apartment."

"Any idea when you might be coming home?"

"No, babe, I am sorry."

"Ok," she perks. "I will keep writing you. Do you need anything?"

"June, listen very closely to what I am about to say. You are all that I have ever needed. I love you."

"Oh my god, the ring! I forgot to say thank you for the ring and the car!"

"They aren't enough to measure what you mean to me, but I will keep trying."

"Why do you love me so much, Jacob?"

"You are part of me, June. I am so sorry, baby. I have to hang up. I will call again if I can."

Static.

....⁻ ..⁻⁻⁻ ⁻⁻⁻..

Jacob sleeps until 0705. It is believed around camp that he never slept, so no one dared to wake him. At 0715, he starts his two-mile run, then showers and arrives in Operations at 0759. He is given a list of wounded and killed soldiers, signs form letters for the killed in action, which he always personalizes, and is given a list of outgoing and incoming soldiers.

Two names of the incoming soldiers stand out to him: Sergeant Julian Davis and CW4 Alex Brown. Alex is assigned to an Attack Helicopter Battalion 10 minutes north of where he is, and Julian is twenty minutes south with the 10th Mountain Division. He leaves the Lieutenant Commander in charge and flies up to see Alex.

....⁻ ..⁻⁻⁻ ⁻⁻⁻..

War dissolves all barriers. Jacob isn't going to see Alex, June's ex. He is going to see his oldest friend and battle buddy. Alex runs across the complex when he sees Jacob approaching. He stops, snaps his heels, and salutes Jacob. "What the fuck? You got your bird! Congrats, man!" He grabs Jacob and hugs him, slapping his back hard.

Jacob smiles for the first time since he has been in there. "How the hell are you, Chief, W4?"

Alex brushes off his rank.

"So, you are running this bitch, I hear," says Alex.

"Doing the best, I can. You know what a crisis we face trying to gain any ground here."

"Yeah, shits getting real."

"Hey, I hate to just get into it, but I only have about thirty minutes before I need to get back."

Alex looks over at a group of soldiers burning shit in barrels. He takes a deep breath and looks back at Jacob. "Look, man; let's just call it good with June. Dana and I are happy. I haven't spoken to her since that night she went to the hospital."

"Alex, that isn't what I need to talk to you about, but thanks for that. Meyers is here."

Alex looks around frantically, "Where?" he demands.

"I transferred him to the Operations Center."

"Why the fuck would you do that?"

"Keep your enemies close, right?"

Alex has only seen Jacob lose his composure once. As he looks at him now, his eyes are those of a savage, but his physical move- ments are calculated, like a warrior.

"Alright! What are you going to do?" asks Alex.

"Wait for the universe to present a solution," he says.

Alex twists his mouth. "Well, let me know if the 'universe' needs a fucking hand."

"Will do, Chief. You look great, man. If you are around Ops, stop in. I will brief you on what our goals are here."

"Check, Sir. Give June my best."

With those simple words, Jacob knows everything is for- given. "And give Dana and the kids my best."

....⁻ ..⁻⁻⁻ ⁻⁻⁻..

June has been trying to reach Julian for months, but his phone has been disconnected, and the letters and cards she has sent him are returned. He is infamous for disappearing, so she assumes that is the case. She is curious about how Devan had found him years before, but she refuses to call him. She has disconnected from all her support system except for Pippa.

Pippa has struggles of her own. She suffers from manic depression and self-medicates with illegal drugs. They sit on the floor in June's living room, both crying as June relates her most likely betrayal with Devan.

"June, that is some heavy shit to carry." She takes a drag of the blunt she has just lit. She holds it out to June, who waives it off.

"It is killing me not to just tell him, but he's fighting a fricking war, for God's sake."

"Right!"

"But! I don't want him to hold on to me when I am such a piece of shit."

"Right!"

"Give me the damn blunt, Pip," says June. She breathes it in, and her anxiety begins to soften. "Maybe I should just write it in a letter. That way, he could just not write back if he is pissed?"

"He's going to be pissed."

"Thanks, Pippa."

"I'm here to give you the real! Anyone can feed you that feel-good bullshit."

"So, should I tell him on the phone?"

"JB, are you going to fuck Devan again?"

"No!"

"Alex?"

"No!"

"Anyone but Jacob?"

"Probably not."

"Then that's your answer." She lies back and takes the last drag.

June lies back too. Maybe she shouldn't tell Jacob. She looks at the ring on her finger but really feels she doesn't deserve it.

The next day June quits her job at the VA. She says it is because she wants to get a nose ring, but it is really because she can't handle seeing Abelle every day. She takes a job at the coffee shop down the street as a barista. She loves that most of the people she sees are too busy to talk to her.

....⁻ ..⁻⁻⁻ ⁻⁻⁻..

Jacob has gotten word of some reported rapes at three of his subordinate units, so he calls the company and battalion commanders for a meeting. The room is clamoring when he enters. "Attention!" barks the Battalion commander of Operations.

"At ease," says Jacob. "Listen, this is not going to be a free-for-all. If you have something to say, raise your hand, wait to be acknowledged and then speak. When you are finished speaking, I will address you. There will be no side talking or commentary. Am I understood?"

They collectively say, "Yes, Sir!"

Everyone raises their hands, but Jacob calls on the 10th Mountain Division Commander. "Yes, John," says Jacob.

"We have three reports of male soldiers being attacked in their sleep and waking up with apparent sexual assault."

"Ok, I am sending Sergeant Harris around with pieces of paper. Give me the total of reported cases for each Battalion."

There are 14 cases.

"It is my understanding that the Military Police have been notified and are investigating each case. The soldiers have been given medical attention and processed home. Is that accurate?"

Sergeant Smith acknowledged it was.

Lieutenant Colonel Anderson raises his hand.

"Yes, Arthur."

"Are we looking into the gays?"

Jacob took one of June's meditation breaths. "Arthur, what exactly do you mean? Do you have any proof that the offender is gay?"

"Pardon my language, Sir, but would a straight man ass fuck another soldier?"

"Arthur, I have known you for a decade. I have to say that I am extremely disappointed that you are taking this stance. Rape is an act of violence-- period. It has little to nothing to do with sexuality, and I will not allow a witch hunt on my watch. Is that completely understood?"

"Yes, Sir!"

Jacob addresses the group. "I stated at the beginning of this meeting that I was not interested in your commentary. Is that understood?"

They say, "Yes, Sir!"

"Moving forward, submit your cases to me, and I will review the facts and only the facts. We have no idea if this is a soldier or a civilian, so no action will be taken without my approval. Do I make myself clear?"

"Yes, Sir!"

"Dismissed."

Jacob walks over to the mail room after the meeting. He has gotten two letters from June that are scented with a fragrance that made him have to readjust his walk. He makes a mental note to ask her what it is. There is also a letter that has no return address. He puts them all in his pocket and returns to Operations.

Jacob always takes a break from 4-5 pm in the afternoon to shower, eat and read June's letters. He isn't sure how she plans it, but he receives at least one letter when the mail is delivered every three days. He saves the letters by postmark and only reads one per day. He sits on his bunk and looks at the letter with no return address. He decides to open it first. The handwriting isn't familiar to him, so he looks at the bottom of the letter, and it is signed: Devan.

The blood rushes to his face. He skims over the words, *'had sex with...' and 'looking out for you...'* When he closes his eyes, he can feel a sharp pain in the center of his chest. He had justified Tara's cheating to be a result of his own affair. He had understood that June's connection to Alex was because they both shared very painful experiences. He doesn't rush to judgment. He decides to call June, even though it is 3 am her time.

"Hello," mutters June.

"It's Jacob," he says with a Commander's authority.

She is taken aback by his tone. "What's going on, Jay?"

"June, I don't have time to play games with you. Did you have sex with Devan?"

June sits up in bed and runs her fingers through her hair. A flood of guilt and anxiety rushes through her like tiny daggers. She slips off her ring and places it on the nightstand. "I think I did, and I am so sorry, but Amira drugged me."

His silence haunts her. She braces for impact. "June, I know me being away has been hard on you. It isn't fair that I have held you in suspense all this time."

She doesn't move or breathe.

"I need to process all of this. I probably shouldn't have called you. I will get back to you in a few days."

She wants to say I love you. She wants to roll back the days and refuse to see Devan. She wants to die, but all she can do is disappear in his silence.

June traces back Jacob's words, and they are eerily familiar. "Fuck!" she says, knowing that if Alex had been given a Roofee in Korea, there is no way he would have had any control of what happened with Dana. She texts Alex 428, but he doesn't respond.

Thirty

Rules of Negotiation

June looks at her phone every few seconds, turning the volume off and then back on to ensure it works properly. The mail runs at 3 pm every day, and June waits to speak to the mail person every day and has them recheck their bags to make sure that a letter isn't stuck to the bottom. She even rechecks her mail at 3 am to make sure that she hasn't missed a letter from Jacob or that the mail person hasn't come back when they find it in the floorboard of their truck.

After three weeks, she takes the ring off the nightstand and places it in a shoebox with all of Jacob's letters. She places the box on top of the other two boxes she still has of Devan and Alex's letters. She stares at them aligned perfectly in the closet corner and then moves Jacob's box to a separate corner. She walks out of the closet and immediately spins around and grabs Jacob's box and places it on her bookshelf, and then she does the only thing that she knows. She runs.

June runs every morning, up to 9th Ave. SW to SW Morrison St., across the 405, turning left on SW 20th by the Stadium; right on SW Jefferson, and then down to Tom McCall Waterfront Park. She loves the pain and breathlessness of a good run. It is the only part of her life still connected to Jacob.

....- ..--- ---..

Alex has been in Afghanistan for seven months when he runs into Julian. He is flying a joint operation with the 10th Mountain

Division and has to stay over in their camp. He has never really considered himself an officer in the social sense, so he requests to bunk in the enlisted tent.

"Chief!" Julian screams, "Boo bear," he whispers. "How the hell are you?"

"Can't complain," says Alex.

The air is filled with the awkward but unasked question: June?

Alex joins a game of spades that is being played in the corner and laughs uncontrollably when he is caught talking across the board. He loves being a soldier. The distance from his family is soothed by the grit of sand that lingers in his mouth. He has been bitten by the wanderlust that afflicts most soldiers. It is easier for him to have his own space and love his family than share theirs and love himself.

Alex takes a cold shower and walks back to the tent in his t-shirt and shorts. Julian is waiting by his cot.

"Damn," Julian says, seeing Alex in his shorts.

"Easy!" says Alex. "You can still get kicked out for that shit."

"What?" says Julian with child-like innocence.

"Have you heard from June?" asks Alex.

"I actually haven't in a while. There is a lot of drama that orbits that one," says Julian.

"Really? You are going to fault her on drama?" laughs Alex.

"I think the real question is: Have you heard from June?" inquires Julian.

"Look, Julian. I have moved on and allowed her to pursue Jacob freely."

"How's that working for you?"

"It's fine, but the last I spoke to him, he isn't speaking to her?"

"Do I want to know why?"

"He says something about Devan, so I am, assuming she—— "

"Drama! I told you."

"Julian, go easy. After finding out about Meyers, I am surprised she's still standing."

"What about Meyers?"

Alex covers his face. "She didn't tell you Meyers raped her?"

Julian motions Alex to the doorway of the tent. "What the hell are you saying to me, Alex?"

"Jacob found out that Meyers raped June, or we believe he did."

"He's a freak," said Julian. "I thought he was gay."

"Gay?"

"Yes, that mother-fucker was all over me in Korea talking about some freaky shit that not even I am into."

"I don't know," Alex says, lifting his hands. "Jacob and June, both believe it was him."

"Ok, so where is Meyers?"

"He is here. Jacob had him transferred to Operations."

"To do what?"

Alex shrugs. "June told me once she had a nightmare about the guy having a round scar on his right shoulder. She said it was purple. I have never seen Meyers without a shirt, and neither has June, to my knowledge. That will be a weird coincidence if Meyers has that scar."

Julian stares at the stars and his thoughts vanish in the darkness. "It would be weird," he whispers inaudibly.

....⁻ ..⁻⁻⁻ ⁻⁻⁻..

Jacob sifts through the files on his desk. Arthur has sent him a list of "suspected gays." He briefly looks over the list; Julian Davis' name is there. He has never heard June talk about him being gay, so he tears the list into small pieces and puts it in his cargo pocket.

The 'Don't ask, Don't Tell' policy has prohibited this witch hunt mentality. However, a soldier can still be prosecuted and discharged if a substantial proof is provided to the court that they have performed any illegal acts of sodomy.

The sexual assault of soldiers in his command weighs heavily on his conscience. So far, there has been no traceable evidence to connect anyone to the crimes. The perpetrator must have been using a condom, he thinks. He has considered doing surprise inspections and confiscating any condoms he finds but decides against it. He also tries to coordinate Meyers location with any cases and can't find a connection.

He sits behind his desk, watching soldiers move around with purpose, but he can't find his own. On the corner of his desk is a stack of unread letters from June. He has stopped collecting them from the mailroom, so they have them delivered to his desk. He stacks them neatly in a pile, tracing her writing with his finger, and then puts them in the same cargo pocket with the paper shreds. On his way to chow, he tosses the contents of his pocket into the fire of burning shit.

....⁻ ..⁻⁻⁻ ⁻⁻⁻..

June awakes with a sense of purpose. She takes the boxes of Alex and Devan's letters and tucks them under her arm. She drives to Silver Falls and finds a picnic area with a barbecue grill.

She takes a deep cleansing breath and soaks Devan's letters in tequila and places them on the grill with a splash of coke. The fire balloons, then slowly burns each letter to a fine black powder. The rain starts tapping on the pavilion roof, so she quickly soaks Alex's letters in blackberry beer and burns them too. She looks toward the trail and remembers the feeling of holding Alex's hand as he took her to the Falls.

The drops of rain fall onto her face as she looks toward the sky, still hoping for God to show her He is really up there.

She waits.

Nothing.

She breathes in the smoke and then tosses water on the grill to extinguish any fire that might be left.

....⁻ ..⁻⁻⁻ ⁻⁻⁻..

Her next stop is her therapy appointment. Hanna is happy to see June. She brings her right back to her counseling room. "June, it has been a while, but we were making such great progress that I would love if we could just dive right in."

June crosses her legs on the couch and looks directly at Hanna. "I made progress today. I burned all of Alex's and Devan's letters."

"June, tell me how that makes you feel to burn the letters."

"Free."

Hanna smiles. "What made you decide to burn them?"

"Well, I couldn't tell if I was living in a dream or nightmare all this time. I was looking at my life but floating above it. I thought that holding on to the letters would ground me, but instead, it chained me to the ground. My neighbor gave me a date rape drug, so I could deal with talking with Devan, and I think we had sex.

"June, let me try to understand what you are saying. Are you saying your neighbor date raped you?"

"No, she thinks Devan is a demon and takes roofees to help her deal with seeing demons."

Hanna takes a deep breath. "So, you aren't sure if you had sex with Devan. Have you asked him?"

"He won't return my calls."

"June, I don't know a lot about the date rape drug, but I do know that it can cause you to blackout. Do you feel responsible for something you did when you blacked out?"

"I should have said no."

"When you were blacked out?"

"No, I should have said no to seeing Devan."

"June, you have been in difficult relationships. I can understand wanting that closure."

June takes a deep breath. "Jacob found out somehow."

"Where is Jacob?"

"Still in Afghanistan, I think. I keep writing him but haven't gotten a response."

"I am really sorry to hear that, June. "

"June, did it occur to you that Devan wanted revenge?"

"No, I haven't thought about that. Oh my God, I told Jacob it was true."

"June, I wanted to bring this up in your last session. Have you ever heard of Post-Traumatic Stress Disorder or PTSD?"

"Yeah, but I wasn't in the war."

"You don't have to be in a war to have a traumatic experience. Your rape could cause PTSD."

A diagnosis? thinks June hopefully.

She stares at the moving trees glistening with drops of rain. Hanna describes all her symptoms of nightmares, negative behavior, flashbacks of her rape, haunting reminders, and the inability to sustain a relationship or job.

"What can I take for it?" she asks.

"June, there is no medication, but I am not surprised that you said you had a positive reaction to MDMA."

"Really? Molly helps the PT thing?"

"There is a lot of research that indicates it does, IN THERAPY."

June laughs. "It works really well for other things too."

"Let's go forward from here. I need your commitment that you will continue therapy though."

"I will. I want to show Jacob I am not crazy."

"June, you aren't crazy. You have suffered the same level of trauma as someone with a physical injury. You wouldn't call someone crazy that broke their arm, would you?"

"No."

June writes Jacob one last letter telling him about therapy, the possible motive of revenge on Devan's part but mostly apologizing for putting herself in a situation to be compromised. She says that she will return his ring to his apartment in a few weeks and that his plants have died, so she will get him a gift card to Home Depot for new ones. She also sent him a photo of her standing beside their twisted tree. She has a feeling he won't read her letter, so on the outside, she writes: I love you, Jay. She walks down to mail the letter, but Amira blocks the door.

"Hey, Amira," June smiles. "Can I go into the mailroom?" She reaches for the doorknob.

"No!" barks Amira. "The new mail guy is a demon too."

June looks through the window and sees an ordinary human man standing in a mail uniform. "Ok, Amira. I see him, he looks horrific."

Amira looks shocked, "You can see his horns and those gill-looking holes on the sides of his face?"

"Yes, I see him. Could you do me a favor, Amira?" She nods.

"Could you put this letter in the outgoing mailbox when he leaves? I am scared to go in there." June pats her on the back and then kisses her on the cheek. She has tried several times to get Amira to see Hanna, but she runs away each time, screaming that she isn't crazy.

Amira takes the letter and sees the words: I love you, Jay on the back. "Stay with him. He isn't a demon," says Amira.

"I know," says June softly.

June's next stop is the library. She looks up Rimini, Italy. She imagines herself standing on the Tiberius Bridge, looking down at its arches reflecting off the flat surface of the water. She will wear a red dress and walk-through Old Town to find a coffee shop and learn to speak Italian. She checks out four books on Italian for Beginners and Italian Grammar. She has saved up enough money for a plane ticket, and she figures she will have enough to rent a room for a few weeks in a month or so.

.....- ..--- ---..

"Colonel, I have a love letter for you," says the mail guy emphasizing the word love. He holds the letter up so that Jacob can see the, *"I love you, Jay,"* that is written on the back of the envelope. Jacob bites the inside of his jaw as his eyes begin to sting. He carefully takes the envelope from the mail guy's hand and puts it in his cargo pocket. "Private, your commentary about my mail is not required or appropriate. Is that understood?"

"Yes, Sir."

Jacob walks toward the fire pits with his hand on June's letter, but her words sear into his skin as if they have some magical power. He can't will himself to burn it. He walks uncomfortably to his tent and slowly opens the letter. He skims the words and smiles when he reads that she is going to therapy. He wonders why she is still writing to him. He hasn't responded to her in a year. He looks at the photo of her standing beside their tree. She looks amazing. Her hair is long and dark brown, which brings out her golden-brown eyes. She is wearing a red dress, but he can see that she is hiding her running shoes partially behind the tree.

He remembers their first run in Point Defiance Park. He had fallen behind several times to tie his perfectly laced shoe, so that he could look at her hair bouncing with each step. Her body was perfectly shaped, and her legs were strong. He realized that was the day he had fallen in love with her.

He wipes his eyes with his sleeve and places the letter underneath his pillow. His eyes are closed as he walks out of the tent and straight into Meyers.

"Excuse me, Sir!" says Meyers.

"Captain Meyers, what are you doing outside my quarters?" barks Jacob.

"Lieutenant Colonel Austin asked me to come to get you. He's waiting for you in Operations."

"Thank you, Captain. I will head right over there."

Meyers waits for Jacob to leave, then walks into the officer's tent.

"Hey Mike," says Jacob, walking up to Lieutenant Austin.

"Hey Jacob," I just wanted to give you the in, and outgoing soldiers list for review. We are losing Meyers in two weeks. We will need to pull another pilot down here to replace him.

"CW4 Alex Brown, says Jacob without hesitation. "Who did you say is leaving in two weeks?"

"Captain Meyers." I guess his mother died, so he requested an emergency leave. We would have transitioned him sooner, but you know how complex logistics are for personnel."

Jacob can't swallow. He stumbles over his words as he grasps tightly to the papers Mike has just handed him.

"Are you ok, Jacob?"

He wasn't.

"I need you to get Alex Brown here now," he says, clutching his chest. I will lie down for about an hour, but let me know when he arrives."

"Yes, Sir. Should I have a medic come to check on you?"

"No, I am fine. Just get Alex."

"On it, Sir."

Jacob lifts his pillow to read the letter from June again, and it's gone. He looks under the cot, tears through the neatly folded blankets, and turns the cot upside down. Terror collapses around him: Meyers!

He runs back to Ops, grabs the Sat Phone, and dials June's number.

June has just come in from a Yoga class and hears the phone ringing as she is about to step into the shower. She pauses, looks at the phone, and then at the shower. She chooses the shower.

"This is June; I'm probably out for a run, so leave your digits, and I will get back to you."

"June, this is Jacob. I will call you back in one hour; it is 8:03 pm your time. I will call you at exactly 9:03 pm. Please, please pick up."

June gets a bottle of water out of the refrigerator and turns on the radio when she remembers the phone ringing earlier. She didn't recognize the number, so she laid the phone back down, just as it rang again. "Hey, Pippa!"

"Would you want to go have a drink with me?"

"I just got back from yoga. I think I am just going to bed early."

"Please, June, I need to talk to you."

June looked at the clock; it is 8:45. "Ok, I can meet you in fifteen at the dive bar down the street. You know the one with the great cheap cheese pizza?"

"Sure, my treat," says Pippa.

"Wow, big spender. It is only three bucks."

"Well, it's three bucks closer to getting to Italy, isn't it?"

"Right! Right! I will see you there."

June throws on a dress and some rain boots and runs out the door without her phone.

At 9:01 June's time, Jacob dials her number. *"This is June. I'm probably out for a run, so leave your digits, and I will get back to you."*

Where the hell is she at 9 pm on a Wednesday night? He thinks as he looks at his watch and calculates the time difference. "June, this is Jacob again. I really need to talk to you, and I don't want to leave this on a voice mail. I will try you again in two hours. That is midnight your time."

....- ..--- ---..

Alex runs over to the officer's tent when he lands. "What the hell, Jay?" I was doing a training exercise. "Are you ok? You don't look ok. Should I get a medic?"

"I'm fine!" He hands Alex Meyers' orders to return to Fort Lewis.

"Fuck!" says Alex holding the paper to his head. He looks around as if he is searching for something. "What are we going to do?"

Jacob shakes his head in a daze. "I can't reach her," he says, slumping to his knees. "She won't answer my calls."

"Should I call her?" asks Alex sympathetically.

Jacob hands him the Sat Phone.

"It's her voicemail," he looks at his watch. It was 11 pm her time. "Did you try Pippa?"

Jacob looks up. "I don't have her number." Alex has the number of all of June's friends and her family. He scrolls through his phone and finds the number for Pippa that is coded as: *Barracks P Commander.*

"Ok, I am not buying any of your shit, so stop calling me," answers Pippa.

"Hey Pippa, it's Alex. Is June with you?"

Pippa covers the phone and looks a June, who has a mouthful of pizza. She mouths silently, *It's Alex.*

June spits out the pizza in her hand and shakes her head no.

"Pippa, Jacob is trying to reach June. Do you know where she is?"

Pippa mouths, *He's with Jacob.*

June snatches the phone from Pippa's hand.

"Alex? Is Jacob ok?"

"Hold on. He's right here."

June stands up and then sits down. She looks down at how she is dressed as if it matters. She straightens her dress and runs her fingers through her hair.

"Jay-bee?"

She can't breathe. She throws down the phone and runs to the bathroom.

"Hey, this is Pippa. June is pretty upset."

"Hi, Pippa. I know. I am really sorry. I should have called her sooner."

"Yeah, asshole, like maybe a year ago."

"Pippa, it is vital I speak with June. Could you please try to get her back to the phone?

"Oh, so you string her out for a year without a letter or phone call, and now, tonight, you call out of the blue, screw you."

"Pippa, please!"

Pippa walks to the bathroom and holds the phone over the stall for June. "He says it's vital, whatever the hell that means."

June holds the phone to her ear but doesn't speak.

Jacob can hear her sobbing. Tears fill his eyes, and he covers his face. Alex motions that he will be outside. He blocks the door and refuses to allow anyone in.

"June, I am so sorry. I am such an ass for not calling you sooner."

"What do you want?"

He wants to ask her a thousand questions but needs to talk to her about Meyers. "June, I don't have long that I can talk, but I want to tell you that Meyers is here, and he's being sent back to Fort Lewis."

"He's there? How do you know?"

"He's under my command."

"Then stop him from coming here!"

"June, I can't. He's going on emergency leave. Babe, there is more."

"What? You gave him my address and phone number?"

It isn't far from the truth. If he hadn't transferred Meyers to Operations, he would have never had access to June's letter. "June, I think he does have your address. One of the letters you sent me is missing."

June drops the phone to her stomach. Her response is not what he anticipates. "You read my letters? Why didn't you write me back?"

"June, did you hear what I said about Meyers?"

"You didn't answer my question, Jay."

"I only read one, the last one, the one that is missing. I am glad you went back to see Hanna."

"I don't care about Meyers. He won't get past Amira."

He laughs a little.

"June, listen to me. Don't go out alone."

"Jacob, it's my rape. Neither you nor Alex gets to tell me how to handle it."

"I just want you to be safe, June."

"Then stop him from coming here!"

"I can't."

"I will leave all your stuff at your condo before I go to Italy."

"Italy?"

Before he can repeat her name, she hangs up.

....⁻ ..⁻⁻⁻ ⁻⁻⁻..

Alex sees Julian walking by the enlisted tent, and he motions him over. "You are a little too heavy on the collar to be pulling guard duty on the officer's tent, aren't you?" Julian jokes.

Alex doesn't respond. He hands Julian Meyer's orders to go to Fort Lewis.

Julian looks into the distance as the sand swirls into a small funnel cloud behind a passing vehicle.

"What are you doing up this way?" asks Alex noting his lack of concern for June.

"I gotta date," he whispers.

"Julian, you know they are on a witch hunt for the 'gay predator', don't you?"

"How many gay rapists do you know?" he states.

"Julian, these white fucks don't care. They need a pig to roast."

He leans into Alex. "You are right! I have to run by the medic station to see a friend but meet me in the enlisted tent in forty-five minutes."

"Why?"

"Be there and bring shithead."

Alex knows he is talking about Jacob.

The base is quiet this time of day. Most of the enlisted soldiers are out on missions or working around the base. Julian runs into the medic station and then to the pilot's tent. It is empty. He wanders around the base until he sees Meyers talking to a female soldier. He walks by, bumping his arm and slipping a piece of paper into his pocket.

Alex looks at his watch and then walks into the tent where Jacob sits with his head in his hands. Jacob didn't need to tell him how the conversation had gone, or what June's response was to his news about Meyers. He asks the question that lingers in the air. "Do you still love her?"

He nods.

"Then don't let her go. I live with that mistake every day. It's not something I am proud of," says Alex.

"I think she's already gone."

"You really don't know June, do you? She loves for life and imprints her spirit on everyone she encounters. You will never get over her. I can promise you that."

"She asks me to stop Meyers. What am I supposed to do?"

"Stop Meyers."

"Alex, how?"

"The hell if I know, but we have a week to figure it out."

Thirty-One

The Cost of Freedom

June has enough money for her plane ticket and three-week vacation in Italy. She takes the box of cash that she has been hiding in her air conditioner vent and places it on her bed. She has earned most of the money in tips from the coffee shop.

Her mom and sister contributed the rest as a 30th birthday gift.

She walks into the travel agency and places the box on the counter. "I want a ticket to Rome, Italy," she says.

The lady looks strangely at the box. "What is this?"

June proudly lifts the lid of the box. "Money for my ticket."

"Ma'am," the lady looks around nervously. "We don't take cash, only credit cards."

June grabs the box and holds it close to her chest. She is supposed to leave in three days. She will not qualify for a credit card now that she has quit her job. June walks home in tears. She has finally found the courage to do something on her own, and she feels like it is being taken from her.

She calls Pippa. "I can't go to Italy."

"Why JB?"

"They need a credit card for my ticket."

Pippa pauses. "June, do you still have Jacob's card?"

"That is stealing, Pippa!"

"No, it isn't. Just leave the money at his condo and pay for the ticket with his card. It has your name on it, doesn't it?"

"Yes."

....⁻ ..⁻⁻⁻ ⁻⁻⁻..

Alex looks at his watch again. Fifty minutes have passed. He grabs Jacob's arm and lifts him up. They run over to the enlisted tent and fling open the curtain. Julian is lying face down, with his pants around his ankles. Alex and Jacob run over to him, and Alex notices a handkerchief in his hand. He smells it, and it makes him dizzy. He tosses it aside and yells for Jacob to call a medic. Julian is breathing, but there is blood around his waist and legs.

Jacob waits outside the medic's station for a report. As soon as the doctor hands him the report, he sends it to the MP's who arrest Meyers. Arthur contested the arrest based on his suspicion that Julian is gay, but it was Jacob's decision whether or not to prosecute. Still the rumors that circulate, facilitate orders for Jacob to return to Fort Lewis.

....⁻ ..⁻⁻⁻ ⁻⁻⁻..

June walks into Jacob's condo with tears in her eyes. She has the box of cash underneath her arm, which she gently places on the kitchen counter. She traces the edges of the counter to the spot where Jacob had lifted her to kiss her after one of their runs.

There is a pile of mail on his floor that has been shoved through the door slot. She sorts out the junk from the essential-looking stuff and makes three piles with sticky notes that read: Wasn't sure if this was junk, looks like bank stuff, and this looks personal. In the personal pile, she noticed eight letters from Tara. She wants to throw them away but puts them in her purse instead.

She places the keys to the Mustang by the letters with a note about the money, which she hides in the freezer. She puts her ring on her toothbrush in the bathroom and then brushes her teeth with his. She backs out of the hallway slowly, locking the door. She looks at his keys and removes the key he said is to his condo in Rimini. She drops the rest of the keys through the mail slot. A cab picks her up downstairs to take her to the airport. She asks the cab driver to stop by the post office, where she mails all Tara's letters to Jacob.

June's flight attendants aren't as nice as Molly. They look exhausted and rarely smile. She tries to say hi to a lady named Emma in the galley, but she pulls the curtain closed in June's face and says she isn't allowed back there.

....- ..--- ---..

Jacob hasn't told June he is coming home. He knows there will be a long road back to her heart. As soon as he lands stateside, his phone is flooded with missed calls and text messages. There are no messages from June, but several from his bank.

"Customer Service."

"Yes, this is Jacob Edwards, I got several calls from you yesterday about my account. I just got back to the States."

"Yes, Mr. Edwards. Thanks for verifying your information on our automated system. We need to verify some recent purchases on a card assigned to June Brown."

Jacob is taken back that she had used his card. "Sure!"

"We have a purchase of $1323.22 from *You Book It* travel agency in Portland, Oregon, and a $30 charge from Yellow Cab."

Jacob feels too guilty to contest the charges but is shocked that June would use the card after cutting it up five times. "Yes, Ma'am, those charges are ok, but do you have the number of the travel agency?"

....- ..--- ---..

Jacob drops his bags by the door and heads for his favorite recliner. He had brought it from his house with Tara even though it didn't match any of his new furniture. He sits in silence, staring at the photos of June on his bookshelf. He feels her there; he looks around as if he expects June to be hiding somewhere.

He notices the mail stacked in perfect piles with pink sticky notes on each bank. He traces her writing with his finger. He is starved to find more clues about her presence there. He looks in the recycling and finds all the mail she considered trash. He laughs that she had thrown away all the AARP advertisements. He opens the refrigerator hoping for a bottle of water, and it is full of water and Bud Light. He remembers her calling it horse-piss the first time she tasted it, but she drank it with him anyway. He takes a beer and walks toward the bathroom. The keys to her car are on the side table, with a note: Thanks. I loved it. J~

Jacob can hear Alex's words; she *loves for life*. He knows that the imprint she has made on Julian compelled him to sacrifice his own body for hers, yet he has abandoned her because she made a mistake. He can't look at himself in the mirror so he focuses on his toothbrush. It is still damp. *She must have used it. She has a toothbrush at my house. Why would she use mine?*

He looks in the trash and the medicine cabinet for her toothbrush. He finds it aligned perfectly with his toothpaste on the side table he used to hold his towels. On the neck of her toothbrush is her ring, and beside it is a note. *Look in the freezer.* He spins her ring around the toothbrush and then removes it, and tries to place it on his pinky. It is too small.

There is a shoebox in the freezer. It contains $1353.22. All the money she had spent on his card. He throws the box and money across the room and falls to his knees.

....- ..--- ---..

June lands in Rome and takes the metro to Roma Termini. She has carefully planned her trip to the finest details, but when she tries to take the train to her hotel, she sees a sign that the train is *"chiuso."* She looks it up; it means closed. It is a STRIKE. She frantically looks through her book of common Italian phrases, but nothing talks about the trains being on strike.

She waits in line at the Termini for a cab driver that speaks English, waving the person behind her to the cab when she gets a negative response to *Tu parla Inglese?* After two hours, she jumps into the cab and points to the address in her itinerary. "Si Bella!" the cab driver says. June looks up the word Bella, which means beautiful. She looks in the review mirror and suddenly flashes back to when she arrived at Fort Hood. *I wasn't Si Bella that day,* she remembers.

She finds her hotel with the help of a four-year-old little boy and collapses on the bed.

....⁻ ..⁻⁻⁻ ⁻⁻⁻..

Alex stays by Julian's bed until he wakes up. "What the hell were you thinking?" he says as soon as Julian's eyes open.

Julian smiles. "It must have worked," he touts.

Alex shakes his head and smiles. "His ass will be in Leavenworth for quite a while. They charged him with fifteen counts. And, you got the Meritorious Service Medal, courtesy of Colonel Edwards."

"Have you told June he's gone?"

"Meyers or Edwards?"

"Child, you do need help, Meyers!"

"I tried to call her, but she isn't answering. Jacob left two days ago. I am sure he will tell her."

Julian lifts his hand. I had to cut myself. "That bitch was too tiny to make me bleed, so I improvised."

Alex shook his head. "I think you might love her more than I do."

"Alex, do you still love June?"

He turns away.

"Alex, she loves you too. You guys just got twisted."

"How do I give her to my best friend?"

"You realize she isn't yours to give?"

He doesn't.

....⁻ ..⁻⁻⁻ ⁻⁻⁻..

Jacob doesn't know how to wake up in his bed. He had become acclimated to the extreme heat and frigid cold of the desert, the routine of his daily tasks, and the stress of the authority he possessed. Now alone, drowning in silence, he realizes he has made a horrible miscalculation. He decides to call Hanna to see if she will speak with him.

"Hi, Hanna, this is Jacob Edwards. I believe you were treating my girlfriend June Brown."

"Ok, let me stop you there. It is a conflict of interest and a breach of confidentiality for me to speak to you about June."

"I understand that. I am just hoping I could talk to you about some things."

"I don't feel comfortable counseling you, Jacob, but I could refer you to a colleague."

"She went to Italy. I just got back from Afghanistan, and I can't even apologize to her for how stupid I have been."

"Again, Jacob. I am sorry, but I can't speak to you in a professional capacity."

Jacob never misses any details. "What about in a personal capacity?"

"Have you ever visited Italy? I heard Rimini was nice this time of year."

"Thank you, Hanna."

Jacob looks for his keys to the apartment in Rimini. They are missing. He calls Tara to see if she still has kept her keys.

"Hello, Tara. I hope you are doing well."

"Did you get my letters?"

"Tara, I just walked in the door last night. I've been gone for over two years to Afghanistan."

"Why didn't you tell me?"

"We aren't exactly friendly that way, are we?"

She doesn't say anything.

"Tara, do you still have the keys to our place in Rimini?"

"Yeah."

"Can I get a copy of yours? I misplaced mine."

"Are you going to Italy?"

"Maybe. I just want to check on the place if I make it over there."

"Just call the maintenance guy. He will check on it."

"Tara, can I get a copy of the keys?"

"Did you read my letters?"

"Tara, the keys?"

"Just get the maintenance guy to let you in, Jay."

Before he can respond, she hangs up, so he looks on the counter for letters from Tara and then looks in the recycling. *Had June thrown Tara's letters away?* He wonders. Maybe she still loves him. He imagines her ripping Tara's letters into small pieces.

....- ..--- ---..

Alex is excited to get his orders back home to California. He reaches for the phone to call Dana but can't dial the number.

"Hello?"

"Hi, Darlene, this is Alex."

Darlene takes a deep breath. "Hi Alex, what do you want?"

"Dee, I know you are still pissed at me."

She interrupts. "Pissed? I hate you for what you did to my sister."

"I get it, but could you hear me out for one second?"

She takes a deep breath and listens.

"I swear to God, Alex this is the last time."

....- ..--- ---..

June wakes up starving, so she wanders out of her hotel to a bustling street. The energy in Rome is riveting. She walks to a local pizza place, practicing her best Italian phrases repeatedly in her head. She sits at a table covered in red and white checkers. *Like in Paris,* she thinks. The waiter comes over and stands beside her. "Vino rosso della casa per favore?"

"Which red wine would you like, ma'am?"

"Della Casa," she says.

"They are all considered house wine, ma'am."

"Parlo un po' Italiano," she says hopefully.

"We mostly speak English here in Roma," he states.

"Vorrei vedere il menu?"

"Yes, I will bring you a menu."

She looks at the menu and notices spaghetti, but nothing else looks familiar. She points and asks Va bene?" She hopes it's the correct phrase.

"Yeah, it's ok."

The spaghetti brings her taste buds alive for the first time. The pasta is soft but not squishy, and the sauce tastes like tomatoes and garlic have made love to each other. She eats slowly and sips her wine like it is the first and last glass she will ever drink. The cool air wafts through the open door, and she can hear the sound of the city streets as they dance around her with an outreached hand.

....⁻ ..⁻⁻⁻ ⁻⁻⁻..

Jacob walks out of his Commander's office and tosses the papers that he is holding into the trash. He jumps into his Jeep and races down the street as "What Hurts the Most," by Rascal Flatts blares into the cool air. He dials Pippa's number.

"This is Pip!"

"Hey Pippa, this is Jacob."

"And?"

"Pippa, I need to find out where June is."

"She's gone."

"I know she is in Italy. I want to find her. Pippa, I need to find her."

"Why?"

"I screwed up. I know I screwed up. I got scared that she still loved Devan."

"You mean Alex?"

Jacob drops the phone. It weighs a thousand pounds as he pulls it back to his ear. "Does she still love Alex?"

"She will always love Alex."

His eyes sting, and he feels his throat collapse. "Can you please tell me where she is?"

"Ok, but this is the last time."

"Pippa, can you tell her to use the credit card I gave her?"

"Why?"

"So, I can find her."

"Wow, that is smart!" Pippa perks. "Hey, Jay, I think Alex is going to Italy."

"What? Why?"

"Uh, for June. Dee called me. She told Alex that June is in Rome."

"When?"

"Three days ago."

The air is heavy with the sounds of both of them breathing.

"Jacob, Alex always fights for her. If you want to be with her, you will have to man up and fight for her too."

Man up? "I have just been trying to respect her decisions, Pippa. It doesn't mean I am not a man."

"Well, let me explain a few things to you, Jacob..."

Thirty-Two

Bacio

June spends the next week immersed in everything Italian. She even finds a few places that allow her to practice her Italian phrases. She wanders around the city, absorbing the culture that seeps up from the cobblestone streets, floats in the aroma of the coffee, and kisses her lips every time she drinks limoncello. She takes notes about everything she experiences and writes in her journal about Jacob, Alex, and Devan, never crossing their names or thoughts of them on the same pages. She plans to go to Rimini in three days and visit Jacob's condo. It is her way of saying goodbye to what could have been.

As she walks around the outer walls of the Vatican, she begins to have déjà vu. She envisions this child running into the road, and when she rounds a corner where the sidewalk ends, she sees a mother pulling her children back from the street. She follows the Vatican wall around and sees a beautiful golden dome that reflects light on the homes on a nearby hill. She imagines this is what a street in heaven must look like.

She follows the road to a key-shaped courtyard full of hundreds of people. She has never seen anything this big, and all for some religious guy who lives there. *They must really love him,* she thinks.

The next day she takes the train to the Coliseum. She can't believe that they let you walk up and touch it. She watches all the couples taking photos and feels sad that she won't have any photos of her trip. She walks through the Coliseum in awe. *How could so many people gather in one space to watch other people die?* She decides that even if she had a camera, she wouldn't want a photo there, where death and blood had soaked into the ground so many times.

She feels the coolness in the air and heads back to her hotel. She doesn't feel comfortable being out at night alone. She stops by the local Pizza place again for a glass of wine.

"Ciao, Bella!"

"Ciao, Antonio," says June smiling.

"Vino rosso della casa per favore?"

"Si! Si!"

She sips the wine and scrunches her nose.

Antonio laughs, "You don't like it?"

"Molto dolce."

"You don't like sweet wine?"

"No."

"Prova questo," he hands her a new glass of wine. "Bene?"

"Cosi-Cosi."

"Wow, Miss June you are becoming Italian."

"My Italian is better?" she perks.

"No, that is still bad. You are becoming picky about your wine. That makes you Italian."

June laughs and finds a corner table to write in her journal. She flips to the section on Jacob and reads about the night they went dancing before he left for Afghanistan. She could still taste the Bud Light on his lips when he pressed her up against the Jeep. The thought of him still arouses her. She closes her eyes and sips her wine, thinking about his touch.

"Mira?"

June spits her wine across the table, soiling the pages of her journal. She slams the book closed and frantically stuffs it into her bag. "Alex, what are you doing here? How did you find me?"

"The lady at the hotel said you come here every night."

June looks over at Antonio, who is attentive to the conversation. "Bella? Stai bene?"

"Sì, lei sta bene," says Alex sternly.

Antonio walks over and offers a hand to June.

"It's ok. I know him," she pouts.

Alex sits in front of June. Her dark brown hair is braided on both sides; she has a tiny silver nose ring and a tattoo on her right arm. *It looks like butterflies on acid*, he thinks. He searches for that child-like part of her that he was so connected to, but it isn't there.

"Are you going to tell me why you followed me to Italy?"

"June, I need to know if there is a chance to get back to us."

"Well, that is easy. No!"

"June, stop. Can we talk? I haven't even been home yet. I flew straight here."

Her face softens, and she looks at him. He does have a little sand left in his hair. "What are you saying?"

"I still love you."

"Those are words, Alex. Are you planning on leaving Dana?"

"Would I fly all the way to Italy if I didn't want to be with you?"

"Hmm? You didn't answer my question."

"June, how can I answer that unless I know how you feel?"

"It shouldn't matter how I feel, Alex. You either love your wife enough to be with her, or you don't."

"Can I take you for gelato tomorrow?"

"I am leaving tomorrow for Rimini."

"Jacob?"

"No! Not Jacob, he's still in Afghanistan."

"June, he was sent back to Fort Lewis after Meyers was arrested."

"What?"

"Meyers––"

June puts up her hand. "I don't care about that. When did Jacob get back?"

"Do you love Jacob?"

"I did."

Alex stands up. "June, please think about us and what we have. I have never loved anyone as much as I love you. I will be here in the hotel for another week, and then I have to leave."

She brushes past him, but touching his skin is like a drug that penetrates quickly. She turns him around and looks into his eyes. "Bacio?"

He lifts her chin and kisses her softly. "Mi mancherà tu"

"I will miss you too."

Thirty-Three

Misconnections

June boards the train for Rimini and heads straight to the concession's car. They are giving out samples of limoncello. "No, grazie," June says with a Cheshire smile. Then when the man turns to help someone else, June leans over the counter and slides an empty glass into her bag.

She has purchased two tickets for the trip to Rimini, but as the train pulls away, she tosses her bag in the adjoining seat. She looks around cautiously, then opens her bottle of limoncello and pours some into her glass. She has found a bottle for 4 euros at the grocery store.

She gazes out the window with teary eyes and watches the city turn into meadows of grass. Alex said he would miss her, but he didn't come to the train station. She hasn't talked to him in years, and now he wants to be back in her life. She wonders what inspired his change of heart. She thinks back about all their times together and tries to connect to the part of herself that loved him. She is thirty minutes outside of Bologna when she falls asleep. The bottle of limoncello is empty.

....⁻ ..⁻⁻⁻ ⁻⁻⁻..

Jacob lands in Milan early. He stands in line to rent a car looking at his watch. He can make the 7:10 train. He hates the train, but it is a faster route to Rimini. He sits staring out the window, watching as the buildings pass him in a blur. The past few years had passed with no time to think about June or their situation. He was focused on the mission and Meyers when he should have been focused on June. He stares at the empty seat beside him and gains all the clarity he needs.

The train slows and stammers to a stop in Bologna, interrupting his focus. He looks at the sign of the train on the next track. It is going north. He remembers riding that train to Padova with Tara. She wanted to see the town that inspired Shakespeare's play.

He has always wanted to visit Verona but never did anything spontaneous. There is something alluring about the train, though. He has an urge just to go. Instead, he stays focused on his mission, grabs his bag, and steps off the train to the smell of fresh Italian coffee.

He and Tara had stopped at this station several times on their way to Rimini. He loves coffee and cannoli. He sits with a mouthful of cannoli as he watches the train slowly move forward to Padova. He thinks again of just jumping on the train to visit Rovigo and the park by the Torre Donà. Every town in Italy is full of great war history, and he feels a connection to those places.

Jacob takes this opportunity to call Pippa to see if June has used the credit card he gave her.

"Dude, it's like. I don't know what time it is, but it's late or early. The sun isn't out yet."

"Pippa, have you heard from June?"

"No, but she called Dee from Rome."

"Pippa? She's in Rome?"

"Didn't I tell you that?"

"You said Rimini."

"Yeah, I think she is going there too. Jacob, she thinks you are still in Afghanistan. She isn't going there to see you."

"Why is she going to Rome?"

"It's a free country. Italy is a free country, right? Any-who, she said you promised to take her there, and since you dumped her, she was taking herself there."

"Pippa, you told me to go to Rimini."

"Yeah, I had just seen that Serendipity movie. Just follow your gut."

"What movie? Never mind. Please let me know if she uses the card. You can call the condo collect."

"Dude, I just got a text from Dee. Doesn't anyone flipping sleep?"

"What does it say?"

"*Alex is in Rome waiting for June to return from Rimini.*" "There you go! Rimini. I told you."

"Thanks, Pippa. My train is here. Call me!"

....- ..--- ---..

June wakes abruptly as a man in a black uniform taps the seat in front of her. "Biglietto?"

June searches her memory for that word.

"Biglietto?" He clicks the ticket puncher in his hand.

"Oh, hold on. Minuto." She searches her bag and hands him her ticket.

"No, No. Padova."

"Non capisco," says June. "Rimini."

He holds his hand and speaks fast to a lady across the aisle.

"Look, dear, this train is going to Padova. Do you have your ticket?"

"I am going to Rimini," says June with tears in her eyes.

"You have to change trains in Bologna for Rimini, dear. I will ask him if you can buy the ticket now to Padova. You will have to repurchase new tickets to Rimini from there."

June covers her face.

"It's 45 euros, dear."

June tries to hand the man the money.

"No, No. Carta di Credito." The man holds out his hand.

She nervously shuffles through her bag and hands him Jacob's credit card. She closes her eyes, waiting for it to decline.

"Grazie!" He hands her the ticket.

She looks at the lady. "Grazie."

"Dear, it isn't safe to drink on the train." She points at June's empty limoncello bottle that has fallen out of her bag.

June goes to the concession car, gets a coffee, and waits there, out of the glare of judgment, until the train slows near Padova.

....- ..--- ---..

It has been ten years since Jacob has been to the condo in Rimini. He would have sold it, but Tara wanted to keep it. He has called ahead to have the furniture uncovered and the refrigerator stocked with Peroni. He asks the doorman to allow anyone who comes by access to the condo, even if they don't have a key.

He pushes the door; it is unlocked. Jacob walks, hopefully into the living area looking for June. He looks around and sees a tattered envelope on the counter, and when he opens the refrigerator, it is filled with Bud Light. He looks around, anticipating June's voice, but the apartment is empty. He opens the envelope that has no return address. It is Tara's letters. He tosses them to the side and runs out to the terrace. He doesn't see her by the pool. *Maybe she is at the beach?* he thinks.

....- ..--- ---..

June hops off the train in Padova with her large suitcase. She drags it across the tracks to a small café and plops down on a barstool. The next train back to Rimini isn't for six hours.

She orders a coffee and pastry but doesn't even try to ask for it in Italian. She is still tipsy from the limoncello, so she slowly sips the coffee and watches people bustling through the train station.

She has a sense of peace because she doesn't understand the Italian conversations around her. Weirdly, as she sits in her thoughts, she doesn't think of Alex or Jacob. She focuses on a tall and attractive man waving his arms as he talks to a woman near the train. He looks back over his shoulder and waves at June. She looks behind her, but no one is there. Why *would he be waving at me?* June can tell he is brushing the woman off by the gestures he is making. *It's funny how dramatic they are.* She notices that the man is running toward her. He plops down in the chair next to her.

"Ciao, Bella." He leans over and kisses both her cheeks.

June stares at him in delight. She has no idea what is going on.

"English?" she asks.

"Si, yes." He leans close to her ear and watches as the woman he was talking to walks away.

June looks at him with her head tilted to the side. "What is going on?"

"I needed to get away from la donna."

"Who is Donna?" June looks at him confused.

"Scusi, the woman."

"She's a friend of my wife's."

"Oh, you are married?" June says, a little shocked.

"Si, No, well it is; how do you say?" "Complicato."

"Yes, I know, complicated."

"So, Bella. Why are you so sad?"

"It's complicato too."

"I have the times, uh *the time*."

"I really have to get to Rimini, so I am just waiting for the train."

"But you just got to Padova. Let me show you around, and then we can go back to my place and make love."

June smiles at his boldness. She has never met a man so forward with his thoughts. She stands up to leave.

"Look, the Universe has brought you to Padova. Stay a few days to see if you love it. I can get you a room at the Inn. I will get you settled in, and then come back for you for our dinner tonight."

June looks down at her feet, sways back and forth, and says "yes," softly. June takes his hand and follows him to an Inn, by a big church. She drops off her bag and then hops into the passenger seat of his car. He shows her most of the city, as she tells him all about her life, the rape, and even about Ballentine. She feels free not to know, or be accountable for, what he thinks about her.

He drives her to his apartment and parks in a small garage area. They sit in his garage, and June looks at his profile. He has a beautiful olive skin tone and very full lips. For a moment, she is tempted to lean over and kiss him, but she realizes she doesn't know his name and he hadn't asked for hers.

June follows him into his home as if she knew him. She sits on the couch with her arms crossed, searching the room for clues about this man she just met. There isn't an object out of place, no dust on top of the shelves, no dirty dishes in the sink. *He must have a maid*, she thinks, assumingly.

"What is your name?" inquires June.

"Marcello. You?"

"Juniper," she says without thinking twice about it.

Marcello drops his keys into a small wooden container by the door. "Would you like a drink, Juniper?"

"No. Yes. Hey, I should go."

Marcello looks at Juniper and smiles. "Sure, would you like me to take you back to the Inn?"

That was too easy, she thinks. *Does he not want to spend time with me?*

Juniper stands up and walks to the door. She sees a photo of Marcello with two little babies on the table beside the keys. She picks up the photo. "Are these your daughters?"

Marcello nods.

"What are their names?"

Marcello mumbles something unintelligible as he walks out of the room.

"I'll take that drink," she says, as she gently places the photo back on the table. They sit and drink red wine as they laugh over the stories of their lives. He shares his great love story with his wife and how she left him alone with his daughters. He refuses to divorce her because he believes so strongly in their love. As the evening fades into night, he offers to host her for the evening. He goes into the bathroom for a few moments, then leans around the corner.

"I ran you a bubble bath Juniper," he says, winking. Somehow her name sounds better with an Italian accent. She walks into the bathroom and undresses. She tests the water with her toe. Of course, it is perfect. A glass of red wine sits beside the tub on a small table. The glass sparkles in the candlelit room. She slides into the tub and smiles. How had she gotten to this place with this man? She has felt that she has never done anything brave in her whole life, and now she is in a sexy stranger's bathtub, feeling safer than she ever had in her entire life. A tap on the door interrupts her fantasy of living in Marcello's bathtub forever.

"Please be careful with the glass, my love. It is a very expensive crystal," he whispers through the door.

Juniper looks down at her bubble-covered hands. There is no way she is touching that expensive glass. As she dozes off in the bathtub, Marcello peeks through the door.

"Did you not like the wine?"

"I haven't tried it. My hands are wet."

"Juniper, try it."

She looks at the glass and then covers her face. "I would die if I broke your glass."

Marcello smiles, "Juniper glasses are for drinking, not for sitting on a shelf and being looked at." He kneels by the tub. He slowly lifts the glass to her lips and tilts it forward. He notices that her mouth opens just enough for the glass to touch her bottom lip. She smells lavender before she tastes chocolate and some fruit she can't identify. The wine tastes slightly sparkling and lingers on her tongue. It is the most erotic experience she has ever had. Marcello has kept his promise to make love to her, and he hasn't even touched her sexually.

Juniper spends the next two days learning every detail about Padova, through Marcello's eyes. She can relate to his conflict with the church and God, and she loves that he cares about her opinion, unless it is based on American sensibilities. He hates the way Americans waste their lives on nonsensical things and how they neglect the most important aspects of what living is about.

....⁻ ..⁻⁻⁻ ⁻⁻⁻..

"So, what is wrong with putting sugar in my espresso?"

"Juniper, you drink the coffee to taste the coffee, not overload it with the taste of sugar."

Juniper adds the sugar to her espresso and drinks it quickly. He smiles when he sees her childlike response to his scolding. He understands why she has a trail of American men chasing her to Italy.

Marcello owns a local coffee shop and takes Juniper to it, only after explaining to her that she can't share anything about his life with his employees. They walk into the space, and she falls in love. She would design her own the same way if she had a coffee shop. There are small tables positioned around couches and comfortable chairs, and even a couple of swings attached to the open rafters. Local art hangs on the walls, and a woman plays guitar in the corner. It feels more like Portland than Italy, but that makes her love it even more. They sit on the adjacent swings and hold hands.

"I have to leave soon," she says.

"Why?"

"I still haven't made it to Rimini, and I barely have enough money to make it there and back to Rome."

"Work here. We can work out the details later."

Juniper looks at the women behind the bar and then back at Marcello.

"Si!" she says.

June watches Marcello on their train ride back to his car. She notices everything about him. He touches his bottom lip when he thinks, and he is always kind to older women. She loves the way he dresses, a little younger than his age would dictate. She even thought it was sexy when he smokes. The way he allows the smoke to linger around his lips before he blows it away. They walk into his apartment, and she doesn't speak. She just grabs him and kisses him, backing him up to the bedroom. He moves slowly and feels every moment with her. He kisses her face as he undresses her and slows her movements to allow her to be in the moment too. There isn't anything exotic about their connection, but it is the first time Juniper stays in the moment completely.

....⁻ ..⁻⁻ ⁻⁻..

Jacob hears the phone ring in the condo and runs to answer it. It's Darlene. "Hi Jacob, this is Dee, Juniper's sister."

"Hi," he says nervously.

"Look, I honestly don't think you or Alex or Devan deserve JITTERBUG, but I am more concerned that I haven't heard from her in a few days. Pippa said you are letting her use your bank login. She said June used your credit card on the train to buy a ticket to a town called Padova. There was also a hold on the card for an Inn in the town called Il Giardino Nascosto, but there are no charges."

"I am on it, Darlene. I will take the train to Padova in the morning."

"You mean tonight, right?"

"Yes, ma'am. I will head out tonight."

Jacob arrives in Padova close to 4 pm and starts the investigation. He has years of experience building battle plans and executing strategies, but he isn't sure that June will want to see him. He has already violated her privacy by interfering with the search for Meyers, and he doesn't want to ruin his chances to reconnect with her. But the one thing he knows without a doubt is, that he has no chance with June if he pisses off her sister.

The woman at the Inn doesn't provide a lot of information except for Marcello's name. She knows him well and often spends time at his coffee shop. He gives Jacob the address. He also informs him that she hasn't stayed in the room. Jacob rents a room at the same hotel and plans to visit the café the next day.

....⁻ ..⁻⁻⁻ ⁻⁻⁻..

Juniper is in a daze when Jacob walks into the café. He looks twice before he realizes that she is the barista. A thousand questions run through his mind, but he can't get passed how much she has changed. Her dark hair is in braids, and she has an adorable nose ring. She is wearing an orange-flowered dress with quarter-length sleeves, but he can see that she has a tattoo. He bites his lips in anticipation of what it might be. He is happy to see the child-like version of her has gained quite a bit of sass. She doesn't look up as he whispers his order for a café latte and a cannoli.

He finds a seat in the corner and watches her interact with everyone around her. He sees a tall Italian man with dark hair, brush by her and whispers something in her ear, making her laugh. She turns and touches his nose. Jacob felt uncomfortable, it is like watching her make love to someone. He stands to leave, but she sees him.

"Jay?"

He tries to act casual. "June."

"Juniper," corrects Marcello.

Jacob looks at June but doesn't recognize the woman standing in front of him. She wouldn't allow anyone to call her Juniper, and he had never even considered calling her that. There is part of him that is hurt that it's something she shared with someone else besides him, and the other part is so fucking proud of the progress she has made.

"Can I still call you Jay-bee?"

"That's the first question you want to ask me," she bends forward, laughing.

"Will you marry me?" he jests.

"Better!" She grabs his hand and pulls him over to the counter to meet Marcello.

She acts as if she had just seen Jacob the day before. He is confused but intoxicated by her energy. "Don't speak Italian," she whispers.

"Marcello, this is Jacob." She nibbles on her thumbnail.

"My pleasure," he says, grabbing Juniper by the waist. Marcello follows Jacob's gaze to June's hips, where he has his hands. "I love this one," he says, kissing her cheek.

Jacob rubs his beard. "I do too."

Juniper pulls away from Marcello and points to the corner where Jacob has been sitting. They walk close together, not touching.

"Sit down," she boldly directs.

"You coming here took a lot of courage and arrogance. It almost feels that you and Alex are in a competition, and I am just another one of the prizes."

Jacob holds his face at attention and doesn't react in any way.

"Jay, you do know that Alex is here too?"

"I heard that."

"I saw him in Rome, but I didn't have sex with him."

"June, I don't need to know that."

"I did have sex with Marcello."

"That either." He covers his mouth.

"The thing is, Jacob. You do need to know it. You have judged me for the past few years without considering my side of things. I don't need your permission or Alex's to figure out my life." She hands him 45 euros for the ticket to Padova.

"I'd like to hear what you have figured out," he whispers, sliding his hands over hers.

She pulls her hands back. "I can't leave Alex waiting in Rome. Can I meet you in three days?"

"Sure. Where would you like to meet?"

She doesn't answer. "Did you read Tara's letters?"

He is taken aback by her redirection. "No, I saw that you left them in the condo."

"I've never been to your condo in Rimini. I fell asleep on the train," she laughs.

Who left the letters?

"I came up from Rome and drank too much limoncello. I was supposed to change trains in Bologna, but I fell asleep. That is why I needed to use your credit card to buy a ticket here, so I wasn't arrested." She bends forward, laughing again.

"What day were you in Bologna?"

"Four days ago."

There is no way, he thinks. He laughs, thinking of his conversation with Pippa about following his gut.

"Would you like me to go to Rome with you? I promise I will eat at my favorite restaurant and wait for you while you talk to Alex."

"What is your favorite restaurant?

"Gusto al 28 near the Piazza de Popolo."

"Let's meet there in three days, but go to Rimini and read Tara's letters first."

"June, I don't need to read Tara's letters."

"You do if you want to meet me in three days."

He looks at her with her hands perched on her hips, and her head turned sideways. She is different but still very much the same. "I like the Sass. Can I see your tattoo?" He tugs at her sleeve.

She smacks his hand and then crawls into his lap and grabs his ears, pulling him toward her. She brushes his lips but doesn't kiss him. "I waited for you, so now it's your turn."

He salutes her. "Yes, ma'am, I receive you loud and clear."

"Ok, now go," she says, as she hops off his lap.

"June, I need a minute to sit here. He readjusts his pants. Could you bring me another cup of coffee?

"Sure, how would you like that?" She knew how he liked his coffee.

"Café latte, you just made me one."

"Would you like the next one without the Molly?"

"He looks down at his cup. No, the Molly is fine," he smiles.

Jacob sips his coffee as slowly as possible, taking in every detail of June. He has held her at a distance for years, but he knows well how it felt to hold her close. As he looks at her now, he hates the time he has already wasted. Three days seems like an eternity.

He walks by the counter to say goodbye. "Can we get a photo before I go?"

"You have a camera?" she perks.

"Two. I brought a Polaroid for nostalgia, and I have a Canon. I even brought a small printer so we could see what the photos look like."

She is stuck on "we" as she watches his lips moving, wanting desperately to kiss him.

She has Marcello take two photos, one for each of them. Then she asks to borrow the Polaroid for the three days. He gave it to her with twelve cartridges of film. That is one-hundred-twenty photos. He turns slowly, looking back several times. Marcello shoves Juniper in his direction. "I thought you said you loved him?"

"I do."

He throws up his hands in confusion and disgust.

Jacob disappears around the corner, and June sprints to catch him. She grabs his arm and spins him around. He smiles. She pulls at his shirt until his lips are close to her. Then she kisses him as if her desire can only be fulfilled by the taste of him. He gives in to her completely for the first time.

"You have my trust and my heart, Jay Bee. I hope you can find a way to trust me again with yours."

"I never took back my heart. You gave it back."

He tucks in his lip as his eyes begin to burn. Then to her surprise, like a child, he falls to his knees and sobs, holding her waist so tightly she could barely stand. She runs her fingers through his hair.

"I can't carry your shit, Jay. I only have the strength to carry my own."

He stands up quickly and wipes his nose with his arm. "I don't need you to carry my shit, June. I just need your forgiveness for not standing beside you like I promised."

She wipes the snot from his nose with her thumb and then smears it on her apron. "I really don't know how to hate. Not even Meyers. Maybe that is my problem. You don't need my forgiveness, Jay. My love is the same as it always was."

He knows that means her love is the same for Alex and Devan too. It suddenly makes sense to him why she can't let go. Why she won't hold on to the same kind of hate that he has toward Meyers.

June even sent him love letters from Tara. He knows there is no way he would have ever done that if the situation were reversed. She is one of those rare souls who understand what agape love actually means.

He doesn't know the words to say how he feels, so he kisses her.

She understands completely.

"Go! I have to make coffee for the rest of the day to afford a ticket to Rome."

He knows not to offer to pay for her ticket but wishes he had left a bigger tip.

"I have to be honest. I talked to Pippa and Darlene. That is how I found you."

"Oh, shoot. I need to call Dee. I was so wrapped up in Marcello that I forgot."

He hopes she means that figuratively. "I just don't want there ever to be anything unsaid between us again."

"I will need a pass on that. The last time I was honest with you, it didn't serve me well."

He reaches into his pocket and pulls out a pretend pass. "I hear you and understand completely, but I will change that too."

"I have a huge task for you in the next three days."

"Ok?"

"I need my Jacob. Not Colonel Edwards. I can't deal with Colonel Edwards."

"Ok. I will try my best. I resigned, so that will be great practice."

"What?"

"I resigned before I came here. I didn't know how long it would take for you to forgive me."

"Jay!"

"However, I think Alex has to report back in a week. I know he loves you, June."

She closes her eyes for a long blink and takes a deep breath. "You don't get it, Jay! I will see you in three days."

He scoops her arm. "Explain it to me, please. I am really trying."

"Fight for me, Jay!"

"Pippa said that Alex always fights for you. I thought that was arrogant, but I would fight to the death for you, June."

"I can't kiss you if you are dead," she jests.

"I won't lose the fight."

She smiles. "Don't!"

He kisses her forehead. "I love you so much. I won't lose you."

She turns and skips back into the coffee shop.

He stands in awe, watching her bounce.

....- ..--- ---..

The train ride from Padova to Rimini is torture. He plays over scenarios in his mind. How can he fight for June when the man who wants her is one of his dearest friends and his *battle*? Then he realizes that The Art of War says, the best strategy in battle is distracting the enemy. Jacob catches a cab to his condo and immediately picks up the phone to dial a very familiar number.

"Dana?"

"Yeah, who is this?"

"Jacob Edwards. Please listen and try not to scream at me..."

....- ..--- ---..

Marcello grabs Juniper's hand as they walk out of the coffee shop and lock up. He swings her hand back and forth but doesn't say anything on their walk to the train. Juniper is floating above the ground and doesn't notice Marcello's mood. She feels vibrant and encouraged for the first time in a very long time. She finally returns to Marcello when she sees him push his way by an older woman without excusing himself.

Juniper has never considered how her interactions with others impacted their lives. She has always been surviving the encounters she has created. There is something about Marcello that is different to her. There isn't a judgment or expectation that comes with his relationships. She wants to experience that kind of freedom with him without regret.

She walks over to him and grabs his hand. He kisses hers and says, "Sei più perfetta di quello che riesci a immaginare." He only speaks to her in Italian when they are in bed, so she turns to him as her lover and kisses him in a way that lasts a lifetime. "Vorrei che tu rimanessi qui con me," he says, spinning her around to hold her from behind. She understands that *'con me'* means with me, and gets an ache in her heart. Part of her wants to stay, but she knows from his story that his heart belongs to someone else. His mood softens, and he grabs her waist tightly, holding on to their moment. "Non voglio aver bisogna di te," he whispers, as they step off the train. She has heard him say this before and knows it means something he needs or doesn't need.

They walk quietly around each other as the day falls into the evening. He shows her how to make pasta the Italian way and scolds her about Americans that break the pasta before putting it into the pot. They laugh over dinner and fall asleep on the couch watching Io Sono L'amore.

Juniper wakes up early, but Marcello isn't in bed with her. She isn't even sure how she got into the bed. She walks into the kitchen, and there are several bouquets of flowers on the table and a stack of CDs. She makes a coffee and sits at the table, waiting for him to return. Marcello runs through the door carrying a bag full of wine and cheese. June is intrigued. "Cos'è questo?" she asks in a very Southern accent.

"This! This is all about you!"

Juniper smiles widely and claps her hands.

Juniper, what kind of music do you like? June thinks a few minutes and then says, "I like that Bocelli guy."

"Fuck Bocelli! Who do you like, Juniper? I didn't ask you to pick an Italian artist."

June puts her hands through her hair. "I like Sarah Harmer, Sarah Bettens, Gemma Hayes. She has a great song called: "Chasing Dragons;" it makes me cry every time I hear it. Oh! Oh! I love Kacy Crowley and Tracy Bonham. They are both bad-asses. There is a guy I heard on MySpace, too; Tom McCrae. He has a song: "You Only Disappear"; it kills me. I think I listened to it a thousand times when Jacob stopped writing to me. When I have nightmares, though, Deva Premal's music is the only thing that helps me sleep."

"Music says a lot about who we are and what we feel. It's ok if your musical tastes don't match those of the person you are with."

He has her close her eyes and smells the different flowers in the room to pick her favorite flower; it is the Iris. Her favorite wine is an Allegrini Amarone della Valpolicella Classico DOCG and her favorite cheese is smoked gouda.

When he is finished with his exercise, he kisses her forehead. "I think it is ironic that Alex calls you Mira."

"Why?"

"Mira means to look, but he never has. He has no idea what an amazing woman you are. Devan couldn't find a nickname for you because he could only relate to you in one way. We are always evolving."

June looks up at Marcello. "What about Jacob?"

"I think he is terrified to fall in love with you because he does see how amazing you are. Losing you would devastate anyone." He grabs her and pulls her tightly to his chest.

"You'll never lose me. Amore Mio?" she says, looking up to check that her Italian is correct.

"Ma non ti avrò nemeno," he says as he walks to the balcony to smoke.

....⁻ ..⁻⁻⁻ ⁻⁻⁻..

June catches the 2 pm train to Rome. She changes trains in Bologna, then snuggles in and closes her eyes. As she drifts off into the unprotected state of sleep, she has flashbacks of Meyers. Knowing him in Korea worsens her nightmares. She knows his voice and how his body moves, bringing the horror of his touch to a vibrant forefront. She turns on her CD player and hears the soothing voice of Deva Premal, and drifts back off to a peaceful sleep.

When she wakes up, she thinks about Marcello. She remembers Marcello saying the phrase to her in Italian: *Siamo tutti l'albero contorto;*

we are the twisted tree. She has always claimed the tree for herself, but Marcello made her challenge a lot of her thoughts about things.

The train pulls into Roma Termini, and she hops off and runs the five blocks to where Alex is staying. She is excited to share the new things she has discovered about herself with him. She skips up the steps to his room and notices a note: Hey Babe, I am across the street at the gelato place. They have WiFi. Meet me.

How did he know I was coming? She laughs when she thinks of him leaving a note for her every time, he leaves the room. She straightens her dress and runs her fingers through her hair before she opens the door of the gelato shop. When she swings open the door, Alex is sharing vanilla gelato with Dana. *He hates vanilla!* She hides behind the column by the door and watches him touch her trying to find fault in his movements. He kisses Dana's nose as they laugh over the dripping gelato. *He loves her.*

June covers her face and runs out of the shop, slamming the door. Alex looks up to see her darting around the corner of the building. She hides behind a dumpster in the alley.

"Mira!"

She doesn't answer.

"Mira, I see you behind the dumpster."

She peeks out like a child with her hands behind her back.

"I didn't think you were coming back."

"So, you called Dana?"

"I didn't call her. She just showed up. I am not even sure how she knew I was here."

"You hate vanilla ice cream."

"It's her favorite," he says.

"Of all the foods in Italy, you had to go for ice cream with Dana?"

"It's gelato," he says, as if that will lessen the act of betrayal.

"So, you changed your mind about us?" asks June.

He doesn't answer, he just pulls on his bottom lip and stares at her feet.

"Alex?"

"June, I love you. I will always love you. That is why I keep circling back to you, but I need things to work with Dana."

"Did she know Meyers raped me?"

"What?"

"She was dating him in Korea and set you up to get her pregnant. How could she not know how evil he is? Have you asked her?"

"No, I haven't, June."

"Then I will." She pushes past Alex and runs toward the gelato shop.

Alex runs after her and grabs her arm before Dana sees her. "Stop it, June. This won't change anything."

"It just did," she says. She turns and walks past Alex, but then pauses. Her feet won't move forward or backward. Alex grabs her arm gently, "June."

She looks up at him with tears in her eyes. "Andiamo Alex!"

Alex releases her arm and looks back at the gelato shop. "I can't," he says, not looking at her.

"Andiamo!" she screams, burying her head in Mira's pocket.

"I am sorry," he says, pulling her off his chest. He looks around nervously and turns back toward the shop.

She doesn't speak, but her feet are freed to move. She turns toward the train station and walks slowly without looking back. Her pace quickens the further she gets from him, until she is in a sprint to the train station.

....⁻ ..⁻⁻⁻ ⁻⁻⁻..

She has an hour before the time she had set to meet Jacob at the restaurant. She walks in circles around the Piazza del Popolo, most of the time. She wonders if she is choosing Jacob because Alex isn't available. She needs to know before she sees Jacob. She closes her eyes and imagines them both standing in front of her. They both ask her to come with them, and nothing is standing between them. She smiles when she thinks of the passion she has for Alex. She would miss Mr. Pierre. Then she thinks of Jacob. He felt she betrayed him, and he still came to Italy to find her, but Alex came too. She sits in the middle of the Piazza, waiting for a sign.

...- ..--- ---..

She is annoyed by a tickling on her nose. She swipes it away as she opens her eyes. Towering over her is Jacob. He is dropping white rose petals on her face.

"Ballentine," she whispers with tears in her eyes.

He reaches out his hand. She knows what taking his hand means, but she doesn't hesitate.

"It should be me looking up at you," he says as he gets down on his knees. "June, I have never loved anyone as deeply and completely as I love you. I don't deserve to have you in my life, but I pray that God will shine down upon me, and you will see me through that kind of grace."

She feels panicked; she pulls him to his feet. The gleam in his eyes darkens, and his smile fades as his bottom lip disappears. He waits for her to speak, but she is silent and focuses on his feet. She grabs his waist and hugs him as tightly as she can. "Don't ask me," she says.

Tears fill his eyes. "Ok."

"Can we go eat?"

He smiles. "Of course, you will love this place."

They eat in silence, chewing slowly so they can't hear themselves crunching their salad. Jacob watches June eating. She tastes every bite and closes her eyes a few times to take in the pleasure of the food.

"Have you made any decisions?" Jacob asks.

"Nope," she says with a pop sound on the "p."

Jacob never expected June to take him back after all the silence and the lack of assuredness that he had put her through when he was deployed. He actually fell more in love with the stronger, more vibrant woman that he has watched mature over the years.

"June, I don't need your answer. Dammit, I don't deserve it right now." Jacob looks at June, and she isn't expressing any emotions toward him. There is a distance between them that he knows he created.

He wants to touch her hand but feels the barrier between them. "Do you want to talk about what happened with Alex?" he bites the inside of his mouth in anticipation.

"To whom?" she asks.

"To, uh–– Me?"

"Who are you?"

He knows how difficult that question is to answer after all he has done to her.

"Well, not Colonel Edwards. He's an asshole," he smirks.

June looks up from the wine glass where she has buried her nose and laughs.

"Yeah, he is."

"Shit. June," he blows out all the air in his lungs. "If you lined us all up: Alex, Devan, Me, and that Italian god, I'd pick the Italian guy. I don't know why you'd choose me, Devan, or Alex." He grabs her hands.

She thinks about Marcello and smiles. She pulls away on of her hands, licks her index finger and runs it around her wine glass until it sings.

"I am happy to just be here for you, as a friend," says Jacob.

He isn't.

"Do you realize that you were my choice? Not Alex. Not Devan. I loved you more than both of them combined, and you hurt me more than both of them combined."

Jacob knows what defeat feels like, and he lowers his head and releases June's hand.

"Jacob, I can't make you fight for me, but I tried to fight for you. Did you read any of my letters after we talked about Devan?

He didn't.

Jacob looks at his half-eaten food. He can't look at June. "I didn't read your letters, June, and if that means you walk away from me, I'll understand."

June reaches into her bag and grabs copies of all the letters she had written Jacob. "I was going to make a book of our love story," she drops the letters on the table with enough money to pay her bill. She stands up and turns around with an "about-face" motion.

"Jay-bee!"

June's eyes sting as she holds back her tears. The burning sensation in her nose makes her sneeze. Jacob stands up and walks toward June. The waiter yells, "Signore, non hai pagato!" Jacob tosses 100 euros on the table and catches up with June.

"Jacob, don't speak to me until you have read all my letters."

He doesn't speak. He doesn't ask where she will be. He knows the answer is Padova. He realizes he has left the letters on the table. He runs back to the restaurant, and a couple is already sitting at their table. He frantically looks around for the waiter and finally sees him in the corner, reading one of the letters. Jacob grabs the letter out of his hand and the others sitting on the table. "Have you read those letters?" the waiter asks sincerely.

Tears fill Jacob's eyes. "No."

The waiter motions over a waitress who brings a bottle of wine and sparkling water. "Siediti! Tu leggi!"

Jacob opens the first letter. *Jacob, I love you. I have never imagined that those words from my heart wouldn't be enough for you.* Jacob looks up, and a group of the wait staff is in the corner watching him. Everything in his character wants to stand up and leave, but he craves June's words. He takes a sip of his wine and keeps reading.

....⁻ ..⁻⁻⁻ ⁻⁻⁻..

June stands at the Roma termini looking at the overhead monitor for train times to Padova. She's startled when someone grabs her shoulder. It is Alex.

"Dammit, June! I have looked all over the city for you."

June looks at Alex but doesn't hear what he is saying. Her eyes fill with tears as she is again caught in the precipice. Alex grabs her head and pulls it to her spot on his chest by his shoulder. "Mira, can I take you somewhere to talk?"

She doesn't want to go. She wants to stand there in that spot forever. But she nods yes.

Alex takes her to a small restaurant on a quiet street behind the Vatican. The entrance is covered in broken plates, and she walks down into the basement restaurant behind Alex, who has to bend down to get through the doorway. The waitress serves them wine in small water glasses and brings them warm bread with butter.

"How did you find this place?" she asks, sipping her wine and touching the warm bread with her finger.

"I was walking through the streets just trying to grasp all that has happened, and I saw this place. It made me think of you, Mira."

"Where is Dana?" she redirects.

"She had to fly back. The kids are with her mother."

Kids? She wonders but doesn't ask.

"Where are your bags?" he randomly asks.

"Luigi took them for me."

Alex can feel his throat tighten. "Ok," he says, as his bottom lip disappears.

"June, I have never really said how sorry I am about everything. Our life was almost perfect in Korea. At least I thought it was."

She looks down at the bread as he slices it and puts it on the plate in front of her. It isn't warm anymore, and the butter has already melted into a perfect little square of yellow gue. She moves the softness around with her finger and then licks her finger. *How could butter taste so freaking good?* She realizes that Alex has stopped talking, so she looks up at him and nods yes with her mouth twisted to the side.

"I wanted to be with you, June; you said you couldn't handle my son."

Wanted? That's past tense. She tastes the butter again and smiles.

"June, I fucked up, I know that. I just can't find a way to let you go."

She takes the last sip of her wine, and Alex automatically refills her glass.

"Do you still love me? June, say something."

June looks up as the waitress returns to the table. "Dov'e' il bagno?"

The waitress points to the bathroom.

June scrunches her nose at Alex and slides slowly out of her seat, and tiptoes to the bathroom.

Alex takes a mouth full of bread and chases it down with a whole glass of wine.

June sits on the toilet-paper-covered seat and stares at the Italian graffiti on the bathroom door. *Vaffanculo:* she wonders what that means.

Her thoughts interrupt the flow of her pee as she retraces the day's events. She cracks the stall door, still sitting on the toilet. *The window is too small to escape.* She raises both hands when she suddenly realizes she doesn't want to be there with Alex. She doesn't want to talk to him. He doesn't have the right to explain his way back into her life.

"Vaffanculo!" she says loudly, hoping it means something terrible. She hears the woman in the stall beside her gasp. "Mi scusi signora! So sorry." June quietly exits the bathroom, trying to hide from the cracks of the other stall. She walks confidently back to the table and sits down.

With all her newfound confidence, she looks up and Alex and immediately softens when she looks into his eyes. She remembers the day they sat across from each other at the Dairy Queen in Killeen, when he asked her to marry him. She remembers falling in love with him again when they sat in the park and he made Mr. Bear talk. "Don't speak," she says. "Just listen."

He nods.

"I love you more than the stupid air in my lungs, but I love Jacob more than that. That is all the energy I am giving the topic. I am going to stand up and leave now. I forgive you. I hope you will always be happy." She doesn't look at Alex as she stands up to leave, and part of her doesn't hope he'd always be happy.

....⁻ ..⁻⁻⁻ ⁻⁻⁻..

Jacob finishes the last letter and looks up at the waitresses in the corner, motioning him to go. He offers to pay for the wine, but the waiter says, "E' per amore. Tu vai!" Jacob runs out of the restaurant and all the way to the subway. He gets off at the Termini and searches for June. The next train to Padova is in over two hours, so he is sure she is waiting somewhere in the station. He wanders around several times, and then he sees her luggage behind the counter of a newsstand. "Dov'e' lei?" he asks Luigi, pointing to the luggage.

"She left with Alex," he says in perfect English.

" Alex?"

Did The Art of War fail me? He wonders.

"Yes, the tall, handsome guy. She was crying. Did you make her cry?"

"I did."

"Then I will not tell you where she is," he says frankly with a *vaffanculo* gesture.

"Can I please just leave her a note?" begs Jacob.

"Si, but I will read it."

"Ok, give me a moment, please." Jacob writes: *I read all of your letters. I love you that much too. Please come to the condo in Rimini. I left you a ticket for the train.*

Luigi reads the letter and stares blankly at Jacob. "It's not enough! Tell her you are stupid and don't deserve her because you don't."

Jacob adds those exact words to the letter and returns it to Luigi. He wants to make sure June gets the note, but he also knows the words are true.

He takes the next train back to Rimini to wait for her.

Thirty-Four

Finding Ballentine

Luigi gives June the note, and she smiles when she sees the words that he is stupid are underlined several times. Instead of going to Rimini, she exchanges the ticket for one to Padova. She waits a few days for Marcello to return her phone calls before going to the coffee shop. The new barista tells her he is on a family vacation with his wife. June is hopeful this means they have reconciled, but she stays in Padova just in case he comes home heartbroken. She waits outside the café until she sees him walk up with his wife smiling and laughing.

Does she know how amazing and loving he is? June watches her lover holding hands and looking around cautiously. *His wife doesn't know.*

She wants to run-up to the woman and tell her that she learned more about love in a few days with Marcello than she has in all the previous years of her life. He made her body beautiful and whole again. He freed her from the darkness that crawled onto her the night of her rape. This man made her feel safe to be sexual again. She tries to understand why we get so twisted up in other people and barely notice that they are there. She thinks of her dream and understands why the tree wants to be untangled and why it dies when it is. *Siamo l'albero contorto. We are all the twisted tree.*

....- ..--- ---..

June walks slowly back to the train station. A part of her just wants to go back home to Portland, and a part of her wants a fresh start in

Padova. She doesn't realize until she reaches the train station that she doesn't have enough money for a ticket anywhere, so she calls Jacob.

"Hello, love," he answers, then bites his lip anxiously.

For her those words change everything.

"Hey, Jay. Is it ok if I use your credit card to buy a ticket there?"

"Of course. Did Luigi not give you the ticket?"

"He did." She doesn't offer any more explanation.

"Well, use the card anytime June. When can I expect you?

"In a week."

Jacob tries to hold back his enthusiasm. "Well, I will see you in a week."

After wandering around the city for the day, June decides she doesn't want to wait a week to see Jacob. She catches the next train.

Before June realizes it, she is standing quietly outside the door of Jacob's condo, listening. She can hear the sound of the ocean through the door, which is framed in bright white light. She rummages through her bag and finds the key that she took from Jacob's condo in Olympia. She slowly opens the door.

There are Gerber daisies everywhere. Some were dying in the vase in the kitchen, so she knew that he had been anticipating her arrival for weeks. She imagines the room full of Irises. She loved how Marcello tickled her nose with each flower and then blew softly through the pedals so she could get a good smell of each of them. The Gerbers that she thought she loved didn't have much fragrance, but they tickled her nose the most.

The condo smells fantastic. Someone is preparing lasagna, and two glasses of wine are on the counter. She smiles when she realizes that he is working really hard to please her. *He must have seen the credit card charge and knew I was coming.*

The ocean breeze draws her out to the balcony. A not of the sliding glass door reads: *Hey Girl, just meet me at the Mercato Centrale Coperto. I also need cheese from Lattincini e Formaggi for the lasagna. If I am not there, I stopped by the Il Capannone.*

Hey Girl?

June yawns and wanders around the condo, debating if she has the energy to find this market he is talking about. She finds the bedroom and instinctively bends over to smell the covers. They smell like Jacob. She has missed that smell for so long. She buries her face in the blankets and drifts off to sleep.

Jacob comes barreling into the house with arms full of groceries. He plops them down on the counter and looks around the apartment for Tara. As he looks out on the beach, he sees her talking to someone and texts her to come back for dinner in an hour. He goes into his bedroom, where June is lying on the bed, and throws off his clothes to get into the shower, covering her face with his shorts.

....⁻ ..⁻⁻⁻ ⁻⁻⁻..

June wakes up and hears the shower running. She peeks into the steamy room and sees Jacob naked and covered in soap from head to toe. She wants him. She misses his touch and the way he grabs the back of her neck when he kisses her. She slips off her clothes and runs to the shower. She grabs him from behind and rubs his body up against his. He is startled and gets soap in his eyes to the point he can't open them. He grabs her to push her away, not realizing it is June. "What the fuck? Get the hell out of here!"

June, already wounded by his rejection, pulls her hands away from his body and steps backward out of the shower. She wraps a towel around her soapy body and runs back into the bedroom.

"Hey, Little Bit," says Tara as she walks into the condo. "I am thrilled you made it. Tarzan in there wouldn't have made it another week."

What just happened in there wasn't welcoming.

"What? I am sure there is some mistake. You are all he has talked about since I got here. It's actually a little annoying."

"Tara, why are you here?"

"Two reasons: I owe you an apology for how I treated you with the boys in the war. We had our shit to deal with, and I wasn't a good friend to you. Second, and here is the best part. I brought Julian over with me. It turns out he is really terrified to fly. I had to give him a pill to sleep most of the way. June can't stop smiling. "Where is he?"

"He will be here tomorrow. He went to Naples, something about a side piece. I am not sure what that means."

June giggles, but doesn't explain.

Jacob steps out of the shower, his eyes are still burning. "Tara! What the hell kind of bullshit are you pulling?" he yells from the bathroom.

"Jacob, come out here now!" she screams through the door.

"Do you have your clothes on?"

Tara and June both start laughing when they realize Jacob thought it was Tara in the shower.

"Yes, sweet thang, we both have our clothes on."

Jacob puts on a pair of shorts and comes into the kitchen. He sees June wrapped in a towel with soap still in her hair. "Wait!" he looks back at the shower. "That was you? Can you please come over here so I can hug you?" he whimpers, meeting her halfway across the room.

Tara is texting on her phone and then slams it closed. "Well, I officially have plans with Tony from the dive shop. You both have a lot of catching up to do."

"Tara, you don't have to go," says June.

"Of hell yes, she does," counters Jacob. "I love you, Tara. Get the fuck out of here," he says playfully.

Tara laughs and salutes Jacob and then June.

Jacob breathes in deeply, trying to hold on to her with all his senses. "I have wine, and I am making lasagna. Are you hungry?"

She is.

June walks over, grabs the glass full of wine, takes a small sip, and says, I really like Allegrini Amarone Della Valpolicella Classico DOCG. She shows him the note she made in a small book she had in her pocket. He saw the other notes as he slowly writes down the name of the wine. She pulls the book away quickly, but he had made a mental note of *Irises, Smoked Gouda, Sarah Harmer, and Deva Premal.*

He texts the list to Tara, who rolls her eyes but responds, "Got it."

"Tara is picking up some of that wine for dinner."

"How much time do we have?"

Jacob looks at June. She has the same look in her eyes that she always had when she wanted sex.

"The only thing is–– Well, I still have all this soap in my hair." She runs her fingers through her hair and bites the side of her lip.

"There is a lot of soap in your hair," he brushes the hair away from her face.

June smiles and walks back to the bathroom. He can hear the water from the shower. He walks to the bathroom feeling a little nervous. He hasn't been with anyone in years, and June isn't just anyone to him.

He walks back to the kitchen, drinks the full glass of wine, and takes a deep breath. He suddenly remembers June's breathing techniques and smiles. He never thought this would be the context in which he needs them the most.

The bathroom is filled with steam when he arrives, and June is already in the shower. She stands with her face under the water, and her hair is a fountain on her small arched back. He finally sees the tattoo on her arm. It's a stunning addition to an already intoxicating vision. He steps apprehensively into the shower behind her, trying to control his physical response to her. He gently puts his hands in her hair to guide the water to the soapy parts of her body. She leans back, placing most of her body weight onto his chest. "I've missed you," she says, hiding her tears in the water that is still splashing on her face. He slowly moves her hair back to kiss her neck, but gets a mouth full of water. He turns her to face him and lifts her chin to kiss her. Their lips are quivering as they touch again for what seems like the first time. June can taste the wine, and she smiles. "I guess you need a drug to be with me this time?"

He looks into her eyes and sees that brightness he has always loved. Her eyes aren't sad like they had been the last few times he saw her. "I needed some courage to touch you again since I know I don't deserve you."

"Luigi thinks that, not me," she giggles, because she had watched their interaction at the Termini that night. June turns off the shower and grabs Jacob's hand. She leads him to the towels so neatly folded on the shelf and starts to dry the parts of him she can reach. "Why are you so dang tall?"

He smiles, then takes a fresh towel and dries her off, starting with her hair, then her shoulders, the small of her back, her hips, and then positions the towel to dry between her legs. She pushes him back against the wall. "I like that wet," she says as she continues to push him toward the bedroom. She pushes him down on the bed and then runs to the front door and latches the chain. *Too many people have keys to this place*, she reasons.

She grabs another glass of wine to take with her to the bedroom. "Do you want some more of this?"

He did, but not the wine.

She takes a small sip of the wine, then climbs on top of Jacob and kisses him, allowing the wine to swirl into his mouth.

"That is strangely erotic," he whispers.

She grabs the glass and continues kissing him. He raises his hips to meet her, wraps his legs around hers, and flips her onto her back.

"UFC?" she inquires, laughing.

He nods and continues to kiss her body, leaving a slow trail of incandescent kisses on her stomach and hips. He toys with her breast as she moves down her body, kissing her hard enough to leave pink marks along his path. He looks up at her before gently opening her legs and tasting that moisture she diligently protected. His heart races as he has flashbacks of those times they had been together and the pain of being without her. For him, this is new and more exciting than he has remembered. He notices everything about her. The way her body moves in sync with his touches, how her skin smells after he kisses her, and the sound of her breaths as he gets closer to pleasing her. He notices when her heartbeat quickens, and holds on to her hips so she can't pull away from her climax.

"I like it when you drink wine," she smiles.

He crawls up and lies beside her. He starts tracing her silhouette from her forehead to her nose and then slides his finger quickly down to her mouth. She chomps at his finger. June leans over the bed and grabs her purse, pulling out a condom. Jacob tries not to react; he just puts it on. She moves her body on top of him and whispers in his ear, "Do you want me, Jay?"

"I do."

June positions him perfectly and starts moving her hips back and forth slowly, whispering in his ear and kissing his neck. "Harder?"

He grabs her hips and moves her body back and forth. He flips her on her side with another UFC move and pulls her hair back, and bites the back of her neck.

"Oh my god, I love that! Keep doing that."

He pulls a little harder at her hair as he moves in sync with her moans.

"Right there–– oh my god, right there," her body suddenly relaxes, and so does his.

They lie in bed, still intertwined, until they both fall asleep.

....- ..--- ---..

June wakes up when she hears Tara trying to get into the condo. She is drunk and dragging along an attractive younger guy in nothing but shorts. She wakes up Jacob to deal with them and whispers, "I am starving. Let's gets dressed."

"Lasagna or onion veggie pizza?" he laughs.

"Wow, you can't let that go after all these years."

"I still taste those onions on your breath."

"Oh, now you have jokes." She twists his ear and pulls it.

"Is there another room in this place?"

"Yeah, Tara can take the boy to that room."

"Stop! It's her choice, and he's charming."

"Oh, hell no, he has to leave now," jokes Jacob.

"It's ok, Babe. I like them old. I mean older men."

"That's great, but I am getting them a place tomorrow. I want you all to myself."

"I'd like that too, but I must see Julian as soon as he gets here."

"June, I need to talk to you about that."

"About what?"

"About Julian and how much he loves you, but can it wait until tomorrow?"

"I guess so. Since I don't know what you will tell me that I don't know about our friendship."

Jacob turns his back toward June. He didn't know how he would tell her that Julian risked his life to save her, and to put away Meyers. He didn't ever want to have to bring up Meyers again to June, but if Julian shared it with her, he thinks she would feel that he had betrayed her again.

When the lasagna is baked, Jacob decorates two plates like masterpieces and grabs the bottle of wine Tara has brought back. He points June toward the balcony.

"Wow, this is amazing," says June. "I love when men cook for me."

He knew he couldn't ask.

They mainly sat quietly, listening to the ocean waves.

June is happy for the first time in a very long time.

Jacob is worried his news about Julian will steal her happiness all over again.

The sound of the ocean waves floats over June as she sinks into her chair. In moments she is asleep. Jacob scoops her up and carries her to bed. He returns to the dining room to finish the project he has been working on. After it's completed, he snuggles beside June and watches her sleep until he drifts off to sleep.

June wakes up early and goes straight out for a run. She hasn't run in almost a year, and it feels like this is the morning to re-connect with that part of herself. She heads straight for the beach, takes off her shoes, and runs with them in her hands until she reaches the market area.

She runs through the city streets and finds a bridge to stretch out and cool down. She watches the water flowing under the bridge for a few minutes before she walks back toward the condo.

She feels peaceful for the first time in a long time. She grabs some fresh oranges and berries for breakfast and grabs a cannoli for Jacob. She tastes the cream and laughs. She knows he will know she licked it, but he'd never say anything to her. She is excited about seeing Julian later that day but more interested in what Jacob needs to tell her, so she runs back to the condo as fast as possible with a bag of groceries.

The apartment is quiet. Jacob must have awakened Tara and the boy early to have them move to the place he found for them. She juices the oranges and makes a plate of the fruit for herself and one with the cannoli for Jacob. She sees a book on the kitchen table, moving it aside to arrange a romantic breakfast. She finds some candles in the drawer and salvages some of the surviving Gerbers for the arrangement.

She sits for almost an hour, waiting before thinking about the book. Jacob would never accidentally leave a book on the table. She takes it over to the couch and opens it. Tears fill her eyes, as she frantically flips through the pages. He has made a book of their letters, but he responded to each of them. She starts reading his letters one by one, and the voids of space start closing in her heart. He has found a way to fight for her that she had never expected. He has even found the photos they took together at his aircraft for the 4th of July and all the photos she had sent to his phone. He had written little notes about how each of the photos had made him feel on his steps to falling in love with her. She is amazed at how he looked at her, even back then when they were friends.

Jacob walks into the condo smiling when he sees that June has found the book.

"Thank you," she says holding the book tightly to her chest. He is thrilled to see a smile on her face. He walks over and hugs her and the book.

"I am sorry it took years to answer those beautiful letters. I know I made a huge mistake June. I just hope you'll give me a chance to keep that smile on your face."

His stomach sinks as he says the words because he knows he must tell her about Julian. Jacob sits down beside her, and his mood changes. "Well, I need to talk to you about Julian."

June puts her hand over his mouth. "Don't! If Julian wants to tell me, he can, but I don't need to know any details. I know how much he loves me. He has never made me doubt that."

Jacob sighs. He knows that she should be able to say that about him. He looks over at the table. "Is that a cannoli?" he says, wildly licking his lips and rubbing his hands together. He kisses June and then pauses to look at her. "You are the perfect person for me, June." With a mouth full of cannoli, he asks, "So, when can we talk about having babies?"

June looks out the window but doesn't speak. Jacob hits himself in the head. *Why are you so fucking stupid, Jay?*

"June, I am so sorry. I know it's way too soon to talk about kids."

"I killed our baby, Jay. I don't deserve to be a mommy."

"June, you don't know that what you did is what caused the miscarriage."

"Yes, I do."

"You know, June, some people believe that little souls are up in heaven waiting to pick their lives down here. Even though Ballentine didn't get to come down then, she will still find her way here again someday."

"Do you believe that, Jay?"

He moves to sit beside her. "With all my heart ,June. You will be a great mommy."

They are both startled by a knock at the door. June runs to open it, and there stands Julian. She grabs him and holds him as tight as she can.

"Alright now, you know I hate that love-shit you keep throwing my way."

They both laugh. Julian walks over, shakes Jacob's hand, and pulls him in for a one-armed hug. "I knew you were the better man; he whispers."

Jacob smiles.

"So, what have you been up to? Are you enjoying Italy?"

"He means how is your side piece?" June giggles

"All is good. I can't complain."

"What are you doing these days for work?" asks Jacob

"Mostly nude modeling, but I get in an occasional dancing job here and there."

Jacob looks at June, who provides him no comfort. "That's awesome, man."

June and Julian both start laughing.

"I went into Information Technology. I work for a company in Portland."

"For how long?" asks June sternly.

"Keep your shorts on. I have only been there a month. I looked for you, and that's how I found Ms. Tara."

"By the way, what's up with that Amira chick? She told me to watch out for the mailman. She said he was a demon?"

"She is lovely, but I think she has some issues." She looks at Jacob. "Maybe we could invite her here for a vacation?"

Jacob twists his mouth, "The demon lady?"

"She isn't a demon lady. She just says she sees demons."

"So, she has a mental disorder?"

"She seems fine, Jay. How do you know that she can't actually see demons?"

"God, I hope not."

June wants to tell him that Amira thought Devan was a demon, but she changes the subject instead.

June looks a Julian, "So what do you want to do today?"

He looks a Jacob and then back at June. "Don't ya'll have some babies to make?"

Jacob bulges his eyes at Julian.

June walks out to the balcony.

"Too soon?" asks Julian looking at Jacob.

"Yes," says Jacob patting him on the shoulder.

"I got this one," says Julian. He walks out to the balcony and sits down beside June. He doesn't speak for a few minutes until she looks over at him. "Girl, this world has thrown you some crazy blows, but that man in there, he points at Jacob. He loves you. Not that selfish love like Alexhole. Jacob is your ride or die."

She understands.

"Now I have some plans for this free vacation you have me on. Go jump on your man."

"Are you coming back here tonight?"

"Girl, not if I still have it going on." He brushes off the imaginary dust on his shoulder. "So, your answer is NO."

"Ok, have fun, but stop and see me before you leave Italy."

He rolls his eyes and kisses her on the cheek. Jacob, she is ready for you now. Jacob stands up and spills his coffee. "Thanks, man!"

Jacob turns on his CD player and plays the mix-tape he had made for June. He walks over to her and reaches out his hand. "Will you dance with me?"

June looks up with tears streaming down her cheeks. She stands up and falls into Jacob's arms, sobbing. He pulls her head toward his chest and holds her, afraid to move his feet.

"I," she whispers.

"June, you deserve a baby. You deserve love and peace and a safe place to explore who you are. Let me at least be that safe place for you."

She looks down at Jacob's feet that are planted into the ground. "I thought we were supposed to be dancing," she laughs.

He lifts her chin, wipes her nose on his sleeve, grabs her hand, and spins her around. "I will plan a night for Julian and us before he leaves. I know that is important to you."

She nods.

"I never saw Marcello when I was in Padova. Do you mind if I go up today to find him?"

He did.

"No, do you want me to go with you?"

"I am fine going alone."

....⁻ ..⁻⁻⁻ ⁻⁻⁻..

June takes the 2:30 train to Padova. When she arrives at the station, she sits at the same coffee shop that she had visited that first day she had fallen asleep on the train. She feels destiny had brought Marcello into her life, and she wants to test fate by waiting there for him. June sits uncomfortably, scanning the horizon for hours, looking for Marcello.

....⁻ ..⁻⁻⁻ ⁻⁻⁻..

Jacob paces back and forth, trying to think of something fun for them to do with Julian before he leaves. It is extremely out of his comfort zone to coordinate anything fun or light-hearted, so he calls Pippa to see if she wants to surprise June in Italy. He thinks of inviting the "demon" girl but chooses not to.

Pippa has been having a few rough months and is excited to get away for this amazing adventure. Jacob has to figure out how to be the fun guy in the room and not the hard-ass he has become so comfortable within his military career. It's then he remembers the Carnaby Bar. *Perfect,* he thinks.

....⁻ ..⁻⁻⁻ ⁻⁻⁻..

June hears the sound of a little girl laughing, and it sends chills down her spine. She turns around, and there is Marcello with a beautiful little brown-haired girl, swinging his arm back and forth. She waits silently at the café until he notices her.

"Bella, what are you doing up this way?"

June looks at Marcello and then down at the little girl who grabs her hand. "Mama," she says, reaching for June.

Marcello pulls at his daughter's hand and then looks strangely at June with one eye squeezed closed. "They call everyone *Mama* at this age."

"What is your name?" asks June.

"Shaqueline," says the little girl.

"Ja-Ja Jaqueline," says Marcello.

June looks at the little girl. Her daughter would have been three. She wants to believe that maybe this little girl is Ballentine. Perhaps she came down to Marcello so that she could meet her. She drops down to her knees and looks at Jacqueline. "It's you, isn't it?" she asks.

"Si, I me," says the little girl. "You, mama," she points at June.

June kisses her on the forehead. "Well, of course, you are you. I am just being silly."

She stands up and kisses Marcello on the cheek. "I don't want to say goodbye."

Then we will say, "Vediamo cosa ci reserva il destino."

"What you said," she laughs. "Now, write that down in my book so that I can look it up."

....⁻ ..⁻⁻⁻ ⁻⁻⁻..

Jacob has coordinated everything for Julian's last night in Italy. Julian and Pippa are waiting for June and Jacob to arrive at the bar. June wears a blue dress and heels and puts up her hair. Jacob coordinates her color blue exactly, with a blue polo shirt and black slacks. They order drinks at the bar, and Pippa comes up behind June and covers her eyes. June turns around and screams when she sees her standing next to Julian. Pippa hugs her hard and whispers in her ear. "Have you danced out all your crazy yet?"

June nods with tears in her eyes.

Jacob is meticulous about details, but he forgets a little bit of his plan with each drink. By the time he has had his fourth drink, he stands up in a grand gesture and walks to a piano. Julian sits down behind the piano and starts playing a song. June looks oddly at Pippa, "Do you know what this is about?"

Pippa shrugs.

Jacob says, "The love of my life is here." His voice is breaking. "She doesn't know this, but I have a special talent for not being able to sing, and I have decided to humiliate myself tonight to show her how much I love her." The crowd cheers and Jacob starts singing: "*You Are Everything*" by the Stylistics. His voice is high and cracking. Pippa and June are laughing and falling over each other.

"You know this takes a lot for Mr. Perfect Pants to do," says Pippa.

June smiles. She knows very well how difficult it is for Jacob not to fall into the personality of Colonel Edwards.

"Go up there, June. Don't leave him hanging after all that."

"Ok, but you and I are going to Rome tomorrow. I am keeping track of all I spend, though, I have to pay Jacob back."

Pippa knows she will, every penny.

June walks up to Jacob and whispers in his ear, "Let's go home and make a baby."

"Really, June?"

"Yep."

Jacob smiles, puts his arm around her neck, and kisses her head. "If I had only known, all I had to do was humiliate myself."

"You sounded great!" she laughs. "You need to work on the dance steps, though. She demonstrates by snapping her fingers and scooping her arms left to right.

June looks over at Pippa, who is sitting staring at her glass. "Are you ok?" she asks. "Yeah, June. You go! This is your happy ending, not mine." She kisses Pippa on the forehead, grabs her hand, and then grabs Jacob's. Julian runs up behind her and points to a guy in the corner.

It's understood.

"Tomorrow, Pip. You and I are taking the 5 am to Rome."

Jacob walks to the door with June and then looks back at Pippa sitting alone. He runs back to the table and grabs her hand. "I make great lasagna, or would you prefer onion pizza?"

Thirty-Five

The Box

Both Julian and Pippa have been gone for weeks. June and Jacob have found a comfortable routine. June has taken a job at a local coffee shop, and Jacob is consulting at Longare.

June sits staring out the window, listening to the sound of the waves, when she sees a box. She walks over to this ornate, but dirty box. It looks old but has a modern digital lock on the front. The dust that has settled in the grooves, is greenish and smells like sage. She lifts her finger to her nose.

She is startled when Jacob walks into the room. "What's in the box?"

"I don't know. I found it at an antique store in Portland when I was down for a run. The shop owner said it was a basic skeleton key, but he couldn't figure out the three-digit code to open the other lock on it. I was going to take it by the base and see if they can figure out the code, but you can only put in one code every four months. It's weird."

"It's a beautiful box. What are you going to do with it?"

He hopes to put a wedding ring in it.

"I don't know yet. I'd like to see if it holds a treasure, though."

"When was the last time you tried a code?"

Jacob counts back the time in his head. "About six months ago."

"Ok, did you try 666?"

"Yikes. No, I didn't, but if that opens it, we are burning it."

June tries to reason it out. Maybe destiny brought the box to you, so perhaps it's something related to you?"

"I have spent two years trying to open it, here are the numbers I tried."

June looks at the numbers. One is her birthday, 2/18, and the other is the prefix to her address in Portland. She smiles. She looks at Jacob and scrunches her face, and then presses 666. She hears a tumbling sound, then three beeps. It's still locked.

"I love that you are brave enough to be friends with a demon girl and put 666 in a code to open a magical box."

"Hey, I know that there is something out there watching out for me. I should have died. The tourniquets were perfect."

June has never mentioned tourniquets to him when describing her rape. He feels sick to his stomach. "June, I swear, I will never allow anything evil like that ever to get close to you again."

She touches his chest. "God allowed that evil to get close to me. How can you make that promise?"

"I am making it, June."

There is a long pause. Then he says, "Why do you think you survived?"

"I am glad you finally asked me that. I feel like it was Ballentine, but I ruined that."

"If you truly believe in destiny, June, you can't ruin anything."

June runs into the bedroom and grabs the little book she keeps in her pocket. "What does this mean?" She points to Marcello's phrase: *Vediamo cosa ci reserve il destino.*

Jacob takes a deep breath. He knows it isn't written in June's handwriting. "It means let's see what destiny holds for us."

She hops onto Jacob's lap. "Vediamo cosa ci reserva il destino," she whispers.

Jacob pushes June forward and climbs on top of her.

"Take me to bed, Colonel." He grabs her waist and lifts her. She can taste his desire for her. He kisses her while simultaneously undressing her. The cool air from the open window causes her nipples to stand at attention. He tastes each one, taking care to divide his attention equally. He tries to move slowly down her body, but she has an urgency to feel him inside her. She pulls at his pants until he unzips them and then she kicks them savagely to the floor. Then she uses her feet to remove his underwear.

"I want you," she pleads, hungry for the warmth of his body against hers.

He moves his hips and takes her to the place she desires.

She breathes him in and out until they find no distance between them, then he flips her over and bites her neck again.

She likes having sex with Colonel Edwards.

Thirty-Six

Destino

The ocean breeze blows into the condo and swirls around June's nose. She feels vibrant for the first time in her life. She sneaks into the bedroom where Jacob is sleeping and kisses him softly on the cheek before heading out.

The streets are full of beach goers, heading to the local fair, for the summer activities. The thoughts of Devan and Alex have faded into a story-like memory, and she is focused on the wonderful feeling she has when she snuggles up next to Jacob.

In the last couple of months, she has developed migraines and has agreed to see a local doctor at Jacob's behest despite her lack of concern.

She sits in the doctor's office, staring at her reflection in a jar of cotton balls on the counter. She is startled by the puffiness in her face and pokes at her cheeks several times before being interrupted by a nurse. "Hi, Miss Brown."

June cringes that she still has Alex's name.

"Can you please call me June?"

"Sure."

"Well, we ran some tests, and I am happy to tell you that you are pregnant."

June stares at the wall in desperation, holding her stomach.

"It's pretty early along, so be careful and start taking your prenatal vitamins. The Dr. is estimating your due date to be around June 5th. Do you have any questions for me?"

"Are you sure I am pregnant?"

The nurse laughs. "Yes, dear, you are very pregnant."

June stops by the market on the way home and grabs fresh fruit and a cannoli for Jacob. She tiptoes into the apartment and drops the bag before running into the bedroom. Jacob wakes up as she pounces on the bed.

"I bought you a cannoli, on my way home, but I ate it like a crazy person."

"Did you?" He rolls over and kisses her. "I can taste it."

"All I taste is–– "June covers her mouth and runs to the bathroom. She crouches over the toilet, breathing deeply so she doesn't puke. Slowly she stands up and grabs his toothbrush and overloads it with toothpaste. She walks into the bedroom with her nose pinched and extends her arm to him.

He laughs as he grabs the toothbrush and brushes his teeth while talking. "What did the doctor say about your headaches?"

"I'm fine," she says abruptly. "Can you ask me again?"

Confused–– "What did the doctor say about your head-aches?"

"I am fine, ask me the other question." She looks down at her bare ring finger.

Jacob stops brushing and looks at his dresser drawer. He wipes his mouth and then stumbles to the dresser. He searches frantically for the box with June's ring in it, but it isn't there.

June runs to the kitchen and grabs the ring from a box of dishwasher soap. She has hidden it so that he wouldn't ask her again.

She hands the ring to him and then snatches it back from him to brush off the powdered soap.

He gets on one knee and holds the ring close to his heart.

"Juniper, soon to be Edwards, will you do me the honor of being my wife?"

"Oh, you are so sure I will say yes?"

"No, but I will keep asking until you do."

She nods. He tries to place the ring on her finger, but it doesn't fit. She grabs it and puts it on her pinky." My hands must be swollen," she says. "Could we get married today?"

"Today?"

"Yes, I want to marry you today."

Jacob looks at his watch and then grabs his phone, accepting the mission wholeheartedly. He dials a number and asks to speak to the base chaplain. June stares at him anxiously, motioning him to fast forward his conversation. He asks the chaplain, then waits for what seems like an eternity for a response. June has her face covered, so he taps her on the shoulder and gives her a thumbs up.

....- ..--- ---..

June listens to every word the chaplain says, and she is excited to say yes. Jacob tries to pick her up to carry her out of the church, but she resists. "It's safer to walk," she says.

"So, tonight will be our honeymoon," says Jacob smiling.

June wonders silently if it is safe for the baby for her to have sex. She is bursting with excitement when they finally get back into the condo. "Hi, husband."

"Hello, wife."

She grabs her stomach. I want to introduce you to our baby. She is gleaming as she holds her stomach and sways back and forth.

Jacob kneels to her stomach and kisses it. "I told you that you will be a great mommy."

"The doctor said, 'be careful,' so we need to throw out all the chemicals in the house, get a water and air filter and start buying food from that fresh market down the street."

Jacob just smiles and salutes her.

"She looks down at her stomach. "Will you love me when I am fat?"

He clears his throat, "Pregnant isn't fat, and I would love you if you couldn't squeeze your body through the front door."

He spins her around and kisses her on the forehead. "You think Bee will come back to us?"

"No, I think she is already here. I can introduce her to you if you come to Padova with me sometime."

He smiles wildly. "I would love to."

June looks around the room for her prenatal vitamins and sees the box on the table. "Do you think I should try my due date?"

Jacob bites his lip, "Sure, do it."

June walks over to the box to press the number 605, but she stops. "Oh, my Buddha!"

"The box."

"Portland."

"What? Did it work?"

"Jay, how do I call the States?"

He dials the number for her and hands her the phone. June's hands are shaking.

"Who is this?" answers Amira.

"Hi, Amira, it's June."

"It's not June. It is September."

"Amira, June, your neighbor."

"Hi, I didn't know the pill was a drug for raping."

"Amira, it is ok. Hey, when is your birthday?"

"April 28th."

"Ok, sweetie. I will talk to you soon."

June hangs up the phone and looks at Jacob. "I think I have it."

"What?"

"The code." She presses the code: 428 and hears cylinders moving. There is a long beep and then the box opens.

She desperately looks at Jacob. He pushes June behind him and grabs a knife from the kitchen. He gently lifts the lid.

"What's in it?" squeals June.

Jacob looks in the box and sees an envelope covered in sage. On the front are the letters A M I R A.

I wrote this book because it took me a lifetime to realize there is no way past rape. However, there is a way through it. There is a way to regain your dignity and your sexuality. I hope by sharing Juniper's experiences through her trauma, that others will find their voices too.

There truly is an "art of letting go." My hope is that you will see the beautiful person you are. That you allow the wonderful wild woman inside you the freedom to scream from the top of a mountain.

This is also dedicated to those soldiers who carry their own hidden scars from PTSD. Talking to someone helps. Please reach out to a professional counselor.

If God could have responded to Juniper's questions, with a song, I think it would have been this one: "Rescue," by Lauren Daigle.

If reading this inspired you to share your story, feel free to write me at: authorsarlew@gmail.com

Respectfully,
SarLew